An adolescent girl 1
and flopped directly across

eyes wide, Adidas-clad feet kicking in the air...Dagmar bent to help her rise, then gasped as a dark figure loomed between her and the sun—a man in a helmet and a blue uniform, dilated mad eyes staring at her through the plastic goggles of a respirator, weapon raised to strike...

"*This* way." A hand seized Dagmar's sleeve and snatched her away from the descending club. Dagmar felt the breeze of its passage on her face. The policeman raised the club to strike again, and then Tuna lunged into the scene: the big man clotheslined the cop neatly across the throat just under the respirator's seal, and the man flew right into the air, feet rising clean over his head, before he dropped to the grass with a satisfying thud.

In what seemed about two seconds, Tuna ripped the gas mask off, grabbed the cop's club, and smashed him in the face with it a half-dozen times. At which point Ismet took Tuna's shoulder as well, firm grip on the sturdy tweed jacket, and repeated his instruction.

"*This* way."

Praise for *This Is Not a Game*

"*This Is Not a Game* is a tale every bit as engaging as one of the intrigues its characters might have dreamed up." —*Bookpage*

"Williams' dialogue is razor-sharp, his plotting breakneck, his eye for trends keen and his empathy with his characters deep."
—scifi.com

"The characters are realistic and absorbing, and the story deeply compelling." —*Publishers Weekly* (Starred Review)

By Walter Jon Williams

DEEP STATE

WALTER JON WILLIAMS

www.orbitbooks.net

Orbit
Hachette Book Group
237 Park Avenue, New York, NY 10017
www.HachetteBookGroup.com

First Edition: February 2011

Orbit is an imprint of Hachette Book Group, Inc. The Orbit name and logo are trademarks of Little, Brown Book Group Limited.

The characters and events in this book are fictitious. Any similarity to real persons, living or dead, is coincidental and not intended by the author.

Library of Congress Cataloging-in-Publication Data
Williams, Walter Jon.
  Deep state / Walter Jon Williams. — 1st ed.
    p. cm.
  ISBN 978-0-316-09804-5
  1. Video gamers—Fiction. 2. Turkey—Fiction. I. Title.
  PS3573.I456213D44 2011
  813'.54 — dc22
                              2010026563

10 9 8 7 6 5 4 3 2 1

Printed in the United States of America

For Kathy Hedges

ACKNOWLEDGMENTS

With thanks to the usual fine intelligence of Critical Mass: Daniel Abraham, Melinda Snodgrass, Terry England, Emily Mah, SM Stirling, Ian Tregillis, Ty Frank, Victor Milán.

Special thanks to Charles Stross and Stefan Pearson for improving my Scots.

In the days when Sussman was a novice, Minsky once
  came to him as he sat hacking at the PDP-6.
"What are you doing?" asked Minsky.
"I am training a randomly wired neural net to play
  Tic-Tac-Toe," Sussman replied.
"Why is the net wired randomly?" asked Minsky.
"I do not want it to have any preconceptions of how to play,"
  Sussman said.
Minsky then shut his eyes.
"Why do you close your eyes?" Sussman asked his teacher.
"So that the room will be empty."
At that moment, Sussman was enlightened.

—anonymous hacker koan

PROLOGUE

Jerry left the warmth of the station building and walked out into the parking lot. Packed snow crunched beneath his Nikes as frigid air burned its way down his throat. He blew warm breath onto his hands and looked west, where the light of the setting sun illuminated the curves of the Tigris far below on its rolling plain. Hills and scarps obscured much of the river, leaving scattered loops of gilded water that were laced across the brown and white terrain countryside like fragments of some ancient Syriac alphabet graven on the land.

Rearing up above the Tigris were the spectacular crags of the Hakkâri Dağları, all dark stone, white snow, and formidable black shadows. And above Jerry were the domes and antennae of the CIA listening station, perched here at eight thousand feet, with convenient electronic access to Syria, Iraq, and Iran, the Middle East's perpetual stormy petrels.

Jerry had been delighted to learn that the Hakkâri Dağları were also known as the High Zap Mountains, because the High Zap was what he and his partner had done four days earlier—reached electronic fingers down into the plain below and performed long-distance surgery on crucial electronics controlled by a clutch of malign foreigners.

The operation had been a brilliant success, at least until the news had come that had left Jerry stranded on the mountain.

Sunlight dazzled Jerry as a frigid wind numbed his cheeks.

Tears leaked from his eyes. He wished he had been allowed to bring a camera to take a picture of the scene, but things were so secret here that cameras and cell phones were forbidden, even to station personnel.

This was simply the most beautiful and spectacular place he'd ever seen in his life. He'd been born in the flat Iowa cornfields and now lived outside Annapolis. Giant rearing untamed glacier-capped mountains were a completely new experience to him. He just wished he could leave the station and visit some of the towns he could see on the plain of the Tigris, far below.

On his one and only drive, coming to the station, he had looked out the window as they passed through the square of a small village and he'd seen old Arab women with tribal henna tattoos on their faces. It was like a visitation from another universe.

Being stranded up here at the station sucked. Totally.

Jerry flapped his arms and shuffled his feet for warmth. When he and Denny had flown out to Turkey, they'd had no clear idea where they were headed, and they hadn't brought clothing suitable for living on a mountaintop in the middle of February.

The deep mountain shadows expanded as the sun neared the horizon. Jerry scanned the horizon one last time, then turned and shuffled his way back toward the main building.

The listening station lacked any trace of glamor. Four acres of windswept limestone had been scraped flat by bulldozers and surrounded by chain fence draped with rusting signs reading "Danger" in English, Turkish, and Arabic. The main building was a prefabricated steel structure that sat on a concrete pad. Two more structures served as garage and generator room. Above the main building were the huge golf ball–shaped domes that concealed the station's dishes and antennae, their bulging geodetic surfaces an echo of the domes of the mosques on the plain below.

The air was glacial and snowfalls were frequent. The only reason the station wasn't absolutely buried in frozen H_2O was that the wind blew most of it away — though still there were drifts here and there, and occasionally the station personnel had to get on a ladder and sweep snow off the roof before it collapsed.

The gate was padlocked shut, and an old Mercedes truck, with icicles dripping from its bumpers, was parked behind the gate as a security measure—another obstacle that a jihadist car bomber would have to push aside in order to blow up the installation. But the gesture seemed halfhearted—the regular station crew didn't seem very interested in the possibility of attack, and in fact Jerry couldn't see the station as a high-profile target. You wouldn't get many headlines blowing up an anonymous, prefab site on a remote mountain in some place called High Zap. Much better to blast a café in Istanbul or an embassy somewhere else.

Jerry walked into the main building, stomped snow off his boots in the anteroom, and headed straight into the ops room with its coffee machine. He took his cup—a souvenir mug from Perge, where he'd never been—and filled it with hot coffee. The coffee was unbearably strong.

"You know," said his partner, Denny. "You can watch the sunset perfectly well from the window."

"Not the same," Jerry said. He had a hard time keeping his teeth from chattering.

Around him data flashed across flat-screen displays, intercepted transmissions from Syria, Iraq, or Iran. The material wasn't analyzed here; it was encrypted, sent to a relay satellite twenty-two thousand miles above the planet's surface, then beamed down to a facility in northern Virginia where it was either inspected or, most likely, ignored and filed away—in any case, the data itself wasn't any of Jerry's business.

Neither Jerry nor his partner, Denny, were members of the station crew, nor were they CIA employees. They were special contractors who had flown to Turkey on a special assignment eight days ago.

What had surprised Jerry was the discovery that, despite working at a CIA facility, *none* of the station personnel were CIA employees. They were all contractors working for one corporation or another. But then he'd realized that, in fact, they *all* were CIA—the corporate identities were just ways of sanitizing the identities of Agency employees.

He'd realized that when absolutely none of them expressed curiosity concerning the task that Jerry and Denny had been sent to perform. The lack of interest in the Zap had been professional all right, but it wasn't in any way *corporate*.

But now Jerry and his partner were stuck here on the mountaintop. While they were engaged in their special assignment, transmitting the High Zap to sites below, the Turkish government had changed suddenly and violently. The prime minister, on a state visit to Spain, found himself deprived of his office by the military. The president was under arrest in an undisclosed location. The entire country was under martial law—particularly the Kurdish areas, such as those on all sides of the listening station.

The attitude of the military government to the U.S. installations on Turkish soil seemed ambiguous. On the one hand, Turkey was a NATO ally of the U.S. and its military had enjoyed a long collaboration with the Americans on security matters. On the other hand, the Turkish generals were ultranationalists who might view with suspicion any foreigners using Turkish soil for their own purposes—a suspicion enhanced, no doubt, by the possibility that the listening stations might now be listening to *them*.

The orders that came down to Chas, the soft-spoken engineer who was in charge of the station, seemed to Jerry to be contradictory. Chas had sent half his people away—it wasn't clear where, exactly—and was now running the station with a skeleton crew of eleven. Jerry and Denny, by contrast, were forbidden to leave the station at all.

Jerry had asked Chas why.

"Because," Chas said, "the regular personnel won't be able to tell the Turks anything they don't already know."

Jerry and Denny were confined to the mountaintop by their

own importance. They knew about the High Zap, and the High Zap couldn't be allowed to fall into foreign hands.

Another frustrating aspect of the situation was that even though they were bored and had nothing to do and the station was now shorthanded, Jerry and his partner weren't allowed to use any of the station's regular equipment. Denny and Jerry weren't authorized to use the station's gear, any more than the station's personnel were allowed to use the laptop that Jerry and Denny had brought with them from the States.

It left Jerry with nothing to do but watch the sunset. Or the sunrise, if the desire took him.

"Wanna play *Felony Maximum*?" Denny asked.

Denny was a short man of twenty-eight years. He'd been a fat kid and had grown into an obese adult, but two years previously he'd put himself on a severe diet that consisted solely of vitamins and an assortment of Progresso canned soups. Denny had lost seventy-five pounds and his body was now of svelte proportions, for all that he still had no muscle tone — he had managed to lose all the weight without any exercise at all, and even climbing a stair left him out of breath.

The odd thing about the diet was what had happened to Denny's *face*. Its moon-pie proportions had shrunk, but the skin hadn't ebbed to the same degree as his flesh, and the results were deep creases that hadn't been there before. Jerry thought his partner now looked like a very intelligent monkey.

Despite the peculiarities of his appearance, the weight loss had nevertheless achieved its objective: it had given Denny the social confidence to court and marry a young woman named Denise, who was now pregnant and installed in a minimansion off in the Blue Ridge.

Right now Denny was sitting in the cubicle he and Jerry had been assigned, which featured a desk, two chairs, and a flat-screen monitor that hadn't been connected to anything, because they weren't permitted to touch any of the equipment.

"*Felony Maximum*," Jerry repeated. *Felony Maximum V* was one of the two games Jerry had brought along with his Xbox, and the other, which involved World War II fighter combat, had already been played to death.

"Fine," Jerry said. "Let's play. But this time, *I* get to use the MAC-10."

Jerry and Denny had managed to get the game's convict protagonist out of Ossining and into Manhattan when they were called to supper — hearty lamb stew in the local style, fresh bread, and strawberry Jell-O for dessert.

Meals at the listening station were taken mainly in silence. If you were the sort of person who was a spy and who furthermore lived in a small near-monastic community on a mountaintop, you were also likely to be the sort of person who didn't talk much. Jerry and Denny sat at the same table and chatted to each other about the progress of the game and how best to get revenge on the mafiosi who had sent the game's protagonist to Sing Sing.

A phone rang in the ops room, and Mauricio, the short Dominican guy, answered. He called Chas in, and twenty seconds later Chas returned, his face set in a look of cold resolution.

"The army's coming," he said in his soft voice. "We need to erase or shred every piece of data in this place."

There was a clatter of plates as the station crew pushed back their chairs and stood. Jerry stood as well, though he didn't quite know why.

Chas looked at him.

"We need to get the two of you out of here," he said. "Get your stuff together."

Jerry left the remains of his dinner on the table and hustled to the little cell-like room he'd been assigned. He unplugged the Xbox and put it in its case, then began stuffing clothes into his duffel.

The laptop, with the High Zap encrypted on its hard drive, had waited in its case in the corner for the last four days. Once he'd understood that the contents of the laptop were what was confining him to the mountain, Jerry had asked permission to erase the drive, which would guarantee that it wouldn't be captured by rogue Turkish generals or indeed anyone else—but to his surprise, his employers in Virginia had balked. He was supposed to return the program in the same condition in which he'd received it and otherwise not use the laptop except when authorized to do so. It was there in black and white—Jerry had signed a contract to that effect, a contract that included a twelve-page nondisclosure agreement.

When permission was refused to erase the hard drive, Jerry had realized that the program almost certainly contained a log on it that would inform his employers when and in what circumstances the program had been accessed. The return of that log intact would be the only way the Company would know that the High Zap hadn't been misused or copied.

His bosses, Jerry realized, were too paranoid, or bureaucratic, for their own good.

Jerry threw the duffel on a chair and headed for the bathroom for his toilet kit. Chas appeared in his door, a set of keys in his hand.

"Take the VW," he said. "Go warm it up now; then we'll load it."

Jerry took the keys and threw on his thin nylon jacket and ran out to the garage, through the ops room where the document shredder was already in operation, and past the techs bent over their keyboards, intent on zeroing every file on the hard drives. The Volkswagen's door handle was bitterly cold to the touch. The plastic seats sucked the heat out of Jerry's bones.

The car didn't start the first try, the cold battery reluctantly heaving the starter over. Jerry swore, switched off, and then ground again and the engine caught. He shoved the heater lever all the way over to the right and turned up the fan as far as it would go. He put the car in neutral, set the hand brake, and stepped out into the still air of the garage.

The garage door shot up with a great boom and the high

mountain wind roared into the building in a stinging swirl of ice crystals. Jerry gave a convulsive shudder as the cold hit him. Chas, looking warm as toast in a huge blue fur-lined parka, came into the garage.

"Open the trunk," he said.

Jerry bent into the driver's compartment again and spent a few useless seconds looking for the trunk latch. Chas reached in past his shoulder and popped the trunk lid.

"Okay!" he said. "The army's coming up from Hakkâri. You've got to get to the crossroads before they arrive."

"Right," Jerry said. The crossroads were a good ten klicks down the mountain, where the switchback road that led to the listening station met the two-lane road leading west from Hakkâri. If the army got to the crossroads before Jerry did, there was no way the car could escape.

"When you get to the crossroads, turn left to Şırnak."

"Check."

"Here's your stuff."

Denny rushed into the garage, burdened with his carry-on and his suitcase. Denny was followed by Mauricio with other bags, including Jerry's duffel. The luggage was heaved into the trunk, and the trunk slammed shut.

"When you get to Şırnak—" Chas began.

Jerry turned to Mauricio. "Do you have the laptop?" he asked.

Mauricio flashed a bright smile. "I took care of it, man."

"Okay!"

Denny opened the passenger door and dropped into the car. Chas leaned close to Jerry's ear. "When you get to Şırnak," he said again, "call your contact at Langley and ask him for instructions."

Jerry stared at Chas.

"Call him with what?" he asked. "We weren't allowed to bring phones."

A savage grimace crossed Chas's face. Jerry shuddered in the cold.

"Okay," Chas said. "In that case, get on the E90 and head west till morning. Then buy a phone with prepaid minutes and make your call."

"Fine."

Jerry decided that he officially no longer gave a damn about his instructions. He just wanted to get out of the freaking cold.

"I'll open the gate and get the truck out of the way," Chas said.

"Fine." Jerry's teeth were chattering. "Bye."

He dropped into the driver's seat and slammed the door. The car wasn't any warmer, but at least he was out of the wind.

Jerry experimented with the VW's dashboard controls while Chas got in the Mercedes truck and backed it out of their way. He put the car in gear and inched forward, then when Chas swung the gate open put the accelerator down. The tires spun on ice, then caught bare rock and hurled the car forward. The VW sped through the gate and began the long trip down the mountain.

The road had been plowed after the last storm, but the wind was ever present and there were new drifts everywhere. The road surface was stone or gravel plated with ice. There were no guard-rails, and a mistake would send them over a cliff, or into a stand of pine where they'd hang suspended until they starved or someone came and rescued them.

The idiocy and danger of their situation drove Jerry into a fury. He attacked the mountain as if the Volkswagen were a tank rather than a reasonably priced coupé. Twice he skidded off the road and bounced the car off banks of snow piled up in corners by the snowplow. He smashed through drifts as if the car had a blade on the front. He cursed continually as he worked the stick shift, and in his terror and anger he forgot all about being cold.

"Jesus, Jer!" Denny said. "Are you sure you know how to drive on ice?"

"Better than you do, Florida Boy," Jerry said.

Denny's weird shrunken monkey face contorted with fear. "I went to MIT!" he said. "It snows in Massachusetts! Maybe I better drive!"

"You didn't have a car when we were at MIT. You had a Schwinn. I remember."

"*Fuck!*" Denny shrieked as the wheels spun uselessly on ice and the car began a sideways drift toward yawning, empty space… and then one wheel hit some gravel, gained purchase on the road, and the car lurched back onto the correct trajectory.

"*Will you please take it easy?*" Denny cried.

"Shut the fuck up." The drive was taking too much of Jerry's concentration for him to deal with anyone's fear but his own.

The VW lurched and skidded its way down the mountain. Short of the T-intersections Jerry turned off the lights so that if the army was in the area, they wouldn't see the VW turning off the road to the listening station.

"What the—" Denny began.

"Shut up."

Jerry pulled up to the intersection, the darkened car skidding the last few meters, and then turned left and pulled onto clean, dry, two-lane asphalt. Denny gave a cry of relief.

"Look behind," Jerry said. "See if they're coming."

Denny turned to peer through the rear window. It took a moment for the banks of snow on the side of the road to open and give Denny a view of the mountain behind them.

"Holy crap," he said. "There they *are!*"

"How many?"

"Looks like four or five vehicles. Like a convoy. I can see their lights like a mile away."

Jerry backed off the accelerator and downshifted. He didn't want to have to brake and give their position away with a flash of the brake lights.

"Tell me what's happening," he said. The VW bounced over frost heaves.

Denny rocked back and forth to keep the vehicles in sight. "I— I can't see them," he said. "Trees in the way."

"Keep looking."

The tires drummed through potholes as Jerry took the VW

through an S curve, and then he ended up on a broad curve of mountain that provided a perfect view of the road behind them.

"I see them!" Denny said. "They're coming up to the intersection!"

Jerry slowed again to let Denny keep the vehicles in sight.

"They're stopping! They're turning! They're heading up to the station!"

Relief gushed out of Jerry's throat in a long sigh. He accelerated and shifted into third and let a curve carry him out of sight of the vehicles behind. When Denny assured him that they were out of sight of the other vehicles, Jerry snapped on the lights and accelerated to eighty kilometers per hour, which was as fast as he was willing to go on a strange mountain at night.

"That was close!" Denny said.

"I don't want you complaining about my driving again," Jerry said.

Denny took several long breaths, like a runner at the end of a sprint.

"Can I turn down the heater? It's really warm in here."

It wasn't just warm now; it was hot. Jerry hadn't noticed.

"Sure," he said.

Jerry drove on another ten klicks and then saw the sign for the Monastery of Didymus Thomas. The monks, ethnic Kurds, were Assyrian Christians, a sect of which Jerry had been completely ignorant until he'd been driven past the monastery on his way up the mountain. The monastery was literally perched on a cliff face, the monks living in caves hollowed out of the mountainside. The only way out of the monastery was to be lowered to the ground in a huge basket.

At the moment, presumably, the monks were all in their eyrie, shivering in their beds.

Jerry downshifted and swung the car into the monks' parking lot.

"What's the matter?" Denny said. "You want to change drivers?"

"Get the laptop out of the trunk. I want to zero the hard drive."

Denny looked at him doubtfully.

"We're not supposed to do that," he said.

"Look," Jerry said. "We're going down into the Kurdish part of the country. There's *got* to be a big Turkish military presence there, and I don't even know *if* there's a curfew or not. We're very likely to get stopped, and I don't want to get stopped with a software bomb in the trunk. We look suspicious enough as it is."

Denny thought about this for a moment and then nodded.

"On your head be it," he said, and opened his door.

Thanks a lot, Jerry thought, and sprang the trunk latch.

When Denny returned, Jerry saw the case and knew that they were totally fucked.

Totally, he thought. *Totally totally totally. Totally.*

Denny saw Jerry's stricken expression. He looked at Jerry with his strange monkey face.

"What's the matter?"

Jerry pointed at the case.

"Dude," he said. "That's my Xbox."

ACT 1

CHAPTER ONE

FROM: LadyDayFan

Hey! I have received word of a Facebook site featuring this coded message.

Not to give it away or anything, but it looks like James Bond needs our help!

FROM: Corporal Carrot

The blond or one of the others?

FROM: ReVerb

George Lazenby could *really* use us!

FROM: Vikram

Why us? Is Q on vacation or something?

FROM: LadyDayFan

I have started the usual series of topics under the title From Isfahan, with Love.

Newcomers to this forum should check out Tips for Beginners. I also recommend my latest guide on Netiquette, which might just stop some flamewars before they begin.

FROM: HexenHase

Excuse me, but I must have missed something. Why Isfahan?

FROM: Corporal Carrot

For the Isfahan thing, check out this link.

FROM: HexenHase

Oh. Sorry. Got it now.

FROM: LadyDayFan

If you'll look here you'll find a crossword puzzle, which seems to have been left behind by an enemy agent. Does anyone know a six-letter word for "Meleagris covers mostly Anatolia"?

FROM: Corporal Carrot

TURKEY! We're off again!

CHAPTER TWO

Primary Turns Solid Dangerously

The explosion smelled of roses. The scent was strong enough to turn Dagmar's stomach.

It was a conflation of memory, she knew. It was only after the explosion that she'd smelled the roses in her car. But here the two memories were mashed together.

It wasn't one of the flashbacks, Dagmar thought. It was a dream. She knew it was a dream because she could take some measures to control it.

She couldn't alter the dream's subject, that last explosion in LA. The green Ford parked with its view of the city, beyond it the webs of lights strung across the night, Century City a brilliant outpost in the darkness. Then the bubble of fire that exploded from the car, the light magnified a hundred times by gridded reflections on the glass-walled office building that stood over the parking lot. The clang as the car roof landed on the asphalt, followed shortly by the hood, and then the little sparkles as the incendiaries rained down like the remains of an Independence Day firework...

The explosion repeated itself over and over—not with startling rapidity, as it had in real life, but in ultraslow motion, like in an action film. It was the fact of its being so much like a movie that helped convince Dagmar that this was a dream.

Over and over again, the life in the car ended.

She couldn't manage to alter the event itself—she couldn't make the pieces of the car fly back together, couldn't restore her lover's life—but she could act in other ways to make the dream harmless.

Dagmar gave the image a sound track—Rossini's overture to *The Thieving Magpie*. The music was filled with drama so overblown as to become comic, the tension undermined by the oboe and flutes chortling away in the background, parodied by a platoon of rapping snares... the humorous sounds helped to neutralize the horror of the image, introduce a farcical element.

She distanced the image still further. She built a proscenium stage around the explosion, in hopes of reinforcing the idea that this wasn't really happening, that it was just opera or melodrama or some kind of boring art film hoping to make its point by showing the same dumb thing happening over and over.

She thought about pulling back the camera a little farther, showing the heads of the audience as they stared at the explosion, and at that point she woke up.

She was in a hotel, and for a moment panic flooded her, and she thought she might be having a flashback for real.

It wasn't the hotel in Jakarta, she told herself. She wasn't lying naked in the tropical heat, helpless amid a civilization that was coming apart, that was dying in riot and arson and looting.

Dagmar was in the hotel room in Selçuk, and she had taken steps to make certain it was not and could never be the room in Jakarta. She'd turned the bed at a diagonal, instead of square to the wall as it had been in Jakarta, and she'd made sure the windows were to her right and not to the left, and therefore there was no reason, none whatsoever, to have a flashback at this time...

She turned on the light. The room was not at all like the one in Jakarta, with its television and its minibar and its tropical heat. Instead she was in a boutique hotel with a view of the mosque and a tile mosaic of an old man gazing down at a group of turtles, some Turkish folk motif that she didn't understand.

This was not Jakarta. But the terror that was Jakarta was still somewhere in the back of her mind, threatening to break out, and that terror kept her awake, kept her sitting in bed with the light on until long after the muezzin called out the early morning prayer and light began to glint on the mosque dome and she heard the first sounds of traffic filling the streets.

Saint Paul Railed Against Breastwork Here

Dagmar watched as the gamers poured into the great stone theater. It was just after eight in the morning and the theater was still in the deep, long shadow of Mount Panayir; the air was cool and scented by the pines that lined the long walk from the entrance. Mourning doves called nearby; a stork clacked from the untidy nest it had built atop one of the stone arches.

The usual crowds of visitors, reinforced by tourists bused in from cruise ships docking in Izmir, had not yet arrived—aside from the doves and the storks, the gamers had the place nearly to themselves.

Cameras were held high overhead as they panned across the stone seats. Cameras in the hands of Dagmer's employees gazed back—the whole event was being streamed live to players who couldn't attend in person.

The flood of gamers slowed to a trickle, and then Mehmet entered. Mehmet scanned the crowd till he saw Dagmar and then gave her a nod from under the brim of his ball cap.

Dagmar gave him a half salute, raising two fingers to the brim of her panama hat. Then she stood and joined him in front of the worn pillars of the proscenium.

The gamers occupied a small fraction of the twenty-five thousand stone seats that the Greeks and Romans had dug into the flank of the mountain. In this theater the works of Aeschylus, Sophocles, and Plautus had been performed. Gladiators had fought and died here. The stage had been flooded for aquatic spectacles, perhaps miniature naval battles. Saint Paul had preached in this place, and been driven out by rioters calling on the name of holy Artemis.

Even Elton John had performed in this place, Captain Fantastic himself, a concert broadcast to the whole world.

The Theater of Ephesus had seen all this in the two thousand years of its history, and now it was going to see something new.

"Günaydin!" she called, Turkish for "good morning." "Can you hear me?"

The theater's superb acoustics echoed her own words back to her. She had more or less worked out she wouldn't be needing the lapel mic she had pinned to her T-shirt, and she didn't turn on the battery pack clipped to her waist.

"On behalf of Universal Exports, Limited," she said, "I would like to thank you for your help in assisting our salesman, Mr. Bond, escape from his troubles in Antalya. And I know you will join with me in sending condolences to the family of Semiramis Orga."

She signaled to Mehmet, and he translated the words into Turkish. Of the six or seven hundred gamers present, most were Turks, and most of these were new to alternate reality games.

They were picking up the basics pretty quickly, though.

"Unfortunately," Dagmar continued, "we are still unable to locate Mr. Bond. We believe that he may be in this area, and one among you discovered what seems to be a crossword puzzle partly filled out in his hand. I have provided copies for each of you, and you're each welcome to take one. The puzzle is called 'Ephesus,' and the answers seem to mostly involve this area. Perhaps the answers may help you determine Mr. Bond's location."

While Mehmet translated this, Dagmar returned to her seat and a large wheeled cooler, which she pulled out along the front of the proscenium. She opened the cooler to reveal stacks of printed crossword puzzles. The clues were written in both Turkish and English, and the answers, most of which had to do with Ephesian history and with inscriptions on the monuments, would be the same in any language.

She broke the stacks of puzzles into smaller stacks and distributed them between the many pillars of the proscenium. Then she invited the gamers to come down and each take one.

Which they did. At great speed. And then, organizing into groups, they dispersed all over the ancient city with their cameras, their phones, their maps, their Baedekers, and their Lonely Planet guides. Dagmar's camera crews followed them, eavesdropping on their conversations.

The puzzle and the clues would be scanned and uploaded to networking sites so that people off-site could work on them. People would be calling up the Internet on their handhelds so that they could google answers to the clues. Turkish clues would be translated into English, and vice versa, in hopes of gaining additional insight. Pictures would be taken of inscriptions, and of maps, and of monuments, and then the players would share the pictures with one another, or upload them so that others might have a crack at deciphering any mysteries they might contain.

And somehow, when all those pictures and clues and answers were jigsawed together, they would provide a form of aid to the world's most famous fictional spy, who lurked somewhere in the landscape near Ephesus, just beyond your eyeblink, or humming somewhere in the electronic landscape, or in the stream of celluloid running before the great blazing unwinking eye, images focused on the blank white screen that might just exist solely in your mind…

Type of Whiskey Minus Two

Dagmar walked with Mehmet down the pine-shaded road that led to the entrance to the site. Behind her, gamers and cameramen were flooding over the ancient city like an invasion of driver ants.

She had gotten her ass saved by James Bond four months earlier. She supposed that might make her a Bond girl—possibly, at thirty-three, the oldest ever.

Six or seven years earlier, when her creative skills had been paired with her friend Charlie's money, she had built her company, Great Big Idea, into a powerhouse in the world of alternate reality games, or ARGs. But then Charlie had died—been murdered, actually—and his various business interests had been "rationalized," as the jargon had it, by his corporate heirs. Great Big Idea had been cut loose, left to fend for itself in a sea now swarming with other companies promising to deliver equally terrific cross-platform viral advertising.

The company in fact did reasonably well most of the time, but there were times when Great Big Idea needed injections of cash to pay rent and make its payroll. In the past she could go to Charlie for a short-term loan from one of his other businesses, but now she had to establish relationships with financial institutions, like banks.

Explaining an alternate reality game to a banker was a daunting experience. *It's an online game?* Yes, except when it's out in the real world. *The real world?* Yes, we send players all over the world on live events. *And the players pay for this entertainment?* No, we give it away free and charge sponsors for our services.

Banks seemed unable to entirely reconcile themselves to this business model.

During the dry periods she'd kept the company going with her own money, paying herself back when she found a client. Until, earlier in the year, she had failed to find a client at all.

In March she had fired eight of her friends. She would have fired the rest in April except that James Bond had come to her rescue.

The new Bond movie, *Stunrunner*, would open in August. It was pretty much a remake of *From Russia with Love*, itself a film shot largely in Turkey—though instead of the maguffin being a Soviet coding machine that needed to be smuggled across the Balkans, it was Iranian nuclear secrets that needed to be got across Anatolia, with a climax filmed as a boat chase through the Basilica Cistern in Istanbul.

James Bond would be played by a new actor—Ian Attila Gordon, a Scots pop star new to the business of acting. He was also the first Bond since Connery to speak with a Scots accent and the first with a visible tattoo, a large, colorful one on his neck that loomed above the wing collar of his tuxedo.

The studio seemed a little nervous about the film, and about the Bond franchise in particular, which was suspected of being on the wane.

At any rate, Dagmar was told that the studio would very much like a state-of-the-art viral-marketing campaign for the film and would like it to take place in Turkey, tracing Bond's route across the country.

"Turkey?" Dagmar had asked. "Isn't Turkey like a military dictatorship now?"

"The movie was shot before the coup," Lincoln had explained. "And sad though the political situation may be, the studio would like its investment back."

And so would I, Dagmar thought, thinking of her savings that were on the brink of extinction, all eaten by her company.

"I don't have a good history with military governments," she said. In a dark corner of her mind she could hear automatic weapons rattling, see bodies sprawled on the street, a great pillar of smoke that marked a massacre, roads lined with broken glass and burning autos.

Lincoln gave her a mild look.

"You handled yourself well," he said.

"I was scared spitless the whole time."

"This time," said Lincoln, "you'll have a whole posse to keep you out of trouble. I'll be there myself."

The game, Dagmar considered, would bring some money to

Turkey, of which the generals would no doubt get their share. But Dagmar could make sure the game wouldn't have to support the generals in any other way.

And she could make payroll. Her friends wouldn't all be thrown out into the world.

And all that was required was she pretended that a few generals didn't exist. And, it had to be admitted, she already did that every day.

"There's never been a full-scale ARG in Turkey," Lincoln said. "I expect it'll be huge."

"Is there enough of an IT backbone in Turkey to run one of these?"

"Turkey is supersaturated with IT," Lincoln said. "They're completely wired. A goodly percentage of the world's hackers come from Turkey."

Lincoln Jennings worked for Bear Cat, a public relations company that represented the studio. Dagmar had met him before, but not under that name—she'd encountered only his online handle, which was "Chatsworth Osborne Jr." He was a complete alternate reality geek—a dedicated player of ARGs himself— and now he had the budget to stage one himself.

He was pretty well over the moon about it. This was some kind of long-buried dream for him.

A six-week game in two languages, with live-action meet-ups in a foreign country? Dagmar charged Lincoln a *lot*. She had to pay herself all the money she'd loaned the company, she had to rehire as much staff as she could, and she had to have enough left over to survive the next dry period. She built escalator clauses into the contract, getting a bonus if more than the usual number of people actually signed up to play. During the course of her job, she'd be getting several checks, each for seven figures.

The game she created took place around the margins of the movie's action. *Stunrunner* had a straightforward script: a long series of encounters, some violent, some sexual, separated by chase scenes that took Bond through Turkey's most iconic scenery, from

Mount Ararat to the dome of the Blue Mosque. In Dagmar's hands the story became much larger, sprawling out from the movie's spare story line. She made use of the characters from the movie and added a couple dozen of her own, either on Bond's team, the Iranians', or members of a freelance group of mercenaries who wanted the Iranian secrets for their own reasons. She was tempted to make them SPECTRE but decided against it. The Bond films seemed to have forgotten about SPECTRE.

The film's Operation Stunrunner, in which Bond first was inserted into Iran, then made his thrilling escape, in Dagmar's hands took on a far more Byzantine aspect, now not simply about the mullahs' nuclear secrets but about security in the Strait of Hormuz, about the mercenary outfit's attempt to hijack an oil tanker, and about Semiramis Orga's attempt to establish herself as an opium smuggler.

Semiramis Orga, by the way, was a character from the movie, the bad Bond girl who gets killed about a third of the way in. (The less bad Bond girl, the one converted to virtue by a night with Bond and who flew off with him in the end, was a Brit named Evelyn Modestbride.)

Dagmar's story was told in many different ways. Radio plays, short films, coded messages, comic strips, pictures with coded messages between the Photoshopped layers, sound files with text hidden in the code.

Then, as if the story wasn't complex enough, Dagmar broke it up into bits, fragments that would be hidden online on Web pages, buried in source code, sent in email, and even available in plain sight if you just knew where to look.

Many of the game's puzzles had a crossword theme. That was Dagmar's idea, inspired by the notion that the answers—if they stuck very carefully to the Turkish setting and to elements of the *Stunrunner* story—would be the same no matter which language the clues were given in. Turkish, like English, was written in the Latin alphabet. She wouldn't have to explain to players how the puzzles were supposed to work or cut across too many cross-cultural divides. Dagmar hired a crossword designer and signed her to nondisclosure agreements the length and complexity of which surprised her.

It was the task of the players—ostensibly working to assist Bond's front company, Universal Exports—to tease out the hidden history of Operation Stunrunner, to locate the fleeing Bond and help him escape from his enemies. In the early days of the game the players had kept running across an ad for the Mystery Tour, a twelve-day journey across Turkey, with *absolutely no itinerary given.*

Within the game, there was a lot of hype given to the Mystery Tour. The players were always overhearing nonplayer characters talking about it.

There was a certain amount of suspense about this game element. Everyone wondered if players would actually fly across an ocean on just a few weeks' notice, all in order to get on a bus with absolutely no idea where it was going.

Indeed they would. And they were joined by a lot of Turkish players who were deeply enthusiastic about such a large-scale game appearing in their country and in their own language.

Even though the work schedule was still frantic and though there were two live events after this one, Dagmar had felt a giddy sense of relief ever since the Mystery Tour's passenger manifest had topped two hundred and then kept growing till the buses were filled with nearly seven hundred people. Nearly 2 million others were participating online.

The Mystery Tour players had witnessed a villain's breathtaking helicopter escape past the great stone heads of Mount Nemrut. They had pursued clues through the canyons and spectacular stone chimneys of Cappadocia and tracked the killer of Semiramis Orga through the ruins of ancient Perge. Now they were hunting Bond through Ephesus while conferring online with others who were playing from their homes and offices.

This was another freaking great triumph for Dagmar and Great Big Idea, is what this was.

Give me a big enough budget, Dagmar thought, *and I'll convince millions of people that you're cool.*

And how much, she asked herself rhetorically, *is* that *worth?*

Lots, she thought. To certain people, anyway.

Her thoughts froze at the sight of a pair of armed police. They were ambling along the tree-lined road toward Dagmar and Mehmet—paying them no attention, grinning and bantering with each other.

But the machine pistols they carried weren't banter. They were the voice of the new regime.

Maybe, she thought, these two weren't supporters of the generals. Maybe they were just ordinary cops, not fascists or murderers. Maybe they hated the new government, the new restrictions, the new gangster paramilitaries who were strutting in the sun of the generals' protection.

And maybe they didn't. Maybe they were loathsome creeps who supported martial law and tortured suspects with cattle prods.

The point was that Dagmar couldn't know what they were, nor could anyone else. She had no *choice* but to be afraid. It was the only rational option.

And the police would sense that. Even if they didn't support the junta, they'd sense the fear and resentment of the population, and that would put the police and the people on different sides of a gulf that was going to get wider and wider as the situation went on.

The first thing that totalitarianism did, she thought, was equalize suspicion among the whole population. Anyone could be a suspect; anyone could be an informer; anyone could be a killer, in or out of uniform.

Mehmet protectively stepped in front of Dagmar as they walked, leaving the rest of the road to the police. The cops smiled and nodded as they passed, and Dagmar smiled and nodded back. She felt that they had to know that her gesture was clearly forced, clearly false.

The police passed and went back to their own conversation.

The tension trickled slowly out of Dagmar's spine, the fear as it ebbed being replaced by anger.

Damn it, she thought. This was a lovely country. It wasn't fair that she had to be afraid of the people who ran it.

Learned Chatter Scrambles Peen

Alaydin says:

6 Across. Gaius Julius Caesar Octavianus Augustus_____.
   WTF? Something after that?

Classicist says:

Imperator, maybe?

Alaydin says:

11 letters.

Hippolyte says:

"Ant Only Loses 1, Clips Her."

Desi says:

Ant Only minus 1 is Antony. Was Mark Antony here?

Corporal Carrot says:

The Roman or the singer?

Alaydin says:

Elton J. was here.

Corporal Carrot says:

If you clip her, does that turn her into a he?

Hippolyte says:

7 ltrs.

Classicist says:

ARSINOE. Antony had Cleopatra's sister Arsinoe IV murdered in Ephesus. Right in the Artemisium.

Hippolyte says:

Thanks! Artemisium answrs 5 dn, btw.

Burçak says:

omg! 6 across! mithridates!

Classicist says:

How do you know?

Hippolyte says:

I'm standing right next to B'cak and looking at it. C Julius Caesar Octavianus Augustus Mithridates. Inscribed on the biggest gate in town!

Classicist says:

There's got to be a story behind *that*!

ReVerb says:

I'm standing next to a building marked "porneion." Does that mean what I think it does?

Hanseatic says:

Hey! There's a wreath on Arsinoe's tomb! Semiramis Orga's name is on the ribbon! I'm uploading a picture!

Culinary Institute of America, Initially

Dagmar and Mehmet walked through the gate of the ancient city into the parking lot, where tour buses and visitors' cars were parked next to stands offering guidebooks, postcards, porcelain, soft drinks, Turkish delight, jewelry, apple tea, textiles, ice cream, hand-carved meerschaum pipes, brassware, and camel rides.

Dagmar hadn't yet seen a camel in Turkey that didn't have a tourist on it. But then she was here on the wrong day for the camel fighting, apparently another local attraction.

As Dagmar stepped into the parking lot she was immediately surrounded by hucksters offering their wares. *Ten postcards one euro. Scarves genuine pashmina pashmina. Guidebook Ephesus, beautiful pictures. My place has everything but customers, please come in. Ten postcards one euro. Ten postcards one euro. Ten postcards . . .*

Dagmar smiled at them all politely but otherwise didn't respond. Not even to the sign that offered, with unusual frankness, GENUINE FAKE WATCHES.

One bus stood out from the others, with a telescoping antenna that towered as high as the nearby cypress trees. The antenna captured the live feed from Dagmar's cameramen and relayed it to nearby Selçuk, where Lincoln's technicians had installed a colossal IT structure that featured high-bandwidth connections to the Internet along with a satellite uplink. The rig provided many more baud than Dagmar would actually need, though she was grateful for the room to maneuver.

Dagmar knocked on the door, and the bus driver, Feroz, opened the door with a hiss of hydraulics. Dagmar bounced up into the interior, happy to be liberated from the hucksters and their polite insistence that she buy their tourist crap. Mehmet came aboard, and Dagmar made way for him as she looked around at a mobile headquarters that would have done Ernst Stavro Blofeld proud.

The side windows in the fore part of the bus had been blacked out. Flatscreens were everywhere, most of them carrying live feed from the cameras that were following the players around Ephesus. Others were turned to sites where gamers were meeting online and exchanging information, others to pages from the game that were due to receive updates.

Another screen showed a site with the crossword puzzle, where Dagmar's crossword designer Judy Strange was monitoring the players' progress in solving her clues.

"I thought they'd take forever on the one about Lysimachus," she said as Dagmar looked over her shoulder. "They got that right away."

"Never underestimate their mastery of trivia," Dagmar said.

"No, I won't," said Judy. She was a short, intense woman with dark-rimmed glasses and abundant dark hair partially confined by a rhinestone-studded plastic tiara. A dozen semiprecious stones glittered on the piercings in each ear. She wore long sleeves to cover tattoos that ran down to her wrists—she and Dagmar had both judged that Turkey wasn't really ready for a glimpse of Judy's body art.

Her body was craned forward to study the screen from just a few inches away. Judy wasn't shortsighted, Dagmar had concluded, she was just overintense.

"'Imperator,'" she muttered. The players had just solved another one.

Dagmar patted Judy's shoulder, a coach encouraging a valuable player, and made her way toward the rear of the bus. On the way she paused by the cooler built into the aisle behind the side door and opened the lid. Briefly she contemplated a beer— drinking an Efes in the city, Ephesus, that had inspired its name would be a singularly appropriate thing. But she decided that a beer shortly after eight in the morning was degenerate behavior even for her and dutifully pulled out a plastic bottle of water. She went to the door that sealed off the rear third of the bus, knocked, and entered.

The back of the bus had been transformed into a lounge/study for Dagmar and her senior project heads. There was a long central table and plush benches along the sides and back. And, because this was the sort of place it was, there were the flatscreens and keyboards, too.

Lincoln sat on one of the benches, eating a honeyed pastry he'd bought from one of the vendors. He pointed vaguely at the screens.

"It seems to be going well," he said.

"So far," Dagmar said, crossing her fingers, "so good."

She had never bossed a game so logistically complex as this one, concluding as it did in a twelve-day tour of a foreign country, with six live events scheduled in six locations—unique in the annals of gaming, and something Dagmar hoped she'd never have to do again.

Yet Ephesus was the fourth event, and so far nothing had gone wrong. If only fortune held through Ankara and Istanbul, she would dutifully give thanks to her long-overstretched luck and return, for a week's vacation, to the beaches of Antalya.

Dagmar opened the water bottle, took a long drink, and sat opposite Lincoln. Lincoln gave her a blissful grin, and Dagmar was reminded that while she was working, Lincoln was having the time of his life.

Lincoln was, she supposed, in his sixties. He had a large, noble head, with graying hair worn over the tops of his ears and sideburns stretched halfway down his jaw. He wore metal-rimmed sunglasses that would have done credit to the face of Elvis.

Dagmar supposed Lincoln had been quite a lad, back in the days of Disco Fever.

He licked honey from his fingers.

"How are plans for Ankara shaping up?" he asked.

"Pretty well. Too much depends on how the players react to today's update." She took off her panama hat and ran her fingers through the hair that had gone gray while she was still a teenager.

"Sometimes I hate our kind of synergy," she said.

"The synergy's the coolest thing about it."

"I know."

"So you hate the *coolest* thing about the work you do."

Dagmar shrugged. "Who among us is not a mass of contradiction?" She looked at him narrowly. "You, for instance," she added.

He returned an amused look as he brushed crumbs from his embroidered Guatemalan peasant shirt.

"Oh yes," Dagmar insisted. "My tech guy Richard has been with your techs on all your installations. You've been installing these colossal servers heavily wired into the local infrastructure, and everything's got all satellite uplink capability."

Lincoln affected surprise at the question. "*You* do that, when you have to."

"Sure, when I have to. In places like rural Cappadocia and Mount Nemrut. But in *Ankara*? And *Istanbul*? They're all heavily wired already; it's easier to get bandwidth that's already in place."

He lifted his shoulders. "There's a lot of money at stake. I want to be thorough."

"And *we're* the people who know better than anyone what kind of hardware we need on-site. Normally *we* install everything and link it up. But you have your own people for that."

"I'm in the media business myself," Lincoln said. "Why should I pay you to do a job that can be done by my own employees?"

Dagmar pointed her water bottle at him.

"When we install stuff," she said, "it's just for the live event, just to transmit the live feed; we take it out later and reuse it. But Richard tells me that it would take a *lot* of effort to rip your hardware out. For all intents and purposes, it's permanently installed, as if you expect this game to go on past the final event on Saturday."

She cocked her head and looked at him.

"What game are you running, Lincoln? What are you really doing here?"

He laughed.

"I'm not going into competition with you," he said, "if that's what you're worried about."

"If you were, you wouldn't be doing it from here anyway. And if you want to run Turkish ARGs, be my guest."

Lincoln shook his head.

"We ran the numbers," he said. "It was cheaper to leave the gear in place, and resell it to local IT companies."

"Local IT companies wouldn't leave them in place," Dagmar said. "They'd move all the equipment to their own server farms. So mooring everything the way you have doesn't make sense."

He shrugged his shoulders.

"I must be incompetent, then."

Dagmar fixed him with a long stare.

"I don't think so," she said. "I think you're up to something I'm not supposed to know about."

He looked away.

"I can't say yes or no to that," he said.

Anger sizzled along Dagmar's nerves.

The last time she'd had a boss who kept secrets from her, people had been killed.

Rather than screaming and smashing Lincoln on the head with the water bottle, she decided to use sweet reason.

"We're in a military dictatorship here," she said. "I need to know if this is something that will put my people in danger."

Lincoln seemed surprised.

"No," he said. "Not at all."

"You're not *helping* the generals, are you?"

He shook his head.

"Maybe I can tell you soon," he said. "But not now." He turned to her, and she could see his blue eyes gazing at her from behind his Elvis glasses. "But in the meantime," he said, "there's some important diplomacy in your immediate future."

Dagmar was instantly wary.

"With whom?"

He smiled.

"Have I mentioned that I enjoy your correct grammar?"

"Who with?" she said.

He sighed and put both hands flat on the table.

"The junta," he said. "I've received an invitation for you, from General Bozbeyli's office. They've invited you and your staff to a reception at the presidential palace, two nights from now. Thursday."

Dagmar was horrified.

"You're joking!" she said.

"The game's been getting a lot of publicity," Lincoln said, "and the movie is going to be the best thing for Turkish tourism since the *last* Bond movie shot here. So the generals want to associate themselves with all this glamor and success, and show how hip they are to modern technology and culture. So you are going to the palace to be thanked for all you've done for the nation."

"There's a live event on Thursday," Dagmar said. "And after that there'll be plenty of work to do, preparing for the finale in Istanbul."

He looked at her levelly. "Dagmar," he said, "refusing this invitation *would* put your people in danger. And yourself. And the hundreds of civilians you're carting around the country by plane and bus. Not to mention the millions invested in the game."

"I don't want to be used to validate this government in any way."

"You can say whatever you like after you leave the country," Lincoln said. "But two nights from now, you're going to talk to Bozbeyli about what a wonderful time you're having in his country, and compliment him on his choice of ties."

Fear and fury pulsed through Dagmar with every throb of her heart. She gave an angry laugh.

"I have a personal history with military governments," she said, "and it's not good."

"Last time," said Lincoln, "they didn't invite you to the palace."

"Ha. That's supposed to make me feel *safer*? I —"

There was a knock on the door.

"Come in!" Dagmar snarled. She didn't want an interruption now, not when she had a full-blown tantrum she wanted to throw.

Mehmet opened the door far enough for his head and his baseball cap.

"The crossword puzzle has been solved," he said. "Time for the update."

"Did they find the wreath?" Dagmar asked.

"Yes."

"And the coded message on the back of the ribbon?"

"Yes, they did."

Dagmar grabbed her hat and her water bottle and rose. The players had done their part; now she would have to do hers.

The players had solved all available puzzles, and now an upgrade would refresh some established Web pages with new information, and this information—much of it in puzzle form—would lead to other Web pages and other puzzles, all newly uploaded.

Dagmar would stage-manage the update from the trailer in Ephesus, but the update wouldn't actually be happening from there. Her staff in the Simi Valley offices were much better able to handle the technical details, but she wanted to be on hand in case there were problems.

Not that she could fix them; she just wanted to fret anxiously alongside her team.

She took her phone out of its holster and pressed the speed dial for the Simi Valley office, where—after midnight, California time—Helmuth and Mike and the others were presumably standing by. Her phone used Voice-over-Internet Protocol, which made sense because it could grab the signal from only a few feet away, right in the trailer, and because the phone came right out of the box with military-grade encryption, which minimized the chance of any of the players stealing her signal and trying to read game clues.

As she passed the door she turned to look back at Lincoln, who looked pointedly at her faded T-shirt and khakis.

"Buy a nice dress," he said. "Shoes, clutch purse, et cetera. And put the boys in suits and ties."

Dagmar glared at him.

"This is *so* going on your bill," she said.

CHAPTER THREE

Dagmar spent much of the next two days in a frantic search for appropriate clothing—and not just for herself but for the two members of her team who were to accompany her. Tuna Saltik, her Turkish co-writer, at least *owned* a suit, even if he didn't have it with him, but Richard, her tech and security specialist, had never worn a suit and never even owned a tie. She not only had to find her own outfit she also had to shepherd Richard through the process.

Richard was known in the office as Richard the Assassin, a name derived from the highly imaginative acts of vengeance he carried out upon players who tried to hack illicit information out of Great Big Idea. He was a trim, olive-skinned young man who favored white Converse sneakers that contrasted with the ninja-dark shade of his T-shirts and jeans. Dagmar couldn't remember when he'd dressed otherwise.

It was only to be expected that on his first trip to a boutique he revealed himself as a closet fashion slut and, furthermore, a fashion slut with luxurious tastes in fabric and style. He'd chosen a gorgeous suit of cashmere, gray with a subtle blue pinstripe, a tie of hand-painted Chinese silk, and Italian wingtips allegedly made by hand. Dagmar had flat refused to authorize the shoes for the expense account, but Richard had brought out his own credit card for the shoes and had then gone on to accessorize himself with a Girard Perregaux chronograph on a gold band—"chronograph" being what you called a watch when it cost over ten thousand dollars. Dagmar wasn't aware that she paid Richard enough to afford such things.

Dagmar was even more surprised to discover that this was the first watch he'd ever owned.

"Up till now," he said, "I just looked at my phone when I wanted to know the time."

"You *do* know you can get a Timex for under fifty bucks, right?" Dagmar said.

He held out his arm to admire the glittering object on his wrist.

"I'll never have to buy another watch, ever," he said.

"At these prices," said Dagmar, "you'd better hope so."

"By the way," Richard said, "can you teach me how to tie my tie?"

Auditing Richard's luxurious tastes wasn't Dagmar's only problem. Tuna Saltik, the novelist and essayist she'd hired to make certain the game worked in Turkish, hated the new government and didn't want to go to the reception; he balked at being dragged to the boutique, and he made Dagmar pick out his clothes for him.

"Maybe I'll be sick tomorrow," he said.

"You'd better not be," Dagmar said. "The generals are going to know who shows up and who doesn't. You don't want to end up on the wrong list."

"I'm not afraid of them," Tuna said.

"Yes, you are."

He glared at her, and she realized that she'd made the mistake of challenging his machismo, or whatever it was Turks possessed that filled the same slot as machismo on the mental motherboard.

He was a big man, broad shouldered, shaped like a brick. He had a mustache and heavy brows and big hands, and maybe — just maybe — he actually *wasn't* afraid.

"Look," she said. "You're a *writer*. Writers have more ways of subverting the dominant paradigm than anyone else on the planet. Come to the palace with me, pay attention to what happens, and then you can write savage satire about the generals, their wives, and their taste in furniture. Or whatever. *Just don't put the rest of us in danger.*"

"This is not acceptable," he said, weakening.

"This is what has to happen. We're in business; it's not our job to go to jail."

Tuna turned sullen. "My friends will learn about this, and then they'll think I'm one of *them*."

"Tell your friends," Dagmar said, "that your Nazi boss made you do it."

Which was, she thought, precisely what she was going to tell *her* friends about Lincoln.

Time was running out on Thursday when she heard a knock on her hotel room door. She opened it to find a young man dressed soberly in a tan blazer and tie and carrying a netbook in a shoulder bag. He was, she figured, in his late twenties; he was slim and a little bit boyish and had studious brown eyes behind dark-rimmed spectacles.

"Lincoln sent me," he said. "We haven't met, but I'm your advance man. I've been doing publicity for you for weeks now."

He spoke American English, with only a trace of an accent.

"You're Ismet Kadri?" she said. She'd spoken to him on the phone, and they'd exchanged a lot of email.

"Yes. Pleased to meet you."

Dagmar shook his hand. "Come in," she said.

Papers, belongings, and electronics were scattered over her hotel room. Ismet gazed at the disorder with mild eyes.

"Can I help in any way?" he asked.

"That depends. What can you do?"

"I can translate for you at the palace. And I can... help arrange your schedule."

"Do you have a car?"

"I have a rental."

"Do you know Ankara?"

"Pretty well. Not like a native, though."

"Right. I need to get Tuna and Richard to the tailor for the final fitting. I need to buy some shoes, and get a haircut. And I need to pick up my dress, which should be ready by four o'clock."

Ismet looked at his watch.

"We have very little time," he said.

He and Dagmar managed everything except for the haircut—the stylist was backed up, with customers already filling the available chairs. Dagmar hoped that her prematurely gray hair would make up in novelty what it lacked in elegance.

Fortunately for these last-minute expeditions, Ankara was the capital of the country, a sophisticated, cosmopolitan city with up-to-the-instant shops. Ankara also featured over a dozen universities, the presence of which guaranteed a large number of boutiques overflowing with stylish, often eccentric, and reasonably priced styles.

Dagmar bought her shoes in one of the latter—chunky yet strangely endearing Bulgarian footwear that looked like something Rosa Klebb might have worn to a fatal meeting with 007. In a more upmarket place in Kizilay she found a glossy Donna Karan gown, slate blue that would set off her gray hair; in another a beaded handbag just big enough to carry a cell phone, a compact, and a tampon; and from a woman at a restored Ulus caravanserai she bought a flowery pashmina shawl to drape around her shoulders.

She figured she'd be all right as long as she didn't use the shawl to cover her hair. The military junta were ultranationalists and ultrasecularists, who would rather shoot a pious young Muslim girl than allow her into a school building in a headscarf.

Dagmar herself had no sympathy for religious fundamentalists, but she had every sympathy for their children and thought it was more important to educate young women than to bar the school door with bayonets.

She managed to get her posse to the hotel lobby on time. Tuna, bulky and uncomfortable in his new suit, was sulking. Richard kept admiring his chronograph. Ismet was all quiet efficiency. And Lincoln was discovered in the hotel lobby, lounging by the fountain in his Guatemalan peasant shirt, duck trousers, and tobacco-colored moccasins.

Dagmar raged up to him.

"*You're not ready?*" she demanded.

Lincoln gave her a mild blue-eyed look. "*You're* the bright future of multiplatform entertainment," he said. "I'm just the PR guy. I wasn't even *invited.*"

"So what will you be doing while I'm kowtowing to the junta?"

"The hotel offers Turkish massage." He smiled. "I think I owe myself a little relaxation after the rigors of our journey."

"Rigors?" she demanded. "*Relaxation?*" Fury blazed through her. "When do *I* get to relax?"

Lincoln winked at her.

"Saturday night," he said. "After the game's over."

Dagmar's hands turned into claws, half-ready to gouge Lincoln's flesh.

"Our ride is here," said Ismet.

The generals had sent a sky blue limousine to pick up Dagmar's posse from the hotel, an extended, customized, mirror-polished version of the Grosser Mercedes that movie villains were always driving in seventies action films. Dagmar herded her posse into a passenger compartment that smelled strongly of cigarettes, and slumped onto the backseat, her task done.

From now on, her fate was up to the gods.

The gods promptly wrapped the limousine in a traffic jam. Ismet looked out at the cars inching along Atatürk Boulevard, then looked at Dagmar and smiled.

"You've done your best," he said, "but the rush hour will make us late."

As long as it wasn't her fault, Dagmar didn't much care. Tuna seemed pleased by the delay. Richard looked again at his chronograph.

"Ankara is built on hills," Ismet said. "All the traffic runs into the valleys and gets jammed up."

"We worked that out when we were planning our live event," Dagmar said. "That's why we had our live event this morning in Anıt Kabir Park—lots of ways for Bond to make his escape from the black hats."

"Very smart." Ismet looked at her. "I watched the event online. It seemed to go well."

"So far." Crossing her fingers.

"The players were enthusiastic. Especially about the Aston Martin."

Double-oh-seven's escape vehicle had been shipped in from a dealer on Cyprus, riding in a truck the entire distance, and would be packed up and taken back the same way.

"Are you enjoying my country?" Ismet asked.

"Good beer," Dagmar said, "and the best fast food in the world. I'm hoping to enjoy everything else once this is over."

Ismet grinned. "You haven't bought a carpet yet?"

"No."

"My people are slipping."

Dagmar laughed. "I suppose you have a brother or a cousin who'll give me a good deal?"

"An uncle. But he's in Istanbul."

"We'll be there tomorrow."

"He's in the Cavalry Bazaar," Ismet said. "I can show you." He was quite serious.

Dagmar smiled to herself and turned to watch Ankara roll past. The car lapsed into silence. Hemmed in by tall modern buildings and Ankara's steep hills, Dagmar began to feel tendrils of claustrophobia sinking into her mind. As the Mercedes moved farther south, she saw the police and military presence deepen. As they passed the Confidence Monument, she saw a group of young men in pearl gray uniforms and baseball caps, machine pistols slung over their shoulders.

"Gray Wolves," Ismet said.

Tuna muttered a few disgusted, inaudible syllables and turned away from the sight.

"What are they?" Dagmar said. "Some kind of secret police?"

"Not so secret anymore," Tuna said in a leaden tone.

"Officially they're the youth auxiliary of one of our political parties," Ismet said. "But now they're the pets of the new regime."

"Like the SS," Tuna said.

"More like the Brownshirts," Ismet said in his precise way.

As the conversation made this alarming swerve, Dagmar cast a sharp glance at the driver, who of course might well be a fanatic supporter of the junta.

The driver was behind a glass window, impassive. He probably hadn't heard anything.

But still.

"Maybe," she said, "we should change the topic of conversation."

Tuna made another disgusted noise. A faint smile touched Ismet's lips. He adjusted his glasses.

"Many of the hills here," he said, "are covered with illegal settlements. People move onto vacant land and build their homes — entire neighborhoods, small towns. When you came here from the airport you probably saw them."

Richard looked up, calculation glittering in his eyes.

"You have earthquakes here. Do those off-the-grid buildings survive?"

Ismet shrugged. "Usually not," he said. "Sometimes the government resettles entire communities because they're so worried about earthquake. But they can't afford to do that with everyone." He made a gesture that took in the city, the surrounding country. "In Istanbul the problem is worse. They have eighteen million people, and maybe a third are illegal. They vote for the politicians who promise to give them infrastructure."

"Who do they vote for now?" Richard asked.

Silence answered him.

Dagmar was trying to wrap her head around the idea that one-third of a city could be squatters. They'd be squatters with jobs, or a hope of a job, and families and at least some money, just without a place to live until they'd built it themselves. And they'd come for the same reason that all immigrants came, because even a fragile jerry-built home on an earthquake-prone hillside was better than the poverty and lack of opportunity in the place they came from.

She'd seen it before, in all the developing world. She'd run games or consulted with other game designers in India and China, and she'd seen a revolution firsthand in Indonesia, where the children of poverty had overrun the glittering hotels and office blocks of the privileged.

Overrun them and dismantled them and carried them away to build new things with the scraps.

"We're coming up to the palace now," Ismet said.

A pair of armored cars squatted before the stone walls on either side of the bronze gate. Soldiers with white helmets and gaiters and chromed assault rifles stood on guard. An officer spoke briefly to the driver, glanced into the back of the car, and then signaled his soldiers to open the inner gate and pull up the spike strip.

Once they were past the barriers, a large, brilliant park opened on all sides. Ankara seemed to specialize in parks, but this one was truly exceptional. The grounds blazed with scarlet gladioli and purple lilac, brilliant lilies and soft-petaled lavender. There were several buildings, ranging from the old Ottoman mansion where Atatürk had first lived to modernist office blocks, but the reception was to be held in the president's residence, a pillared mansion called the Pink Villa.

Dagmar tried to imagine an American president living in a pink building, and failed.

Pink stone pillars loomed above them as the Mercedes drew up to the steps. Functionaries in white jackets and aides-de-camp in uniform clacked their way down the stairs in hard leather heels to open doors and offer hands to the passengers.

Dagmar emerged into bright August light and blinked. The scent of lavender wafted to her nostrils. "This way, please," someone said, but Dagmar waited for her party to join her before she followed the young uniformed man up the stairway and beneath the mansion's pink pillars.

Here there was another security check and the party had to surrender their phones. Richard had to offer his chronograph and shoes for inspection; the rest passed. And then they were shepherded into a drawing room, where a trio of somber, dignified photographers snapped their pictures while other cameramen pointed video cameras at them. Dagmar patted her hair and waited, feeling unnecessarily self-conscious. Functionaries ignored them and talked to each other. Dagmar saw that two plush chairs had been placed on either side of a side table. She wondered if she was supposed to sit.

Then there was a stir among the onlookers. The military men clicked to attention, and everyone else straightened. Dagmar turned to the far door and saw the junta march in.

President Bozbeyli hadn't been seen in a uniform since assuming office: today he wore a soft gray Italian suit and a dignified blue tie. He was very short, seven or eight inches shorter than Dagmar, which put him at an inch or so over five feet. He smiled warmly, took Dagmar's hand, and bowed over it with olde-world politeness.

Dagmar gazed in surprise at the general's lavish use of cosmetics. The makeup and rouge failed to entirely conceal the lines and spots of age — and she couldn't help but see that his hair and mustache were suspiciously black.

Bozbeyli straightened. He and Dagmar held hands and smiled while the photographers' flashes went off, the cameras went *click-click-click*, and Dagmar scrutinized the general's makeup.

The cosmetics were clearly intended for the cameras, not for someone standing a short distance away. The effects were too glaring at close range.

Neither of them had yet spoken a word. It was all dumb show for the cameras.

Words might not even be necessary. The picture of Dagmar

shaking hands with the president was probably enough for the regime's purposes.

"Adoring American media figure endorses president." That's the caption they'd put on it.

Unlike the caption she'd use herself: "Dagmar Shaw sells integrity to keep dream job."

The cameras stopped snapping as if someone had given an order. Then Bozbeyli introduced the prime minister, a white-haired former air force general named Dursun—he wore his age without quite so much cosmetic—and again Dagmar clasped an age-scored hand and gave a close-lipped smile while the photographers clicked away.

Bozbeyli introduced his minister of defense—an elderly admiral who still wore the uniform, along with rouge—and the photographers clicked again. Then there was a pause while the junta looked expectantly at Dagmar, and she realized she was supposed to present her team. She did so—the cameras clicked only a few times for each of them—and then with a gracious gesture Bozbeyli offered Dagmar a seat.

They sat opposite each other. Each entourage stood behind its principal. The cameras clicked some more. The admiral, distracted, fished in his pockets for cigarettes and a lighter.

"I would like to thank you for the work you are doing in bringing modern Türkiye to the attention of the world," Bozbeyli said, in very good English. "Your efforts are inspiring many of the brightest minds of the nation. We are always conscious that the road to the future is paved with technology."

Perhaps, Dagmar thought, that metaphor worked a little better in Turkish.

"The technology infrastructure here is very good," Dagmar said. "We've had very few problems."

She figured that Turkey's IT backbone was a safe subject for conversation.

The little president gave a grand wave of his hand. "I gave orders that you be allowed to proceed without interference."

Dagmar was startled.

"Thank you," she managed. "Everyone has been very cooperative."

"You wished to have your game in Anıt Kabir Park," Bozbeyli said. "My security people said—" He changed to a mocking voice. "'No, that's too close to the Atatürk Mausoleum. There might be terrorists hiding in this game, and they might destroy the monument.'" Bozbeyli made an abrupt gesture. "I said, '*No!* This game will be good for Türkiye! Many people will play this game and see this film and then come to see our beautiful country!'" He shook his finger at imaginary security officers. "'You must put more guards on the Mausoleum to keep it safe, but do not interfere with this game!'"

Bozbeyli sat back, crossed his arms like Napoléon, and smiled.

"That was very good of you," Dagmar said.

"If anyone offers you trouble," he said, "you will let me know."

What power, Dagmar wondered, was Bozbeyli handing her? The power to have someone arrested? Beaten? Jailed?

Whatever power it was, Dagmar decided to ignore it.

"Everyone," she said, "has been very kind."

Behind Bozbeyli, the admiral lit his cigarette. Tobacco tanged the air.

"Under the former regime," said the president, "I could not have guaranteed your safety. Extremists and terrorists were allowed to proliferate. Radical Muslims were on the verge of a coup d'état. It was necessary to act."

His hands made a series of chopping movements as he spoke. Maybe, Dagmar thought, he was simply unable to sit still.

"I'm afraid," Dagmar said, "that your country's politics are a little beyond my scope. I design Internet puzzles."

She hoped to detour around the whole subject of the regime and its announced purposes. It was regrettable that she was here at all—but if she *had* to be in the Pink Villa with the generals, at least she could avoid an explicit endorsement of their rule.

But Bozbeyli persisted.

"Surely," he said, "you must recognize the danger of religious terrorists."

"The whole world has recognized that danger," Dagmar said.

"Then you understand"—again the chopping gesture—"the need for action."

"Civilization here is five thousand years old," Dagmar said. "Can it seriously be threatened by a few madmen with bombs?"

Bozbeyli twitched his sable mustache. Behind him, the admiral drew on his cigarette.

"Public safety can be threatened," the president said. "Lives of ordinary people can be put in jeopardy. The existence of our secular republic was in danger."

"Indeed," Dagmar said, "the danger exists."

That danger, she thought, chiefly being the president and his clique.

Bozbeyli stared at her, as if seeing into her secret thought. As she looked back at him, a mad giddy urge to laugh possessed her. These people—this ancient trio of military mummies, held together with cosmetics and cellotape—they *wanted her approval*. They had gone to all this effort to get it. And now Bozbeyli was badgering her because she hadn't provided what they desired.

She leaned close to the president and lowered her voice as if in confidence. "You know," she said, "I'm really just here to help James Bond."

Bozbeyli laughed and chopped the air with his hand.

"Well," he said, "we must give him all the help we can! He fights the terrorists in our country!"

Dagmar responded with her wordless smile.

Bozbeyli turned to view his colleagues.

"My colleagues and I—we did not want this terrible responsibility," he said. "But the nation was in danger—it was necessary to step forward and act to prevent a catastrophe."

Dursun and the admiral looked a little bored by this. Perhaps they had heard this speech too many times.

"Every time the military has intervened in our nation,"

Bozbeyli went on, "we have stepped down once the country's security was assured." He tapped a finger on his knee. "I assure you, we all wish for the day on which constitutional government may be restored."

Dagmar nodded and smiled.

"Then we have something in common," she said.

She knew immediately that this was the wrong thing to say. Bozbeyli's face hardened, and he stood.

"This way, miss," he said, and marched out without waiting for her. His colleagues followed.

And that was it, as far as hospitality was concerned. Dagmar and her party followed the junta into another room where a long table had been laid with a buffet. Others were there, men and women, to meet the guests, but Bozbeyli's attitude was very clear, and no one approached.

Dagmar and her party stood at one end of the long table and Bozbeyli and a score of others at the far end. They talked to one another in low voices and every so often turned to look at Dagmar's group as if sizing them up for their coffins.

Even the waiters didn't approach. Dagmar helped herself to a glass of tea from a buffet.

"And here I thought it was going so well," she said.

"Fuck him," said Tuna darkly. Dagmar glanced at the other party, to make sure no one had heard.

No one was looking at them at the moment.

The grim standoff ended after twenty minutes, when a man in a tailcoat approached and told Dagmar that her car was ready. The group was reunited with its cell phones and returned to the Mercedes and its silent driver.

"Screw it," Richard said. "It's been a long day, and I'm hungry."

Dagmar decided that Richard had the right idea. She turned to Ismet.

"Can you see if the driver will let us off someplace other than the hotel?" she said. "Let's see if we can't find someplace good to eat."

A few minutes later, standing outside a bustling restaurant in Kizilay, Dagmar hit Lincoln's speed dial.

"Hi, Dagmar," he said. His voice was languid, and Dagmar imagined him stretched out on a divan, tingling with the aftereffects of his massage.

"I pissed off Bozbeyli," Dagmar said.

There was a moment's silence. Lincoln's voice, when it returned, was less languid than before.

"You'd better tell me about it."

Dagmar described the conversation as well as she could remember it.

"He said he was longing for democracy," she concluded. "All I did was agree with him."

"Where are you now?"

Dagmar glanced up at the restaurant sign. "Restaurant Harman," she said. "Turkish-International cuisine, whatever that is."

There was a moment of thoughtful silence.

"Call me before you come back to the hotel," Lincoln said. "And I'll check to see if there's anyone hanging around outside."

"And if there is?"

"You'll check into another hotel for the night."

"What about our things? All my work's on my laptop. And I can't wander around for the next few days in heels and a Donna Karan frock."

"If necessary," Lincoln said, "I'll get your things myself."

"How?"

Amusement entered his voice. "I'll bribe the hotel staff," he said.

Dagmar had to admit that this made perfect sense.

"Don't let this spoil your dinner," Lincoln said. "In all likelihood it means nothing."

"I told you at the beginning," Dagmar said, "that I have a bad personal history with military governments."

"Noted," said Lincoln. "Have a nice dinner anyway."

The staff at the Harman seemed a little surprised at so well dressed a party so early in the evening but behaved with an impeccable, bustling courtesy that only mildly concealed their all-encompassing avarice.

In France, Dagmar reflected, you'd be made to feel second-class for dining so early, but the Turks didn't care about such things. If you wanted drinks at nine in the morning, or dinner at four thirty, or breakfast at midnight, they'd do their best to accommodate you. They had an ancient tradition of hospitality to which they adhered with easy grace. Besides, good service was their way to a better paycheck, and they seemed to have no notions about either the proper time to eat supper or the proper time to earn money.

President Bozbeyli, she reflected, was the only rude Turk she'd ever met.

Dinner lasted a couple hours, and featured rakı and Efes, olives and anchovies, spiced meatballs and grilled fish, and a form of *kofte* that, according to Ismet, translated as "ladies' thighs." When the group left the restaurant the sun was just on the horizon and the first cool touch of evening was on the air. They walked along Atatürk Boulevard while the muezzins sang the call to evening prayer—a sound that sent a primeval shiver down Dagmar's spine.

The people in the streets ignored the call. Kizilay was busy and modern and filled with young people just beginning their evening. None of the women wore headscarves. It was like any European city.

Dagmar called Lincoln, and he said he'd take a look at the hotel lobby and the street in front, to see if some kind of unpleasantness waited.

Buses and trucks rolled past. Dagmar recoiled from the scent of diesel.

Ismet glanced around. "Want to see something different?" he said. "Have you been up to the castle?"

"There won't be soldiers?" she asked.

Ismet shrugged. "No more than anywhere else."

He hailed a taxi. With the three men crammed in the back and Dagmar riding shotgun, they sped north to Ulus and turned where a big equestrian monument of Atatürk stood foursquare on its plinth. Illuminated by spotlights, birds circled over the head of the great man but dared not alight.

To the east rose the walled mass of the city's old citadel on its steep hill. A spotlit Turkish flag waved above the ramparts. Cell phone towers and the masts of broadcasters speared the evening sky.

The overloaded cab chugged slowly uphill, past a pair of silent museums, along the ancient Byzantine wall, and then through the gates of the citadel. Crowding the road were mansions dating from the Middle Ages, all built with ground floors of stone and wooden upper storeys that jutted out over the street and turned the road into a dark canyon. Some salesmen stood smoking in the doors of souvenir shops, alert to the possibility of oncoming profit—but most of the homes were family residences in varying states of repair, and Dagmar realized that there was an entire self-contained town standing within the citadel walls, a town of children with footballs, men playing backgammon in front of their doors, and old women in headscarves carrying plastic laundry baskets up steep, narrow streets. A town where cooking smells floated on the air and where television's blue light shone through upper windows.

It was an older presence that she sensed here and much poorer than fashionable Kizilay. Even the little girls wore headscarves, something Dagmar hadn't seen anywhere else. The present was compounded here with the timeless, present-day Ankara with Hittite Ankuwash and Roman Ancyra, with Byzantine Ánkyra and Ottoman Angora, all blended together in the deep blue Anatolian twilight.

The taxi groaned up a steep road and halted in a cloud of biodiesel that tainted the air with the scent of stale olive oil. Ahead was a gate in another wall.

"I'll tell the cab to wait," Ismet said.

A guitar strummed chords somewhere above them. Dagmar followed Ismet up a stair and through the gate. She found herself inside a wide tower, perhaps a hundred feet across and fifty high, its courtyard broad enough for some boys to kick a football around. Ismet led the party to a steep stair leading to the battlements. Climbing, she tottered on her Bulgarian heels as one hand brushed the old Byzantine wall for balance. The stair was too much toil after a long meal: she was out of breath when she came out beneath the brightening stars.

She stood on the battlements of the tower, on a wide stone walk. Courting couples embraced in the shadows. Dark shapes sat on the outer wall, kicking their feet over the edge of the abyss. Farther along the wide walkway, some teenage boys clustered around a friend playing a guitar and stared at these formally dressed new arrivals with interest. Across the fort, a tourist in khaki shorts was setting up a camera on a tripod.

"The best view is from there," Ismet said, pointing to a bastion that stood out on the edge of the hill.

Dagmar gazed doubtfully at the path that led to the bastion. She would have to walk to the outpost along the top of an old wall, with no rail to keep her from falling to a stony landing twenty feet below.

Ismet walked out onto the wall and turned, waiting for her.

She walked to the wall and hesitated, then removed her Bulgarian heels and took a hesitant step onto the smooth old stones. Ismet took a step toward her and held out a hand. She reached for the hand and took it and allowed him to lead her to the bastion. Tuna followed, unimpressed by heights, and Richard more cautiously.

A group of teenage girls in headscarves and long coats were on the bastion, snapping one another's pictures and giggling. Ismet led her to an unoccupied corner and gestured out at the view.

Below her, Ankara was a stormy sea of red tile roofs, rising and falling with the hills. The towers of isolated developments clustered on hilltops like Crusader castles. A deep red gash on the horizon outlined Ulus in crimson sunset fire, and in the opposite direction the purple shadow of the citadel stretched its long hand toward a rising darkness in the east. To the south, the modern towers of Kizilay stood wrapped in smog.

Dagmar's heart gave a joyous leap, and she took a deep breath of the night-scented air.

"This is wonderful," she said to Ismet. "Thank you for suggesting it."

"I used to come up here when I was a kid," Ismet said. "My uncle had a shop a few streets north of here."

"I thought your uncle sold carpets in Istanbul."

Ismet smiled. "That's Uncle Ertaç," he said. "It was my uncle Fuad who sold manuscripts up here in the castle."

"Manuscripts? Like original handwritten manuscripts?"

"Old Ottoman books," Ismet said. "Printed books. They were in the old Arab script, which no one reads anymore, but they had beautiful illustrations done by hand. So Fuad cut up the books and sold the pages that had pictures on them."

Dagmar wasn't sure how to view this literary vandalism.

"Is that allowed?" she said.

Ismet shrugged.

"Apparently it is. Now that the original books are becoming rare, he finds vintage paper and then hires artists to paint pictures in the old Persian style."

Dagmar was curious. "Does he tell his customers that the pictures are modern?"

Ismet smiled thinly. "I'm certain that he does."

Dagmar looked up as the teenage girls began to shriek with laughter. Still laughing, they walked rapidly along the old wall to the main body of the tower.

Dagmar's handheld began to play "'Round Midnight." She answered.

"If the wicked are lurking," Lincoln said, "they're pretty well hidden."

"They generally are," said Dagmar.

"If the government's going to give us trouble," Lincoln said, "it's going to be in Istanbul."

"Thanks so much," Dagmar said, "for massively increasing my paranoia."

"It's my *job*," Lincoln explained. "Have a lovely evening."

Dagmar returned her handheld to its holster. Ismet, Richard, and Tuna were looking at her expectantly.

"Lincoln says the hotel's okay," she said, and then added, "for now."

Tuna curled his lip in contempt of the government, stuck his hands in his jacket pockets, and walked back along the top of the old wall to the main body of the tower. Richard fell into his wake. Ismet and Dagmar were left alone on the bastion.

"You were raised in Ankara?" Dagmar asked.

Ismet adjusted his spectacles.

"I lived here for a while. My father is an economist and has worked all over the world—China, Egypt, Germany, England, and Canada. He spent three years in Ankara teaching at the university."

"You speak American English."

"I got my degree in the States. In Bellingham."

"You were planning a career in public relations?"

He looked at her. "No. My degree is in journalism. I still free-lance, but PR is a better paycheck."

"Yes. Print media is dead, or so I keep hearing."

"You changed your career, too," Ismet said.

"Yes." Once she had been a science fiction writer. "How did you know?"

"I looked up your Wikipedia entry."

She did that herself, now and again. Originally out of vanity, she supposed, but now just to count the inaccuracies. Her biography was really an astounding collection of misinformation, alleviated only by wild speculation.

She never corrected the inaccuracies. She understood that the subject herself could never do that. She'd have to find some authority to quote in rebuttal—but she didn't know any authorities on herself other than herself.

"The entry mentioned that trouble you had," Ismet said. "When your friends were killed."

A chill wind brushed Dagmar's spine. She felt herself straighten.

"I don't want to talk about that," she said.

Ismet was alarmed. "Oh!" he said. "I didn't mean to offend!"

"No offense," Dagmar said, and waved a hand dismissively. But she wasn't about to talk about any of that to a journalist, not even if she was off-the-record.

She realized she had better look up her Wikipedia entry as soon as possible.

Sometimes, she reflected, it was possible to access too much knowledge.

They stayed on the battlements till the last of the sunset faded from the western horizon. All about them were the soft lights of the city, the tall office buildings, the flashing lights on the broadcast towers. Then they went back down the steep, dark stair to their waiting taxi.

Dagmar had the driver drop them a block from their hotel, and they approached carefully and scouted the lobby through plateglass windows before entering. No one paid them any attention except the young blonde woman behind the desk, who smiled in greeting.

When Dagmar arrived at her room she changed into her khakis and an old giveaway T-shirt from a long-forgotten start-up. Everything else, except for her bathroom case, she packed, and then she blocked the door with her bags to keep anyone from forcing his way in.

She was ready to hit the ground running.

Experience had shown her the value of a fast getaway.

CHAPTER FOUR

Dagmar's posse rose early and were first in line for the hotel's breakfast buffet. They saw no secret police; they saw no gamers. The players had been booked in a different hotel, to discourage them from harassing the puppetmasters or breaking into their rooms in search of information.

Where the secret police might be hiding was another matter.

Dagmar carried her bags down to breakfast, not wanting to leave her hard drive in a place where someone could steal or damage it. Afterward she piled her bags into a taxi for an uneventful ride to the airport. While waiting for the Turkish Air flight, she heard from Mehmet that the players had gotten into their buses without incident and were on their way to the airport. To avoid unnecessary interaction with the puppetmasters, they had been scheduled on later flights.

Another meal was served on the flight to Istanbul — Dagmar was amazed at the efficiency of the cabin attendants, who got food and drinks served and cleared in only forty minutes. Two vans had been hired to take them to their hotel. Their luggage nearly filled the first van, leaving room for two people: Dagmar found herself in the van with Judy, the puzzle designer, who was chatting happily on her handheld. The van pulled away from the curb.

"Love you!" Judy said cheerfully into the phone, and holstered it.

Judy wore a long-sleeved blouse that left only rag ends of her tattoos visible at the wrists. She held back her black hair with a plastic headband that had a crown on it, gold-painted points that haloed her head and made her look like a somewhat less spiky version of the Statue of Liberty, albeit one with a lot of mascara and corpse green eye shadow. Her necklace stared out at the world with a couple dozen blue eyes, made up as it was of Turkish evileye amulets mounted in silver; she also wore matching earrings and a bracelet.

"Who were you talking to?" Dagmar asked.

"My dad." Judy grinned. "He worries when I fly—I always call him after I land to tell him I'm okay."

"You must be close."

Dagmar didn't know what it was like to be close to a father—it was an alien concept to her, like knowing what it was like to be an Australian aborigine or a member of the Rosicrucians.

"The funny thing is," Judy said, "is that Dad flies all the time and it doesn't bother *him* at all. He only gets all worried when *I* fly."

"What does your dad do?" Dagmar asked.

"He's a rock star."

Dagmar smiled. "I guess he must be, if he worries about you like that."

Judy laughed. "No, really!" she said. "My dad's Odis Strange, of Andalusian God."

Dagmar blinked.

"You know," she said, "when a person says that someone else is a rock star, usually it's a *metaphor*."

Andalusian God had been *huge* when Dagmar was in nappies. Her parents had their discs, and their single "Nad Roast" was always playing on the jukebox in whatever depressing Cleveland bar her father was working.

She remembered Odis Strange on the cover of *Living the Life Atomic*, Andalusian God's first CD. He wore a dark five o'clock shadow, a Levi's jacket with the sleeves ripped off, lots of stainless-steel jewelry, and hair that was greased up high in a mock-rockabilly pompadour.

She didn't see much of a resemblance in Judy. Probably she took after her mother.

"I didn't really know him till I was sixteen or so," Judy said. "That's when Dad sobered up and remembered he'd had a family back in the nineties." She laughed. "He's really sweet. He looks after me. He paid for my new teeth." She tapped a brilliant white incisor with a fingernail. "Implants. Even when he was away, his management sent money."

"That's great," Dagmar said. Father-daughter bonding was *really* not her thing.

"We've known each other for months," Dagmar said. "Why haven't I known about your dad?"

"People try to use me to get to him," Judy said. "I'm cautious about who I talk to."

"That's sensible," Dagmar said.

Judy's eyes blinked brightly at Dagmar from behind her black-rimmed glasses. "And *your* dad?" she asked.

"He was an alcoholic," Dagmar said. "He's dead now."

"Oh." Judy's face fell. "Sorry."

Dagmar shrugged. "It happens."

Her mother had worked hard to keep Dagmar from becoming one of those kids who came to school smelling funny. Trying somehow to evade or at least ignore her downwardly mobile status, Dagmar had found refuge in geek culture: science fiction, fantasy gaming, computer-moderated social networks where people didn't know or care that she lived in a shabby flat off Detroit Avenue in Cleveland.

And there had been books. Cleveland might have been a decaying postindustrial polis that had failed to negotiate the collapse of its tax base, but in its glory days it had built great public libraries, and libraries were cheap, a big advantage in a household where the television could at any moment be sold to pay for vodka. Even at his most intoxicated, Dagmar's father knew it was pointless to try to pawn library books.

"My dad was never around when he was high," Judy said. "And he was high for *years*. But he wasn't violent or anything."

"Nor mine." Dagmar really didn't want to talk about this. "He was a sloppy drunk, not an angry drunk."

And a thieving drunk, whom Dagmar did not propose at any point in the next several centuries to forgive.

"Look at all the ships," Dagmar said.

Judy seemed relieved to change the subject. They turned toward the Sea of Marmara, where dozens of cargo ships schooled in the blue water, waiting for a crew, a destination, a cargo, or a pilot to take them up the Bosporus.

The ships were freelancing, Dagmar thought, just like herself and her crew.

Give them a destination and they'd amaze you with how they got there.

In Istanbul the Great Big Idea crew was booked into a small boutique hotel, a converted Ottoman mansion in the tourist paradise of Sultanahmet, while the players stayed in a pair of larger, more group-oriented hotels in Beyoğlu, across the Golden Horn. The party's rooms weren't ready when they arrived, at 8:45 in the morning, so Dagmar and her planners agreed to gather in the rooftop lounge to plan the next day's live event, the game's finale.

The lounge had a bar at one end, closed at this hour of the morning, and glass walls that gazed out upon the Sea of Marmara, the deep blue water where dozens of freighters waited their turn to steam up the Bosporus or to moor at the piers of the Asian shore. In the other direction were the dome and six minarets of the Blue Mosque, pale gray against the azure sky.

When Dagmar came up the clanking old elevator, she found Lincoln sprawled on a couch gazing at the sea, his loopy grin on his face. He was still having the time of his life.

Dagmar, less sanguine, stood by the glass wall and watched a host of gulls, wind beneath their wings, sweep in a perpetual gyre around the minarets of the mosque. Anxiety scrabbled at her nerves with rusty iron claws. The lack of information made speculation impossible.

She didn't know if she was safe, if any of her group were safe.

She didn't know if the players would be molested when they assembled in Gülhane Park on Saturday morning.

The most ambitious ARG of all time could end up with people dead. That wasn't how she had intended to go down in history.

She hadn't killed *players* yet, though with other people her record wasn't quite so pristine.

The doors to the creaking elevator rolled open, and Ismet arrived carrying a stack of newspapers. He paused, looking for Dagmar, and then offered her the papers in a hopeless gesture.

"I'm afraid you're famous," he said.

He spread the newspapers over one of the low tables. There was a picture of her with Bozbeyli on every paper, either shaking hands with him or sitting next to him. In every picture he was erect and masterful, his eyes alert and commanding. In each image she looked humble and submissive, her eyes turned to the Great Man for instruction.

None of the pictures hinted at the quantity of the president's rouge and hair dye.

"Would you like me to translate the text?" Ismet asked. "It's pretty much the same in each paper."

Dagmar felt her stomach turn over.

"I can imagine what it says."

Lincoln picked up a section of newspaper, took reading glasses from the pocket of his shirt, and held them halfway between his eyes and the text. "You're quoted as saying that the whole world knows the danger of terrorism," he said. "And that even a civilization five thousand years old can be threatened by the bombs of madmen."

Dagmar stared at him.

"You read Turkish?"

She hadn't heard him speak the language to anyone, not beyond more than a few tourist phrases.

Lincoln shrugged and put away his glasses.

"I read a lot of languages," he said.

"You were also on the television news this morning," Ismet told her.

Dagmar sank into her chair.

"This is going to be everywhere," she said. "On blogs, on Our Reality Network, on Ozone, everywhere."

"You can issue a denial," Lincoln said. "A correction. When you get home."

"I know how memes propagate on the freakin' Web," Dagmar said. "No correction will *ever* catch up with the original story. For the rest of my life I'm going to be the game designer who brown-noses dictators."

She closed her eyes and let herself pitch backward onto the cushions, as if falling into her own personal hell.

Behind her, the elevator doors rattled open.

"Dagmar?"

She opened her eyes, turned, and saw Mehmet. He had a concerned look on his face and his cell phone in his hand, and— because Mehmet wasn't part of the creative team and it wasn't his job to be here—his arrival set a new anxiety gnawing at Dagmar's vitals.

"Yes?" Dagmar said.

Mehmet approached.

"I got a call from Feroz. The headquarters bus was stopped and he was arrested."

The news startled her. Dagmar jumped to her feet.

"Arrested? Can we get him a lawyer?"

"Stopped where?" Lincoln asked.

"Just outside Izmir." Mehmet turned to Dagmar. "He's been released," he said. "But they beat him, and then they took the bus."

"*Beat* him?" Dagmar's bafflement warred with her rising outrage. "Why beat Feroz? He's just the bus driver we hired." She turned to Lincoln. "Can we contact the embassy?"

"Feroz is Turkish," Lincoln said. "Our embassy can't help."

Dagmar was disgusted at the idiocy of her own question. She threw out her arms in annoyance at her own thundering great stupidity.

Lincoln continued to ponder the issue. "Probably that's why they picked Feroz, because they could punish us without causing a diplomatic problem."

Dagmar turned back to Mehmet.

"Does he need a hospital?"

"He says he's afraid to go. They might get his name from the hospital records."

"They don't have his name?"

"They didn't look at his identification. They just took him out of the bus and started hitting him."

Dagmar pulled out her handheld and went over her list of contacts.

"Zafer Musa?" she asked, to no one in particular, and then pressed the Enter button.

Zafer Musa, a matronly woman married to an Australian, was Dagmar's go-to person in Izmir—Zafer had helped to set up lodging and transportation for the gamers and had cleared the game with the various bureaucracies that had a say in whether Ephesus could be used as a site for the game.

Zafer answered. A many-sided conversation ensued, in which Zafer agreed to pick up Feroz and take him to a clinic, have him use a false name, and pay for his treatment with cash. Dagmar would reimburse any expense.

"Have her take a camera," Lincoln said. "We want pictures."

Dagmar gave Lincoln a look, then nodded. She told Zafer to take pictures and then ended the call.

She turned to Lincoln. "We need to hire a bus driver. Quick."

Mehmet shook his head.

"You don't understand," he said. "They kept the bus. The Gray Wolves kept the bus."

So now all the electronics were gone. The cameras, the satellite uplink, the wireless net, the displays. Dagmar reached down to the table, picked up Ismet's newspapers, and hurled them against the glass wall overlooking the sea.

The papers proved a completely inadequate weapon. They blossomed out, touched the wall with a sigh, and drifted to the floor.

"We are hopelessly in the shit," Dagmar said. "We are the fucking falling newspapers, and someone's going to come along and step on us."

The elevator wheezed open, and Tuna entered with Judy Strange. They carried cups of Turkish coffee and plates of vegetables and *gözleme*, cheese-stuffed pancakes, all of which they'd carried up from the hotel buffet. They looked at the tense little scene, the scattered newspapers, Mehmet with his cell phone half-raised.

"What is it?" Judy asked.

A long, disjointed explanation followed.

"It's not the end of the world," Lincoln said. "Tomorrow's event can still take place. We just won't be able to carry it live."

Dagmar shrank from this idea. Carrying the live events as they happened, to connect the players on the ground with the many more players who participated only through electronic forums, was a Great Big Idea trademark.

"Not necessarily," Dagmar said to Lincoln. "You still have your massive server set up in Istanbul, right? What the bus has is all the equipment we need to connect the camera feed to the servers — and it's got all our vidcams, too. So what we need to do is get some new cameras, and then get a connection between our cameras and your server. We don't technically need the bus for that, but we need *something*."

She looked at her speed dial. "I'll get ahold of Richard."

Richard wasn't answering his phone, so Dagmar left voice mail. She holstered her handheld and looked at the others.

"Whether it's safe to continue at all," she said, "is another issue."

"Bah," Tuna said. "Let them do whatever they like."

"No," Dagmar said. "Let's not." She looked ruefully at the furniture, the scattered papers, and nudged a chair with her foot.

"Have a seat, everyone," she said.

They sat—except for Lincoln, who hadn't ever risen from his chair. Before Dagmar sat, she walked to the window, stooped, and picked up the scattered newspapers. She stacked them in a rough pile, dropped them on a table, and then took her seat.

"We have permission to run an event in Gülhane Park tomorrow morning," she said. "So the government knows where we're going to be, and when. And they've taken away our ability to cover the game live, so maybe they think they can take some kind of action against us—attack us, even."

"The players are going to all have cell phone cameras," Judy said. "And a lot will have video cameras, as well. There's no way"

Ismet knotted his long fingers. "But does the government *know* that?" he said. "The Internet didn't exist when the generals were young. I don't know whether they understand anything like what your game represents."

Dagmar recalled the three elderly men and felt doubt slide into her mind.

"Presumably they have younger advisors," she said uncertainly.

Tuna made a fist of one big hand and bounced it on his knee.

"They know nothing," he said. "They're fools; they're ridiculous."

"Dare we take the chance?" Judy said. "If they know nothing, doesn't that make it *more* dangerous? They could order these Gray Wolves to attack us thinking no one would ever know, and even if a thousand pictures are taken on cell phones, we'd still be attacked."

Dagmar turned to Lincoln, who was frowning down at the floor between his sandals.

"Lincoln?" Dagmar said.

"I'm thinking," he said. "I'm trying to work out how much the generals care about world opinion."

"They seem to care about *my* opinion," Dagmar said.

"This game is *huge,*" Lincoln said. "The generals have every reason to want it to succeed. Attacking a bunch of foreigners in a park isn't the sort of thing that would bring millions of tourist euros to their country, and so..."

He let the words trail away. He closed his eyes and was silent for a long, long moment. He nodded a few times. Dagmar began to wonder if he'd fallen asleep.

And then Lincoln lifted his head, looked at Dagmar through his Elvis glasses, and shook his head.

"Nope," he said. "You can't risk it."

"Why?" Dagmar asked.

"Because," Lincoln said, "I could be wrong."

Anger clamped around Dagmar's heart like a grim little fist. She wanted to jump, rage, wave her arms. Instead she took a long breath and spoke.

"I really want to stick it to these people," she said.

"Yes!" Tuna said. He pumped a hand in the air. "Yes, very good!"

Lincoln was still looking at Dagmar, his eyes narrowed, as if he was studying her.

"How?" he said.

"I don't know."

"What are our goals?" Lincoln said. "To damage the regime in some way? To cock a snook at the generals?"

"Cock a what?" This clearly was a new expression for Mehmet.

Lincoln continued as if he hadn't been interrupted.

"Or are we abandoning the game?" he said. "Or carrying it on in spite of the possible dangers? Or altering the gaming experience somehow?"

The options spun in Dagmar's head. She returned Lincoln's look.

"*You* hired *me,* Lincoln," she said. "You have to approve whatever gets decided. And more importantly, you have to fund it."

"I'm not the creative presence here," Lincoln said. "Before I can endorse an idea, I have to know what it is."

Judy Strange took a sip of her coffee, then made a face and put the cup on the table.

"Well," she said, "if it's dangerous to run the live event, we'll have to cancel it."

Dagmar felt a stubborn resistance build in her to the idea.

"With all respect to Lincoln's list," she said, "I think it's a little out of our league to damage the regime, though I don't mind cocking the odd snook..." She raised a hand as Mehmet was about to interrupt again. "...so long as it won't get us thrown in jail." She turned to Judy. "And as for the game," she said, "maybe we can alter it so we won't be running a risk."

Judy leaned closer to her.

"How?" she said.

Dagmar shifted her gaze to the others.

"I don't know," she confessed. "We'll need to work that out." She felt the urge to move, to think on her feet, and she surged to her feet.

"Let's take a walk. Let's go to Gülhane Park."

The park was within easy walking distance of the hotel. Their path took them past both the Blue Mosque and its great, crumbling ancestor, Hagia Sofia, which faced each other across tourist-choked roads and a large garden blazing with summer flowers. Along one side of the mosque was the old Byzantine hippodrome, still a long ovoid in shape but now another park. Vast numbers of tourists, far outnumbering the locals, moved among the radiant flowers, past the silver waters of the fountains. Sometimes the tourists swarmed in huge packs, marching along behind their guides, amid air scented with roses and diesel.

She wondered if she could hide her players among the tourists, her buses amid the tour buses. It certainly seemed possible.

But then she looked up and saw the streetlights with their quaint, lacy white heads, and the CCTV cameras attached. A group of soldiers stood by one of the fountains.

It wasn't necessarily the malevolence of the generals that had put these measures here, she thought. There were all sorts of reasons that this area should be secure—many foreign visitors, irreplaceable public monuments, heavy traffic.

But even so, the brilliant sun-filled park flanked by the two huge domed structures now seemed just a little sinister, just a little too much like a trap waiting to be sprung. Dagmar headed north, skirting Justinian's old church, then descended a steep road while streetcars hummed past her. Men on the sidewalk shilled for carpet stores and restaurants.

At the bottom of the hill they encountered the outer wall of the shambling Topkapı Palace, with two arched, open gates. Soldiers in white helmets stood by the entrance.

Feeling a shiver of apprehension, Dagmar walked through the gate.

Topkapı was built in a series of irregular, walled courtyards, one set inside the next like nesting dolls. In the center was the harem, where the sultan would have lived with his concubines, children, and mother.

During the course of scouting locations for the live events, Dagmar had learned from Mehmet that the sultan's harem had been a far cry from the sybaritic paradise imagined by the Western—male—imagination. The harem had actually been run by the sultan's mother, who made all the important decisions, including which of the concubines slept with the sultan and when and how often. The sultan wouldn't have gotten to arrange his household to suit himself until his mother died, if then.

But Dagmar wasn't going farther into the palace, let alone to the harem. Instead she turned left, passed a group of pushcart vendors selling roast chestnuts and *simit*—a kind of cross between a bagel and pretzel—and walked into Gülhane Park, which was actually between the outer two walls of the palace. The ground sloped down toward the Golden Horn, the path bordered by flower beds and a double row of giant plane trees. The rest of the palace loomed above them on the right, invisible behind the wall that crowned the hill.

A ship's horn sounded up from the harbor below. Soft morning light filtered down through the leaves of the trees. Somewhere a child laughed.

"It's a pity we're not here in spring," Ismet said. "During the Tulip Festival, there are tulips in all these flower beds. Some of them very exotic."

"I always thought tulips were a Dutch thing," Judy said.

"The Dutch got their tulips from Turkey," Ismet said. "That's why there was such speculation in tulips at first—they were Eastern and exotic."

"Speculation?" Judy asked.

"Let's talk about Tulip Mania later," Dagmar said. She slowed, then stepped off the path to stand before a statue of Atatürk. Uptilted eyebrows gave the Republic's founder an elfin caste. She returned his skeptical gaze, then looked at the park around her for the first time since her original scouting trip nine weeks before. Lincoln voiced her thoughts aloud before she could speak.

"This place is unusable," Lincoln said. "I know why we picked it for the live event—it has limited access, so the players won't get lost, and yet it's open, and we can hide a lot of things in here for the players to find. But as far as keeping our people secure, it's hopeless." He waved a hand up to the palace. "People on that wall will see everything we do. And we can be completely bottled by closing the two entrances."

Judy looked around with apprehension on her face, as if she were already seeing the tanks closing in.

"Where else can we go?" Dagmar asked.

There was silence for a moment. Then Ismet cleared his throat.

"Does it have to be Istanbul?" he said. "Can we move the players out of the city?"

"The players are already in Beyoğlu," Judy said. "Can we do the event there?"

"Taksim Square?" Dagmar said hopefully. It was the only Beyoğlu landmark she could remember.

"No," Ismet said. "Beyoğlu is full of foreign embassies. The security's too high."

"My wife and I live on the Asia side, in Üsküdar," Mehmet said. "We could drive the buses across the bridge, and stage the event there. There are plenty of parks."

Ismet frowned. "And also the military barracks at Selimiye."

Mehmet's expression fell. The group stood for a moment, their general gloom a contrast to the cheerful green of the park, the packs of children with their ice cream, the teens with their MP3 players, the gulls calling overhead.

Ismet looked up and shaded his eyes with his hand. "Look there," he said, and pointed.

Dagmar followed his gaze and saw a small aircraft silhouetted against the sky, orbiting a few hundred meters above the palace.

"Surveillance drone," Lincoln said.

High-tech military surveillance drones—the kind that could fly thousands of miles, loiter for hours over the target, and drop bombs or missiles—these were expensive and cost millions of dollars each. But low-tech drones, essentially large model aircraft with Japanese lenses, digital video, and uplink capability, could be built in someone's garage, for a few thousand dollars.

They were all over the place in California now, where Dagmar lived—floating above the freeways to clock speeders, racing to crime sites to track felons, shadowing celebrities on behalf of paparazzi, and ogling sunbathers at the Playboy Mansion. The drones were cheap enough so that the highway patrol could afford them, as could local TV stations, celebrity magazines, private detectives, and hobbyists who collected candid videos the way other people collected stamps.

"Do you think it's tracking us?" Judy asked.

"Probably not," said Lincoln. "I doubt we're worth following. It's probably looking for suspicious people around the historic sites."

Anger simmered in Dagmar as she scowled up at the drone. If the military government was using these cheap flying remotes, they could shift their focus of attention from one place to another very fast. One place, she thought, might be as dangerous as the next.

She let her gaze fall from the bright sky and blinked the dazzle from her gaze as she looked at the silver-green bark of the nearest plane tree. The sound of a ship's horn floated again on the air.

"There," she said, pointing north, toward the Golden Horn.

"Yes?" Lincoln said. He peered at the tree-shrouded horizon and narrowed his eyes as he tried to see what she was pointing at.

"We have the event on the water," she said. "Rent some excursion boats, take a cruise. They won't be able to harass us unless they scramble the navy and board us."

Lincoln turned to Mehmet.

"Can we rent boats for seven hundred people on twenty-four hours' notice?" he asked.

Mehmet gave a slow, thoughtful nod.

"There are a lot of excursion boats in Istanbul, and a good many are tied up three deep waiting for customers. But it would depend on what you're willing to pay."

Lincoln raised a hand in a gesture of pure noblesse, like a grand cardinal-archbishop giving a blessing.

"Whatever it takes," he said.

Mehmet smiled. So did Dagmar. She knew that she could trust in the Turkish willingness to inconvenience themselves in the name of profit.

"What shall I tell them?" Mehmet asked. "Bosporus cruise?"

Dagmar nodded. "Why not?"

Mehmet reached for his handheld and began to page through his rather substantial list of contacts.

Dagmar turned to Lincoln.

"Thank you," she said.

"Thank *you*," said Lincoln. "I'd much prefer my brilliant PR coup not end in broken heads."

Dagmar turned to Judy.

"I'm afraid this means we've got to come up with a whole new crossword puzzle by tomorrow morning."

Judy was looking inward with her usual fierce concentration.

"I know," she said.

"Can you do it?"

"I'll have to, won't I?" Judy looked across the park at the Golden Horn. "What's on the Bosporus, anyway? What is there to put in the puzzle?"

"Dolmabahçe Palace," Ismet said. "The Bosporus Bridge. Selimiye Barracks. And..." His voice trailed away. "I'm not sure. I've never actually been up the Bosporus."

"How," Dagmar asked, "did the Bosporus Bridge avoid being named after Atatürk, like every other major structure in this country?"

He smiled. "There already *was* an Atatürk bridge, over the Golden Horn."

"I am enlightened," Dagmar said.

The party began heading upslope, back to their hotel.

"Fortress of Europe," Tuna said, adding to the list of Bosporus sites. "Fortress of Asia. That big mosque in Ortaköy, I don't remember the name of it."

"Our hotel will have a brochure for cruises," Dagmar said. "It should list the sights."

Dagmar's handheld began to play " 'Round Midnight." She reached for it.

"This is Dagmar," she said.

"This is Richard. I had my phone off. What's the problem?"

Dagmar was nettled that he had made himself unavailable during work hours.

"Why was your phone turned off?"

"I was with Ismet's uncle Ertaç, haggling over carpets. I didn't want to be interrupted."

Dagmar shook her head and sighed.

"What did you buy?"

"Six carpets. One runner for the hallway. Two kilims that I just couldn't resist."

She saw Ismet looking at her and lowered the phone to speak to him.

"Uncle Ertaç just scored big," she said.

Ismet laughed. Dagmar returned to her phone.

"Richard," she said. "Have you ever been in a foreign country before?"

He was surprised by the question.

"I've been to Cabo San Lucas," he said.

"When you went to Cabo," said Dagmar, "did you buy everything that was put in front of you?"

"I was in *college*," Richard said. "I bought all the beer and tequila in front of me, and maybe even some of the food."

There was a buzzing overhead. Dagmar looked up to see the drone swoop low and then head out of the park toward the southwest.

"I'm kind of worried that I've led you into some kind of horrible temptation," Dagmar said. "Are you sure you can afford all these things you're buying?"

"I *did* have to call the credit card company and argue them into raising my limit," Richard said. "But the carpets are actually *investments*. Now there's more opportunity for women in this country, they're not going to spend their time sitting at home weaving. The carpets are going to become more rare, and that means more expensive. In time, I'll be able to sell the carpets for a profit."

He spoke rapidly, trotting out these ideas with what sounded like considerable pride in their form and originality.

Uncle Ertaç, Dagmar realized, might just be the greatest carpet salesman in the world.

"It might take you twenty years to realize your profit," Dagmar said.

"It's a more solid investment than the dollar," Richard said. "Remember what happened to the currency a few years back?"

Dagmar remembered all too well. It occurred to her that she was perhaps the last person on earth to advise anyone on investment strategy.

"Well," she said, "go with God." And then she remembered why she'd called Richard in the first place. She explained about Feroz and the missing bus.

"We need to replace everything on the bus, and get the receiver and uplink somewhere above the Bosporus where everyone on the boats can broadcast to it."

"Well." Richard was suddenly thoughtful. "I think it's do-able. What kind of expense account do I have?"

"You have whatever's necessary," Dagmar said.

Richard's tone brightened instantly. "Excellent! Are you at the hotel now?"

"We're on our way there."

"Avoid the hippodrome, then. There's some kind of political demonstration going on."

Dagmar glanced up as she remembered the aerial drone speeding off. Anxiety roiled in her stomach.

"We'll do that," she said.

The soldiers at the palace gate seemed more alert. Their officer was talking urgently on a cell phone.

Dagmar warned everyone about the demonstration at the hippodrome. She and her party panted up the steep road, past the great shambling mass of Hagia Sofia, and into the area between the old church and the Blue Mosque. A scrum of tourist buses stood like a wall across their path. Diesel exhaust brushed her face with its warm breath as she wove between the buses. Her head swam as it filled with fumes. As she stepped from the road to the park on the far side, a solemn Japanese man aboard one of the buses raised a camera and snapped her picture.

Ahead were paths, flowers, palm trees, hedges, a broad circular fountain, and the Blue Mosque. The surveillance drone turned gentle ovals overhead. Dagmar dodged a carpet seller before he could even begin his sales pitch—her reflexes were improving with experience—and then her nerves jolted to the sound of gunfire.

Shotguns! she recognized, and hunched involuntarily as if expecting a round of buckshot between the shoulder blades. She wasn't hit and then looked wildly for the source of the firing.

White smoke poppies blossomed across the park, followed by

the hollow roar of a crowd, a roar mixed with screams and shrieks. Dagmar knew the sound too well and realized the shotguns hadn't been targeting people but had lofted pepper gas into a crowd that, on the far side of the park bushes, she hadn't realized was so close...

"Run!" Tuna bellowed. Perhaps it was the wrong thought.

Adrenaline boomed in Dagmar's veins. She couldn't think of any place to run *to* except for the hotel, diagonally across the park, and she started a dash in that direction, knowing even as she ran that her path would take her unnervingly close to the spreading white smoke.

Behind, she heard Tuna's cry of disgust, or despair, but her feet were already moving.

Dagmar was nearing the fountain when a wave of people came stumbling out of the smoke, weeping. The demonstrators had dressed well that morning: the men were in coats and ties, the women in neat suits or headscarves. They were less neat now: crying, sobbing, cursing, faces stained with slobber or with blood... Some dragged signs and bedraggled Turkish flags. A few threw themselves bodily into the fountain in order to rinse pepper gas from their eyes.

The refugees lurched across Dagmar's path, stumbling over hedges or sprawling across the neat white shin-high cast-iron rails intended to keep people off the lawn. Dagmar dodged, jumped over one of the white rails, ran madly across a brilliant green lawn. The air was full of shrieks.

An adolescent girl tripped and flopped directly across Dagmar's path, eyes wide, Adidas-clad feet kicking in the air... Dagmar bent to help her rise, then gasped as a dark figure loomed between her and the sun—a man in a helmet and a blue uniform, dilated mad eyes staring at her through the plastic goggles of a respirator, weapon raised to strike...

"*This* way." A hand seized Dagmar's sleeve and snatched her away from the descending club. Dagmar felt the breeze of its passage on her face. The policeman raised the club to strike again, and then Tuna lunged into the scene: the big man clotheslined the cop neatly across the throat just under the respirator's seal, and the man flew right into the air, feet rising clean over his head, before he dropped to the grass with a satisfying thud.

In what seemed about two seconds, Tuna ripped the gas mask off, grabbed the cop's club, and smashed him in the face with it a half-dozen times. At which point Ismet took Tuna's shoulder as well, firm grip on the sturdy tweed jacket, and repeated his instruction.

"*This* way."

One hand on Dagmar's shoulder, the other on Tuna's, Ismet efficiently guided them through the park, past the berserk masked cops, the shrieking demonstrators, the bewildered, terrified tourists clumping together for safety... The girl in the Adidas had disappeared. Ismet led Dagmar and Tuna to the steep stair that led down to the Cavalry Bazaar. Dagmar and her escort funneled down the stair along with a couple dozen other refugees, then jogged as quickly as they could through the narrow lane between tony shops selling textiles and ceramics, old cavalry mews converted to a high-class shopping mall.

"Where are Lincoln and Judy?" Dagmar gasped, looking over her shoulder.

"We were following *you*," Tuna said.

"Are they all right?" Dagmar asked, completely conscious of the uselessness of the question. Either they were okay or they weren't.

Tuna looked at the bloody club in his hand and then hurled it aside with an expression of disgust. The sudden bright clacking sound of the club hitting the pavement made bystanders jump.

Ismet guided them out of the bazaar and to their hotel. In the street they encountered Lincoln, Judy, and Mehmet, who had taken a more rational route around the trouble. They looked at Dagmar with relief.

"You ran right into it!" Judy said to Dagmar.

"Yes," Dagmar said. "I did."

Whatever *it* was, Dagmar thought, she was always running toward it, or knee-deep in it, or falling face-first into it, or failing to claw her way free of it.

"It's how I roll," she said.

CHAPTER FIVE

Dagmar spent the next fifteen minutes shivering in the bathroom of her hotel room. She knew there were police standing just outside the bathroom door — Indonesian cops, with riot shields and samurai helmets with metal plates protecting their necks — and that they were waiting for her with weapons raised. She knew that she would be smashed to the ground the second she left the security of the bathroom.

In Jakarta she had learned to recognize the smell of burning human flesh. Shuddering on the commode, she wept as the scorching, greasy smell filled her nostrils.

Reality returned in its slow, relentless way. The scent faded. Dagmar spent a moment just staring at the washroom door, then rose, wiped her eyes, washed her face, and took the elevator to the rooftop bar of the hotel.

Her team awaited her. The day's newspapers, with their pictures of Dagmar and Bozbeyli, had been neatly folded and placed on a glass table; a smiling, efficient employee in a bow tie now stood behind the bar, waiting for the day's drinkers.

How normal it is, Dagmar marveled.

The waiter offered her tea and poured it into a tulip-shaped glass with great efficiency, from a copper teapot decorated with elegant filigree.

The Turks were damned serious about their tea, Dagmar thought. Thank God.

She clutched the teacup like a *Titanic* survivor snatching a life preserver. It had been a little over an hour since she had left the bar on her reconnaissance to Gülhane Park, but it seemed like days ago. As she was looking through the glass walls over the roofs of Sultanahmet, it was impossible to see that there had been a disturbance at all: the gulls still circled the Blue Mosque; the Sea of Marmara still blazed with azure beauty; the sound of the muezzins still echoed in the streets.

The demonstration seemed to have fallen clean out of history. Dagmar assumed there would be nothing in the news about it. Pictures snapped by tourists might be the only evidence that anything had ever happened, that and the broken heads and bones of the regime's victims.

"I *told* you not to go there," Richard said. He had avoided the demo entirely by detouring around the back end of the Blue Mosque. "What were you doing in the middle of it?"

"You said not to go to the hippodrome," Judy said. Her voice was intense. "We went through the *park*."

"We couldn't see any of it until they were *there*," Dagmar said. "And then it was too late."

She reached for her glass of tea. Her hand shook, so she held the tulip glass in both hands and sipped from it. She looked at Ismet.

"I should thank you," she said. "You kept me from being clubbed."

"You're welcome," Ismet said. His brown eyes looked at her through his dark-rimmed spectacles. His face took on a look of concern.

"Are you all right?" he asked. "Can I get you a drink or . . . something?"

"Sorry. Bad memories." Dagmar shivered to a surge of adrenaline. "I'm as all right as I'm going to be."

She turned to Tuna.

"You saved us both," she said. "If you hadn't taken that cop out of the picture . . ."

"Bastard deserved it!" Tuna said.

"No doubt. But—"

Lincoln made a covert finger-to-lips gesture, then nodded to the ultrapolite barman. Paranoia seemed to flood the air like a faint whiff of tear gas. Tuna saw the gesture, shrugged, and changed the subject to something else equally explosive.

"I did military service when I was a young man," he said. "I was stationed in Şırnak Province—lots of Kurds there. And do you know what my commander was doing?"

His voice grew louder, more indignant. Lincoln made his gesture again and was ignored.

"The army was in the spare parts business," Tuna said. "People—just ordinary people—were being shot for their kidneys. Then the kidneys were sold on the international market for fifty-five thousand euros apiece—and the sad bastards who got shot were written up as Kurdish terrorists."

Dagmar was staggered. "Organlegging?" she said.

Judy seemed equally appalled. "Has this been *confirmed?*" she asked. Like there were some NGOs that could be called in to verify a story like this, Pathologists Without Borders or something...

"I *saw* it," Tuna said. His mouth quirked. "Or I saw the bodies, anyway. The colonel had some special killers who did the shootings for him. Everyone out there knew what was going on." He made a pistol with two fingers and mimed a shot. "And do you know who the colonel reported to? General Dursun." He slapped himself on the chest. "Our new prime minister." He looked at Dagmar. "One of the old men you met at the Pink House. The fucker."

There was a moment of silence. Dagmar sipped her tea, put the clear tulip glass back in its saucer. Glass rattled.

"Well," Lincoln said. "That's who we're dealing with. The question is, do we go on with the live event tomorrow?"

Tuna waved a hand. "Of course we should."

Dagmar decided that Tuna's breezy confidence was perhaps a little premature.

"The players are across the bridge in Beyoğlu," Dagmar said. "They're far away from what happened this morning."

"And they won't hear about it," Ismet said.

Which meant, Dagmar thought, that *the situation hasn't changed, as far as the game went.* The idea struck Dagmar with surprising force. She resisted the notion: she preferred to think that because she had changed, so had everything else.

But no. It hadn't. She still had six or seven hundred gamers on buses—at this hour scheduled to visit the Grand Bazaar, fine shopping since 1461, a last chance to buy carpets or meerschaum, spices or ceramics, brassware or leather goods, before they bade farewell to James Bond's glittering world on Saturday.

Later this afternoon they would visit the Suleiman Mosque and then Hagia Sofia, assuming the authorities hadn't closed it in the aftermath of the riot—but by that point, she reckoned, any sign of the demonstration would have been long since cleaned up.

The gamers were in no more danger than they had been two hours earlier. Or no less danger. It was all a big unknown, but for the life of her Dagmar couldn't see why the government would bother to harass them.

"Let's go," she said. "We can always call it off tomorrow, if there's a revolution in the streets—and if there's trouble, we'll just distribute the puzzles in the hotel instead of on the excursion."

Judy sighed and adjusted her spectacles.

"I suppose," she said, "that means there have to *be* puzzles."

"I'm afraid so," said Dagmar.

Laptops, netbooks, and phones were deployed. The history and sights of the Bosporus were brought to blazing life on screens and salient facts and images copied to files. Judy had a program for creating crosswords: she and Tuna huddled over her screen, working in intent collaboration as they tried to find clues that would be roughly equivalent in both Turkish and English and to find answers that would work in both the Turkish and English alphabets. This was accomplished by instructing the program to ignore the difference between *c* and *ç*, *i* and *ı*, *Ş* and *s*. Fortunately, the program didn't care how the words were actually *pronounced*.

Ismet watched with interest—he hadn't actually seen one of

these brainstorming sessions before—and offered some helpful suggestions. Mehmet turned up to let them know that Zafer Musa had taken Feroz to a clinic in Izmir and that the bus driver had been patched up. Lincoln told Dagmar to see that the bus driver got a generous bonus, then got brandy from the bar, sipped and listened, and—judging from the smile on his face—went to his happy place, wherever that was.

Richard, with help from Mehmet, found all the hardware he needed online or by phone and set off to collect it.

The waiter produced menus, and food was ordered from the restaurant downstairs. The bar was filled with the scents of *kofte*, baked chicken wings, kebaps strong with the aroma of cumin. Baklava made its appearance, Turkish-style with pistachios, and the waiter offered small cups of Turkish coffee that soon had everyone as wired as if they'd been mainlining Red Bull for the past three days.

In late afternoon, Lincoln received a call from the police. The permit to use Gülhane Park had been canceled, due to "unforseen complications." Lincoln thanked the caller and hung up.

The plotting session went on.

By evening, Richard had his gear in a rented van and he and Mehmet and the team's three hired cameramen were practicing with the technology. The crossword was finished, and Judy dashed off to her room, where she had a printer that would run off hundreds of copies in the next hour.

The bar was filled with drinkers, cigarette smoke, and ghastly Central European pop music. Tuna went to the bar to smoke a cigarette and order a celebratory *rakı*. Lincoln went out onto the balcony, away from the music, to phone the operator of the excursion boats they were renting and to give the man the number of his corporate credit card. That left Dagmar and Ismet sitting in adjoining chairs. Dagmar shifted the weight of her laptop in order to ease a cramp in one hamstring.

"Thanks again for helping," she said.

"I enjoy watching you work," he said. "It's all so intricate. Do you normally do your job under such pressure?"

"Normally we don't work under the threat of physical violence," Dagmar said, "but there's always a lot of things that have to be done at the last second. And we have to keep things away from the spies."

He was genuinely surprised. His brows lifted well up above the line of his spectacles.

"Spies?"

"There are players who stalk us—try to hack our computers, or steal scripts from the actors, or follow us around in hopes that we'll drop a clue."

Ismet seemed delighted.

"Do you get good at escape and evasion?"

"Escape and evasion?" It sounded like a course in commando school. "I don't know about that," she said, "but I've gotten good at hiding things."

He smiled. "Tomorrow," he said, "you're going to hide seven hundred people."

"Let's hope," said Dagmar, "that I do."

He raised his Efes to his lips. "I think we'll be fine," he said.

She looked at Ismet with a sudden flare of interest. She'd met him only the day before, but since then he had so efficiently inserted himself into her process that she hadn't noticed till now.

"You keep saving me," she said. "Yesterday from social embarrassment, this morning from getting knocked into the hospital. Is this sort of thing normal for you?"

One of Ismet's small hands made a circular motion in the air, a local gesture that Dagmar knew meant something like, "Oh yes, I've done that countless times."

His actual words were a little more modest.

"Lincoln told me to be useful," he said.

She narrowed her eyes. "How long," she said, "do I get to keep you?"

Dagmar saw a little flare of light behind the spectacles, as if he'd only just now realized that there was flirtation going on.

"I work for Lincoln," he said. "Or rather, my PR firm does.

You could request that I be kept around to rescue you when necessary."

"Maybe I shall," Dagmar said.

Tuna came barging up, a drink in his hand and wrapped in a cloud of harsh tobacco fumes.

"Shall we eat?" he said. "I'm hungry."

Dagmar turned her eyes from Ismet with a degree of reluctance.

"Yes," she said. "It's probably time we did."

Hippolyte says:

Oh, goodie! A boat ride!

Burçak says:

I wish I had brought a coat. Going to be cold out on the water.

Corporal Carrot says:

Wish I had Dramamine. I get seasick.

The next morning Dagmar stood above the golden span of the Bosporus Bridge from the vantage point on the steep hill of Ortaköy. Excursion boats drew their wakes across the deep slate of the straits below, tiny little water bugs alongside the enormous tidal surge given off by a brilliant white cruise ship so enormous that it seemed like a piece of the continent broken off and adrift.

A blustery cold wind blew from the Black Sea, and Dagmar wore a jacket against the chill, with the brim of a baseball cap shading her eyes from the sun, still low in the eastern sky. Behind her was Richard's new electronic marvel, his rented gear packed into a Ford van, with an antenna strung from the van to a nearby plane tree, and another directional antenna mounted on a long wood plank aimed at Lincoln's bunkered router up above Seraglio Point. A generator rumbled from a yellow trailer, spitting diesel smoke into the brisk wind.

They could have just grabbed a local signal—the area was saturated with IT—but the local bandwidth might not be up to the task. Their own gear, however improvised, was to be preferred...

"Reception is *brilliant!*" Richard called. "If only the rest of the world is getting it..."

He was busy on the phone to Great Big Idea HQ in Simi Valley, where it was late Friday night. Tens of thousands of American gamers, it was hoped, were awake to watch the game's conclusion on live feed.

At least they would, if Richard's jury rig worked.

The live event had gone perfectly to this point. Buses had taken the gamers from their digs in Beyoğlu to the quay in Ortaköy, where they filed happily aboard their excursion boats in the shadow of the district's elaborate Mediciye Mosque, a structure that looked—to Dagmar, on her hill—like a Mississippi steamboat, with two filigreed funnel/minarets, an arched dome with a silhouette like an amidships paddlebox, and gingerbread dripping from the Texas deck...she wondered if the mosque's nineteenth-century architects had in mind the era's steamboats, chugging up and down the Bosporus in plain sight of the structure.

"*Five by five! Five by five!*" Richard shouted. By which Dagmar concluded that Simi Valley was receiving the transmissions just fine and that soon the finale of the *Stunrunner* game would be played out to its worldwide audience.

Dagmar got out her handheld and was aware of Ismet by her side mirroring her gesture. She looked over her shoulder to see Richard making a third call from his own phone, so that the guides on the three boats would get the message at the same time, and all three feeds would soon offer the last set of instructions given to the players.

"*Universal Exports thanks you for your assistance to our sales associate Mr. Bond. We are pleased to report that he has returned to England in complete safety. But we would appreciate your assistance in helping to clarify a few final details...*"

And the players were off.

Alaydin says:

"Foundation laid by Io's grandson, where Yeats invoked mechanical bird." wtf? 9 ltrs.

LadyDayFan says:

Googling Yeats + mechanical + bird gives a poem called "Sailing to Byzantium."

Classicist says:

BYZANTIUM. Io's grandson was Prince Byzas, who founded the city.

ReVerb says:

"Abdülmecid filled the Sultan's garden here." 10 letters.

Burçak says:

EZ, if yr Turk. DOLMABAHÇE Palice. Dolma + bahçe = filled + garden

Hanseatic says:

"Motivated by gadfly's tongue, heifer drives Henry's car." 8 ltrs.

Desi says:

Henry's car would be a Ford.

Classicist says:

BOSPORUS. Io was turned into a cow and driven across the Bosporus by a stinging fly. Bosporus is Greek for "cow-ford."

Corporal Carrot says:

Do you have to have a doctorate in classics to get this stuff?

Maui says:

"Where snakes, pink lions, and Mad Fuat got their yah-yahs out."
(7 ltrs)

Classicist says:

I suspect my degree isn't going to help with this one.

Burçak says:

Yah is Turkish for "mansion on water." But which one?

LadyDayFan says:

Googling like fury here...
Snakes, Pink Lion, Egyptian, and Mad Fuat are all *yahs* along the
    Bosporus.

(*Crescent and Star*, Stephen Kinzer, p. 197.)

Hippolyte says:

But where are they?

Corporal Carrot says:

Realty Web page says Egyptian *yah* is for sale. Address in
ORTAKÖY.

ReVerb says:

Brilliant! We're on our way!

The players in their boats laid little white tracks on the blue.
Standing on the hill of Ortaköy, Dagmar finished her call and
cast a glance at Ismet. He was dressed in his tan blazer and tie,
and the blustery wind had brought a little color to his cheeks. He
looked down at the distant Bosporus traffic as he held his phone to

his ear, then nodded, smiled, and returned the phone to his pocket.

He looked up and smiled. The wind tossed his hair.

"What are you doing after this?" she asked.

"Back to working for our regular clients. I think the next job has to do with advertising a new series of electronic switches, mainly in trade journals."

"Sounds peaceful."

"Oh yes." Ismet threw out an arm, at the spectacular Bosporus scene, the electronic world, at *Stunrunner* sizzling invisibly through the ether, its video streams reaching to outer space and back.

"This is the most fun I've had in ages!" he said.

"Other than the riot and the anxiety."

He made an equivocal gesture.

"That's my country now," he said. "That sort of thing can happen at any time."

Dagmar hadn't been able to continue her brief flirtation with Ismet during the group dinner of the previous night, with everyone talking at once and passing mezes and drinks back and forth—and afterward she'd been too tired, her system having crashed after too many early mornings, too many nights on the go, and always worried that she, her friends, her charges, could end up on the points of bayonets...

And besides, she'd been having second thoughts. She had a bad history with office romance.

Her last lover, an actor she'd hired for one of her projects, had (1) turned out to be married and (2) been savagely murdered and, furthermore, had been killed on her account. That was *two* reasons for feeling guilty and miserable—more if you considered the wife.

He hadn't been the last to die, either.

In the aftermath Dagmar had decided that the only remaining morally defensible position was to forget the world of relationships and concentrate on work. Which she had, for three years.

But still, she was planning a week's vacation after the live event, the first vacation since the one that had gone so disastrously wrong in Jakarta. And the week could be a lot more fun with someone else along.

"Where do you actually live?" she asked.

He nodded across the water. "The Asia side, in Üsküdar. I share an apartment with a colleague."

"So you take the ferry every day?"

He made an equivocal gesture. "The ferry, the train, aircraft... I travel all over the place. I rent a single room in Ankara because we lobby the government, but I may have to give it up. The generals have their own structures in place, and a very firm idea of which interests they have to placate. They don't respond to our efforts." He tossed his head back. "Call me another dissatisfied customer of the regime."

Richard stuck his head out of the van.

"Look at this! It's beautiful!"

She turned and stepped up into the van and duckwalked to a better view, leaving the world of reverie for the more immediate sphere of video. The multiple feeds were indeed beautiful, digital icons of the packed tour boats hissing through the water, flags snapping, old Ottoman mansions lining the shores, most of them beautifully restored and probably worth millions, gamers bent over their puzzles, the sharp wind ruffling their hair... astern loomed the towers of the Bosphorus Bridge, the roadway suspended by a web of sun-etched cable. Dagmar's heart leaped.

"Are those *dolphins*?" she cried.

"Yes." Ismet peered into the van, shading his eyes with a hand. "'*That dolphin-torn, that gong-tormented sea.*'" Quoting Yeats.

Ismet looked at her curiously. "Did you say *gong*?"

Dagmar smiled.

"Yes," she said. "I did. But Yeats said it first."

They were back to the hotel in time for lunch. Richard would return his borrowed electric gear and everyone would have the afternoon off, after which they'd drive over the Golden Horn to a farewell dinner with the players, held in an enormous hotel ball-room. After that the players would go to a specially arranged screening of *Stunrunner*, which had opened worldwide the previous night, while the puppetmasters—who had already seen the movie dozens of times, on discs that came complete with their very own nondisclosure agreements and prepaid FedEx return envelopes—would go with the techs to the VIP suite in a Beyoğlu club, where the celebration would go on until exhaustion overtook them all—in Dagmar's case, most likely before midnight.

Lunch, though, was not a planned event. Dagmar thought she might see if Ismet might want to join her for a midday snack at one of the cafés up the street.

But first she ran into Lincoln in the lobby of the hotel. He'd watched the game finale on his laptop, and when she walked through the door he rose to give her a rib-shattering embrace.

"Brilliant!" he said. "Absolutely brilliant!"

"Thank you," she said. She felt as if her lungs had just been crushed.

He released her and stepped back. Dagmar gasped in oxygen.

"Dagmar," Lincoln said. "Could I see you privately sometime this afternoon?"

"Sure."

She cast a glance over her shoulder, where Richard, Tuna, and a half-dozen techs were trooping into the hotel. Cameras and tri-pods were tucked under their arms. Cables dragged empty metal sockets across the brown tile of the hotel foyer. Ismet was visible through the front window, talking on his phone.

"After lunch?" she suggested hopefully.

He nodded. "Call me when you have a moment. I'll probably be somewhere in the hotel." He looked up at the party of techs. "Can I help you with anything?"

Dagmar let Richard and the technicians sort out the gear, with Lincoln's help. She took a turn around the lobby, waiting for Ismet to finish his conversation. Standing by herself, she felt a sudden rush of triumph surge through her veins, the heat of victory racing through a brain already a bit dazzled by its own ingenuity. Game brilliant, cool, and *over*; military thugs confounded; vacation in sight; nothing to do but celebrate.

Optimism seized her. She decided that she would ask Ismet to lunch, spend the night dancing with him in the Beyoğlu club, maybe drag him off to bed—assuming of course that she didn't collapse first out of sheer exhaustion.

Maybe he'd be able to beg off from the week's work of selling electric switches, head south with her to Antalya, spend a week dividing their time between lounging on the beach and having massively satisfying sex in a darkened hotel room...

Ismet finished his call and came into the lobby, neatly avoiding the electronic gear now being sorted into piles. He came to Dagmar and said, "I'm afraid I've got to leave."

"Is something wrong?"

"My sister called." He gestured with his right hand at the phone held in his left. "My grandma fell and had to go to the hospital."

"Oh no!" Dagmar felt her carnal dreams spin down the drain even as her face and voice made the proper responses. "Is she badly hurt?"

"Broken arm. But she's very frail and..." He hesitated. "Well, she doesn't do well in settings like a hospital. She was raised in a nomad family, and had an arranged marriage to my grandfather, who was from the city..." Ismet gave an apologetic smile. "Anyway, I should go translate between her and the modern world."

Dagmar's mind swam with questions that she had never before asked any human being: *Nomad? Your grandmother's a nomad? What kind of nomad? Do you still have nomads in your family?*

"If you can come to the dinner tonight," Dagmar said, "or the party afterward, please feel free to join us."

He seemed agreeable.

"If I can," he said. "But I should say good-bye now."

She hugged him and sensed his surprise at the gesture. He had an agreeable scent, a blend of Eastern spices, with a faint under-tone of myrrh...

He returned her hug, gently, then went to the others and said his good-byes. Dagmar, aware of a host of possibilities silently drifting away, carried on a tide toward the Dardanelles, turned to Lincoln.

"You know," she said, "we might as well have that conversation now."

Lincoln had a corner room on the top floor of the hotel, with a wide bed, a rococo desk with an Internet portal, and broad windows that displayed spectacular views of the Blue Mosque. Another wall featured a dormer window complete with a window seat, and beyond the shambling bulk of Hagia Sofia.

"Nice," Dagmar said, going to the broad window just as the muezzin began his call. He was echoed almost instantly by the muezzin in the small mosque behind the hotel, the one down by the old Byzantine gate, and then by calls from other small mosques in the area.

It was, Dagmar thought, one of the last times she'd hear this.

"You're planning on going to Antalya tomorrow?" Lincoln asked.

"Yes," Dagmar said. "Shouldn't I?"

"I wouldn't advise it. I'm not going to be happy until you're on the far side of the border."

She shrugged, another dream gone. She turned to face him.

"So much for my vacation," she said.

"I've taken care of that." Lincoln went the rococo desk and shuffled through folders: he took out an envelope and handed it to her.

"Compliments of Bear Cat," he said. "First-class train tickets, and a week's vacation in the beach resort of Aheloy."

Dagmar blinked. "Where's that?"

"The Moesian Riviera. Bulgaria."

"Bulgaria?" Dagmar could only repeat the word.

"Fifty-six thousand square meters of beach in Aheloy," Lincoln said. "Someone counted. Better beach than the French Riviera, too. Organic farms and vineyards just up the river — you'll eat and drink extremely well in the local cafés."

"Okay." Cautiously. Bulgaria was not exactly what she'd planned.

Lincoln smiled. "I was there a few years after the Wall fell," he said. "It was very quaint and olde-world, but I imagine it's more twenty-first century now. And you'll be just five kilometers from Sunny Beach, which is a hugely overdeveloped beach resort with boutiques and discos and bars, if that sort of thing is your preference." He peered at her over the metal rims of his Elvis glasses. "I wasn't sure."

She looked back at him, into the startling blue eyes.

"Discos, huh?" she said. "Did you spend a lot of time in discos, back in the day?"

"Naturally." He shrugged. "Disco was quite the cultural revolution, before overpopularity and *Saturday Night Fever* wrecked everything. The movie left out the gays and the drugs, and that was half the scene."

Dagmar tried to picture Lincoln young, dancing in the patterned light of a spinning mirror ball, but failed.

Disco. To Dagmar it was just another style of music that had risen and then crashed, back before she was born. Like calypso, or ragtime.

"I don't think discos are high on my list," Dagmar said. "I just want to relax." Her mind spun, trying to come up with objections to Lincoln's scheme. She knew next to nothing about Bulgaria, nothing whatever about its Riviera. She didn't even know enough to raise a valid protest.

"Aheloy is the place to relax, all right." Lincoln was confident. "I put you in a bed-and-breakfast — you have a very nice bedsit, and you've got your own entrance to the garden, so you'll have privacy."

"Ah. Thanks." She fumbled with the envelope, saw schedules, tickets, printouts. No pictures of the garden or the bedsit.

"People from all over Europe go to Bulgaria's beaches for vacation," Lincoln said. "Lots from Russia and Ukraine. And a great many Brits, because Bulgaria's still a place they can afford."

"Okay." She was still not entirely pleased, though she couldn't have said why.

"I've arranged for a car and driver to pick you up at the station, take you straight to the B-and-B; you can walk to the beach and be in the water by one thirty in the afternoon."

"Thanks." She peered again at the documents, then looked up at Lincoln. "Is anyone else coming?" she asked.

He seemed surprised. "Everyone else is going home tomorrow. Or so I thought."

"And you?" Because a sliver of ice-cold paranoia had slipped into her brain and for a moment she wondered if she would arrive in Aheloy only to find Lincoln there, with roses and chocolates and a box of condoms, ready to launch himself on top of her once he'd gotten her in his secluded little love trap...

She'd never gotten anything like a sexual vibe from Lincoln, but then she'd been wrong before.

"I'm flying to New York tomorrow morning," Lincoln said. He peered at her. "Don't you like Bulgaria?"

"I don't know enough to know whether I like Bulgaria or not. All I know is that I like their shoes."

"I considered sending you to Rhodes," Lincoln said. "But there are no air connections between Greece and Turkey right now, you'd have to fly through Bulgaria anyway, so I figured once there you might as well..." He flapped his hands.

"I'm sure it will be fine," Dagmar said. "Thank you."

"If you hate it, you can make other plans. But you'll have to pay for them yourself."

She patted his arm. "That's fine. I appreciate your...kindness."

He smiled, then swept out an arm.

"Why don't you have a seat? Because I have another business proposition for you."

Dagmar glanced around and decided on the window seat. Lincoln took the creaking wooden chair that went with the rococo desk.

"Does Great Big Idea have any commitments after this?" he asked.

"Nothing signed," Dagmar said. "I've got three pitches coming up, one to Seagram's, one to a Korean software firm, and another to a cable company that wants original content."

"Television company?" His eyebrows lifted. "You'll be doing television?"

"Television and game both," Dagmar said. "The two will be linked."

Lincoln was impressed. "Must pay well."

"Television pays well because the content provider has to wade through endless network hassle in order to do her job," Dagmar said. "Frankly, if it weren't for a whole season's worth of checks, I'd rather sell the whiskey."

Lincoln smiled. "Not the software?"

"The Koreans want *us* to tell *them* how to sell their product," Dagmar said. "I don't think they have much of a future in the North American market."

"So you *might*," Lincoln said, "have room for another project."

Dagmar waved an arm.

"Bear Cat wants another ARG?"

"Not Bear Cat."

She settled into the window seat and gave him a level look.

"I suppose you're going to explain to me why you've been emplacing servers all over Turkey."

Gracefully he shifted course.

"You did a brilliant thing in the last twenty-four hours," Lincoln said. "You faked out the generals and made them look a bit silly *and* satisfied your customer base."

"I made myself a nervous wreck."

"I gather that's...*normal* in your line of work."

"Anxiety's normal. Physical danger isn't."

Except for me, she thought. *My friends get to die for me.*

Lincoln placed his elbows on the chair arms and steepled his fingers before him.

"I have...friends," he said. "Contacts. And when *The Long Night of Briana Hall* came online a few years ago, and your friends were killed..."

Dagmar flashed him a warning look. "I don't talk about that," she said.

"I don't want you to." He spoke quickly. "I don't actually want to *know* anything." He relaxed a little, leaned back against the chair's pink satin cushion. "I just want to say that I looked into some things—where your friend Charlie's money came from, for one thing—and I read some reports from the FBI and the LAPD, and I drew my own conclusions."

Dagmar tensed. Lincoln looked at her.

"You handled yourself well," he said. "That's all I'm saying. I'm not making judgments; I'm not making accusations. But from where I'm standing, you did well."

"You don't know what I did."

"I don't," Lincoln said. "Not really. I only have my guesses." He raised a hand as she prepared again to object. "And as I said, I don't want to know—so if you ever have the urge to confess anything, don't do it to me."

What makes you think I have anything to confess? she thought—and then decided she didn't actually want the answer to that question.

"And—as far as the botnet goes—you did well there, too."

A cold shaft of terror pierced her. Panic yammered in the back of her head. Lincoln knew about *that*?

Dagmar decided to counterattack. She glared at him.

"So who the hell are you, really?" she demanded. "I checked out Bear Cat, it's a real outfit, and you're there on the Web page, but who are you really? Publicity flacks don't have access to FBI reports."

He smiled thinly. "I'm not a flack; I'm an account executive. You should know the terminology; you're in the advertising business."

"Sorry." She put as much sarcasm into the single word as she could.

"Sometimes I'm in a position to rain money on Bear Cat," Lincoln said. "And in return they're kind enough to provide me with credentials."

A lightning revelation seemed to strobe across the inside of Dagmar's skull.

"Oh Christ," she said, "you're not telling me you're some kind of *spy*." She began to laugh. "A spy using a James Bond film as a cover! Talk about postmodern!"

"I *used* to be a spy," Lincoln said. "I was a spy for thirty years." He gave a little amused bow from the waist. "Now I'm a consultant. Advertising, and other things. Consulting pays much better."

She just looked at him.

"And you're telling me this because ...?"

"I want to hire Great Big Idea," Lincoln said, "to do just what you've been doing."

"Which is what?"

Lincoln waved a hand in an elaborate pattern as he spoke.

"What do you do in your games, Dagmar? You teach people how to use and break codes, to do detailed research, to solve intricate puzzles. You provide raw data, which the players must put into usable form. You send people on missions into the real world to find information or locate objects. Your players have to find hidden motivations and meanings, distinguish truth from fancy. You organize events, both online and in the real world, in which complete strangers unite to complete a common task."

He blinked his blue eyes at her.

"Do you know what those skills are, Dagmar? Those are practical intelligence skills. I want you to do a project for *us*."

She blinked at him. "So you want me to create a game? For the CIA, or the NSA, or whatever it is you actually work for? To train people how to do their jobs."

"*That*," said Lincoln, "would tread on too many toes. We already have plenty of training facilities and trainers."

"What, then?"

Lincoln smiled and then told her.

She would have laughed, if she hadn't been so surprised.

ACT 2

CHAPTER SIX

After Bulgaria—which was *lovely*, exactly the vacation Dagmar needed, sipping gin and tonics as she reclined on a chaise set on a couple of Aheloy's fifty-six thousand square meters of beach while about eighteen varieties of barely clothed male flesh competed to keep her drink topped up—so after the return to California, and after the set of pitches failed, there was nothing to do but take Lincoln up on his offer. So she found herself on the island of Cyprus, in a set of offices overlooking a British runway baking in the Mediterranean sun.

The building was old but well maintained, and featureless in what Dagmar came to recognize as a military absence of style, efficiency combined with cheapness and an almost fetishistic lack of anything approaching aesthetics—aluminium-framed windows overlooked the runway's vast expanse, high ceilings with fans and ranked fluorescents, walls thick with decades-old ochre yellow paint and featureless save for pinholes where picture hooks had once been, or placards announcing what to do in case of fire or in the event of an interruption in electric service. Out of some warehouse had come graceless furniture made of metal and painted in unaesthetic colors that only the military employed, as if marking their property by the application of a coat of Ugly.

The noise from the runway was continuous; the windows rattled in their frames; the fluorescent light seemed to strobe in some hard-to-define, headache-inducing way. Air-conditioning had been retrofitted into the building in ways that made sense only to the British, resulting in zones of wintry climate that alternated with areas of Sahara heat. The lavatories featured the world's most useless and inefficient toilet paper, which Dagmar could only conclude was created to some ancient wartime government specification, from a time when only cheap pulp paper, filled with little chunks of actual undigested wood, was available.

Piled on the metal desks were cardboard boxes full of thousands of dollars' worth of computer equipment: flat-screen monitors, office towers crammed with the latest in graphic interfaces, a million times more processing capacity than the entire Manhattan Project, DVD burners, modems, printers. Other boxes held software: office suites, programs for editing video and graphics, software packaging for budgeting and ultrafast communication.

"The T3 connection is already installed," Lincoln said.

He showed Dagmar and her posse their work space with what seemed to be a sense of pride. They shuffled along after him, jet-lagged, not quite believing they were actually here.

Lincoln made a grand gesture taking in the room, the metal desks, the computers and software in their boxes.

"Welcome to the ops room," he said.

Ops room, Dagmar thought.

"Back home," she said, "we'd just call it an office."

It was almost as if Dagmar had decided to remake *Stunrunner*. Richard the Assassin had come along, tickled to use his computer-ninja skills on real-world applications. Dagmar had hired Judy again, not so much because she needed a puzzle designer as because Judy had a talent for creating and controlling intricate situations. And Dagmar had brought along her head programmer, a German who bore the name Helmuth von Moltke, a moniker he'd inherited from an ancestor who had once conquered France.

Helmuth dressed better than anyone else in the party, in gray cashmere slacks, a starched white shirt with chunky gold cuff links, and a dark Nehru jacket, a fashion choice that put him in a league with a whole series of Bond villains, including Dr. No, Hugo Drax, and the impeccably groomed Ernst Stavro Blofeld.

Helmuth was, generally speaking, a match for any creature of Ian Fleming's imagination. In his circuits of the Earth, the sleekly blond Helmuth occupied the Party Orbit: he girdled the world looking for bars, music, and lonely females. In LA, he seemed to spend half his life on the Sunset Strip and had apparently done away with any need for sleep—a useful skill in a programmer at any time.

The rest of the Great Big Idea staff remained in Simi Valley, though their expertise and advice could be called upon at any time. In any case, they would all be very busy—the Seagram's people had reconsidered, and Great Big Idea was now prepping a full-fledged ARG for them. This was the first Great Big Idea game that Dagmar would not actually write herself, and even though she'd hired a substitute who seemed professional and imaginative and who was even willing to relocate to California for three months, a low twelve-volt anxiety now hummed in Dagmar's nerves, sixteen cycles per second of uncertainty and unease.

Lincoln invited Dagmar into his office while Helmuth, Richard, and Judy began to pillage the cardboard boxes. The ops room and the hardware would be set up and configured to their specifications.

Lincoln's office had the same bare, dull yellow walls as the ops room, and he had a metal desk identical to the others. There was a safe with a digital lock, and Lincoln had also equipped himself with an Aeron office chair, a marvel of lightweight alloy, pneumatics, and material science. He sat in this and leaned back with a blissful smile.

"You've pimped out your office," Dagmar observed.

"Note the other feature." He pointed at the wall, to a poster where a silhouette of a sinking aircraft carrier was accompanied by the slogan LOOSE TWEETS SINK FLEETS.

"This has all the potential of a security nightmare," Lincoln said. "We've got to be very strict, very correct, from the start. Particularly about code names."

"We did all right during *Stunrunner*," Dagmar said. "And we were in Turkey then, right in the security zone, with hundreds of gamers surrounding us and eager to find out our secrets."

"The problem with Cyprus," Lincoln said, "is that it's lousy with spies."

"Ha. You should feel right at home."

"Cyprus is a crossroads," Lincoln said. "Here we've got Turkish nationalist fanatics and Greek nationalist fanatics. We've got Greek spies, Turkish spies, Syrian and Egyptian spies, Israeli spies, British and American spies."

"And there's *us*," Dagmar said.

Lincoln looked at her with great seriousness. "We're not actually spies," Lincoln said. "We're special ops."

"Oh," she said, startled. "Sorry."

"I want to give a special warning." Lincoln gave her a stern look. "There's a Russian colony down the road in Limassol, and I want you to stay away from them."

Dagmar smiled. "Afraid I'll spill everything to Rosa Klebb?"

"I'm afraid you'll be drugged, raped, robbed, and murdered," Lincoln said. "Some of those guys are old-school Russian Maffya left over from the day when Cyprus was the money-laundering capital of the world."

Uneasiness fluttered in Dagmar's belly. Her smile froze to her face.

She had a bad history with the Russian Maffya.

"I was station chief in Nicosia in the nineties," Lincoln went on. "At least a couple hundred billion dollars flowed through here to tax havens in the West, and I drove myself crazy trying to keep track of it all. Russia went bankrupt, but Cyprus practically had a golden age, if you don't count the bombings and shootings." He saw Dagmar's face, and his expression softened. "Sorry," he said, misinterpreting. "I didn't mean to shock you."

Dagmar decided she wasn't going to think about Austin's death right now.

"I'm not shocked," she said. "But sometimes I forget that we're here doing something, uh, real."

"Maybe," Lincoln ventured, "it's best if you think of it as a game."

Dagmar thought of bullets, bodies, smoke floating over cities. From the nearby runway came the sound of a flight jet aircraft launching into the air, a sound that lent an uneasy reality to Dagmar's thoughts.

"I don't know if I can," she said.

"Games are what you're good at," Lincoln said. "Leave the rest to me."

"I'll do that." The affirmation, she thought, was something closer to a prayer than to anything like a firm resolution.

"And—speaking of the Russians..." Lincoln's face took on an amused caste. "There are a lot of Russian women here, in the bars. Some are prostitutes, some aren't, but they're all looking for husbands to carry them off to the good life in the West."

Dagmar raised an eyebrow and looked at him.

"And you think this would interest me *because*...?"

"Not you," he said. "But you might pass a warning on to your boys. We wouldn't like to have any of them rushing to the rescue of someone named Natasha and ending up paying thousands of dollars to a Russian pimp."

Dagmar considered Richard's habit of going to a foreign country and buying everything on offer and nodded.

"I'll spread the word," she said.

There was a knock on the door. Lincoln looked up.

"Come in," he said.

The man who entered wore a uniform. He had tight-curled black hair, Mediterranean blue eyes, and a brilliant white smile.

"Chatsworth," he said. For a moment Dagmar wondered if Alvarez knew Lincoln from online gaming, but then she remembered the code protocols.

"Ah." Lincoln rose, and shook hands across the desk with the new arrival. "This is Squadron Leader Alvarez, our RAF liaison."

"Good to meet you, Briana," said Alvarez. Dagmar rose and shook his hand and was proud of herself for answering to the alias without hesitation.

They needed an RAF liaison because Lincoln and Dagmar were running their operation from England. It just wasn't the England made up mostly of a big island off the northwest coast of Europe.

The operation would be run from England-in-Cyprus, from RAF Akrotiri—an air base that was, legally, British territory, as British as toffee and binge drinking.

Dagmar's team of game geeks would work from rooms overlooking Akrotiri's enormous runway. The British air base was vast, and Dagmar's people would hide in plain sight amid thousands of RAF personnel and civilian employees, who in turn were dropped amid the population of the island of Cyprus. Dagmar and her friends would share housing in the married officers' quarters, shop for food at the NAAFI, and run their games through British servers.

Alvarez turned to her.

"Are you settling in?"

"So far," Dagmar said, "it's been enlightening."

Dagmar left Lincoln with Squadron Leader Alvarez and returned to the ops room, where her heart gave a leap as she saw Tuna Saltik standing on one of the office chairs, pinning to the wall an enormous poster of Mustafa Kemal Atatürk. Her heart jumped again as she recognized Ismet standing next to him, helping him hold the poster straight. There was another with them, a man with shockingly bright blond hair. All three wore summerweight coats and ties.

She ran up to Ismet and gave him a hug from behind. He stiffened in surprise, then turned around. His eyes widened with pleasure, and then he hugged her and kissed both her cheeks.

"Lovely to see you!" he said.

"How's your granny?" Dagmar asked.

"Much better, thank you. Back in her home."

"You mean her tent?"

Tuna grinned down at Dagmar from under his arm as he held out the poster.

"Good to see you!" he said. "I'll hug you later."

"I'll look forward to it."

Ismet offered a hand. "I'm Estragon, by the way."

Dagmar took the hand. "Briana."

"I'm Vladimir!" called Tuna from somewhere in his own armpit.

Vladimir and Estragon, Dagmar thought. *Right.*

"You're showing off your college education," Dagmar said.

Ismet flushed slightly. "Maybe," he said. He nodded at the man with surfer blond hair.

"This is Rafet."

"Pleased to meet you." Rafet and Dagmar shook hands.

"Rafet," said Ismet, smiling, "is a dervish."

Dagmar turned to Rafet.

"Do you whirl?"

He smiled with brilliant white teeth.

"No," he said. "I'm not in the Mevlani organization. I follow Hacı Babur Khan."

Dagmar's question had been facetious — she had thought Ismet was joking when he said Rafet was a dervish. But now Dagmar began to think that Rafet really *was* a dervish, whatever being a dervish meant in the modern world.

She decided to make the next question a bland one.

"Where did you learn your English?"

"My dervish lodge is in the U.S. In Niagara Falls."

"Ah," Dagmar said, uncertain how to respond to this without demonstrating her own abysmal ignorance.

"Rafet," said Ismet helpfully, "represents the Tek Organization."

Dagmar decided not to ask any more questions and instead to quietly, privately wiki everything as soon as she could.

Tuna jumped down off the chair and gave Dagmar a one-armed hug while his other arm gestured at Atatürk.

"Is the picture straight?"

Dagmar looked up and received the poster's full impact. The picture was based on an old photograph, but somewhere down the line the photograph had been hand-colored in eerie pastels, and the result was nothing short of terrifying. Larger than life-sized, the Father of the Nation wore a fur Cossack hat and a civilian tail-coat with a standing collar and tie. He scowled down from the wall, his unnaturally pink cheeks a startling contrast to his uncanny blue eyes.

The look in the eyes sent a shudder up Dagmar's spine.

In her time in Turkey, Dagmar had seen a great many pictures of Atatürk. Most businesses had a photo displayed somewhere, and Atatürk busts and statues were common in Turkish towns and public buildings.

What had surprised her was the variety of Atatürks on display. There was no standard representation. There were benign Atatürks, dignified Atatürks, and amused Atatürks that emphasized the impish upward tilt of his eyebrows. There were Atatürks with mustaches and Atatürks without mustaches. There were dapper Atatürks wearing tails and carrying a top hat, statesmanlike Atatürks standing amid a group of ministers and comrades, commanding Atatürks in military uniform.

And then there were the scary Atatürks, a surprising number of them. This one, with his glaring eyes and upswept eyebrows, looked absolutely diabolical. He looked like the villain in a bad fantasy film. Below the image, in a blue typeface that matched the Gazi's eyes, were the words *Biz bize benzeriz.*

Something in Dagmar shrank from having this frightening icon gazing down at her for the length of the operation.

"The picture looks straight enough," Dagmar said. She pointed at the letters. "What does it say?"

Ismet answered. "It says: 'We are like ourselves.'"

Dagmar looked around the room, at the piles of cardboard boxes, at Helmuth and Richard and Judy all laboring under Atatürk's iron gaze.

"Well," she said. "That's true enough."

What she actually wanted to say was, *Are you sure you want* this *Atatürk?* But she couldn't quite bring herself to speak the words aloud.

The cult of Atatürk was something Dagmar understood only in part. The United States of America had many founders: Franklin, Washington, the Adams cousins, Hamilton, Jefferson, Madison, Tom Paine, and even people such as Benedict Arnold and Aaron Burr had done their bit to define the new republic...but Turkey had only Atatürk. He was the arrow-straight dividing line between the shambling old Asiatic Ottoman Empire and modern, Western-leaning Turkey. Like any decent Founding Father he had thrashed the British, and after that he'd remade the country in his own stern image: he'd adopted the Roman alphabet and Gregorian calendar; given civil rights to women; made Turks adopt surnames; driven religion and its symbols out of public life; built a public education system from scratch; defeated enemies foreign and domestic; created a parliamentary system; promoted Western ideas of art, music, and culture. He'd also done away with the Muslim prohibition of alcohol — a mistake in his case, as he died young of cirrhosis.

Turks revered Atatürk the way hardline Marxists revered Lenin, the way gays revered Judy Garland, the way Americans revered their pop stars up till the very second before they pissed all over them. Dagmar got that.

What she didn't understand was this fiendish image on the wall of the ops room. She didn't want it there, but she didn't know how to say it without setting off some kind of atavistic Atatürk-inspired defense mechanism and getting her Turkish comrades mad at her.

"We brought presents!" Tuna said. He reached his big hand into a pink plastic bag and pulled out a fistful of blue and white amulets, the kind that Turks deployed against the evil eye. He, Ismet, and Rafet immediately began fixing the amulets to every vertical surface.

Judy watched them with interest. She turned to Dagmar.

"Do they really believe in the evil eye?" she asked.

"I don't know. But we need all the mojo we can get."

"And here's one for your office." Ismet, handing Dagmar an amulet.

"Thank you."

It was a nice one, shaped like a military medal, with the dangling eye made of heavy glass, better quality than the cheap plastic amulets available everywhere in Turkey.

After the amulets were hung, everyone pitched in with putting the ops room together. By early evening flat-screen monitors glowed from the walls and from each of the desks, towers hummed, printers were set up in corners, and Mr. Coffee sat atop a table in the break room.

"The rest of the team will be here tomorrow," Lincoln said. "First briefing at oh eight hundred."

Dagmar raised a hand. "Will we always be using military time?" she asked.

He smiled. "You should be thankful we're not using Zulu Time," he said.

Dagmar had never heard of Zulu Time in her life.

"I guess I should be," she said.

Before the flight to Cyprus, Dagmar had a series of meetings with Lincoln in California. They met at a sushi place in Studio City, where they talked about gaming and other harmless topics—the actual purpose of their meeting couldn't be discussed in public places like restaurants.

Chopsticks in his hand, Lincoln lightly dipped his Crunchy Crab Roll in soy sauce. Dagmar observed the hand.

"You don't wear a wedding ring," she said.

The crab roll paused halfway to Lincoln's lips.

"I was married twice. Divorced both times. The job is hard on marriage." His mouth quirked in a little smile. "Though I have to admit that, sometimes, what I do is *insanely fun.*"

"Any children?"

Lincoln, chewing, nodded. He swallowed, then took a taste of iced tea.

"Two daughters," he said. "Both grown, both doing well." He looked wistful. "One of them lives in New Zealand. I see her every two or three years. The other blamed me for the divorce, and I haven't heard from her in more than a decade."

Sadness brushed Dagmar's nerves. She shook her head.

"Sorry," she said.

"I keep tabs on her," Lincoln said. "Because, you know, I *can* — so I know that she's all right." His mouth took on a rueful slant. "But part of me wishes she'd run into the kind of trouble that only her dad can get her out of."

Dagmar's sadness swelled. She had similar foolish fantasies herself, that Charlie or Austin or Siyed would walk through the door, surprisingly alive, and with an elaborate story that explained how it had been someone else who had died, somebody else's corpses that Dagmar had seen, and that the whole affair had been an elaborate but necessary deception in order to thwart some unimaginable villainy...

But of course that wouldn't happen. Austin and Charlie wouldn't be coming back from the falls at Reichenbach, and sometimes families came apart that shouldn't, and sometimes families stayed together that should have come apart. And sometimes two lonely people consoled themselves with sushi and avoided talking about what had brought them together in the first place.

After lunch Lincoln took Dagmar to the Bear Cat offices to discuss their plans for the Cyprus excursion. Lincoln had an office with an Aeron chair, a view of the Santa Monica Mountains, and framed photos of media campaigns in which he'd been involved, with *Stunrunner* given the pride of place, Ian Attila Gordon in his tux gazing out of the frame, his elegant little Walther automatic in his hand.

"You get to pick your code name," Lincoln told her.

"Wow," Dagmar said. "We really are living in Spy Land."

"Special ops." Patiently. "We're not after intelligence; we *do* things."

"Sorry." Dagmar was amused. "I'll try to remember."

"The computer has to approve the name," Lincoln said. "You can't take a name that's already in use, and you can't do anything obscene, but other than that, you're reasonably free. It should be something you can remember and easily answer to." He looked at her over his Elvis glasses. "I'm using Chatsworth." From the handle he'd used in online games, Chatsworth Osborne Jr.

"Does the name mean anything?" Dagmar asked. "Or did you make it up?"

He offered a little smile. "Chatsworth was the name of a playboy character in a sixties sitcom," he said.

She looked at him, at the bubble hair and Elvis glasses.

"Were you a playboy?" she asked.

"What makes you think I'm not a playboy *now?*" he asked. She laughed. He considered being offended, then shrugged. "But no, it's kind of a complicated joke. The Company was founded by a certain type of character—East Coast, Old Money, loyal Republicans—and I fit that description, sort of, at least when I was younger." He smiled nostalgically. "I worked for Barry Goldwater alongside Hillary Clinton, do you believe it?"

"You really knew her?"

He waved a hand vaguely. "We met, here and there. I didn't know her well." He smiled. "She was too serious for me."

"Ah," Dagmar said. "You *were* a playboy, then."

"I was a spoiled rich kid," Lincoln said. " 'Chatsworth Osborne' is what I'd have become if I hadn't gone into government service, so it's the name I use when I'm enjoying my harmless entertainments."

"Like overthrowing a foreign government."

"Like that." Lincoln said. He cocked his head and looked at her. "Your code name?"

Dagmar thought for a moment.

"Briana," she said.

After Briana Hall, the fugitive found alone in a rented room at the beginning of Dagmar's best-known game, and whose dilemma mirrored certain aspects of Dagmar's past.

"*Motel Room Blues,*" Lincoln said. "Very good."

Dagmar's other employees were given code names as well. The problem with renaming her employees, Dagmar considered, was that she knew all of them by their real names. She was bound to slip sooner or later.

Judy decided, logically enough, to name herself Wordz. Richard the Assassin called himself Ishikawa, after—of course—a famous ninja. The programming chief, Helmuth, decided he wanted to be called Pip. Dagmar did not think the reference was literary and decided she didn't want to know what other inspiration might have leaked into his alcohol-tolerant brain.

She hoped she could keep all the names straight and remember to use them in front of other people. Lincoln said to use the code names all the time, but Dagmar was sure she couldn't.

It was at the Bear Cat offices that Lincoln presented her with the contract, pages and pages of documents that featured, on the first page, a sum even greater than that she'd earned for *Stunrunner.*

"I'll have to show this to our lawyer," she said.

"He can't see Appendix A," Lincoln said. "He's not cleared for that."

In the two-bedroom apartment she shared with Judy in the married officers' quarters, Dagmar opened a bottle of Bass Ale and fired up her laptop. She looked up Zulu Time, which was apparently military-speak for Greenwich Mean Time, and then googled both "dervish lodge" and "Niagara Falls."

Naturally, Rafet's dervish lodge had a Web page. Rafet and his comrades followed Hacı Babur Khan, a Sufi saint who had lived in Herat three centuries ago. There he founded an order of dervishes that followed his regulations for spiritual practice, among which included, according to the article, "ecstatic drumming." "Which," the article continued, "has resulted in occasional persecution by more orthodox Sunnis."

The dervishes lived in communal lodges, practiced austerity and poverty, drummed, and sang hymns written mostly by Hacı

Babur Khan and his successors. The Web page maintained by the Niagara Falls lodge mentioned that it was founded in 1999, played host to a couple dozen dervishes at any one time, and offered demonstrations of drumming to the public several times each year.

That led to a query about the Tek Organization, which Dagmar at first misspelled as "Tech." The search engine obligingly offered a correction, and she found that a Turkish imam named Riza Tek had founded the worldwide eponymous religious organization, which had branches in at least fifty countries. The Tek Organization ran charities, schools, and broadcast stations; it owned hospitals and newspapers; it had a large publishing house that put out books, magazines on news and religion, and a very impressive-looking science magazine . . . none of which, alas, Dagmar could read, as they were in Arabic and every known Turkish dialect but not English.

Turkish nationalists thought that Riza Tek was a fanatical God-inspired reactionary. Fanatical God-inspired reactionaries, the sort who belonged to or spoke for organizations that practiced suicide bombing, had a contrary view: they thought Riza Tek was a creation of the CIA.

Any relationship between the Tek Organization and the dervish lodge in Niagara Falls remained purely speculative.

Dagmar looked up from her laptop as Judy came into the room from the bathroom, where she'd been taking a shower. She wore a tank top that showed off her tattoo sleeves, color reaching from her wrists up her arms, over the yoke of her shoulders, and down her back. The tattoos didn't seem to represent anything concrete but seemed inspired by physiology: they suggested, rather than depicted, muscles, bone, and a circulatory system. This gave Judy's body an unearthly aspect, as if there were some whole other form, or other creature, hidden just beneath her skin. Dagmar would have found it repellent if she hadn't so admired the art of it.

As Judy walked she clicked her tongue piercing against her teeth, giving her movement a rhythm track. A scent of honeysuckle soap trailed her to an armchair, where she sat, picked up her netbook, and booted it. While she waited for the first screen to appear, she looked up at Dagmar.

"Is there some reason," she asked, "why you moved your bed so it's on a diagonal?"

Dagmar's nerves hummed a warning. She didn't know Judy well enough to trust her with the answer.

For that matter, she didn't know *anyone* well enough.

"It's a luck thing," she said vaguely.

Judy nodded, as if that made sense.

"I notice that you drink," she said.

Dagmar glanced at her Bass Ale, then looked back at Judy.

"I do," she said.

"Aren't you worried you might have inherited your father's alcoholism gene?"

Dagmar looked at her drink again and considered telling Judy to piss up a rope.

"I'm not going to worry," she said, "until I find myself drinking the same cheap crap my dad did."

"With my dad's history," Judy said, "I'm not getting high, ever."

Dagmar looked at the tattoos, the rows of piercings lining Judy's ears.

No, she thought, *you don't use; you just got addicted to pain instead.* Getting jabbed thousands of times with a needle—now *that* wasn't extreme, was it?

In any case, Dagmar was not in the mood to be dictated to by some kind of tattooed Goth puritan. She picked up her ale and waved it vaguely.

"Whatever works," she said.

"What do you think of Rafet?" Judy asked.

Dagmar offered her laptop. "I can show you my research."

"I think he's totally hot," Judy said with sudden enthusiasm. "D'you think he's free?"

"I think God's got him," Dagmar said. "He's supposed to be some kind of monk."

Judy's eyes widened. "They have monks?"

Dagmar offered the laptop again. "Check it out."

Judy set aside her netbook and took Dagmar's computer. Her brows drew together as she read about the Niagara lodge.

"It says they're committed to poverty and austerity," she said. "There's nothing about chastity."

"Well," said Dagmar. "Good luck with all that."

Judy handed the laptop back.

"Whatever you do," Dagmar said, "don't try to seduce him with alcohol."

Lincoln—in his hotel room in Istanbul, the tickets and itinerary for Dagmar's Bulgaria trip scattered on the table—watched Dagmar's turmoil with perfect calm.

"Are you *serious?*" Dagmar asked, staring into Lincoln's blue eyes. "You want me to *astroturf an entire country?*"

"A little guidance is all they need," Lincoln said. "They'll do all the hard lifting, not us."

"They're going to get *killed,*" Dagmar said. "Look what happened in Iran. In China. They were trying to do exactly this kind of thing and the government answered with bullets."

Lincoln affected to consider this.

"If we do this right," he said, "maybe not so many. Maybe none at all."

"*Tens of thousands* died in China!"

Lincoln's lips firmed.

"They didn't have us to guide them. But if people choose to take that risk—if they think their political freedom is worth risking their lives—then they also deserve our help."

Dagmar resisted this logic.

"If people got killed," she said, "it would be my fault."

"No." Lincoln was firm. "It would be the fault of the bastards who killed them."

Dagmar was beginning to suspect that there were a few too many bastards in this picture.

*   *   *

The 0800 briefing began with a buffet of local breads, olives, tomatoes, cucumbers, hard-boiled eggs, and the best watermelon Dagmar had ever tasted in her life. She looked sadly at the buffet and regretted the Weetabix she'd just had for breakfast. Nobody had told her there would be food.

A pack of strangers filled the room, and Dagmar wondered if they'd just come for the buffet before she realized they were all Lincoln's people from the States. Magnus was tall, well over six feet, and thin—what Dagmar thought of as a Geek, Type One— and was a programmer. He wore a Daffy Duck T-shirt, and his scrawny, hairy legs were revealed by a Utilikilt, a signal garment of the geek.

This was, Dagmar reflected, a British air base, the personnel of which were certain to have a fair number of Scots. She wondered what the Scots would think of Magnus and his Utilikilt and what Magnus would think of the Scots.

Scots, she thought, looked very well in kilts. Or at least those who didn't knew better than to wear one.

Why was it so different for the Americans?

Lola and Lloyd—whose names, echoing each other, demonstrated the hazards of letting people coordinate their own code names—were well-dressed white people in their early twenties whom Lincoln introduced as interns. Efficient, wavy-haired Lola, businesslike in a gray summer suit, was in charge of the buffet and also of the ID badges that she handed out. The interns were Company, here to learn what Dagmar did, so that they could do it without her later.

Dagmar hoped to hell that they wouldn't take their skills into the private sector and become her competition. They seemed fearsomely intelligent.

She was just getting acquainted with these when a dignified, well-dressed man entered and was introduced as Alparslan Topal, the observer from the Turkish government-in-exile currently residing in Rome. Dagmar figured he wasn't using a code name.

Topal had a white mustache and exquisite manners and bowed over Dagmar's hand as he was introduced.

"Pleased to meet you," Dagmar said.

Topal's soft eyes looked into hers.

"I hope you will be able to relieve my distressed country," he said.

Dagmar was a bit startled by this direct appeal.

"I hope I won't disappoint," she said.

The last man to arrive used the code name Byron. He was a short, pinch-faced man who wore a tropical shirt and sandals made of auto tires and in no way resembled the poet. Unless, of course, the poet had shaggy hair on the backs of his hands.

"Sorry I'm late," he told Lincoln. "I was off trying to help out Camera Team C."

"They were having a problem?"

"Unfortunately, your tech guy didn't quite understand the fine points of the uplink."

Lincoln raised his eyebrows. "I hope you straightened him out."

"I did," Byron said. He looked over the ops room, at the blank displays, the evil-eye amulets, the oversized portrait of Atatürk.

"Quite a group, is it?" he said.

Inspiration struck Dagmar. She grinned.

"We're calling it the Lincoln Brigade," she said.

"As I understand it," Dagmar said later as she stopped by Lincoln's office, "the Gray Wolves are *your* people, right?"

Lincoln adjusted himself in his Aeron chair.

"Not anymore," he said. "That was an arrangement between *our* grandfathers and *their* grandfathers."

"But the Americans," Dagmar persisted, "*created* them, right? Created the Deep State and Counter-Guerilla and Ergenekon and the Gray Wolves?"

She had made a point of doing her homework, looking up decades-old history on Web sites that glowed with speculation and paranoia, all of which suggested that Turkey had been run for seventy-odd years by a creepy little cabal of military men and politicians known euphemistically as the "Deep State."

Lincoln seemed just a little bit sullen.

"Stalin shifted whole armies to the Turkish border in '48," he said. "He demanded that Turkey open the Bosporus. For all anyone knew, he was about to invade." He shrugged. "So yes, *we*— our grandfathers—created a lot of things," he said. "We created stay-behind organizations in every state in Europe, to lead the resistance in case the Russians marched in."

"Gladio used Nazis," said Dagmar.

"Not in Turkey," Lincoln said. "No Nazis there. But yes, Gladio used lots of people. People who were willing to do things to communists, and not all these people were Gandhi." His look was severe. "But let's not forget that Stalin wasn't Gandhi, either. He killed something like fifty million people, half of them his own citizens."

"Granted," Dagmar said.

Lincoln's mouth narrowed into an angry line. "But what we *didn't* do," he said, "was tell the Deep State to take over the heroin traffic running through Asia Minor. And we didn't tell them to start overthrowing democratic governments *once the damn communists went away.*"

"Without a Soviet invasion," Dagmar said, "they were bound to get into mischief. My, uh, *grandfather* might have foreseen that."

Lincoln's expression was savage. "We need to get rid of those dinosaur generals. They're a fucking *embarrassment.*"

"Kill the dinosaurs," Dagmar said. "Check."

Maybe she could embarrass them to death.

Dagmar had imagined clandestine agents inserted into Anatolia, then working under deep cover to build networks that would strike when the time was right. But Lincoln informed her that the networks already existed.

There were the networks of the political parties and their supporters, all of whom were out of power, out of work, and already organized. There were government workers, annoyed at interference from their new superiors. The religious who wanted to practice their faith free of government harassment. Members of the military and police who had been dismissed as politically unreliable. Students furious at restrictions on academic freedom and rejoicing in their own natural anarchy.

Members of the cultures, and subcultures, spawned by social networks such as Facebook, Ozone, and Taraa.

And there were the poor, especially the urban poor who squatted around the major cities in their improvised, ramshackle communities. The generals were busy placating—or threatening—the rich and powerful, whom they viewed as a greater threat to their legitimacy: they had no time or funds or inclination to raise the hopes of those living in poverty with anything except rhetoric.

All these networks already existed. All that was necessary was to mobilize them and to convince them that they could act with reasonable safety.

Even the poor, Dagmar was told, had cell phones.

The bus was back. The bus that the police had confiscated outside Izmir had been returned to Lincoln's company once *Stunrunner* was over and it no longer mattered. The bus was so heavily customized that it would be difficult to sell, so Bear Cat had garaged it till now, when Lincoln was going to make use of it.

Right now the bus was across the Green Line in the Turkish part of Cyprus, following the unit's three camera teams. The camera teams—all Turks—were making videos of towns and scenery, nothing remotely governmental, military, or classifiable, so as not to attract official interest...the bus captured the video, streamed it along the uplink to a satellite, and then down again to RAF Akrotiri, where it appeared on the Lincoln Brigade's monitors. There the ops room team practiced storing the raw video, editing and manipulating the pictures, then uploading them to dummy, practice sites to which only they had access.

The satellite link with the camera teams was theoretically two-way, with the ops room able to ask the cameramen to give them specific shots. This was the element that caused the most trouble: an alarming percentage of the communications failed, mostly through human error.

Dagmar was supposed to be in charge, under Lincoln. She'd done this sort of thing before, at most of Great Big Idea's live events, but in California she had a practiced, well-drilled team and they knew what videos to take without her telling them. Dagmar kept making the mistake of thinking her current team knew more about what they were doing than they actually did.

Part of the problem was the enormous variety in the hardware. There were covert cameras hidden in sunglasses or ordinary spectacles, complete with a laser heads-up display that would imprint incoming text messages right onto the retina. But these weren't very flexible and didn't record as many megapixels of reality as would sometimes be required, so the techs were required to get comfortable with other gear: small video cameras that would fit into the hand, cell phone cameras, large professional units capable of sucking up vast amounts of bandwidth.

The team was aided by what they were calling Hot Koans, their own pronunciation for Hôt Xoán, the Vietnamese company that produced them. These were small, battery-powered wireless repeaters capable of spontaneously assembling into an ad hoc mesh network. Each of the repeaters, which came in a small, plastic box colored bubble-gum pink, had a range of a few hundred meters, and signal could be passed up and down the network to a receiver well out of sight of the camera, computer, or cell phone that had produced it. The repeaters would keep working as long as their battery lasted, which was around forty-eight hours.

Richard had found these and had ordered thousands of them. An area could be saturated with Hot Koans, providing massive redundancy to any communications and keeping the receiver well out of danger.

The Hot Koans—which turned out to have a much greater range than advertised—were about the only success on that first dreary day of training. The team was overwhelmed by all the new technology. By four in the afternoon Lincoln called it a day: "We'll get more practice tomorrow."

Dagmar was exhausted. She dropped into her chair, winced at the sudden pain in her lower back, and wished she'd had the foresight to buy herself an Aeron.

"I have a Hot Koan," Richard said.

Dagmar turned to him. "Yes?"

Richard tented his fingers. *"A player came to Dagmar and asked, 'Does the ARG have Buddha nature?'*

"Dagmar replied, 'That would make a pretty good story.'

"Hearing this, the player was enlightened."

Richard's effort was well within a well-established tradition of creating enigmatic hacker koans that had to do with computers and computer people. Dagmar grinned, then winced at a stab of pain from her back.

Helmuth, however, seemed impervious to fatigue. He jumped up, turned to the room in general, and said, "Anyone for finding something to drink off base?"

Byron turned toward him, looking as if he was interested. Magnus stood, grinned, raised an arm.

"A drink sounds good," Magnus said.

Byron hesitated, then frowned. "Too much jet lag," he said.

Dagmar considered that Byron might have just had a narrow escape. Neither was quite aware of the hazards of a night out with Helmuth, of waking draped over some piece of furniture, a headache stabbing shivs into your eyes, your mouth tasting as if it had been used to put out cigars, the bathroom sink splashed with vomit, your cuffs spattered with someone else's blood, and your underwear turned backward. At Great Big Idea this was known as "being Hellmouthed."

Not that Helmuth ever Hellmouthed *himself*; he would always turn up at the office in the morning perfectly groomed and perfectly tailored and from his own invincible height survey his victims with a smile of brilliant white cosmopolitan superiority.

Perhaps, Dagmar thought, she ought to give the lads a warning.

"We start again at oh eight hundred," she said. "Don't lose too much sleep."

Judy stood. She wore another of her series of rhinestone-covered plastic crowns, this one tiny and pinned to the crown of her head, like that of a beauty queen.

"You could just walk to the officers' club," she said. Then she raised an arm and sniffed her armpit. "I'll go if I don't smell too skanky," she added.

"You're no worse than me," Dagmar said. Which was, unfortunately, true. She turned to the others. "Officers' club, everyone?"

"Not me," Helmuth said. "I want to go somewhere I don't have to hear jets taking off every three minutes."

He and Magnus retired to whatever desperate pleasures awaited them. Lincoln went into his office. The interns began to clean up what was left of the buffet. That left Dagmar, Judy, and Byron for the officers' club.

Dagmar gave an automatic glance around the room for Ismet, then remembered that he, Rafet, and Tuna were elsewhere. They weren't techs; they weren't part of Dagmar's game except as pawns. They were being trained as field agents, and what they did they would do in Turkey.

All of which left Dagmar uneasy. She didn't want to send people she actually knew into danger.

It would be bad enough if her pawns were faceless.

The trio walked to the officers' club over burning hot pavement that smelled of rubber and jet fuel. They were all honorary British officers, with photo ID cards worn on lanyards around their necks, and entitled to drink with the RAF's finest.

The club was a little bit of Britain: dark paneling, brass, slot machines, a snooker table, Real Ale, the scent of chips frying. Yorkshire-accented hip-hop rocked from the jukebox. Not a lot of customers, even though Happy Hour had just started.

They found a round table in what passed for a quiet corner.

Photos of 1950s aircraft decorated the walls. Dagmar got a gin and tonic, Judy a ginger beer, and Byron a single malt, water back. Thirsty, he gulped the water first. As he dropped his glass to the table, Dagmar saw the wedding ring.

"You're married?" she said.

Byron nodded. "Wife. Daughter. I'll call home later tonight."

"How old is your girl?"

"Six weeks." He pulled out a billfold and offered a picture of a goggle-eyed infant. Judy and Dagmar made appropriate noises.

"I have more pictures on my laptop," he said. "But I'm not allowed to bring it into the ops center."

"If I remember the security briefing correctly, you're not sup-posed to show us even *this* photo," Judy said. "Let alone in a public place like a bar."

"Right," Dagmar said. "We will stop oohing over Byron's child at once."

"Can I see the picture again?" Judy asked.

Dagmar sipped her drink, looked around the club once more, and caught a number of the officers casually scoping the two new women who had just walked into their dark-paneled sanctum and doubtless wondering which of them belonged to Byron and whether the other was free . . .

When in contact with the locals the Lincoln Brigade had been told to say they were here to do something with the computers. Local curiosity probably wouldn't extend much past that—if it did, they could just say that they couldn't talk about their work.

Dagmar turned to Byron.

"Have you ever done this sort of thing before?" she asked.

Byron seemed doubtful. "I don't think anyone has."

"I mean—you know—covert, secret stuff."

"Oh. Sure." He tasted his drink, splashed a bit of water into it, then tasted again. "I mean, I'm a contractor, Magnus and I work for the same company, and they work almost exclusively for the government. And that includes three-letter organizations that make me sign secrecy agreements." He shrugged, sipped again at his whisky. "The security rules are usually idiotic—in fact, it's impossible to do my job if I follow them all."

"What do you mean?"

Exasperation distorted his pinched face.

"The hoops I have to jump through to take my work home are ridiculous," he said. "And often I *have* to take it home—there's no way to do the work on-site."

"Why?" Judy asked.

"There are a whole long list of Web pages that I'm not allowed to access from government computers—but often as not, these are the pages that contain the information necessary to do my work, or that have the software tools I need to do it. So"—snarling—"I have to take the classified material home, so that I can put it on my own computer, from which I can access the necessary information." He shook his head. "It's all maddening. Someday the military and intelligence branches of the government are going to completely freeze, because no one will be allowed to see or do *anything.*"

"I've never worked for the government," Dagmar said.

"Hoh. You have such a treat in store for you." Byron's face reddened. "Uncle Sam is about fifty years behind in their computer protocols, which still assume that everyone is working on a big mainframe. You have to do certain tasks in a certain order, and fill out all the paperwork on it in a certain order, and the odds are about ninety-nine to one that the tasks and the paperwork *have nothing to do with the actual work you were hired to do.*" He looked up at her with a glare of surprising hostility.

"There was a period when I was doing computer security at a major government lab—I won't mention which one. The computers we were working on were riddled with unknown intruders— *hundreds* of them!—I mean, those people were practically *waving* at us! But I couldn't do a single thing about them—*not a single thing!*—because I spent about seventy hours each week dealing with assigned tasks and paperwork. And after I broke my heart on that job for a couple years, I quit and went into the private sector."

He shrugged. "At least I'm making a lot more money than the idiots I was working for back then."

Dagmar, whose whole business was based on secure computers, was startled by this outburst.

"Computer security isn't exactly rocket science," she said.

"I don't know if you've noticed," Byron said, "but the U.S. doesn't exactly do rocket science anymore, either."

Dagmar decided to change the subject before she completely lost any faith in her own project.

"Have you worked with Magnus before?" she asked.

"Tell you the truth," Byron said, "I'm surprised to see him here."

"How so?"

"Well, I *have* worked with him before, and he's not the best at the kind of improvisation you're doing."

"Really?"

"He really needs a script to work from. I'm much better extemporizing than he is."

"I'll keep that in mind," Dagmar said.

She tried to view this information by considering the source. Byron's character type was not exactly uncommon in computer circles: he was boastful about his own abilities and disparaging of everyone else. He was also, Dagmar thought, very, very angry.

Byron was Angry Man, she decided. And Magnus was Kilt Boy. At this point Lola and Lloyd weren't anything more than the Interns. She'd get to know them better later.

At this point a pair of RAF officers, Roy and McCubbin, the latter known as the Mick, appeared and offered to freshen their glasses. The officers were fair and freckled and pilots, with splotches of pink sunburn on their cheeks and noses, and Dagmar and Judy were pleased to invite them to the party.

The lads were delighted to learn that Dagmar and Judy were unattached. They were also pleased to learn that Dagmar had lived in England, having once been married to a Brit. It required quite a lot of amiable conversation to establish the fact that they had absolutely no acquaintances in common.

Roy was drunk when he arrived and got more drunk as Happy Hour went on, though pleasantly so. Eventually, though, he grew nearly comatose and the Mick's wedding ring became impossible to ignore, and so Dagmar and Judy collected the lads' cell phone numbers, and—declining the offer of escort—walked along with Byron to their apartments in the married officers' quarters, long, low apartment blocks with tiny little yards strewn with the bright plastic toys of the officers' children. The scent of charcoal was on the air, from the backyards where pink-skinned RAF officers, cold bottles in their hands, congregated in the evenings around grills with their mates and families.

Palm trees, bottles clinking, the scent of proteins cooking, and the sounds of sports floating from TV sets...to Dagmar it seemed like some kind of retro LA scene. Like Hawthorne, maybe.

"I'm going to call my wife," Byron said, and gave a jerky wave of his arm as he turned onto the walk that led to his apartment. Dagmar and Judy kept on a few more doors, then passed into their own unit. Dagmar held up the napkin with the pilots' phone numbers.

"Do you want this?"

Judy flicked her hair. Her plastic crown glittered. "Toss it," she said.

Dagmar dropped the napkin into the trash. Judy went into the bathroom to take her evening shower. Dagmar opened the fridge, poured herself a glass of orange juice, then went to the dinette and booted her laptop.

She was not yet finished with her work for the day. Back in Los Angeles, her company was hip deep in the run-up to the Seagram's game. She had to check her email for the updates, then make phone calls if intervention seemed necessary.

Dagmar slipped her keyboard out of its tube, then unrolled it. She preferred a full-sized keyboard to the smaller one on her laptop and carried one with her—flexible rubberized plastic, powered by a rechargeable battery, with genuine contacts beneath the keys that gave a pleasing tactile feel beneath her fingertips. It connected wirelessly to her laptop—she'd turned the screen around so that she wouldn't have the unused keyboard between herself and the image.

The Seagram's game seemed to have a greater reality, even at this distance, than her own enterprise here in Cyprus. Possibly because the goal—to sell whiskey or, at any rate, to make whiskey cool—seemed more well defined than her own.

She was used to telling people what to do—her fictional creations, her employees, the players—but she lacked confidence in the idea that she could really give orders to an entire nationality. Somehow her vanity had never extended to that.

She waved a hand, like a sorcerer incanting a spell.

You all be good, now, she thought. And then added, *You, too, Bozbeyli.*

A conventional insurrection stockpiled arms and explosives. Dagmar's revolt would stockpile cell phones.

Cell phones had already been acquired and warehoused in safe houses in major cities. So were video cameras, transmitters, antennae, satellite uplinks, and of course the Hot Koans.

The revolution *would* be televised. And tweeted, blogged, attached to emails, YouTubed, Ozoned, googled, edited, remixed, and set to a catchy sound track. It would be bounced to High Earth Orbit and back. It would be carried live on BBC, on CNN, on Star TV, on every other electronic medium dreamed up by an inventive humanity.

What Dagmar could only hope was that none of these media would be transmitting pictures of a bloody massacre.

"The lawyers aren't going to let any of this happen," Lincoln said, "unless the President signs an executive order. He hasn't done that yet, but I think he will before too much longer."

"This is too much for me," Dagmar said.

The call for the midday prayer had gone out from the Blue Mosque. Dagmar sat among her travel documents for Bulgaria, still stunned by what Lincoln was asking of her.

Less than twenty-four hours earlier she had been cowering in her bathroom, trying to hide from phantom Indonesian attackers. She wondered if Lincoln would want her for this job if he knew she was mentally—what was the appropriate word? *Challenged? Compromised?*

He looked at her, the gray light of the mosque shining off the metal rims of his shades.

"Look," he said. "Once that order is signed, this operation is going forward. I have some talented people I can employ, and I'm sure they'll do a good job. But—" He raised a blunt finger. "They won't be as good as you. And if they aren't as good, we could lose some people that we wouldn't otherwise have lost." He shook his large white head. "If you do this," he said, "you could save lives."

It was that argument, Dagmar reflected later, that had overcome her last resistance.

I am such a freaking bleeding heart, she thought. She could only hope that Lincoln was right that she would save lives and not lose them.

CHAPTER SEVEN

Oh eight hundred. Dagmar cycled to the ops center, then realized she had forgotten the ID card she was supposed to wear around her neck, the card that not only held her picture but also could be used on the door's card reader to pass her into the center. She looked up at the camera above the door and gave an apologetic wave, then waited for someone to open the door for her. When this didn't happen, she knocked.

Eventually Lola, the wavy-haired intern, opened the door for her. Lola was dressed in a blue suit — a change from yesterday's gray one — and she looked at Dagmar with cool intelligence.

"Yes?" she said.

"Thanks for opening the door." Dagmar moved to walk past Lola, but the other woman blocked her.

"Don't you have your ID?" Lola asked.

"I forgot it in my apartment."

"I can't let you in without it."

Dagmar looked at her in surprise.

"But you *know* me," she said.

"Yes, but I also need to know where your card is. You can't leave that lying around."

Dagmar opened her mouth to protest, but a look at Lola told her that further argument was pointless, so she turned around, cycled back to her apartment, picked up the ID card from the kitchen table where she'd left it, hung the card around her neck on its lanyard, and returned to ops.

She was beginning to think Byron might have a point about the stupid security rules attending this kind of operation. Besides the fetish for code names and ID cards, there had also been an inventory of every electronic device that Dagmar had brought with her—her handheld, her laptop—which had to stay in her apartment. For the ops room she had a new cell phone, laptop, and desktop computer, all dedicated to the exercise, and which could not be taken out of the ops center. The phones, she noticed, had their camera functions disabled. The computers had most of their USB ports soldered shut, and all data was available only on portable memory, which was locked in the safe at night. Each flash memory or portable drive featured a sticker with a bar code— Lola scanned these when the members of the Brigade checked them out, then scanned them in again at the end of the day. It was not totally impossible to steal data, she supposed, but it would be very inconvenient and require a certain amount of nerve.

The worst threat to security, Dagmar thought, came from the fact that the computers were connected to the Internet. In a truly secure operation, any machine containing sensitive information would either have no outside connections at all or connect only to a secure local area network. Any machine connected to the outside created an opportunity for intruders.

Dagmar would have to trust the counterintrusion skills of Richard the Assassin. He was brilliant about keeping crackers out of the Great Big Idea file system, and those he'd battled on behalf of the company were the best on the planet.

She reflected that she and the world in general were lucky that Richard had chosen to ally himself with the Forces of Good.

On her return to the ops center Dagmar encountered Magnus, whose kilt was hiked up to highly unacceptable levels as he cycled to work on his bike. Fortunately, by the time she caught up to him he'd dismounted and was stowing his bike in the rack.

It was a different kilt, she realized, than the one he'd worn the day before. The man had at least *two* Utilikilts.

That was hard-core Geek.

"Morning," she said.

"Hi, Briana."

He waited for her to finish racking her bike. She looked at him curiously, looking for signs that he'd been Hellmouthed the night before. He seemed fine, maybe a little tired.

"Did you have a good night?"

"Limassol is a happenin' town," he said cheerfully.

She looked at him. "You got the lecture about the Russian hookers, right?"

Magnus laughed. "One of them came right up to me off the dance floor and wiped her face on my T-shirt," he said.

Dagmar was curious. "What did you do?"

"I blew her off." He laughed again. "Jesus Christ, it's not like I want whore sweat on my clothes."

They walked toward the door of the building. Two airmen came out, and one politely held the door for them. Dagmar thanked him as she entered, and then she and Magnus walked up the stairs to the ops center.

"Are you settling in?" she said. "Any problems?"

"None to speak of," he said. "It's a more interesting job than the government usually gives me."

She remembered Angry Man Byron's complaints the previous day and asked if he found the security rules too restrictive. He shrugged.

"They do get in the way. But it's not too bad here—I mean, if we're not all in the ops center anyway, we're not working, right? This isn't the kind of job you bring home with you."

"True enough."

She came to the door of the ops center, waved at the camera, and snicked her card through the reader. The lock buzzed open, and Dagmar pushed the heavy steel door open.

Lola looked up from her desk as they entered. Dagmar waved the ID at her, and Lola nodded expressionlessly.

Dagmar stopped in the door to the break room, where yesterday there had been the breakfast buffet, and saw that today no food had been provided. Yesterday she had eaten breakfast and then found out about the buffet; today she had assumed there would be a buffet and not eaten breakfast.

She sensed that the primary theme for the day had already been set: whatever she did or thought was going to be wrong.

She paused by her office door and let Magnus walk past her into the ops center, T-shirt, kilt, thin hairy legs, and flapping sandals.

Part of the secret of the Scots kilt, she decided, was the long stockings. They limited the amount of unattractive pale flesh visible to the onlooker. They suggested curvy calves even if the calves in question were matchsticks.

Magnus hadn't quite learned what made a kilt work and what didn't. But it wasn't Dagmar's job to tell him.

Though probably she was going to have to tell him how to ride a bicycle in a skirt, just to keep him out of the hands of the RAF Police.

We are like ourselves, Dagmar thought, and walked into her kingdom.

It turns out that Lloyd, the intern, was in charge of the unit's air force. He had been a model rocket hobbyist in high school, and apparently that qualified him to wrangle a whole fleet of radio-controlled drones.

Lloyd invited Dagmar and Lincoln to his workstation for a status report. Lloyd's scarred metal desk was directly beneath one of the ceiling fans; the fan gave a regular mechanical chirp as it drove cold air down on Dagmar's head.

Dagmar guessed that Lloyd had graduated from college a couple years ago. He was a little shorter than average height and had rimless spectacles. He wore soft gray slacks and a Van Heusen shirt with a faint lilac stripe, long sleeved against the artificial chill.

He was Air Force Brat, Dagmar thought. And Lola was the Guardian Sphinx.

"We've got two types of drones," Lloyd explained. He had loaded videos of the tests in his desktop computer. "One is a model helicopter with an off-the-shelf zoom lens." The video showed a flying machine so bare and basic that it looked as if it had been assembled out of carbon-fiber fishing rods and leftover circuit boards. There were two rotors, surprisingly silent, with a package slung between them that consisted of three cameras, each equipped with a different lens and capable of independent tracking. On the video the copter bounded into the air like a jumping spider, then zigzagged around the sky with sufficient speed and agility that the video had trouble tracking it. It made a faint whooshing sound, like Superman passing far overhead.

"It's got GPS," Lloyd said. "You tell it where to go, and it goes there, and if you've got the coordinates of the target, it will point the camera there without a human operator having to manually adjust it. We figure to use these for reconnaissance—keep tabs on nearby police stations or army barracks."

"How close does the operator have to be?" Dagmar asked.

"Doesn't even have to be within sight," Lloyd said. "The operator won't be anywhere near the action, and the helo can automatically return to the GPS coordinates from which it was launched, or anywhere else within its range."

There were more videos, these taken by the copters' onboard cameras, their occasional jerkiness smoothed by computer enhancement. The lenses, generic products of some anonymous Southeast Asian factory, were capable of remarkable performance: Dagmar could make out individual faces as the helos floated unseen, unheard, over Limassol.

The sounds of the operators came over the sound track, all speaking Turkish. Dagmar listened, frowned.

"Is that *your* voice?" she asked.

Lloyd gave her a guileless look. "Yes."

"You speak Turkish?"

"I do."

She waited for a moment in case Lloyd wanted to offer an explanation, but he only offered a tight little smile and then went on with his talk. The rules said they weren't to tell each other anything of a personal nature, and Lloyd was clearly a rule follower.

"Our second drone," he said, "is another VTOL—we can fly them both off roofs, or from roads or parks. But the second one also has anti-air capability. It's a flying wedge, basically."

"Sorry?" Dagmar asked.

Lloyd looked at her, solemn dark eyes behind spectacles.

"Do you ever watch *World War: Robot*?"

"No."

"It's one of those programs where homebuilt robots fight each other. And the basic rule for robot combat is that wedges rule."

Dagmar's mind swam. "Sorry," she said, "but I'm still four-oh-four."

Lloyd's hands swooped descriptively in the air. "A wedge is just a robot with a wedge-shaped cross section," he said. "They're used for ramming—they hit the other robot at high speed and just fling it in the air."

"Okay."

"So what we did was adapt the wedge to aerial combat. We've got a hard plastic wedge kept aloft by arrays of miniturbines. It's got several cameras, a GPS, and a top speed of about forty knots if we really want to burn through the fuel. Stability is achieved by fly-by-wire computer guidance—you really can't turn the thing upside down even if you try. The idea is to fly it against police drones and bring them down by ramming. It's a type of attack the Russians call *taran*."

Dagmar looked at him. "The Russians use planes to ram?"

Lloyd nodded. "They train for it. Even now."

Dagmar blinked.

"That's hard-core," she said.

Lloyd nodded. "Glad we never had to fight those guys."

The video made the tactic clearer. The flying wedge brought down a whole series of target drones. Usually the wedge tumbled for a second or two but righted itself. On a couple occasions the wedge lost control and crashed.

Dagmar had encountered miniturbine-powered drones before — she remembered the thing hovering over her in the humid night, the hydrocarbon smell of its breath. She thought for a moment, then looked at Lloyd.

"This all seems very sophisticated," she said. "But what we're supposed to be leading is a grassroots rebellion springing spontaneously from the population. If we start flying machinery this complex against them, it's going to be clear that someone's behind it."

"This was discussed," Lincoln remarked, from behind Dagmar's shoulder. Dagmar gave a little jump at the unexpected sound.

"The wedge is made from generic materials," Lloyd said. "The miniturbine arrays are available by mail-order. Even the fly-by-wire software is available from hobbyists online — I was kind of amazed to discover that it actually works."

"Hm." Dagmar looked at the screen, saw flying wedges hit drones time after time.

"Well," she said. "I guess it all seems fine."

Lloyd offered a satisfied smile.

"Now," he said, "we need to coordinate the air force with your teams."

"Ha," Dagmar said. "As if my job wasn't complex enough."

Lloyd smiled. "I'll do most of the work, if that's all right with you."

Dagmar could think of no objection to this.

"I was thinking," Lloyd said, "that we might want to give the air unit a name."

"Free Turkish Air Force?" Lincoln said. "Atatürk Air Force?"

"Royal Chatsworth Air Force?" said Dagmar, with a look at Lincoln. He returned the compliment.

"Briana's Airmen?"

"My policy is to remain anonymous," Dagmar said. "How about the Anatolian Skunk Works?"

Lincoln thought about that for a moment.

"I like it," he said.

"Words," Dagmar said. "They're my job."

Over the next two days Dagmar's teams gradually improved their performance. The camera teams shot videos of birds, of the model helicopters, of tractors rolling down country roads, of freighters cruising along the blue Mediterranean horizon. Until Team C's cameras lost their uplink all at once and they failed to reestablish contact.

Dagmar turned to Byron.

"You handled this last time, right?" she said.

He looked up at her.

"Yes," he said. "I'll try to talk them through the fix."

This failed, even with Lloyd interpreting. Dagmar turned to Byron again.

"Can you go north and help them?"

He looked up at her, eyes glittering in his pinched face.

"No way!" he said. "The north side of the island is run by the people we're trying to subvert. I'm not going over there."

"It'll be very inconvenient," Dagmar pointed out, "to have to send all Team C back and their gear through the checkpoints in Nicosia."

Angry Man flushed. "It'll be even more inconvenient if I'm picked up by the Turkish Cypriot police and tortured," Byron said. He pointed down the corridor, toward Lincoln's office.

"Ask Chatsworth," he said. "I don't have to go over the Green Line."

"I'm not *ordering* you," Dagmar said.

Byron folded his arms.

"Doesn't matter," he said. "Orders or not, I'm not going. It's in my contract."

Dagmar paused and felt everyone in the ops room looking at

her. She sensed that her authority was teetering on the brink of an undefined precipice.

She knew she wasn't any good at being a tyrant. She owned a company, but she wasn't an authoritarian boss—rather than imposing her will on her subordinates, she relied on shared enthusiasm to achieve results—and so she wasn't quite sure how to deal with Byron's defiance, especially if he was right.

"Well," she said lightly. "If it's a *contract*, and you can't be tortured over *there*, then we'll have to find a way to torture you *here*." She looked at him for a moment, long enough to see him shift uneasily in his chair, and then she nodded.

"Try and fix their problem again," she said. "And if that doesn't work, try a third time."

It took an afternoon, and eventually Magnus and Helmuth were both called in. It was Magnus who solved the crisis, by moving a certain jumper from its slave to its master setting. It was a nice piece of long-distance diagnosis, and Magnus seemed very pleased with himself for providing the answer.

So much, Dagmar thought, for Byron's claim that Kilt Boy wasn't able to think on his feet.

"Yes," Lincoln said later, when Dagmar reported the problem and its solution. "It *is* in Byron's contract—and Magnus's, too—that they're not to be deployed in the field. In fact, it's Company policy not to use American citizens in situations where they might be in jeopardy."

"Okay," Dagmar said. "I didn't know that."

Lincoln swiveled his Aeron chair toward his safe. Keeping his body between Dagmar and the digital lock, he opened the safe door.

"You're not cleared to view their contracts," he said. "So that's understandable." He looked over his shoulder. "Plus you've seen all those spy movies, where sinister Agency masterminds put ordinary people in deadly situations over and over."

"Is there anything else," Dagmar asked, "that I need to know that's in documents I'm not cleared for?"

Lincoln swung his chair toward his desk. "I'm sure there is," he said cheerfully. "That's how our business works."

"Terrific."

Lincoln opened the safe, then took the day's papers and portable memory and locked them away. Dagmar heard bolts chunking home. An LED on the door turned from green to red. Lincoln straightened and looked at her.

"Buy you dinner?" he offered.

"Sure," Dagmar said. "Why not?"

It wasn't like she had a more exciting evening planned.

Dinner was takeout from an Indian place just outside Akrotiri's gates. Lincoln found a parking place overlooking the Mediterranean, and the two balanced paper containers of vindaloo and steaming-hot samosas on lichen-scarred boulders while white surf boomed against the ruddy, broken cliff beneath their feet.

Dagmar slurped her mango *lassi*.

"When I met him that time," she said, "Bozbeyli said that the army generals who led previous coups all returned to the barracks."

Lincoln tilted his hat to the west, the better to intercept the sun, and nodded.

"They did," he said.

"So why are we doing this, then?" she said. "Why aren't we waiting for the junta to just go home?"

"Bozbeyli's different," Lincoln said. "The previous military governments were composed of genuine patriots who believed they were acting in the country's best interests. You didn't see them behaving like military rulers elsewhere — after their retirement, they weren't living in palaces, they weren't hanging out with movie stars, and they didn't have big Swiss bank accounts."

"But Bozbeyli's in it for the money."

Lincoln cut a samosa with his plastic knife and fork, then thoughtfully chewed a piece. Dagmar caught a whiff of cumin on the wind.

"When Atatürk first created the country," he said, "he called it the Republic of Turks and Kurds. But over time the Kurds got sort of left out, and the government decided as more or less official policy that everyone in Turkey was a Turk by definition. The Kurds, according to this scheme, were just Turks who hadn't quite learned to be Turks yet, and so they had to be *made to be proper Turks*, and they were to be educated in Turkish and forbidden to speak their own language." He waved his plastic fork. "Just as all Turkish Muslims were, by definition, Sunni Muslims — which left out a very large minority of Alevi Muslims... Christians and Jews can have churches and synagogues, but the Alevis can't have mosques and have to meet in private homes, because all Muslims are officially Sunni, and so are all the mosques."

He looked up suddenly. "Are you following this?" he asked.

"What are Alevis?" Dagmar asked.

Lincoln flapped a hand. "Too complicated."

Dagmar reflected that this was not unlike everything else in Turkey.

"Okay," she said.

"I was talking about the Kurds, anyway," Lincoln said. "So — given that the Turks were trying to extinguish their language and culture — a lot of them were less than pleased with the situation, and back in the nineties there was a genuinely dangerous Kurdish insurgency led by a party called the PKK. Which was mainly financed by Syria but also in part by Kurdish heroin dealers who were importing Afghan and Iranian narcotics along the traditional drug highway to the West. The Turkish authorities didn't see why the heroin money should go to the insurrection, so they sent right-wing gangsters and the Gray Wolves and government assassins to kill the heroin dealers and take over their networks — and they largely succeeded. And then the heroin money started percolating up into the system, and before long the war was just too profitable to allow it to end, even after the insurgency had been crushed through the usual deportations, killings, and random acts of terror.

"After which" — waving a bit of tikka masala on his plastic

fork—"there was the Susurluk incident, where a Mercedes truck squashed an auto that held a police chief, a wanted heroin dealer and assassin, and a Kurdish member of parliament, along with the gangster's mistress, drugs, and a hell of a lot of firearms. And the heroin dealer was carrying ID issued by the minister of the interior, which showed that both sides of the insurrection were hip deep in collusion. After that it was clear that the war was just being continued for all the drug money, and the Deep State was exposed and faded away, along with the war. For a while."

But the money, Lincoln continued, was still there. And the heroin was still there. And it became impossible for either the PKK or the authorities to resist all that, and so the war picked up again, and this time the death squads were killing *moderate* Kurds, anyone who suggested compromise was possible...the elected moderate Islamic government kept trying to make peace on terms that were unacceptable to the military, such as admitting that Kurds are Kurds and not Turks...and then the government started making remarkably clumsy efforts to assert its control of the military, by promoting Islamists to field command. And the result was a series of bombings and assassinations that served as the provocation for Bozbeyli and his clique to take command and restore order, essentially by canceling the chaos they themselves had provoked...

"I don't think the junta's going back to the barracks," Lincoln said. "Their profits are too big, and they're finding life pretty easy right now." He gestured toward the booming vastness of the sea. "Bozbeyli and his gang are the last of their kind—Turkey's right on the verge of becoming a glorious twenty-first-century success, and I don't want it devolving into a narco-terrorist state on NATO's southern flank. So that's why we're here."

"Yeah, well," Dagmar said. "I'm good with all that."

"I'm simplifying enormously," said Lincoln.

"I figured."

"And besides," Lincoln said, "what we're going to do is genuinely cool."

Dagmar nodded. "I got that, too."

How many people have to die, she wondered, *before it all stops being cool?*

The jukebox in the officers' club was playing Carl Perkins's "Dixie Fried." It was the end of Happy Hour and the place was full: Dagmar and her crew hadn't been able to get a large enough table, so all six were clumped around a small, round table barely large enough to hold their drinks.

Ismet, Tuna, and Rafet had returned after four days on the other side of the Green Line, working there with the camera teams and the Anatolian Skunk Works. Judy and the Turkish-speaking intern, Lloyd, had also come along. Rafet and Judy were sipping their soft drinks; the rest had lager.

Dagmar looked at Ismet and Tuna.

"Have you been working for Li—for Chatsworth all along?" she asked.

Ismet seemed surprised by the question.

"You mean, during the *Stunrunner* game?" he asked.

"Yes."

"No. We got recruited later."

Tuna put a big fist around his pint glass. "I think, uh, Chatsworth decided we were politically sound."

Certainly, Dagmar thought, during *Stunrunner* they had both demonstrated opposition to the regime. And they knew a lot of people and could bring other recruits into the scheme.

And, of course, that meant no highly trained Company employee would be put at risk: only Turkish natives would be in danger. They were completely expendable. It was this realization that made Dagmar feel as if her ribs were closing in on her heart.

"My boss was willing to let me take leave," Ismet said. "He's not doing that well anyway, since firms with contacts in the government are getting most of the business."

Dagmar cast a glance at Judy and Rafet: they seemed to be having a quiet conversation on their own, inaudible over Perkins's vocal. She turned to Lloyd.

The Air Force Brat was a quiet dark-haired young man, dressed in a soft chambray shirt and cords.

"How did you learn to speak Turkish?" she asked.

Lloyd seemed a little surprised to be included in the conversation.

"I'm, uh—not sure I'm supposed to tell you."

"He speaks with an American accent," Tuna offered.

"Well," Lloyd said. "My father is from Turkey, but I was born in the States."

"Do you have dual citizenship, then?" Dagmar asked.

"I have a Turkish passport," Lloyd said, "but I've never used it."

He was so clearly uncomfortable with the questions that Dagmar decided to change the subject. She looked at Ismet.

"You said your grandmother was raised a nomad," she said.

Ismet adjusted his spectacles. "Yes. She was a Yörük. There are nomads in Turkey, even now."

"Why do they...do what they do? Keep on the move?"

"They follow their herds. In the winter they're on the south coast near Konya—actually most of them now have regular winter houses—but in the summer the sun cooks the grazing, so they move up to the high pastures in the Tauros Mountains and live in big black goatskin tents." He took a sip of his lager. "They're very poor, but then they need very little they can't provide for themselves."

Lloyd spoke, surprising Dagmar.

"Some nomads," he added, "travel *because* they're poor—they don't own any land of their own; they have to keep on the move, and graze their animals on the highway right-of-way or places that no one actually owns."

Dagmar remembered that this was a country where every city was surrounded by illegal settlements, lived in by poverty-stricken refugees from the country. She turned back to Ismet.

"And your grandmother married out?"

"She had an arranged marriage with the son of a merchant.

The son was able to give the Yörük access to things they needed, and the Yörük provided the merchant with a steady supply of cheese, butter, hides, kilims, and so on."

Dagmar asked if he still had nomad relatives.

"Yes, certainly. I used to visit them during my school breaks." He gave a nostalgic smile. "That's really the old Turkish lifestyle, isn't it? Living in a tent, lying on carpets, eating meat and cheese and milk, cooking everything on a brazier. Our ancestors lived that way for thousands of years."

"Sounds like an ideal vacation for a boy."

Ismet shrugged. "I didn't appreciate it as much as I should have—I missed my rap music and the Internet. And I'm afraid I was bored looking after the sheep." He smiled again. "I enjoyed riding the horses, though. I'd shoot my toy bow from horseback and pretend I was a Gazi."

"I'd like to meet your nomad relatives," Dagmar said.

Ismet absorbed this with interest, eyes bright behind his spectacles.

"Once the generals are gone," he said, "I'd be happy to introduce you."

"I wish I was up in the mountains *now*," Tuna said. "It's so bloody hot here." He pressed his pint glass to his forehead but then took the glass away and scowled at it—the lager, not very cool to begin with, was by now room temperature.

"At least you're getting away from Akrotiri now and again," Dagmar said. "I'm tired of being cooped up here within smelling distance of the runway."

"If you have free time," Ismet said, his eyes still bright, "I have a car. I can take you out to see the sights."

Dagmar felt a warm current of pleasure at the thought of Ismet and his car and the whole Island of Aphrodite to lose themselves in.

"Are you all right," Dagmar asked, "here on the Greek side of the line?"

Tensions at the moment were high. Cyprus was still divided

into the official, UN-recognized Greek south and the Turkish north, the latter of which since the invasion of 1974 had been organized as a republic recognized only by Turkey. Persistent attempts to solve the crisis on the part of the UN and the EU had resulted in a certain softening of attitudes: the situation hadn't been *resolved*, but it had grown more blurry, more complex, more nuanced.

But General Bozbeyli's regime had hardened things again, had thrown all of Cyprus into stark light and shadow. Though the situation technically hadn't changed, though no agreements had been abrogated, a series of belligerent proclamations by the military government had heartened the Turkish nationalists and driven the Greeks into a frenzy of resentment. Both sides were demonstrating. No one was brandishing guns yet, but it was clear that guns *could* be brandished, that shots *could* be fired, armies and navies mobilized, the whole of the region brought into bloody chaos.

Was that to Bozbeyli's advantage? Dagmar wondered. Would he start a war if he felt threatened?

It was all too easy to see disaster looming everywhere she looked.

"I'll be all right," Ismet said. "I can pass for an American. And of course I'll be with you, and—" His smile brightened. "If I get into trouble, you can rescue me."

Again Dagmar felt that tingle of pleasure at the touch of Ismet's brown eyes.

Tuna leaned forward over the table, his big fist dropping his empty lager glass on the table. Dagmar turned to him.

"I was wondering," he said, "if you can give me some advice."

Dagmar blinked. "If I can."

"I'm trying to work out how to get published in the States." He frowned. "I get good reviews, but nobody in America reads reviews that aren't in English."

Dagmar almost laughed but caught herself in time. People were always asking her how to get published or how to get into game writing: they were always disappointed when the answer involved hard work instead of knowing some kind of secret password.

But Tuna wasn't a wannabe; he was a successful author in his own country. So she gave Tuna what advice she could—which wasn't very encouraging. American publishers would only look at manuscripts already in English, and even then—with the whole ramshackle edifice of publishing perpetually teetering on the edge of the void—the odds were not good.

"I can translate the work myself," Tuna said. "But I'm not good enough to write literary English; it would need polishing."

Dagmar said she'd try to find someone interested in polishing up the translation of a foreign writer. Tuna seemed disappointed— perhaps he was hoping that Dagmar would volunteer. But Dagmar had no time for such ventures, and in any case her connections in publishing were almost a decade out-of-date.

"Well, thanks." Tuna stood, empty glass in his hand. "More drinks?"

Dagmar considered her mostly empty glass and was on the verge of saying yes when she realized what was playing on the jukebox. Ian Attila Gordon, pop star turned James Bond, singing the bombastic theme to the film *Stunrunner.*

"Hey!" Dagmar said. "It's our theme song!"

They all listened for a second or two, and then laughter gusted out.

"Overproduced," sniffed Tuna.

"We are Bond!" Judy cried, punching the air.

It occurred to Dagmar at that instant that they weren't Bond at all, they were the sort of people that Bond routinely destroyed— the subversive technophiles operating from a secret headquarters on a sea-girt island, engaged in covertly, busily undermining the order that Bond represented.

They weren't Bond. They were the Rebel Alliance from *Star Wars,* trying with desperate idealism and kludged-together tech to restore an imperfect republic that had barely worked in the first place.

Fortunately, she thought, Bozbeyli wasn't Darth Vader, he was just a painted-up heroin dealer.

But Dagmar was very tired and a little drunk and felt unable to explain this to the others. So she punched the air and cried, "*We are Bond!*" and signaled Tuna to bring her another drink.

It was early evening, and the scent of jet fuel mingled with the charcoal smoke from the backyard barbecues. "Do you know," Judy said as they cycled home together, "that you don't have to be a Muslim to be a dervish?"

Dagmar looked at her. "Rafet's kind of dervish, you mean?"

"I . . . guess so." Judy's eyes narrowed in thought, and she clacked her tongue piercing against her upper teeth. "He said that anyone with a heart open to the Divine was welcome at his services."

Dagmar cast her mind back to the Web page of the Niagara lodge, the description of the services. She had to speak loudly over the sound of a landing Skylifter.

"Don't they sing verses from the Koran?" she shouted. "I mean, they may be open to all faiths, but those faiths are going to spend a lot of time listening to the *Complete Works of Mohammed* and singing songs in praise of Allah."

"Rafet only talked about the drumming," Judy answered.

"But you and he are getting on?"

Judy seemed doubtful. Sunset colors glowed on her tattoo sleeves. She clacked her tongue piercing against her teeth in rhythm.

"I suppose. He didn't ask me out or anything."

"You could ask *him*."

"Mm." Doubtfully. "What's my opening? He's talking about God and mystic oneness, and I pop up and say, 'By the way, *Terrorslash III* is showing at the base cinema, want to go?'"

Dagmar had no advice on this matter.

"Ismet offered to take me out," she said.

Judy raised an eyebrow. "The quiet one? You like the quiet ones?"

"I like the intelligent and undemanding ones."

"I see." Nodding.

"You know," Dagmar said, "this is a military base loaded with guys. Does it have to be the monk?"

Judy laughed. "He's just so pretty!"

Dagmar could only agree. "Maybe that's why God picked him," she said.

Judy gave her an odd look. Then she shook her head.

"By the way," she said, "my dad knows Ian Attila Gordon."

Dagmar looked at her. "Really?"

"Yeah. Ian's a big fan of his. Sometimes they do benefits together." She laughed. "Dad says he's a complete tosser."

"I didn't think he was that great a Bond."

Judy winked. "We're better, yah?" Dagmar smiled wanly. Judy jumped off her bike and turned up the short walk to their apartment. Dagmar followed.

"Dad said that he hoped Ian would make a success as an actor," she said, "because his musical career wasn't going anywhere."

"He's got a big album coming up in a few weeks," Dagmar said. "I saw posters at the airport."

Keys flashed in the light of the setting sun; the apartment door opened. Somewhere, a jet engine fired off its afterburner: the vast noise diminished to a muffled roar as soon as the door was closed.

"Ian's album is a huge mess," Judy said. "That's the word from the producer. It should have come out along with the movie, but it was delayed." She looked up. "Can I use the shower first?"

Dagmar gave a wave of her hand.

It was time to call California and get the bad news about the Seagram's game.

"I'm sorry I was so evasive yesterday," Lloyd said. It was early morning, and he had clearly been waiting for her outside the ops center door.

"No problem," Dagmar said as she racked her bike. "We're really not supposed to give personal information. Especially in public places like bars."

"It's just that my father is an Alevi Kurd and I have to be careful what I say around Sunni Turks."

Dagmar opened her mouth, then closed it and nodded.

"I don't know what their attitude is to Kurds," Lloyd went on. "And I'm pretty sure Rafet would consider Alevis to be heretics— and he's a Islamist and most Alevis tend to be secularists, and that on top of the Kurd thing...And of course he's my roommate, so that makes it worse."

"Right," Dagmar said. "Understood." Not understanding this at all.

Lloyd gave a nervous smile and touched her arm. "Thanks."

"Rafet says that his outfit is open to all," Dagmar said.

"By *all*," Lloyd said, "he may not actually include *Alevi*." He shrugged. "Or he may. I don't know."

"Okay," Dagmar said.

"Look," Lloyd said. "There are a lot of Alevis in Turkey— more than most Sunni Turks think. The head of the last commission that was supposed to arrive at an estimate ended up dead in a mysterious auto accident, and that was *before* the military took over."

Dagmar, pretending she understood, gave a careful nod. For a country of modest size, she thought, Turkey's politics were beyond intricate.

"Sometimes," Lloyd said, "they just kill us."

"Ah." This was the best response she could manage, given the depth of the sea of ignorance in which she swam.

She was unable to decide if Lloyd was a complete paranoid or not, so when she had a moment to herself she wikied as much of this as she could, and then understood even less than she had before.

Sometimes they just kill us, she thought.

Sadly, it seemed, there was no branch of the human race to which this statement did not apply.

Two-cycle engines spit oil-tinged exhaust into the air. Tires shrieked and scrambled for traction on the corners. Dagmar wasn't used to driving this close to the ground: the surface of the track seemed threateningly close as it passed beneath her. Tuna made an effort to pass her on the left; she moved to cut him off.

She had seized the lead early in the race—she was an early adapter of technology, even if the technology was mechanical and considerably older than she was.

RAF Akrotiri was a full-service air base: it even had a go-kart track. And after five days' hard work, Lincoln had decreed an afternoon of fun, a cookout followed by racing. The day had cooperated: morning showers had been followed by mellow afternoon sun.

Dagmar glanced over her shoulder, saw Ismet pulling up on the right, and swerved to block him. He had to brake and fell back. She hugged the inside on a corner; then as she came out onto the straight she swung out into the middle of the track, ready to block any challenger. Tuna rolled up on the left again, and she swerved to stay in his way.

She looked over her shoulder to see if Ismet was coming up on the right. He had pulled up even with Tuna, but his little two-cycle engine didn't seem to have the power to overtake the leader. He looked at Dagmar, and as their eyes met, a silent signal passed between them.

Tuna was boxed in, Dagmar ahead of him, Ismet on his left, the grass outfield on his right. Dagmar slowed, and Ismet turned the steering wheel and swerved to his right, right into Tuna.

The two go-karts collided, then rebounded. Ismet swerved wildly to the far side of the track before he regained control, and Tuna went clear into the grass and hit a wide, shallow puddle left behind by the morning's rain: a tall rainbow sheet of water sprayed high in the air as his kart stopped dead. Dagmar cackled and accelerated away. She could hear Tuna's roars of frustration fade behind her.

When she passed the start line, the race course manager was holding out a sign that said: NO BUMPING. Dagmar gave her a cheerful wave and raced past.

She managed to keep ahead of Ismet until she came up behind Magnus and Byron. She was surprised they were so far behind that she was on the verge of lapping them, and then she saw that Angry Man and Kilt Boy were not so much racing as restaging the naval battle from *Ben-Hur*. The two karts were ramming each other, bounding apart, then ramming again. A considerable slipstream blew up Magnus's kilt, flapping it in his face, but it didn't seem to affect the ferocity of his driving. Neither driver spoke or gestured or gave any other indication they were angry at each other: they let their vehicles do the talking.

It seemed dangerous to go near them—and Dagmar didn't want to see up the kilt anyway—so she slowed and followed the two lurching, ramming, grating go-karts around the track to the start line, where the manager black-flagged both Magnus and Byron and sent them off the course. Dagmar accelerated again and again found herself in the lead, but by this point no one was racing anymore.

Dagmar seemed to have won. Or so she surmised.

"What the hell was *that* about?" Dagmar asked Lincoln later, after she'd unstrapped herself from her kart.

Lincoln wore a tropical shirt and a broad sun hat and carried a bottle of Fanta. In the tropical sun his Elvis shades had turned a deep black. He was amused.

"Healthy competition, I guess. We're going to need that kind of aggression two days from now."

She gave him a surprised look.

"Two days?"

"That's when we hit the first target. The camera crews, the bus, and the air unit are already on their way to the mainland, and Tuna will fly out tomorrow."

Dagmar felt herself rearing like a startled horse.

"Are you serious? Our exercises have been complete shambles."

Lincoln gave an amused smile. "Perhaps from the point of view of someone who produces professional videos. But in fact everyone's gotten better, and in any case we're not trying to make everything look like Hollywood—if all the video looks too professional, it'll be obvious that professionals are involved. It seems to me that everyone's doing well enough."

Dagmar was astounded. "Well *enough?*" she repeated, and shook her head. Lincoln was clearly out of his mind.

"Lin—Chatsworth, it's got to be better than that! This thing could be a catastrophe!"

He raised a hand. "We do not have world enough and time," he said. "We have to move forward."

She looked at him.

"Is there some particular reason why it has to happen now?"

Lincoln waved his Fanta.

"It should have happened *months* ago, okay? And now I don't want any delays, because that gives the people in D.C. time to get nervous, and then fly in to interfere—" His glasses slipped down his nose, and he looked at Dagmar over the metal rims with his soft blue eyes.

"We'll make mistakes," he said. "We won't be perfect. But Bozbeyli's been in charge over there long enough."

"Another week and we could—"

He put a hand on her shoulder.

"You're the best, Dagmar. You're the best hope we have. And I have utter confidence in you."

Frustration and vanity danced an exasperating little tango in Dagmar's skull.

"I'm only one person," she said, suddenly forlorn. "Turkey is a whole *country.*"

"I saw you knock Tuna into the weeds just now," Lincoln said. "I figure you'll know what to do, when the time comes."

If I'm not huddled in the corner, Dagmar thought, *hiding from phantom Indonesians.*

But sensibly enough, she kept that thought to herself.

"There's something not quite right here," Dagmar said.

"I know," said Calvin.

"But I can't put my finger on it."

"Neither can I."

Calvin was the writer Dagmar had hired to script the game for Seagram's. Like Dagmar, he was a science fiction writer whose career had collapsed—in his case, because his publisher had been so enthusiastic about his first novel that they had printed no fewer than thirty thousand hardback copies, of which they had sold six thousand. What would normally have been a very respectable sale for a first novel had become a horrific financial loss for the company, a loss for which the author—as always—had been blamed. The second and third books, already under contract when the first book appeared, had received no promotion, and their publication had been delayed for years when their places on the schedule had been taken by books about which the publisher was more enthusiastic.

By the end of this purgatory Calvin's writing career was as dead as a can of Potted Meat Product, and when Dagmar called he had been supporting himself by ghostwriting erotica for the online journals of porn stars out of the San Fernando Valley. He'd been very happy to accept Dagmar's offer for work that didn't involve rapturous close-up descriptions of the money shot.

Long-distance from Cyprus, Dagmar had to walk Calvin through the process of writing an ARG. Copies of the work were emailed to Dagmar, and she made notes and changes and emailed them back. And at least once each day there was a phone call filled with desperation and last-minute improvisation.

"So we've got Harry and Sandee trying to get to Lake Louise in Alberta," Calvin said. "And all they have is a few dollars, a Swiss Army knife, and a bottle of whiskey—the latter being product placement. And Sandee is falling apart because she's just seen her son murdered, so Harry has to take charge and turn hero."

"With the help of the players," Dagmar said.

"Of course."

Dagmar thought about this for a moment.

"Why," Dagmar asked, "am I not seeing this?"

There was a long silence while Calvin considered his character outline.

"Harry hasn't been a leader up to that point," Calvin said. "All he's done is follow Sandee around, and when she's not around he wanders in circles."

"That's right," Dagmar said.

"The players are going to help him out, of course."

"It still has to be plausible," Dagmar said.

There was another long moment, and then Calvin spoke. The words came slowly, as he thought them out. Dagmar could almost hear the slow clank of gears turning in his head.

"I can put in a flashback," he said. "I can show him being heroic at some point in the past."

"No flashbacks," Dagmar said. "Flashbacks are deadly. They confuse the hell out of everybody because the games take place in a kind of eternal present—flashbacks break continuity."

"Okay." Calvin's gears ground slowly on. "I can—I can fore-shadow it somehow."

Dagmar thought about this.

"You'd have to start back on week one, and week one is launching in two days. You'd have to rewrite scenes that are already completed."

"Well. I *could*."

"You've already written a lot of material that shows that Harry isn't a hero," Dagmar said.

"Well." Thoughtfully. "I could change all that in the rewrites."

"Maybe he's *not* the hero," Dagmar said. "Maybe Sandee is the hero."

"But Sandee's going to fall apart. She's going to have a break-down in week three."

"What if it's Harry's job to keep Sandee together? Maybe that's what he's there for."

There was another moment of silence.

"So what you're suggesting," Calvin said, "is that Harry isn't Frodo, he's Sam."

"Yes," Dagmar said. "That's what I was suggesting." The Tolkien analogy hadn't occurred to her, but it seemed appropriate.

"I don't know," Calvin said. "I had such big plans for Harry."

Dagmar suspected that Calvin was very fond of Harry, identifying perhaps with the character's haplessness. The fondness was blinding Calvin to the character's true arc, which Dagmar was pretty sure meant that Harry wasn't the Hero, he was the Hero's Best Friend.

"I think this will work," Dagmar said. "And the players will like helping Sandee surmount her troubles."

"Maybe they can guide her to a good shrink," Calvin muttered.

"I think this is our solution," Dagmar said. "I think this is how it goes."

Calvin conceded defeat. "Let me think," he said, "how to present this."

I am Plot Queen, Dagmar thought in quiet triumph. *I may sleep in a crooked bed, but I can make a story dance.*

If only, she thought, she was as good at creating a happy ending in real life as in her fictions.

CHAPTER EIGHT

Welcome to Çankaya Wireless Network. Customer service is our most important product! We work constantly to expand our network throughout the Turkish-speaking world.

Anyone signing up to our network in the next month will be entered into a special drawing. Prizes may include cash, a beautiful bouquet of seasonal flowers, or a special photograph session for you and your family! The next drawing will take place by noon on Thursday!

Dagmar's first action—the proof-of-concept—would take place in Istanbul. In Beyazit Square, before the tall gate that marked the entrance to Istanbul University.

Even most of the Lincoln Brigade didn't know the target. Of those remaining in Cyprus, only Dagmar and Lincoln were aware.

Dagmar had the explosion dream the night before the Istanbul action, the Ford blowing up again and again, the fire blossoming in a great golden bubble, the incendiaries raining down, bouncing along the pavement like flaming bystanders fleeing the scene of a catastrophe. Dagmar woke in her cockeyed bed, the room wheeling around her, terror clutching at her throat.

She nerved herself for the day with coffee and her lucky RIOT

NRRD T-shirt, then went to the ops room early and buried herself in last-minute planning.

There would be a lot of spam to send out today.

> Have you considered taking advantage of the 108 digital television channels offered by Çankaya Wireless Network? Each is delivered with crystal-clear perfection! We have six plans, and one of them is certain to be suitable to your budget!

The students at the university were natural allies. Other groups would be called in as well.

Dagmar frowned down at the message glowing in the flatscreen before her. Send the message and everyone was committed. The revolution — or its horrific suppression — was on its way.

It had been Dagmar's idea to use spam as a means of coordinating political action. Not the disgust or annoyance that was the usual response to a message offering penis enlargement, a fortune waiting in Nigeria, or investment advice, but a message hidden somewhere in the text that only an insurrectionist could read.

A 419 scam, for example, could contain instructions — "seven," the numeral 8 — that told the recipient where they could find a clean cell phone. An offer for a drawing could offer instructions for what to bring to the next event — a photograph, a bouquet of flowers — and suggest a time frame, the twenty-four hours preceding noon on Thursday.

The code was simple because it would have to be understood by ordinary people. Dagmar could have used steganography, for instance a message hidden inside the code for a digital photograph of an object displayed on eBay or hidden in the code for an old, obsolete Web page. She could have used public key encryption or more elaborate coding systems provided by her employer. But targets openly receiving coded messages would attract attention and decoding took time, and even so most of the people involved had no technical expertise in using such systems—after all, otherwise intelligent users routinely managed to fumble even simple programs like Outlook Express.

Dagmar had therefore opted for speed over security—she hoped to put her actions together so quickly that even if the government deduced the target, they would be unable to respond in time.

She was putting her revolution together like a flash mob. They would arrive all at the same time, they would make their point, and then they would disperse before the authorities could react.

Or so Dagmar hoped, anyway.

The final message, the one on Dagmar's screen, gave map coordinates for the action based on a standard map of Istanbul— E-8, the numeral 8 in the text, *E* being the first letter of the second sentence. The last sentence gave the time for the action—six P.M. on Wednesday.

It was now a few minutes before four. She looked up at the wall clock, ticking away next to the ferocious picture of Atatürk. *Biz bize benzeriz*, she read.

She looked around the room. Lincoln, Ismet, Rafet the well-spoken dervish, Judy Strange, Helmuth the head programmer, Alparslan Topal the representative from the government-in-exile, and Richard the Assassin in his white Converse sneakers. Atatürk's pale ferocious gaze embraced them all.

Well, she thought. *We* are *like ourselves. And no one else.*

She looked at the wall clock again: 3:58.

Lincoln, kicking his legs as he sat on a table by the window, took pity on her.

"Go ahead and send the message early," he said. "Our kids haven't had much of a chance to practice."

She looked at him with gratitude.

"Right," she said.

And pressed the Send key.

There was a hierarchy in the networks that would respond to the message. They were organized along the classic covert cell structure, with each member of a cell known only to members of that particular cell and to the cell members whom each member would in turn recruit. If a member was caught or turned, there were only a few individuals he could betray. There was also a colossal redundancy built into the system.

Dagmar's message went to the network heads in the Istanbul area—union bosses, academics, political organizers, religious authorities, student leaders. Once they decoded its simple meaning, they contacted those in their cell by whatever electronic means they had agreed on. These contacted those below, and so on, in the model of a phone tree.

All of this happened outside Dagmar's purview. There was very little to do for the next couple hours but keep in touch with the camera teams, with Lloyd's remote-control airmen, and with Tuna. And since communications protocols forbade anything but the most necessary messages, the messages were few and far between.

Dagmar went to the break room for more coffee and ran into Lincoln seated on a plastic chair peeling an apple, the spiral uncoiling beautifully into a serviette unfolded on his lap.

"That's nicely done," she said, impressed.

"It's about the only real skill I have," Lincoln said.

"I don't know about that. You talked all these people into joining you here."

He looked up, amused. "I offered the chance to intelligently use computers in a beautiful foreign location," he said. "To a certain kind of person, that kind of offer sells itself."

"And how did you come up with Lloyd?" Dagmar said. "Turkish-speaking Kurdish-Azeri American citizens with a background in model rocketry can't be exactly thick on the ground in D.C."

Lincoln frowned. "Azeri?" he asked. "Do you by any chance mean Alevi?"

Dagmar felt heat rise to her cheeks. "Yeah," she said. "That's what I meant."

"I didn't know he was Alevi," Lincoln said. "But I damn well know he wasn't from Azerbaijan."

Dagmar nodded. "Lloyd is Alevi, whatever that actually means. And he's a little nervous around Rafet, I guess for reasons of history."

Lincoln seemed annoyed at himself. "He's Turkish, I knew he was Muslim, and I assumed Sunni even thought I should have known better." He decided to be amused. "But his dad wasn't exactly a barefoot persecuted little Kurdish refugee from eastern Turkey; he was a military attaché in Washington for many years, and he retired a colonel."

Dagmar blinked. "Really. Lloyd hadn't given me that impression."

"Oh yeah." Lincoln's penknife neatly quartered the apple as he spoke, then began to cut out the core. "Lloyd's dad returned to D.C. after he retired, joined a company that provides security to businessmen, and started a second family with a much younger American wife. He's still going strong, so far as I know. Lloyd would be their eldest."

Dagmar considered this. "If Lloyd's dad is a high-ranking military officer, does that mean his sympathies might lie with Bozbeyli?"

Lincoln sliced off a chunk of apple, chewed, swallowed.

"His file says not."

"Oh," Dagmar said. "That settles it, then."

The amused sparkle in Lincoln's eye was muted by the shadowy lenses of his glasses.

"Do you think we should send him home?"

"I—" Dagmar was too surprised to formulate an immediate response. "I don't see why we should," she said. "If you believe the file."

"The file's probably crap," Lincoln said. "But I'm less concerned with the father than the fact that the son gave you personal information that he was supposed to keep to himself."

Dagmar felt a sudden flutter of panic that she might have compromised one of her employees.

"He told it to me privately," she said, "by way of explaining why he didn't speak more openly the day before, when Rafet and the other Turks were pressing him for details about his background."

"Ah." Lincoln ate another chunk of apple. "That's probably all right, then."

Relief flew through Dagmar at the thought that she might have shoved Lloyd out of the way of a bullet.

"Besides," she said. "We can't do without the air force."

"No," said Lincoln, and looked at a chunk of apple poised on the tip of his penknife. "I suppose we can't."

"I have another Hot Koan," Richard said.

Dagmar watched on the flatscreen as Tuna walked along Ordu Road toward Beyazit Square. He wore a dark jacket, tie, shades, and polished shoes. Though he had a wide-brimmed hat pulled down to hide his face, his big body and loping gait were unmistakable. Eye-catching as well was the enormous bouquet of lilies he carried in one big hand. He carried a shopping bag with the corner of a manila envelope, an envelope that presumably contained a photograph. *A beautiful bouquet of seasonal flowers, or a special photograph session for you and your family . . .*

Tuna's image was eclipsed by a line of red tram cars. Dagmar shifted her gaze to another monitor, one with a wider angle, and waited for Tuna to reappear.

"Tell me," she said.

"*The novice came to Dagmar,*" Richard said, "*and he said, 'I have tried to hot-swap my PS/2 connector, and now my motherboard has been slagged.'*

"*'In that case,' said Dagmar, "make coffee.'*

"*Hearing this*" — Richard smiled — "*the novice was enlightened.*"

Dagmar laughed. "I wish I was really as wise as you make out," she said.

Richard only offered her a Buddha smile. Dagmar found Tuna again on the video, the flowers flopping over one shoulder.

Tuna and a small group of technicians had spent the morning making certain that the demo would receive full electronic coverage. Cameras and their operators were ready in windows of three of the many hotels that lined the road opposite Beyazit Square. Hot Koans had been scattered like birdseed all around the target, plastic hot pink rectangles sitting under furniture, on rooftops, lying in flower beds, their ad hoc mesh network pumping the signal to the antenna in a rented room several streets away, which then relayed them to the server on Seraglio Point that Lincoln had installed during the *Stunrunner* game.

The two nearby police stations, west on Mustafa Kemal Street and east on Kadirga Limani, were also under video surveillance, both from small battery-operated cameras fixed to buildings and streetlights and from airborne cameras belonging to the Anatolian Skunk Works. Dagmar had worried about the Beyazit Square location simply because it was so close to the police, but hadn't found anywhere else more suitable—there were police everywhere in the modern city, but at least in this area there were no military...

Without looking left or right, Tuna strolled into the square, flowers bobbing. Other people seemed to be carrying flowers here and there.

"Hello, Chatsworth." Tuna's headset carried his words into the ops room. "I'm feeling a little lonely here."

"We see more flowers than you do," Dagmar answered hopefully.

Tuna stood in the middle of the square, conspicuously large, conspicuously colorful. Pushcart vendors sold roasted ears of maize and *simit*. A group of girls in headscarves and long coats entered the frame from the direction of the university, all clustered around a pot of flowers. A man in a neat fedora, carrying long-stemmed roses, walked in from across Ordu Road.

How many people in a given area could carry bouquets, Dagmar wondered, before they all began to look suspicious?

"Here we go!" called Lincoln. He was looking at another monitor, its view provided by a camera with a different angle on the proceedings.

This was focused on the main gate of the university, a Roman triumphal arch as viewed through some kind of strange nineteenth-century cross-cultural Oriental-baroque lens. A line of students was pouring out of the central Moroccon horseshoe arch, each waving a bouquet of flowers on high. Gold sunlight glittered on photographs held above their heads.

Dagmar's heart gave a leap as she realized that this might actually work.

Tuna turned, saw the students pouring into the square, and practically ran to join them, waving his bouquet like a marshal's baton.

Tuna had not been in contact with any of these people. He didn't know any of them, and they didn't know him.

They were the faceless members of an orchestra that Tuna would try to conduct.

Over the heads of the students, a banner unrolled. GENERALS OUT! it said, in English.

Whoever had written it seemed fully aware of the practical necessities of modern international communication, among them the requirement that it be done in a language other than Turkish.

The girls in headscarves had joined the crowd, offering their pot of flowers. People brandished cell phones and snapped pictures. More banners and signs were raised. The pushcart vendors watched in surprise as the square began to fill. Tuna dipped into his shopping bag and pulled out an electric megaphone. Dagmar winced and turned down the volume on her headset as Tuna began bellowing instructions to the crowd.

Dagmar had a good idea what Tuna was telling them. In answer to his call, the crowd began to break into smaller groups.

Make a memorial to the victims of the regime! That's why they had been instructed to bring flowers — a token that did double duty, as identification, so that people would know not to trust anyone who hadn't turned up with the proper tokens

Flowers began to be piled into pyramids, scattered into elaborate designs. Photos were added to the pictures — photos of exiled or imprisoned politicians, national heroes like Atatürk, movie or pop stars, sports figures cut from the pages of newspapers or magazines.

While this was going on, Tuna led a group, including most of those carrying signs, to block Ordu Road on the southern perimeter of the square. If the blocked traffic backed up, police would have a much harder time getting through the demonstration.

The crowd began to sing. The song was in march time and everyone knew the words, so Dagmar assumed it was patriotic.

Blocked traffic on the road honked. Dagmar had spent enough time in Turkey to know the language of the auto honk, which ranged from the little blip that said, in a perfectly friendly way, *Hey, I'm here!* to the deliberate long honk that meant, *Get out of the way,* and the more persistent repeated blasts that might mean, *You are an idiot,* or *I have found your attitude deficient and will very shortly correct it in a vigorous manner.*

The auto horns on Ordu Road progressed through all these stages and then fell into baffled silence. The patriotic singers marched on. Bouquets waved in time to the music. A tram bell rang repeatedly offscreen, but the tram never appeared—apparently jammed autos had blocked it.

The crowd kept getting bigger. Passersby, without flowers or photos, were inspired to join the party. The group finished the song and started on another. Cell phone cameras captured everything.

One of the cameras in the hotel rooms jerked, then shifted and refocused. Dagmar tensed at the sight of a pair of police standing a couple hundred feet down Ordu Road. They were watching the demo with interest and speaking on their walkie-talkies, but they seemed disinclined to interfere.

The fact that they were heavily outnumbered might have contributed to their passive stance.

Dagmar told Tuna about the cops.

"Okay," he said. He didn't sound very alarmed and craned his neck to observe the police who were, at that instant, observing him.

"We've got a police drone over the square," Lloyd said. "We're going to try to take it down."

Dagmar drifted over to Lloyd's station, looking over his shoulder at his multiple screens, each relaying the images sent by one of the drones of the Anatolian Skunk Works. Lloyd pressed one image, and it expanded to cover two screens. The target drone, painted the same shade of blue and white as a police car, floated against a background of gray cloud, its starboard wing dipped as the drone circled the demonstration at Beyazit Square. The picture from the Skunk Works wedge was poured through colossally fast, efficient processors, and it came out as brilliant and clear as if it were being lit and shot by Hollywood professionals.

The hunter-killer wedge hovered closer, and now Dagmar could read POLIS written on the fuselage of the craft.

Lloyd spoke to the wedge operator in Turkish, and the machine oriented itself carefully, then raced forward.

There was a sharp, blurry succession of images, too incoherent for even the fast image processors to make sense of. The horizon seemed to flip a couple times, and then the wedge's guidance program took over, and suddenly it was sailing upright, apparently undamaged, through the sky.

Lloyd punched a fist into the air.

"Wedges *rule!*" he said—and then something caught his eye, and he pressed another image to enlarge it, succeeding just in time to catch an image of the broken police drone, one wing spinning in its slipstream, as it caromed off the roof of a stalled tram.

We own the skies, Dagmar thought incredulously.

The demo went on. More people kept joining, most carrying bouquets, some attracted by texting friends. A young woman, laughing at her own daring, ran up to the two police and handed them each a bouquet. The police politely accepted, and the girl ran back.

"Like wow," said Lincoln deliberately. "I just had a sixties flashback."

There was the hoot of a police siren, and another police officer on a motorcycle came weaving through the stalled traffic to join the two police. Dagmar guessed the officer on duty had arrived. He chatted with the two cops, then spoke into his lapel mike.

"They're mounting up," Richard said. He pointed at the camera fixed at the Mustafa Kemal station. Police were leaving the station, piling into vehicles, motorcycles, and a bus. They wore riot gear, helmets and body armor and plastic shields. Automatic weapons were strapped across their chests.

Dagmar shivered as memory stroked her spine with soft, cold fingers.

Even before the coup, Turkish police had routinely used torture on suspects. "Usually just the ones they think are guilty," Lincoln had said, with small comfort. Suddenly Dagmar felt a strong need to get everyone in the demo to safety.

"Tuna, time to break it up," Dagmar called. "Police coming up Mustafa Kemal." She saw Tuna nod, then raise the megaphone to his lips and bellow orders. The people near him reacted.

Tuna walked back onto the square, shouting. The singing faltered but then strengthened again as the people got the message and began to disperse.

The signs and banners, and flowers and photos, were left behind, brilliant color against the rough gray stone of the square, beneath the big Turkish flag that flew before the university gate. There were pyramids of blossoms, photos of celebrities laid out in suggestive couplings, flowers that spelled out political messages, pictures of the junta defaced with mustaches and beards and devil horns, blooms that formed the Turkish star and crescent, serpents of flowers with human photo heads . . .

The pushcart vendors, covered in flowers, stood amid the colorful debris with smiles on their faces. They'd done good business amid the holiday atmosphere.

One of the advantages of the Beyazit Square location was that there were so many ways to leave the area. People could retreat back into the huge university complex or head across Ordu Road into an area filled with hotels and tourists, places where police might be reluctant to charge. They could go into the Beyazit Mosque that stood on the east side of the square. A few paces farther was the Grand Bazaar, with its maze of narrow streets and its hundreds of shops.

Once they'd dropped their bouquets and photographs, the members of the crowd carried nothing that would mark them to the police, particularly if they dropped the hats and scarves and masks they'd used to shroud their identities.

And Tuna—whom Dagmar had last seen hustling in the direction of the Grand Bazaar—would be clean once he broke the SIM card and dumped the phone in some convenient receptacle.

He was a writer and translator. He lived in Istanbul. He had every excuse for being where he was.

When the police finally fought their way through the traffic tangle, there were only a few pedestrians on the square, along with the flowers and photos and pushcart vendors.

No demonstration, no riot, no reason for police to be there at all.

Dagmar looked at Lincoln standing across the room, standing with a cup of coffee in his hand. He looked at her and silently mouthed a pair of words.

Insanely fun.

She nodded. Yes. It was. She bent over her keyboard.

As soon as Tuna was safely away, she was busy supervising the viewing, editing, and distribution of the masses of video that had been collected during the demo. These were edited into ten- and fifteen-second clips for distribution to television outlets, while the rest was uploaded onto sites with names like downwiththedictators.org and restoretheconstitution.net. The videos were edited slightly, to make the crowd look bigger than it was or to blur images where faces were too recognizable.

Most of the job, however, was out of her hands. The images and video taken by the demonstrators themselves would soon be everywhere, viewed on file-sharing and social-networking sites, sent from one phone to the next, used as wallpaper, submitted to media.

No one had died. It was possible that no one would even be arrested.

The proof-of-concept had proved itself.

The concept showed that action against the government was possible, that it would be seen, and that it would be safe. It showed that *you, too, could prank the government.*

You could make your overlords ridiculous. And all you'd need would be access to a computer, and a cell phone.

They had promised to make the nation safe from people like *you*, but *you* could make them liars.

The fact that the demo hadn't, objectively speaking, *accomplished* anything was irrelevant. No buildings were occupied, no security agencies compromised; no centers of power were seized.

All that would happen later.

The next stage was to make the military government irrelevant. Not merely to congregate at but to *occupy* public spaces and public buildings and meanwhile flood all media channels with propaganda, urging everyone — the security forces in particular — to join them.

That was the essence of the people power revolt — to walk away from the established government and set up your own, virtual government. If the majority of the population chose to recognize the virtual government rather than the traditional one, the generals would end up alone in their palace, trying to get someone to take their phone calls while their own televisions broadcast a message transmitted by their enemies. Recent history was loaded with examples, iconic moments in the transition of power: Enrile crossing EDSA from Camp Aguinaldo; Yeltsin standing atop a tank in front of the Russian White House; Ljubisav Đokić charging the Belgrade broadcast station on his bulldozer; a crowd of Georgians, armed with nothing but roses, driving Eduard Shevardnadze from his own parliament building; Yuschenko taking the presidential oath in a half-deserted room in Ukraine...

All moments when tyranny cracked.

It wasn't a question of whether the generals would use force to maintain their position. That was a given. They'd taken power through a coordinated series of assassinations of journalists, politicians, Christian missionaries, intellectuals, labor leaders, and Kurdish heroin dealers. Presumably they would not be overly disturbed if their tanks' treads were dyed red by the crushed bodies of their enemies.

But the tank *drivers* were another matter. They were vulnerable to propaganda, and more important, they were vulnerable to their own humanity. Once the generals' instruments of power refused their orders, the generals were finished.

In the Philippines, in Serbia, in Georgia and Ukraine, the tank drivers had balked. In Iran and China and Burma, the tankers had obeyed orders.

Dagmar looked around the room in a sudden surge of joy.

We are like ourselves, she thought, *and no one else.*

Within an hour, a bouquet of flowers and a photo of an anonymous seascape had been nailed to the wall of the ops room, just beneath Atatürk's ferocious gaze.

After everything had been collaged together, the demo would be re-created in an augmented reality environment. People could go to Beyazit Square, now or at any point in the future, and if they wore the right goggles or had the right app for their handheld or had the proper helmet with a heads-up display, they would see the demonstration superimposed on the environment. They could participate vicariously in the demo; they could walk through it as if it were actually happening in their present.

They could lay flowers and photographs on the ground and photograph them and then upload them to the AR site, where the pictures would be added to the virtual environment.

It was possible that more people would participate in the demo afterward than were present at the actual event.

For years after the demo — perhaps forever — the AR of the demo would be available to anyone with the right equipment. People taking a picture of the university's baroque gate would see an icon on their phone, or people scrolling along a map of Istanbul would see a symbol and click it, and instantly the demonstration would come to life, flowers and photos and bemused pushcart vendors.

Perhaps they would know it as the moment that Turkey began its entry into the twenty-first century. Or perhaps it would be known as another moment of false hope before the advance was turned back.

But in any case the monument was there, gleaming in the electronic world that lives alongside your own, eternal and evolving, and whatever the Bozbeyli regime did, they could not erase it.

> Have you considered switching to Çankaya Wireless Network? Our customer service is the reason why we are the fastest-growing network in the Turkish-speaking world!
> This link will direct you to a site for our new drawing. Anyone joining our network in the next few days will be eligible to win either a DVD or a beautiful Turkish towel!
> Hurry to sign up. The next drawing will take place at 1700 on Saturday!

There was a grinding sound as the sea came over the shingle, the sound of thousands of small stones tumbling. The sea reached for Dagmar's sandals with foam fingers, failed, withdrew. Stone rattled again on stone. The air tasted of iodine and salt.

"And there," said Ismet, pointing, "the goddess was born."

White clouds tumbled on the horizon. A great ruddy rock reared up above the shingle beach, ran to the water's edge, then fell to the sea. Just offshore was a pair of huge stones, one large and craggy, one smaller and phallic. Maybe there had only been one giant rock on the day when Paphian Aphrodite had risen from the foam, here where the foam after many ages still, perpetually, anointed her birthplace.

There were only a few people on the beach, but they came in pairs. Even now Aphrodite attracted courting couples.

Visions of the Botticelli *Birth of Venus* floated in Dagmar's mind. The delicate Italian scene, seashell and Boreals, the welcoming nymph or goddess or whatever she was in her spangled dress, and the improbably long-necked Venus herself, draped in her own red-gold hair...all these imagined elements were too delicate to have actually taken place in this primal landscape, all sea and wind and stark stone.

If a goddess ever landed here, a goddess shaped by this landscape, the ground would have shaken beneath her footfalls.

"Aphrodite was worshiped here since at least 3800 BCE," Ismet said. Dagmar considered the dates.

"Aphrodite actually goes back that far?"

"She had many names over the years," he said. "The Cypriots just called her Wanassa—the Queen."

Dagmar turned to look at him. He stood farther up the shingle and was therefore a little taller than she; the Mediterranean gleamed in his sunglasses, stone and sea and white foam. He was dressed with care in a striped seersucker summer jacket. A little spot of sunburn glowed high on each cheek.

"How do you know all this?" she said.

He gave an embarrassed smile. "I looked it up in the guidebook on the shelf in the break room," he said.

"Ah," she said. "So you *don't* have hidden depths."

"Apparently not." Politely.

She turned back to the sea and imagined the goddess rising, sea sluicing off naked shoulders. A wave spattered Dagmar's toes with chill water.

"Tell me more," she said.

"The goddess was worshiped till nearly modern times, centuries after the Christians officially suppressed the cult. Girls would come here, or to the ruins of the temple, and make offerings or anoint the goddess with olive oil, hoping for..." He hesitated. "Fertility, I suppose. There was a fourteenth-century Christian writer who complained that if you slept on the ground here, you arose...very lustful."

She smiled to herself. She rather liked Ismet's shyness in sexual matters.

"The statue survived all those centuries?" she asked.

"The goddess was older than any statue. The Aphrodite worshiped here took the form of a cone-shaped rock. It's in the museum in Lefkoşa." Giving the Turkish pronunciation of the capital city the Greeks called Lefkosia, a word that Franks like Dagmar mispronounced as "Nicosia."

Sea boomed on the great stone. A Royal Navy patrol boat ghosted on the edge of the horizon. She turned again to Ismet.

"So Aphrodite was really a stone phallus?"

He turned slightly away, still a little shy.

"Apparently," he said.

"Wouldn't you just know it?" she said, not exactly sure exactly what she meant.

"Ancient coins show the cone beneath a crescent and star," Ismet said. "Just like the ones on the Turkish flag."

The sea heaved, shifting tons of grating stone.

The day after the demo in Istanbul was a day off for Dagmar's crew. Tuna was flying in for a debriefing, and Rafet the dervish was en route to Antalya to set up the next action, which would take place the day after tomorrow.

Most of the Lincoln Brigade had gone to the beach — not the beach here at Kouklia but the British beach on the aerodrome, as much a part of Merrie England as Brighton itself and kept free of waterborne terrorists by gray Royal Navy patrol craft, cutting back and forth on the horizon like metal sharks... Richard and Judy had expressed interest in Banana Boating, an entertainment in which they would straddle a giant yellow banana-shaped craft that would be pulled at a rollicking pace behind a speedboat.

Dagmar had begged off riding the giant banana in favor of history and archaeology, and Ismet had offered to drive.

Dagmar looked up and down the beach.

"Only couples come here," she said.

"It seems so."

She stepped close to him. Ismet accepted her kiss with his usual courtly gravity. Dagmar couldn't quite tell if he was enthusiastic or not, so she kissed him some more. Presently he grew more animated. His skin had a spicy scent of some exotic mixture of aromatic Eastern oils…They put their arms around each other and kissed for a long time.

Dagmar plucked the handkerchief from his jacket pocket and dabbed her lips.

"That was nice," she said.

"It was. Very."

"I've been thinking about doing this for a while now."

"So have I. But"—a ghost of a smile—"I'm just the employee. I couldn't make the first move."

"No," Dagmar said. "Sexual harassment is supposed to come from the boss."

She kissed him some more. Then there was a bang, and she jumped in his arms. She looked up wildly, saw and heard a battered blue Ford truck backfiring another cloud of blue smoke.

"Christ," she said, shuddering.

Ismet stroked her back. "Just a truck," he said. His lips sought hers.

"This may not be a good idea," she said, and slipped from his embrace.

His face showed sudden concern and surprise.

"You're not suddenly worried about being my boss?"

Surf boomed. Dagmar shook her head. His handkerchief was twisted between her fingers.

"I have a bad history with men," she said.

"So it's not that I'm Turkish? Or a Muslim?"

"My last lover was murdered," she said.

His mouth opened, closed.

"And an ex-lover was killed around the same time. And my two best friends. And—" Dagmar gestured at him with his own handkerchief.

"You're a *spy*, aren't you?" she said. She gave a laugh, a little bubble of hysteria bursting from her lips. "You're crossing the border into enemy territory in a couple days, and you could be caught or killed or beaten or put in prison…"

Ismet reached her. She shuddered at the touch of his fingers on her arms.

"I'm not a spy," he said.

"Right. You're special ops."

"I'm a journalist. I'll have reasons for being where I am, for asking questions, for being at a demonstration. Even if I'm arrested, there'll be no reason to hold me."

"Try that line of argument with a bullet or a bomb," she said savagely. "Bullets don't much care about your reasons."

She had firsthand experience with bullets and bombs. And bludgeons. And other forms of death that lurked in humanity's collective dark unconscious.

Dagmar took off her shades and rubbed a hand across both eyes.

"I'm sorry," she said. "I'm just so completely not over it. What happened in LA."

"You said you wouldn't talk about it."

"I am *not* talking about it," Dagmar said.

Ismet scrutinized her. "May I touch you?" he asked.

She lifted her chin, stared defiantly out to sea as if she could see, just above the horizon, some hopeful star that she could follow. Instead she saw only the patrol boat, flashing a signal lamp at some shadowy craft over the horizon.

"Yes," she said. "Please."

His arms went around her. She wrapped herself in his embrace as if it were a blanket.

"You're not some kind of curse." His voice came quiet to her ear. Warm breath moistened her neck. His myrrh scent flooded her senses.

"You don't kill men with your spell," he said. "You've just been in some dark places, that's all. Along with some of your friends."

"How do you know that?"

"I asked Lincoln."

Dagmar was so surprised that she found a laugh bubbling up from her throat. "You asked *Lincoln*?"

"I thought he must have a file on you. I thought he would know."

"What did he say?"

She could hear his smile as he spoke.

"He said, 'Dagmar is definitely not scary, but you should still be careful not to piss her off.'"

She laughed again, leaning against his warm weight. "Right," she said. "Get me mad at you, I'll send the Group Mind to turn your hard drive into porridge."

"No. You'll send someone like me to organize a flash mob and paintball my car."

Dagmar smiled. She looked at one of the other couples walking along the shore, a pair of Brits judging by their sunburns, their trousers rolled up as they waded ankle deep in Aphrodite's foam. The two of them happy, free of the knowledge that a presentiment of death had floated past, just beyond the limit of their perception...

Dagmar's forebodings were usually insignificant—she had the kind of imagination that threw a million obstacles into her path. She could either work to avoid the barriers or—more usually—watch them turn to vapor in the sunlight of reality. But this magical place, this seascape torn from the womb of the goddess herself, seemed to give to Dagmar's fears the chill force of prophecy... She wondered if dread generated in this landscape was more significant than dread generated elsewhere.

But if that was the case, she thought, then so was love. So was desire. So was lying on this magic earth and rising very lustful, to the ranting dismay of medieval theologians.

She let the landscape speak to her. She turned in Ismet's arms and began to kiss him.

"Very nice." This time it was his turn to say it.

She kissed his chin. Surf boiled up from the heart of the sea.

"Let's take a walk, then," she said. She took his hand and led him down the beach, intent on behaving like the other couples, swinging their clasped hands and playing tag with the sea.

And—in Dagmar's case, anyway—trying to ignore the palpable sense of doom that lurked in the back of her skull.

They walked. They kissed. They let the sea stream over their toes. They looked at shells and rocks and some jellyfish tossed on the shore, deflated domes glistening crumpled on the stones like empty plastic bags.

They went up to Kouklia and looked at what remained of Aphrodite's temple—there wasn't much left, not since someone in the Middle Ages had built a sugar works on it.

By the time Ismet and Dagmar returned to Akrotiri, Tuna had come across from the Turkish side of the island and was delivering his report to Lincoln. There were a number of contacts referred to by code names, and even Dagmar didn't know who they were. It made the whole business more opaque than she would have liked. And the whole time she was listening to the report, she was thinking about dragging Ismet off to bed.

Which she finally accomplished at twilight, leading him by the hand to her apartment, where she was pleased to hear the sound of the shower, presumably with Judy in it. Dagmar was happy about this coincidence—it avoided the awkward scene in which Dagmar and Ismet were forced to chat up Judy for an indeterminate period of time, pretending all was normal when all they really wanted to do was shag.

Best to postpone the awkwardness to the next morning, when Ismet's turning up at the breakfast table would explain everything.

She took Ismet straight to the bedroom, then closed the door behind her. He was watching her with what seemed to be extreme interest.

"Why do you have your bed turned at an angle?" he asked.

She shrugged: too long to explain. "I'm an angular kind of person," she said.

Dagmar turned off the light. Ismet was outlined by the yellow streetlight seeping through a chink in the curtains. His glasses seemed to glow, like the eyes of a cartoon villain. Dagmar stepped closer, put her arms around him, and began to kiss him. He responded with enthusiasm. Myrrh swam through her senses. His glasses mashed her cheek. She took them off, along with everything else he was wearing. He was preposterously erect, and she was flattered by this diverting evidence of his desire.

A metaphorically apt jet roared along Akrotiri's long runway and hurled itself into the sky. The windowpane trembled to its acceleration.

Suddenly impatient, she tore off her own clothes and composed herself on the bed. Unable to judge the irregular angle of the bed in the dark, he barked his knees on the frame, then lay by her side. She kissed him again. His flesh warmed hers; his touch lit up her nerves. He shivered as she licked the sensitive flesh of his throat. She began to remember, after this long hiatus, what this sex thing was all about.

Ismet turned out to be something of a technician. He offered experimental caresses, observed her closely, then either increased his efforts or went on to something else. Five minutes of this and Dagmar felt her body on the verge of dissolving into magma.

Dagmar took a breath and decided to let the Wanassa, the Queen, take over.

Which famous sixties spy are you? The old Internet quiz came to Dagmar's mind as she lay curled on her bed, with Ismet sleeping in the fetal position inside her arc, his pale body outlined by the streetlight outside. The sheet was rucked up under them, tangled about their feet. They were two commas, side by side on crumpled paper.

Not spy, she corrected mentally. *Special ops.*

It wasn't like she'd encountered sixties operatives on their first go-around. She'd been born over twenty years after the first Bond film. But she'd seen all the films and read all the books, as homework for the *Stunrunner* game—and the other spies she'd encountered here or there on DVD or late-night cable, and in many cases read the books that had inspired them. The sixties interested her, as the decade when everything that hadn't gone right had gone so horribly wrong.

Ismet wasn't James Bond—he lacked Bond's glamor and gadgets. He didn't have John Steed's brolly or wardrobe. Briefly she considered Quiller—Ismet possessed something like Quiller's omnicompetence, but ultimately he lacked, so far as she knew, his tragic spirit.

She considered and dismissed the Man from U.N.C.L.E. Thoughts of the Man from O.R.G.Y. made her smile and impelled her to kiss Ismet's shoulder. She would have to subject Ismet to more testing before she could report on that hypothesis.

She mentally paged through John le Carré's works. Ismet was too young to be George Smiley and furthermore had never been miserably married to some bitch-queen of an upper-class vampire. She wondered if Ismet could be any of the other characters at le Carré's Circus, but she couldn't remember enough about any of them. (There was a Hungarian named Esterhase, right?)

And then she recalled Deighton's nameless spy from *The Ipcress File*. That role seemed to fit Ismet better: quiet, unassuming, competent, and rather exciting once he took his glasses off.

Well then. Perhaps Ismet should get Ipcress as a new code name.

Ismet shifted in his sleep, rolling onto his back. Dagmar put an arm across his chest and rested her head on his shoulder. One arm came around her, held her close.

She breathed in the scent of him, myrrh and sweat, breath and sex, and closed her eyes, content to be in the circuit of her lover's arms.

Ismet left after breakfast to bathe and change clothes, leaving Dagmar and Judy across the table with its litter of teacups, its plates of goat cheese, olives, bread, fruit, and Judy's jar of Nutella. Judy looked after the departing Ismet, then turned to Dagmar.

"I wasn't entirely surprised," she said.

"You probably heard us," Dagmar said.

"Not me. Slept like a rock." She carefully spread Nutella onto a piece of bread. "Still, I'm a little envious."

"No luck with Rafet?"

"I can't seem to ever *find* him," Judy said. "He's either over across the Green Line doing training, or in conference with Lincoln or with Alparslan the government guy, or working out in the gym, or doing tai chi—I *guess* it's tai chi—in his backyard. And now he's off to…to wherever the next target is."

"No ecstatic drumming?"

She looked forlorn. "No ecstacy of any sort, unfortunately."

Dagmar was tempted once again to remind Judy that they were on an air base loaded with single men, but the thought was interrupted by total surprise at what Judy said next.

"I guess you're just lucky," Judy said, half-yawning as she stretched her tattooed arms out wide, "that you've got your two men."

"Two?" Dagmar said, too startled to manage more than the single syllable.

"Ismet and Lincoln," Judy said.

Dagmar barked out an astonished laugh. "You think I'm involved with *Lincoln?*" she said.

Judy stuck a finger inside her spectacles and wiped sleep from her eyes.

"Not sexually," she said. "But—you know—it's clear that you've got a special relationship with him."

Dagmar was alarmed. She wondered if everyone was thinking this.

"He's the guy I work for!" she said.

"He's a smart, charming older man," Judy said. "And you're someone in need of a father." She cocked her head, considering. "I'm a bit attracted to him myself on that account, my own dad being absent most of my life."

Dagmar couldn't decide whether to laugh or express outrage. She ended up saying nothing.

Judy took an olive from a plate, bit it, grimaced, and swallowed. Apparently her palate wasn't ready for olives for breakfast.

"Put some Nutella on it," Dagmar advised.

"He's *not* your father, is my point," Judy said. "He's here to do a job, and if getting it done means treating you like a favorite daughter, then that's what he'll do. But if the job called for it, he could be someone else's daddy tomorrow."

"Our relationship," said Dagmar, "is professional."

"That's for the best," Judy said, her tone skeptical. "Because Lincoln isn't just some eccentric old geezer with a game fixation, he's a *general* trying to start a *revolution*. And that means he's going to get people killed."

"He's not bloodthirsty," Dagmar protested. "He's not sending out assassins."

"No," Judy said, "not that we know about, anyway. It's our *own* people that are going to get killed if these demos go wrong. It's Lincoln who's decided to accept that loss, if it happens."

So have I, Dagmar thought. Instead she just repeated what Lincoln had said on that last day in Istanbul.

"That would be the fault of the bastards who kill them."

Judy shrugged her inked shoulders.

"I'd say there's enough responsibility to go around."

Dagmar looked at Judy, her eyes narrow.

"And *your* responsibility?" she asked.

A tremor crossed Judy's face. "I'm complicit," she said. "I got carried away by the sheer coolness of it all."

"Well." Dagmar rose and reached for the teapot. "From this point on, I'm going to be heavily invested in keeping my boyfriend alive."

Judy looked at her with bleak sleepy eyes.

"May you succeed," she said, "in all your endeavors."

Have you considered taking advantage of the 103 digital television channels offered by Çankaya Wireless Net-

work? Great care is taken to make all our plans afford-
able! Any one of our eleven plans is certain to be suitable
to your budget!

There was Rafet, his brilliant yellow hair covered by a sun hat,
dancing at the head of several thousand people. He was holding a
double-ended drum and was banging away and jumping up and
down and everyone around him was singing.

Ecstatic drumming indeed, Dagmar thought.

The new anti-government action was under way. It was ten A.M.
on Saturday, and the demo had been swollen by thousands who
had the day off.

The action was taking place in Karaalioğlu Park, in Antalya,
Turkey's largest city on its Mediterranean coast. The park was
blessed with a spectacular location, perched on a cliff above the
sea, so every video on Dagmar's array of flatscreens showed a
spectacular view of ocean, cliff, clouds, rows of palm trees, sail-
boats, fountains, the ochre-colored walls of a castle, all dominated
by the Tauros Mountains, snowcapped even this early in
autumn. There was also some of the oddest public art Dagmar
had ever seen—a statue of a bellicose mustached man with Pop-
eye arms and what looked like a baseball cap tilted back on his
head; an ancient spear-carrying warrior with a flat helmet, Don
Quixote perhaps as conceived by Picasso; something that resembled in silhouette a two-horned Maurice Sendak monster; and
strangest of all a huge groping hand apparently called *Blessing
Agriculture, Geology, Earth, Ground, Land, Soil*, probably every syn-
onym available in a Turkish thesaurus for *dirt*.

Maybe the Turks just hadn't gotten the hang of statues yet.
Atatürk had imposed statues on his nation, which had previously
adhered to the Islamic ban on human representation—and so the
newly liberated citizens had started off by planting statues of
Atatürk everywhere, which no doubt earned the Gazi's approval.
Since then they seemed to have gone a bit off the rails.

Maybe, Dagmar thought charitably, they all made better sense in context.

The crowds had been told to bring DVDs and towels, and they did. The DVDs were held high, glittering in the sun, and Dagmar caught glimpses of packages bearing the images of Rocky, Celine Dion, Sean Connery, ABBA, and Cüneyt Arkın, the actor who had achieved a kind of international infamy as the Turkish Luke Skywalker... The towels, mostly huge beach towels striped green and yellow and pink, were wrapped around faces to conceal identities. Brilliant color danced in the morning light.

"It looks like a *Hitchhiker's Guide to the Galaxy* convention," Dagmar said.

"I was just thinking that," said Richard.

Signs with bloodred letters waved against the blue sky. The crowd sang. The Star and Crescent flapped in the sea breeze. The video jerked and wobbled.

In Istanbul the cameras has been concealed in hotel rooms across the street from the demo. Here there was no way to hide them, so Rafet's crew of support techs wandered amid the crowd. Some carried cameras, others wore sunglasses with video and audio pickups, and they lacked the motion-inhibiting qualities of camera tripods. These did their best to stand still and pan the scene, but every so often they'd get jogged by a member of the crowd or have to move from one setup to another or just get carried away and start dancing. More video came in from the drones of the Anatolian Skunk Works.

Oh well. Dagmar knew they could stabilize the video in postproduction.

Still rapping on his drum, Rafet led the group of dancers away from the cliff, somewhat to Dagmar's relief. Her imagination, the one that obsessed on every conceivable thing that could go wrong, had foreseen a line of bayonet-wielding soldiers driving the protestors over the cliff into the sea.

But, Tuna and Lincoln had pointed out, there would be a lot of foreigners in the park. Foreigners provided a measure of protection: even Bozbeyli would see the disadvantage of conducting a bayonet charge where foreign visitors would be caught up in it. The bad headlines he'd gotten from the hippodrome riot should have been an object lesson to him.

So far Tuna and Lincoln had been proved right: the watchers on the local police stations hadn't reported any movement at all. Maybe no one had even called the police or the army.

Rafet danced along the path, the tails of his towel floating out behind him. He was wearing video shades, but the image he broadcast was a hopeless bouncy blur—looking at it was like jabbing needles into Dagmar's eyeballs. The audio feed delivered a complex series of drumbeats, Rafet's panting breath, and the sound of shoes crunching on gravel.

Rafet led the group past a round fountain that shot a tall spear of foam into the sky, then into the square in front of the Antalya City Hall. The place was a tidy white structure with balconies and a portico and looked as if it had been put up by some European power's Colonial Office—even though Antalya hadn't been colonized since the Turks themselves had done it a thousand years ago, they had somehow locked into the colonial style perfectly well.

It was the weekend and no one was inside the building—the place wasn't even guarded—but that didn't matter as far as the audience for the video was concerned. What the pictures would show would be thousands of demonstrators waving their banners in front of the center of local power...and they would also see no response from the authorities.

The demonstrators began a new song, a triumphalist slow march. Sonorous chords boomed out. Turkish flags waved. Everyone stood still for the song, even Rafet.

Dagmar looked over her shoulder at Ismet. "This would be the national anthem?"

"Yes. 'İstiklâl Marşi.'"

Dagmar nodded. "It just *sounds* like a national anthem."

The song came to a resounding conclusion after two stanzas. Then Rafet rapped for attention on his drum. The sunglass-cameras resolutely pointed away from him: no solid image of the dancing dervish would make it into any of the Lincoln Brigade's videos. Rafet shouted out in Turkish, and the crowd responded. They made the same sort of spontaneous art made at the other demo in Istanbul, DVDs laid out in patterns on the square, stacked in interesting ways, layered on the town hall steps, or set winking in the windows. Enterprising young men scaled the pillars supporting the portico and draped towels off the portico rail. More towels were hung from the rail that topped the wings of the building. Anti-government banners were raised on the town hall's three flagstaffs.

Dagmar could only guess what General Bozbeyli would make of this.

DVDs in the windows? he might mutter. *What DVDs were these? Were they anti-government DVDs? No?* Rocky IV?

What do the DVDs represent? Is this supposed to be some kind of DVD revolution?

And what about the towels? Is this some kind of attack on Turkishness through the symbolism of the Turkish towel? What signals are these people sending?

Call the head of the Jandarma! Call the mayors! We need to find out what all this means!

Dagmar was in on the secret: the items meant nothing. They transmitted no message. In order to fully comprehend the meaning of the demos, you had to be hip enough to understand that the DVDs, the towels, the photographs, and the flowers *meant nothing at all*! They were just convenient articles that people could carry that marked them as part of the flash mob aimed at the government.

The generals would never grok that. Never. They'd grope in the dark for meaning and come up with nothing—which was in fact the *answer*, but they'd never understand that.

A picnic spirit had begun to possess the protestors. More songs were sung. People linked arms and swayed in time to the music. No warning was sent from Lloyd, whose drones monitored the police and army—either the authorities didn't care or were baffled or were waiting for instructions from somewhere up the line or no one had let them know what was going on.

"This isn't a demonstration," Lincoln said, with apparent pleasure. "It's a damn *love-in*."

"Chatsworth," Dagmar said. "What happens if the police don't move? Do we let this go on?"

Lincoln leaned closer to one of the monitors, his Elvis glasses sliding down his nose. He frowned, leaned back.

"The wedges are going to run out of fuel," Lloyd pointed out.

Lincoln settled his glasses back on the bridge of his nose. "No sense in waiting for the police to get their shit together," he said. "We've made our larger point. Let's send 'em home."

"Right."

She told Rafet to end the action and sent additional messages to his support team. Rafet looked at one of the nearby cameras, then nodded.

The demonstrators were enjoying themselves too much to leave right away; the demo trailed off in a diminuendo of song and dance and trailing towels.

Helmuth and Tuna nailed a towel and a DVD of *The Guns of Navarone*, David Niven and Gregory Peck painted in heroic pastels, to the wall next to the towel and bouquet of flowers.

"Who's for a celebration?" Helmuth cried. "Ouzo! Dolmades! Pizza!"

Magnus turned a little pale at the prospect of an entire long day in Helmuth's company. Thus far Helmuth was proving a match for all the cocktails, discos, and desperate Russian women of Limassol put together...

Dagmar looked at Ismet, then looked away.

"Maybe later," she said. "Text me."

She wouldn't go. Helmuth's Rabelaisian idea of a good time had never appealed to her.

And besides, she had to say good-bye to Ismet first.

He was flying away this afternoon to organize Monday's demo

in Izmir. He would cross the Green Line in his car and then fly on to Izmir. To account for the odd stamps on his passport he was writing a series of articles on the Cyprus situation. He had them all on his netbook, along with his notes, if anyone demanded proof.

They had time for a pensive half-hour embrace on the couch in Dagmar's flat before Ismet's departure. Ismet was distracted by his upcoming mission and Dagmar by the ton of melancholy that squatted on her heart.

She'd had two whole nights with Ismet and already she was seeing him off to war. Film scenes ran through her mind, scenes in which the tearful girlfriend, running alongside the train, sees her soldier boy off to the Great War, waving a handkerchief at someone named Clive or Sebastian or Reginald leaning out of his train compartment in his flat helmet, the gas mask container bulking up his chest like an extra layer of fat, one pale doomed hand waving as he chugged off to be turned into chutney at Wipers or Vimy Ridge or Passchendaele...

Each repeatedly reassured the other how astoundingly safe Ismet's task would be, and then Dagmar walked with him to his car. She gave him a fierce kiss and a rib-crushing hug, much to the amusement of an RAF airman sailing past on a bicycle.

"Save some for me, love!" he called over his shoulder, and then ran over a skateboard that some child had left in the road. The bicycle wobbled, and the airman tottered and spilled onto the curb. Dagmar burst into uncharitable laughter.

Ismet got in his Ford and drove off. Dagmar decided not to run alongside waving a handkerchief—*his* handkerchief, actually, which she'd absently put in her own pocket at the beach in Kouklia. She stared after him for a long while, the handkerchief wadded in her fist, while she ignored the airman dusting himself off and pushing off on his bike.

More than ever, she wasn't in a mood to join Helmuth's party, and so decided she might as well get some work done.

She shambled over to the ops center, where she found Lincoln and Byron, beneath Atatürk's fierce gaze, supervising the last remaining details of the Antalya action. The place smelled of stale flowers and cold pizza.

"Rafet and the crew are in the clear," Lincoln said. "Rafet's at the airport buying a ticket back to Cyprus. The rest are back at the safe house with their equipment."

"Lovely," said Dagmar. She looked up at a BBC news program, running in silence, that showed a fifteen-second clip of the demo that she had fed them less than an hour earlier. Towels and flags waved from the town hall, while Rafet—suitably blurred—bounced and played his drum.

"I never figured I'd be working alongside Muslim clergy," Dagmar said. "He *is* clergy, right?"

"No," Lincoln said, "but the people who sent him are. And they're the *right kind* of Muslim clergy. Progressive, scientifically literate, tolerant."

"And extremely polite," Dagmar said.

"Thanks to Riza Tek, all praise to his name." Lincoln's face darkened. "If we fail here, our movement may fall to the *wrong* kind of Muslim theologians."

"If we fail," Dagmar said, "there may only be fanatics left."

Byron gave her a searching look from over his shoulder. His face looked permanently pinched. Dagmar wondered if he'd been ill.

Lincoln scrubbed his hands together.

"But failure isn't going to happen!" he declared. "We're going to conduct a model twenty-first-century people power insurrection, and we're going to make the Turkish generals look like idiots! They've all got a pre-Internet mind-set—they think that once they've got the newspapers and broadcast stations, they have a monopoly on communications. We're going to overthrow them by making them *ridiculous*. We'll make them *irrelevant*! The entire population will *just ignore them*! They'll fold up and leave out of *sheer embarrassment*!"

Dagmar dropped into a chair. "I like it when you get on a soapbox," she said.

"The generals aren't unlike some of my own superiors," Lincoln said. "Start talking about leet, or Ozone, or the IP crisis that's coming up, or even *text messaging* for heaven's sake, and you just get a blank look."

Dagmar looked at him. "How did you get them to approve *me*?" she asked. "How did you explain what it is that I do?"

Lincoln sighed. "I called in a *lot* of favors," he said.

"No kidding," she said.

"Besides," he said, "I reckon we're up against a deadline. Right now the generals are reflexively pro-Western, because *they always have been*. They're nationalist; they're procapitalist; they're anticommunist; they'd never deal with the Soviets. But the Soviets are gone now — and they've left *Russians* behind.

"Everyone's a capitalist now," Lincoln went on, "but there are democratic capitalists and crony capitalists and state capitalists and authoritarian capitalists and everything in between. The Bozbeyli regime has a lot more in common ideologically with Moscow now than with Washington — but they've got such a Cold War anti-Soviet mind-set that they *haven't figured it out yet*. I want to knock them down before they turn into Russia's best friend on the Black Sea."

"And the Bosporus," Dagmar said.

Lincoln nodded. "Indeed," he said.

Sudden insight flashed into Dagmar's mind. She looked at Lincoln in wonder.

"Am I correct in assuming that this operation is really aimed at Russia?" Dagmar said. "That once we do our proof-of-concept, you're planning to scale all this up and go after Kremlin autocrats?"

"Everything," said Lincoln, smiling benignly, "is rehearsal for something else."

It was ten A.M. in California, and Dagmar was on the phone to Calvin, her head writer for the Seagram's game.

"I screwed up bad," he said. "And all because I love my dog."

Dagmar drew her legs up into her seat and contemplated the

gin and tonic in her hand. She could scent juniper berry and fresh-cut lime fizzing from the drink.

"Tell me," she said.

"Harry's got a dog in the story, right? It scares away Murchison when he tries to break into Sandee's place."

"Yeah, okay." Dagmar sipped her drink. She glanced at the kitchen and saw that the water was boiling for pasta.

"So I gave my own dog's name to Harry's dog. Perpetual Misery — Perpy for short."

Dagmar felt a warning prickle on the back of her neck.

"And," she said, "the players googled Perpetual Misery plus Dog and found you."

"Worse than that. Perpetual Misery has a MySpace page."

"Oh my Christ!" Dagmar put her drink down.

"They call me," Calvin said miserably. "They call me to ask for information about Harry and Sandee. I tell them I never heard of them, but they keep calling. When I don't answer, the buffer on the answering machine fills up." He gave a despairing sigh. "Perpy has *thousands* of new friends on MySpace."

"Jesus, Calvin."

"*They're camped out in front of my house,*" Calvin said. "*They follow me when I go to the store.*"

Dagmar tried to suppress her annoyance. Calvin had tried to play cute with the game, to sneak a little joke by the players, and he hadn't realized that they'd jump all over something like that. And now he'd put the whole game in jeopardy.

"They're waiting for you to slip up," she said. "They're hoping you'll leave data where they can find it, or leave a script behind. You've got to secure everything connected with the game."

"I can't believe this is happening."

"Calvin." She spoke as patiently as she could. "Do you have any notes on paper? Any printouts lying around where people can find them?"

Item by item, Dagmar walked him through a procedure for sanitizing his house, his computer, and his handheld.

She hadn't needed Lincoln to teach her these things.

"I'll have Richard call you about computer security," Dagmar said, and pressed the End button.

She looked sadly at her drink, now heavily watered by melting ice, and sighed.

She was trying to run two jobs at a distance, each at least as complex as the other. She didn't feel completely on top of either task, especially as she was working with people who were less experienced than she at any of this.

She comforted herself with the thought that, if there had to be a security breach on one of her operations, at least it was best that it was Calvin's.

If Calvin's operation was breached, no people would die.

The next day Lincoln's predictions seemed to come true, as word arrived of another mass demonstration in Trabzon, a city on the Black Sea. Lincoln called an emergency meeting in the ops room in order to figure out what was happening.

Dagmar scanned video and photos uploaded onto anti-government sites. She saw banners waving under cloudy skies, water looking frigid and gray, ships nosed up to piers.

"It's at the waterfront," Magnus said a little too obviously. He was hungover from the previous day's celebrations and sucked down coffee as fast as he could pour it.

"Video quality isn't bad," Helmuth judged.

"This isn't one of ours!" Lincoln said. "This is going off the rails faster than I imagined!"

Dagmar looked at him in surprise. "That's a good thing?" she asked.

"Look," Lincoln said. "We're *astroturfing* them! We're trying to convince everyone that this is a grassroots Turkish movement. And now it's actually become one!" He gestured grandly at the screen. "These people put it all together themselves!" He frowned at the screen. "Let's hope they don't cock it up for all of us."

The crowd was small but very enthusiastic. Apparently under

the illusion that the items were symbolically important, they carried flowers, DVDs, towels, and photos. They made piles and designs out of these items and spray-painted slogans on the sidewalk. It was everything they'd seen done in videos.

And then they sang "İstiklâl Marşi" and dispersed, presumably to upload their pictures and videos to political and social networking sites throughout cyberspace.

The Lincoln Brigade looked at one another. Lincoln grinned.

"We taught them well," he said.

"I have a Hot Koan," Richard said. They turned to him.

"*Dagmar makes a revolution out of processors, connectors, routers, and Web pages,*" Richard said. "*But take away the processors, connectors, routers, and Web pages and what is left?*

"*Trabzon.*"

The action in Izmir went wrong at the beginning. It was scheduled to take place at noon in the old Konak section of the city, in a large park at the waterfront with more stunning sea views, a pier, and a picturesque gingerbread clock tower. The place was also conveniently close to the city hall should another march on a symbol of authority prove possible. But it seemed that after two waterfront demonstrations in Antalya and Trabzon the authorities must have decided waterfront parks were too great a temptation to sedition. A whole company of police moved into the park on Monday morning, bringing with them an armored car.

The scene had to be shifted at the last minute, a good deal farther east, to Hasanaga Park in the Buca district. The setting was good—there were ample entrances and exits from the park, and the adjoining Dokuz Eylül University provided potential recruits as well as lots of places to hide—but it took time to scout the location, and that meant the action had to be moved up to six o'clock, pushing close to the deadline sent in email messages.

The park was wooded and the demonstrators, carrying stuffed animals and boxes of Turkish delight, took a while to find one another and reach critical mass. One of the tech crew while waiting for people to turn up wasted time shooting video of jack-daws on the lawn.

The demonstrators had been given only two hours' notice when and where to show up, and it was soon clear that insufficient allowance had been made for delays caused by rush hour traffic. By six o'clock there were only a few hundred people at the action, though more continued to swarm in from all directions.

The demo began in a brief rain squall. The sound of raindrops slapping tree leaves dominated the audio, and one of the cameras persisted in tracking the flapping jackdaws. Demonstrators began piling their stuffies into pyramids or perching them in trees. Chants of "Down with the generals!" rose bravely against the sound of rattling rain. Turkish delight was eaten or offered to pass-ersby and to birds. The rain diminished, then died away.

Then there came the first shots, and the startled jackdaws leaped into the air.

Dagmar's body jerked beneath a tsunami of adrenaline. She stared at the screens as her fingers clenched the arms of her chair, physically nailing her to the spot as she fought the instinct that wanted to send her senselessly running from the scene...

The shots seemed to echo forever among the trees. People fell; screams rose; the video image jerked wildly. "Ismet!" she called into her headset mic. "Where are you?"

Memories poured into her mind...she remembered fallen banners, sprawled bodies on the street, the Palms hotel as it burned, the fires lapping upward one storey at a time. The scent of burning flesh stung her nostrils, a memory so strong that tears stung her eyes in reaction...

Hundreds of people sprawled on the wet grass, heads up, looking wildly for the source of the shooting. Pyramids of stuffies were knocked over: plush animals stared at the sky with shiny, dead eyes.

"Are you all right?" Dagmar cried. She could hear someone breathing on the line, Ismet presumably, but he wasn't talking.

"Are you all right?" she demanded. Still no answer.

More shots. More cries. And now the crowd rose to its feet and began to run, a vast screaming mass. The camera crew ran as well. The shooting was a continuous drumroll, full automatic fire spraying the crowd. Dagmar swept tears from her eyes and looked from screen to screen, trying to find a glimpse of Ismet.

"Lloyd!" Lincoln called. "Get a drone over to the shooters! I want their pictures! Get a message to the camera teams!"

Richard, Helmut, and Magnus sent frantic messages. Dagmar was too caught up in her own agony: Lincoln's urgency didn't quite penetrate her own.

Most of the cameramen were caught up in the rout, running from tree to tree and kicking up silver sheets of water from puddles, but the dozens of Hot Koans scattered over the park transmitted the video faithfully. One cameraman put a hand in front of his lens and extruded a middle finger, an answer to the request for close-ups of the assassins. But Lloyd's team answered the call, and one of the helicopter gyred over the park, lens questing, and found two men advancing from the direction of the university. They carried submachine guns in their hands and wore the uniform of the Gray Wolves. They walked among bodies sprawled like stuffed animals, wounded crying or trying to crawl away, piles of rain-soaked animals and spilled boxes of candy.

"Get me their faces!" Lincoln demanded. The helicopter made another pass, this time at a lower angle, and Dagmar could see the killers clearly. Young, laughing, pleased with themselves and the notion that their heroin-dealing superiors were safe for another day. They carried their weapons leveled in front of them but made no attempt to fire into the running crowd. One turned his chin into his collar to speak into a lapel mic.

Lincoln frowned. "I don't like that," he said. He turned to Lloyd. "Tell the pilots to circle the park again. There may be more of them that we can't see."

The image jerked, danced, fragmented.

Where's Ismet? Her eyes turned to the other video feeds. The other camera operators were still fleeing through trees with the crowd, transmitting disjointed flashes of green, of flowers, of scattered, sobbing people. She could hear nothing on her audio. The breathing had stopped.

And then—coming right through the trees—a line of men. Five or six, gray uniforms, guns leveled...and in the fragment of time it took Dagmar to realize what was going on the guns fired.

Bullets ripped into tree trunks, leaves, flesh. Screams echoed from tree to tree. The whole crowd moaned, a kind of universal sigh of despair, and then they turned and began to run in another direction.

Dagmar realized that her VoIP line was dead, that Ismet had hung up or that the phone had been destroyed. She frantically tried to reconnect. She couldn't even get a ring signal.

She looked down at her hands and saw that she was wringing them in an agony of helplessness.

"Camera Three?" Lincoln said. "Who's Camera Three?"

Camera Three was down, lying in the grass, the image tilted. The audio transmitted little determined grunts, as if someone repeatedly was trying to rise but failing.

"Code name Kamber," Termite said.

The shooting had stopped—there had just been that volley to turn them, and then the guns had fallen silent.

"Get me pictures of those new shooters," Lincoln said. The helicopter made another circle, came over the park at another angle.

Dagmar's eyes swept from screen to screen, desperate for a glimpse of Ismet. There was only chaos in the video, fragments of the desperate crowd in motion—all except Camera Three, lying aslant in the grass.

Dagmar wondered if there were more Gray Wolves—if another line of paramilitaries would appear from another direction, turning the crowd again, sending it staggering back into another hail of bullets.

There was motion on Camera Three. Dagmar looked, saw three Gray Wolves step into the frame. They stopped, relaxed, smiled at one another. The one in the middle lit a cigarette, and the others clustered around to share his lighter.

Hot anger replaced Dagmar's helplessness. *Remember those faces,* she thought.

She looked at the other video feeds, and then she saw a camera burst out of the trees, seeing a street, cars, a minibus...signs and businesses and satellite dishes...he was out of the woods.

Other camera operators broke free. Survivors of the crowd staggered out of the trees, sobbing, screaming, supporting one another...Dagmar's heart gave a leap as she thought she saw Ismet, but then she realized it was someone else.

The video images crossed the road, dodging cars, and were free in Buca. Other people bustled toward them, late arrivals carrying stuffed animals and boxes of candy. Dagmar saw the horror on their faces as they saw the demonstrators staggering toward them.

They hadn't been surrounded, Dagmar realized. The Wolves came at them from two directions but left the other exits uncovered.

The helicopters swooped in, providing pictures of the second group of killers. There were six of them in total. None of them heard the whisper of the copters or looked up to see the hovering cameras.

Where is Ismet? Dagmar's brain repeated the question over and over.

Lincoln looked at the flatscreens. In profile he looked like some kind of ferocious Old Testament prophet.

"Get the images of those Gray Wolves," he said. "I want a portrait of each of them that their mothers will be proud of. I want them as recognizable as possible."

Helmuth and the others turned to their keyboards.

"You know," Helmuth said, "when actors on a TV show enlarge a video image, there's actually *more detail.*"

"Can we have that software?" Magnus asked.

Within an hour they had good portraits of the eight Wolves

they'd caught on video and created posters for distribution on the Internet.

WANTED, the posters read. FOR MURDER OF TURKISH CITIZENS.

Within four hours, the public had provided names for each of the faces. An hour after that, they had addresses and other data. Within six, they had names for the others Wolves in their unit.

While this went on, the Brigade worked on creating an augmented reality version of the demo. The piles of stuffed animals, the jackdaws, the rain, the scattered bodies...all would be available, perpetually, for anyone walking through the park.

In electronic form, the dead would die forever.

No word came from Ismet. Dagmar sat at her workstation or roamed aimlessly over the ops room.

Wandering, she looked out the window at the airfield and saw lines of Indonesian police marching down the runway. She shut her eyes, then the blinds.

She wandered to the break room, looked at the lunch she had waiting in the fridge, then closed the fridge door and went back to ops.

Along the way she felt a firm hand on her elbow, and she looked up to see Lincoln. Wordlessly he led her to his office. He sat her in a chair, then took his place behind his desk.

"I need to know," he said, "if you told anyone about the target."

She looked at him in surprise, a surprise that was soon followed by dread.

"No," she said. "You and I worked out where the demo was going to happen, along with Ismet."

Lincoln glanced at his safe. "I lock everything up at the end of the day. I don't commit anything to electronic form."

Dagmar threw her hands wide.

"I haven't talked about this at all, Lincoln," she said.

"Or written it down? Or emailed it?"

"No. Of course not."

Lincoln looked fixedly at a corner of his desk, his jaw muscles working in accompaniment to his thoughts.

"It could be a complete coincidence," he said. "Those Wolves might just have been on the scene — or were pulling some kind of unrelated security detail on campus. And there are a thousand ways our system can be compromised. We could have an informer somewhere in the network, or somebody's girlfriend could have found out he's cheating and told the cops to get even..." He looked up. "Speed is of the essence. We've got to put these events together faster than the authorities can react to informers."

Dagmar pressed her hands together, trying to stop the shaking. Lincoln frowned.

"Dagmar," he said, "I need you to pull yourself together."

She shrank beneath his cold gaze.

"I keep thinking about Ismet," she said.

"There's nothing you can do about him."

"I keep thinking that I've killed another one." Another lover, she meant.

Lincoln's mouth twisted in a kind of snarl.

"Well," he said, "you haven't. And the fact is people have been dying all along — journalists, missionaries, Kurds, Alevis, labor leaders, even the odd tourist... It's been going on all along, and neither of us are going to stop it completely; we can just make it mean something, maybe..."

Dagmar wanted to say that Ismet meant more to her than some political principle, but the words crumbled into dust before she could even utter them.

"I need you to help get those videos into shape, and uploaded," Lincoln said. "I want Turkish public opinion outraged by this. Because we want the outrage *we* feel to be felt by everybody."

Dagmar obeyed numbly. The Turkish government had issued a list of Web sites that were to be blocked. Türk Telekom was too big to ignore the order, but many local ISPs were slow to get the order or slow to enforce it.

Still, Dagmar was staying ahead of the authorities. For the next few hours she edited video, uploaded it, made sure it was posted on new sites that the Turkish government hadn't managed to ban yet. She helped Magnus and Byron create new proxy sites so that people in Turkey could view the videos and send messages to one another without the government intercepting them. Distantly she could hear the thump of shotguns, the cries of wounded and dying, the amplified, incomprehensible snarl of anger coming from bullhorns... it's as if she were listening to a radio station from a parallel world, where the events of her past were repeated over and over again.

As she worked, Atatürk fixed his ferocious gaze upon her from his place on the wall.

It was nearly dinnertime before she heard from Ismet.

His message appeared on a Gmail account they shared. Gmail accounts were perfect for covert work, provided that everyone involved had a password and access to the account.

Dagmar would, for example, write an email giving details of the next demo, then *not send it*. Ismet or Tuna or Rafet, who knew the password, could open the email, make their own comments, then log off, again without sending it. This could continue for any number of iterations, and then the email could be erased without ever being sent.

As long as the email wasn't actually sent anywhere, it couldn't be intercepted. Gmail was a surprisingly secure method of communication, so long as *you didn't actually send any Gmail.*

As Dagmar was working elsewhere, she kept checking the Gmail account she shared with Ismet, and she felt her heart give a lurch as she found an unsent email waiting for her.

> I was pinned down in the park for hours. Had to destroy phone.
>
> IM ok now. Izmir too dangerous, safe house abandoned. I am writing from hotel in Selçuk. Will go to Bodrum tomorrow and fly home from there.
>
> Estragon.

Dagmar waited till her body caught up to her racing thoughts, till she could assure herself that her heartbeat and breath were functioning in the same time as her mind. Then—fingers shaking—she typed her own brief answer.

Love you Briana.

She checked in again for the rest of the night, but there was no reply.

FROM: Rahim

The following proxy sites are still unblocked. Please pass this on to anyone interested in finding out what's going on in Turkey.

128.112.139.28 port 3124

RT 218.128.112.18:8080

218.206.94.132:808

218.253.65.99:808

219.50.16.70:8080

By morning, the official total from the action was eleven dead, twenty-eight wounded. Rumors had it the totals were higher.

How many people have to die, Dagmar thought, *before it all stops being cool? Before it stops being insanely fun?*

One. Just one.

Originally, the government bulletin had claimed "terrorist violence by unknown subversive elements." But faced with the videos, the posters, by ten in the morning it announced that the Gray Wolves had been taken into custody for questioning.

"They're not in jail," Lincoln said. "They're in protective custody to keep them from being lynched by their neighbors."

"Too bad we can't arrange a jailbreak," Dagmar said.

"It was a bad idea to put the Gray Wolves in uniform," said Lincoln. "A government can always use a shadowy, anonymous group for assassination and random violence. Once everyone knows who they are, it's a lot harder to hide in the shadows." He smiled, nodded. "Those bastards have had it."

Dagmar went to bed at midmorning and arose midafternoon to wait for Ismet.

He looked like a wreck—unshaven, pale, smelling of sweat and tobacco. Dagmar held him for a long time after he staggered out of his Ford, then joined him for the debriefing, which was mercifully brief.

"We knew one of these would go wrong sooner or later," Lincoln said. "This one wasn't anybody's fault. We learn and move on."

Dagmar returned with Ismet to the apartment he shared with Tuna. Tuna and Rafet had both gone, on their way to an action in Ankara, and Dagmar relished the chance to be alone with Ismet. But he was exhausted, and when Dagmar left briefly to fetch soft drinks from the fridge he fell asleep fully clothed on the sofa. Dagmar wanted to stay with him, but her mouth tasted foul, her skin smelled of chemical anxiety, and she badly wanted to brush her teeth. She left a note saying she'd be back soon, then kissed Ismet, turned out the lights, and walked to her own place. She'd get a change of clothes and a toothbrush, then return.

Cypress smells were in the air. The airfield was silent. Dagmar's apartment was dark—apparently Judy hadn't expected her to return. She walked onto the porch, fished in her cargo pants for keys, and noticed the door was standing open.

A cold warning finger touched her neck. She stepped to the side of the door, between it and the window into the living room, and then reached around the corner to flick on the living room light.

The curtain was only partly drawn. She looked in to see a man quickly emerge from Judy's bedroom into the hall—a man she didn't know, mustached, dressed in dark clothes. A long pistol was in one hand. He looked up at the window and saw Dagmar the instant that she saw him.

She ducked away from the window as the glass shivered to the bullet's impact. She didn't hear a shot, only a mechanical clacking noise.

She ran, and as she ran she thought to scream. The scream came out wrong—she hoped for the piercing sound of a cheerleader trapped in a horror movie basement, but instead she found that terror had somehow thickened her vocal cords and she could only manage a kind of baritone moan.

"Help!" she rumbled. "Help me!"

Dagmar heard footsteps behind her. A bullet struck sparks from the street near her feet.

"Help!" she groaned. Another bullet cracked past her ear.

However she was saying it, the urgency must have told. Porch lights were snapping on. A door creaked as it opened. The footsteps behind her stopped suddenly, and then she heard the footsteps again, in retreat.

When the RAF Police finally came, they found Judy lying dead in her room.

Which sixties spy are you? Dagmar thought. She was curled in a chair at the offices of the RAF Police, her knees drawn up, her forearms embracing her shins.

She'd decided that Ismet was the character from *Ipcress File.* But who was *she?*

There weren't a lot of options, and the problem was that most of them were superwomen. Emma Peel and Modesty Blaise were too beautiful, too perfect, too intimidating—and besides, Dagmar was absolutely certain that she would not be flattered by a black spandex catsuit.

Mentally she paged through the available options, and then—a cold finger running up her spine—she realized her true identity. She was Jill or Tilly Masterson. She was Fiona Volpe; she was Aki; she was Tracy di Vicenzo. She was Semiramis Orga.

She was the woman who was in the spy business but lacked the necessary skills and experience, who was completely out of her depth, who tried her best but fell afoul of the villain anyway.

Dagmar was the good-hearted but clueless girl who died in the first half of the Bond films.

Of all the characters in the drama, she was the one the audience absolutely knew would not survive.

CHAPTER NINE

The police headquarters filled with RAF Police in their white caps and soldiers from the RAF Regiment in camouflage battle dress. Dagmar, curled on her chair in the hall, felt herself cringing away from the parade of firearms that marched past her.

Squadron Leader Alvarez turned up, the group's intelligence liaison; he scowled as he scanned the room, and went into conference with other officers. A pair of Royal Marines arrived, from off the patrol boats that cruised offshore, and then the first of Dagmar's own people appeared—Lola scowling at the world through a mop of tangled hair, and Byron bewildered, fearful, blinking sleep from his eyes, having been first roused from his bed by a phone call telling him to secure their doors, then taken by military police to their headquarters.

It was time for Dagmar to be the boss again.

So she uncurled from her chair, went to the two, and told them there was a security problem. She showed them where the coffee machine waited, told them to find a seat.

When Ismet was brought in, his glasses cockeyed on his face, she went to him in silence and put her arms around him and stayed there, leaning against him, for a long, desperate moment.

"Judy is dead," she said. "Shot." She spoke quietly so the others wouldn't hear. She felt his muscles tighten at her words.

"The killer shot at me, too," she said.

Being shot at, she realized, was something new that she and Ismet had in common.

"I'm so sorry," Ismet said. His voice was breathless. "What can I do?"

What can I do? That was always his question, as if he saw the world as a series of technical problems to be overcome.

Some problems, she thought, were beyond help.

More members of the Lincoln Brigade arrived, and Dagmar counted heads — everyone was present save for Rafet and Tuna, on their way to the mainland, and Lincoln, Helmuth, and Magnus. Cold terror crawled up her spine as she pictured Lincoln, Helmuth, and Magnus lying slaughtered in their beds, the Brigade's mission a failure, their sole triumph the slaughter of its own recruits . . . and then Lincoln walked through the glass doors at the end of the hall, eyes hidden behind his metal-rimmed shades, his feet marching in step with his two white-capped escorts; and he walked past Dagmar with a curt nod and went straight into conference with Alvarez.

The door closed behind Lincoln, and then through the wood paneling Dagmar heard his voice raised: *"What the hell is going on in this fucking establishment?"* — after which somebody, presumably, calmed him down, because Dagmar heard nothing more.

A police corporal arrived to report that Helmuth and Magnus were not in their quarters. In a burst of relief it occurred to Dagmar that they needn't have been victims of assassins — instead they were probably in Limassol indulging in their usual nightly depravities. She would call them on her handheld if she had it, but she didn't have it with her.

Instead she told the corporal to alert the guard at the gate to escort Magnus and Helmuth to the police station as soon as they arrived.

The door to the office opened, and Alvarez summoned Dagmar. Police officers filed out as she took a chair, leaving only Alvarez, Lincoln, and a police lieutenant Dagmar had never met. Lincoln's jaw muscles were clenched in what seemed to be rage.

The room was a meeting or interview room, with a cheap table and chairs and walls crusted with decades of thick ochre paint. Faded safety notices were posted on the walls. There was a faint odor of disinfectant. The police lieutenant turned on a recorder, put it on the table, and then opened his notebook and clicked his ballpoint.

Recorder *and* notebook. Clearly someone who believed in backup.

On the whole this was not unlike the last police station, the last interrogation in Hollywood, three years ago.

Alvarez looked at her.

"I'd like to begin by saying," he said, "how sorry the establishment at RAF Akrotiri is at the loss of your colleague. And I want to say that we're going to make certain that nothing like this happens again."

Dagmar held his blue eyes for a moment, then turned away. She didn't trust herself to speak.

"You'll all be moved to new quarters," Alvarez said. "And you'll be under constant police guard as long as you remain on Cyprus."

Dagmar nodded. As she looked down she saw the display on the police lieutenant's recorder and saw that it was automatically transcribing the words, little black letters crawling like ants across the glowing screen.

"Miss Briana," said the lieutenant, "my name is Vaughan."

Vaughan was straw haired and lanky, dark eyed, with a trace of Devon in his voice. He was young, twenty-two or -three. Dagmar nodded at him.

"I'd like to know, miss," Vaughan said, "if you got a good look at the killers."

"Killers?" Dagmar looked up in surprise. "There was more than one?"

"Other witnesses saw at least two."

"I saw just one." She called the face back to her mind, then shook her head.

"I only saw him for a second," she said. "He had dark hair and a mustache. He looked like half the men on this island."

"Tall? Short?"

Dagmar thought for a moment. "A little shorter than me. Average for a Turk, maybe."

"How old?"

"Thirty?" she asked herself. "Thirty-five? Not young."

Vaughan looked at his notes.

"Did you by any chance move your bed to an unusual angle in your bedroom?"

Both Lincoln and Alvarez were surprised by the question.

"Yes," Dagmar said. "I did."

Vaughan nodded. "Thank you, miss," he said. "We were trying to figure out why the assassins would move your furniture." He looked up from the notebook. "Why *do* you have your bed like that, by the way?"

"I—" Dagmar started, then shook her head. "It keeps the bad dreams away," she said.

Lincoln and Alvarez were at first surprised, then seemed a little uncomfortable with their new knowledge. Vaughan just gave a brisk nod and jotted briefly in his notebook.

"That makes perfect sense, miss," he said. "Thank you."

Vaughan asked for Dagmar's movements on the night, and she provided them.

Lincoln asked if she'd told anyone outside of the Brigade where she lived. She said she hadn't. While Vaughan was jotting this down, Lincoln spoke up.

"And the action yesterday," he said. "Who knew its location?"

"You already know the answer," Dagmar said. "You and me and Ismet. And though the camera teams were staying in Salihi, they might have had a good idea they were going to Izmir next."

"You didn't tell anyone else?"

"Not till I sent orders to the camera teams."

"Right." Lincoln rubbed the stubble on his jaw. "I suppose that's all, for now."

But Dagmar had her own question ready. She looked at Alvarez.

"How did the killers get on the base? You've got checkpoints, patrols…" She waved an arm seaward. *"Ships."*

Vaughan delicately chewed his lower lip.

"It's a very large perimeter, I'm afraid," he said. "It's difficult to guard it all. They could have gone under or over the fence; they might have come in by small boat." He gave a sigh. "They might have faked some ID. Or the ID may have been real — there are thousands of local civilians who work here at the aerodrome." Determination crossed his features. "At least we can hope that they won't escape."

Yes, Dagmar thought. *Let's hope.*

When she stood to leave, Lincoln rose and joined her. He put a hand on her arm before she could reach for the doorknob.

"We've got to tell them," Lincoln said.

"I'll do it."

"Are you sure?"

She nodded. He released her arm and she opened the door and went into the hallway where the Brigade waited. Helmuth and Magnus, she saw, had returned from Limassol and joined the others.

They all looked at her, and suddenly Dagmar couldn't say a word. She could barely look at them. Lincoln waited barely two seconds before he spoke himself.

"Wordz," Lincoln said, "has been murdered. Briana was shot at but got away."

Dagmar saw them turn to her in shock. Her eyes skittered away from theirs.

"The killers knew exactly where to go," Lincoln added, "and that indicates a very dangerous security breach. So in the course of the next few hours, we're going to be asking you some very serious questions, and I would appreciate truthful answers."

A moment of clarity descended on Dagmar. Someone had pinpointed *her*, had pointed out her apartment to the assassins. Had set her up, and Judy as well, to be murdered.

She rather doubted that person was going to start telling the truth about it now.

Lincoln, Alvarez, and Vaughan conducted the interrogations. Those who weren't being interviewed were given police escorts to their apartments, to pack their belongings and carry them away. Dagmar didn't think she could face the crime scene, so she stayed in the police HQ while two very kind policewomen volunteered to get her things.

After the interrogations were over, the Brigade was carried in police vehicles to the ops center, where without sleep and without cheer, smelling of unwashed bodies and uncertainty, they attempted to do their normal day's work. The hallway to the bathroom was full of personal possessions fetched from their apartments: their personal electronics were stored in metal lockers outside the secure area.

The Brigade stared dully at the screens as they caught up on the news.

The Izmir slaughter had outraged the Turkish nation — the government story had been unconvincing even before it had been shown to be an absurd lie, and the videos and pictures of the massacres were all too available to anyone with access to a computer or to foreign television. Angry posts had appeared on political Web sites, pictures of the dead on lampposts and street corners, copies of the wanted posters everywhere. The junta had failed entirely to keep ahead of the story.

A massive demonstration had spontaneously organized in the city of Konya, where Anatolia's center of conservative Islam was marked by a green-tiled conical tower that stood above the elaborate tomb of Mevlana, the great poet who had founded the Whirling Dervishes. Lincoln and Dagmar had avoided setting any actions in Konya in order to avoid accusations of being religious reactionaries. But the city's residents had managed to mobilize themselves, and it was a vast, angry stream of thousands that circled the city's brown stone Alaeddin Mosque, stopping traffic on the semicircular boulevard and filling the mosque's shady park, shouting slogans and singing patriotic songs. They carried stuffed animals and boxes of Turkish delight, memorials to those who had died two days before.

Lincoln and Dagmar had planned the first series of hit-and-run demos to show the population that it was safe to defy the government. Ironically, it was the demonstration where people were killed that had outraged the people to the point where they were organizing themselves into large actions.

It took at least a couple hours for the police to work up the nerve or gather the reinforcements to deal with the demo, and when they charged the demonstrators they were met with a storm of rocks, bottles, and other improvised weapons. Flowers of pepper gas blossomed among the trees of the park. There was resistance — videos had actually been uploaded by people sitting in jail cells, people whose phones had not yet been confiscated. Dagmar guessed that a few hundred people, at least, were clubbed to the ground and arrested or — if they were lucky — carried in handcuffs to a hospital.

Most of the protestors seemed to have simply found an exit once things got dangerous. They were all networked — only a few would have had to find an actual way out and alerted the rest by phone or electronic text.

The demonstrators didn't have the capability to upload their images real-time, so Dagmar had to search online sources for videos that had been posted hours after the event and try to arrange them in some kind of chronology. Ismet and Lloyd had to translate all the dialogue. All the cumbersome difficulty only added to the frustrations of the day.

Eventually the videos were cataloged and a narrative superimposed on the action. The narrative had to do with freedom-loving resisters in pitched combat with faceless totalitarians and may have possessed only a tangential resemblance to reality — for starters, Dagmar had no idea whether the demonstrators, taken as a whole, were any more committed to democracy than the current regime or would, if given power, set up an equally authoritarian state but with a different agenda. Yet her narrative would serve for present purposes, and the better-quality videos were sent out to the usual media outlets, while the rest were duplicated and catalogued on Web sites hosted throughout the world.

Dagmar worked amid a leaden cloud of despair. It was not just that Judy had been murdered; it was not just that Dagmar worked in a room with someone who had betrayed her; it was not merely that her entire project was now ringed with violence — it was the certain knowledge that her own nerves were not up to coping with any of this.

She could sense panic fluttering in her heart. Sour-scented sweat gathered in the hollow of her throat. Phantom movements in her peripheral vision seemed forever on the verge of resolving into images of Indonesian rioters armed with cleavers, Jakarta police with shotguns, thick-necked assassins from the Russian Maffya. Her mind seemed on the verge of exploding in a bubble of fire, just as the Ford had exploded on that cool Los Angeles night three years before.

Somehow the nightmare did not manifest. Somehow she managed to do her work, think her thoughts, interact with her posse. Somehow she kept herself from crumbling.

Lincoln had spent the morning in his office, talking on the phone or sending encrypted messages to his superiors. He came out at midafternoon, just as Dagmar figured that Rafet and Tuna were landing at the Ankara airport. She was working the Gmail accounts she shared with them, to tell them that Judy had been targeted by assassins.

"Traitor may have given names, dates, and descriptions to the authorities," she wrote. "Make certain you're not under observation and proceed with caution."

She'd argued for canceling the action entirely. Lincoln had overruled her.

"Excuse me, everybody," Lincoln called. The tapping of keyboards ceased; faces turned to Lincoln. Even Atatürk seemed to be paying attention.

"We've got new rules," Lincoln said. "For the rest of our time here, you will be escorted and guarded by RAF Police or other military personnel. You *will not* travel without a guard—if for some reason a guard isn't available to take you somewhere, you are to stay where you are, and call for assistance at a number I'll give you.

"You will no longer have access to your own cars. We don't want anyone putting a bomb under one of them. If you need a ride somewhere, one of your guards will drive you.

"No one will be leaving RAF Akrotiri for any purposes whatever, save as our mission requires." He looked at Helmuth. "No more barhopping in Limassol, I'm afraid."

Helmuth looked as if he was going to comment, then shrugged.

Maybe he figured he could amuse himself by corrupting his bodyguards.

"You are all being moved to a single apartment block," Lincoln said, "where you will be under guard twenty-four hours per day. You will be free to move around the aerodrome, provided you have proper escort."

Byron raised a hand.

"When I took on this job," he said, "I didn't agree to be shot at."

"You haven't been."

Byron reddened. His pinched face turned resentful.

"I've got a family waiting for me in the States," he said. "I'm not going to risk coming home in a box."

"Follow instructions," Lincoln said, "and that won't happen."

Angry Man banged a fist on his desk.

"This isn't in my contract!" he said.

"I think that you'll find that it is," Lincoln said. "If you like, we can go into my office and look at it together."

Byron had turned a brilliant scarlet. His eyes seemed ready to pop from his head. Dagmar wondered if he was going to have a stroke.

"Fuck that!" Byron said. "You can't stop me from leaving!"

Lincoln considered this for half a second.

"I think that perhaps I can. And in any case I have legal options—there's a substantial financial penalty if you walk off the job, as I'm sure you know."

Byron glared but had no answer. Lincoln turned to Dagmar.

"Briana," he said, "can I see you in my office?"

Dagmar gave Byron what was meant to be a sympathetic look, then followed Lincoln into his office. The room smelled of stale coffee.

"Close the door, please."

Lincoln sank into his Aeron chair as Dagmar shut the door. She took her own seat and watched as Lincoln took off his metal-rimmed shades, closed his eyes, and pinched the bridge of his nose.

"I'm in charge of quartering you all," he said, "and I thought I'd ask what kind of arrangements you want. I could put you in an apartment by yourself, but I don't know if you'd be comfortable living alone."

"Put me in with Ismet," Dagmar said.

Lincoln lowered his hand and opened his eyes. The blue irises seemed washed out, and his lower lids sagged down his cheeks, revealing crescents of red flesh.

"I'm not sure that's such a good idea," he said.

Dagmar sighed. "Oh, Lincoln," she said. "Is it that I'll be living openly with a guy, or—"

"No," Lincoln said. "Nothing like that." He reached for his glasses and adjusted them over his temples.

"It has occurred to you," he said, "that it was one of our own group who set you up to be killed?"

She looked at him levelly. "Yes," she said. "That thought had crossed my mind."

He nodded.

"I take it," she said, "that no one rushed to confess."

"It's *possible* the fault might lie somewhere else," Lincoln said. "Someone on the British side. The people who quartered you in the first place, for instance. Someone in the base commander's office. None of them should have known who you actually were, but there might have been some talk, or a document left out of the safe at the wrong time."

"Good luck proving that," Dagmar said.

"It turns out there's a polygraph on the base," Lincoln said. "To deal with security issues, and to vet the civilian workers." His mouth quirked. "I'm kind of surprised. The Brits—and Europeans generally—tend to think of polygraph evidence as voodoo."

"Do you?" she asked.

He gave a silent snarl. "Sometimes voodoo works."

"I thought polygraph evidence wasn't admissible in court."

"We're not going to take the person to *court*," Lincoln said savagely. "Or if we do, it'll be a very private court, which will reach a very private judgment."

"Well," Dagmar said. "Tomorrow the polygraph guy will likely find out something. But tonight I'd like to sleep with Ismet."

"Dagmar," Lincoln said. "Ismet is a suspect."

She was exasperated. "I don't think he—"

"His mission cratered," Lincoln said. "He went missing for hours, completely out of contact. He never called in—never even sent a text message. He said he destroyed the SIM card on his phone, but we don't know that."

Indignation seethed in her blood. "He was pinned down!"

"He could have been captured." Insistently. "He could have been threatened with torture and turned."

Dagmar spoke with icy logic. "He flew here the very next day. He didn't have time to—"

"When you turn someone," Lincoln said, "you get him back to his normal life as soon as possible, before he has a chance to reconsider and before anyone misses him."

Dagmar's mind whirled. "That is absurd," she said.

Lincoln shrugged. "Maybe," he said.

"The killers!" Dagmar said. "Are you saying that the assassination was set up *after* Ismet was turned—*if* he was, I mean? In less than thirty hours? I'm not the professional here, but I'd imagine those sorts of ops require a little more planning time."

Lincoln gave a controlled nod.

"Normally," he conceded. "Unless you've got the team already prepped and they just need a location and an order to go." He gave an uneasy shrug. "No lack of nationalist fanatics with guns over on Turkish Cyprus."

"It still doesn't sound very likely. Not if they have to plan to get through a secure perimeter."

His tone turned savage. He made a cutting gesture with one arm.

"It doesn't matter what's *likely*. It only matters what's *possible*. I've got to take *every possibility into account!*" He spread his hands. "Otherwise, we're wrecked."

Dagmar considered this.

"Aren't we wrecked anyway?" she asked. "This operation is no longer covert. Bozbeyli can reveal what he knows whenever he wants, and show that all the demonstrators are nothing but foreign puppets. And instead, he decides to *kill* us." She waved a hand. "Why is that?"

"I..." Lincoln hesitated. "I don't know."

"Maybe we'd better start trying to work that out."

"I would like to do that—" Lincoln picked up papers from his desk and waved them. "But I keep being distracted by mundane tasks, such as the necessity of *finding places for you all to sleep!*" He dropped his hand and the papers to the desk with a thud. Then he sighed, shook his head, and lowered his voice.

"I was going to ask if you wanted to share my suite. I've got a spare bedroom, and it's in a very secure building normally used by visiting VIPs. That's probably why they didn't try to whack *me*."

Dagmar's temper faded. She dropped her hands into her lap.

"That's very kind of you," she said. "But I'd much rather have my own place. And whether Ismet is officially my roomie or not, I'll be spending the night with him."

Lincoln put on his glasses, reached for the papers, and made a note.

"Done," he said. He looked at her from over the rims of his glasses. "Now that it's morning in the States, I've got to call Judy's mother and tell her that her daughter is dead."

Dagmar tried to speak and failed to find the words. Lincoln's blue eyes seemed to bore into her.

"She was here working on a game," Lincoln said. "An ARG, for the Turkish market. She was killed in what we believe to be a case of mistaken identity."

Dagmar nodded dumbly.

"Just in case anyone asks," Lincoln said. He made a flipping gesture with one hand.

"I think that's all," he said.

She rose and left the room and walked back to ops. The Lincoln Brigade was mostly finished for the day and were quietly packing up their drives and running the bar-code stickers under Lola's scanner. Dagmar checked the clock on the wall, then went to her own office and sent out the day's spam.

> Welcome to Çankaya Wireless Network. Customer service is our most important product! We work constantly to expand our network throughout the Turkish-speaking world.
>
> Anyone signing up to our network in the next month will be entered into a special drawing. Prizes may include cash, a beautiful scarf, or a box of lovely greeting cards! The next drawing will take place by noon on Thursday!

She had just hit the Send key when her office door opened and Helmuth slipped in. He wore an open-necked shirt and a jacket and trousers of linen. He sat on the brown metal chair and waited for her to acknowledge his presence.

"Yes?" she said.

He gave her a hooded look. "Dagmar," he said. "What the hell are we doing?"

There were any number of commonplace responses she could

have given him, but she didn't bother. She knew well enough what he meant.

"Jesus, Dagmar," Helmuth said. "We're getting people killed. We got *Judy* killed."

"I know," Dagmar said.

"Now we're in protective custody, stuck in an apartment building surrounded by guards with guns. We're *prisoners*." Helmuth leaned across Dagmar's desk and spoke in an urgent whisper: "Dagmar, we're game designers. *This isn't our job.*" His hands groped the air as if he were physically searching for words. "Our job is to be cool, to make things cool. We can't make killings and riots cool. We're amateurs and we're fucking everything up."

Dagmar couldn't disagree. "What do you want us to do?"

"Leave," Helmuth said. "Just leave. Go home."

Dagmar looked down at her desk. "What does Richard think?"

"He's your happy Zen warrior. He just sits at his desk and makes up koans and pretends to be a ninja. He'll do whatever you tell him." He sighed. "You should just quit. That's all."

"Like Byron?"

Helmuth's mouth quirked. "Byron's afraid for his skin. I'm afraid for the people we're putting in danger."

"Wouldn't they be in more danger if we left?" she said.

He gave her an appraising look. "I'm also afraid for your safety. And your soul."

Dagmar didn't have an answer for that. She tried to speak, failed.

"You've put everything you've got into the company," Helmuth said. "You can't put that kind of energy into fixing a whole country. It's just not possible."

She licked her lips. "I've just sent out notices for tomorrow's demo."

Helmuth's eyes turned stony. "Dagmar, *Lincoln and his crew failed us.* They were supposed to keep us safe, but instead they put us in the same room with someone who sent a hit squad to kill you. It's their fuckup. Nobody's going to blame you if you walk out."

"Let me think about it," Dagmar said. "I'll give you an answer soon."

A dissatisfied look crossed Helmuth's face. He rose from the chair.

"Think hard, Dagmar," he said. "And let's get the hell back to California."

He left, closing the door softly behind him. She looked after him and tried to think of nothing at all.

Dagmar took the hard drive and her memory stick with the addresses on it and gave them to Lola to be locked in Lincoln's safe. She went to the ops room, where most of her crew were standing around waiting for the police escort to their new quarters.

Ismet stood behind his desk. He was looking across at the picture of Atatürk. His eyes were dark wells behind the spectacles. She drifted to his side, but he seemed not to notice her.

Ismet appeared to come to a decision. He bent down to his desk, opened a drawer, and took out a small stuffed bear and a box of Turkish delight. He went to the wall, picked up the hammer and box of nails that waited there, and nailed the items next to the trophies from the other missions, the flowers, the towel, the photo, the DVD.

He turned and faced the others. His expression was defiant.

Dagmar's heart soared. She wanted to applaud.

Ismet marched back to his desk and she put her arms around him.

Lola came to tell them that their escorts had arrived. Lincoln appeared from his office, shambling stiff legged, his face haggard.

"We will be retaining your personal electronics for the next twenty-four hours," he said.

"God *damn* it!" Byron said, and swung a fist through the air so hard that it spun him around ninety degrees.

"We'll be cloning your hard drives," Lincoln said, "and looking through them."

"I have a *family*, damn it!" Byron called. "I need to talk to them!"

"If you wish to contact your family or send messages," Lincoln said, "you'll have to do it with me or Lola observing—preferably soon, because we'll want dinner at some point."

"*Fuck! Fuck! Fuck!*" Byron kicked a chair across the ops room. Angry Man, Dagmar thought, throwing a tantrum.

Dagmar felt her nerves go nova. She strode to Byron's side and shouted in his ear.

"Shut the fuck up, you useless whining cocksucker!" she screamed. He jumped and turned to her, round eyes white in his red face.

"We lost a friend today, and all you can do is *snivel!*" Dagmar shouted. "*Snivel like a little bitch!*"

Byron began to back away. Dagmar pursued.

"It's time you learned that *this isn't all about you!*" Dagmar said. "If I hear another complaint from you, I'm going to *kick you down the fucking stairs!*"

Byron had backed up against a desk. Dagmar crowded him close.

"Jesus, Dagmar!" he said.

Dagmar pointed to the exit.

"You have my permission to leave the ops center," she said.

Byron edged down the length of the desk, then stepped into the aisle and walked toward the exit, putting his feet down carefully, as if he might cut himself on glass. The others silently parted for him. Dagmar found herself shivering and realized her chin was wet.

Lord, she thought, had she been shrieking at Byron and *drooling?* Here he was pitching his little emo fit and was then confronted with a shrieking, dribbling madwoman, rabid as a vampire bat.

With a quivering hand she reached for a hankerchief and swabbed her chin and lips. Her knees suddenly seemed very weak, and she leaned against the desk.

Gunfire crackled dimly somewhere in her awareness. She tried to shut it off, concentrate on the sound of the ceiling fan ticking over her head.

No one seemed to be looking at her. In the wake of the scene they all seemed to have found something else with which to busy themselves.

Dagmar thought of the break room and thought that perhaps her knees would support her the short distance. She passed by Helmuth at his desk, and he looked at her sidelong.

"Guess that was my answer," he said. Dagmar said nothing.

In the break room she sat on the little yellow plastic-covered love seat and got a lemonade from the fridge. She sipped her drink and waited till she heard the others leave, then rose and went back to the ops room.

Lola, the Guardian Sphinx, was still at her desk at the end of the hall, her head bent over her work. Dagmar walked across the room to the hall, checked her own office to make sure everything was turned off, then closed the door and walked on.

Lincoln's door was open. He sat behind his desk, stretched out on his Aeron chair like a piece of driftwood left by the tide. He saw Dagmar and offered a weary smile.

"You go on knockin' them into the weeds, okay?" he said.

"I'm embarrassed," she said. She raised a hand to the pain in her throat—she'd strained her vocal cords shouting.

Lincoln waved a dismissive hand. "It was educational," he said. "I'm sure we all learned something."

We all learned that I'm crazy, Dagmar thought.

"If you want your phone and laptop," Lincoln said, "you can have them. I know you aren't working with the black hats."

She took her electronics, walked past Lola and down the stairs to meet the two kind, soft-spoken policewomen who had gathered her belongings and moved them to her new quarters.

She had been put into a room with a single bedroom and without Ismet in evidence—evidently Lincoln had conceded on the point of sex but not on living arrangements. Her apartment was on the second floor of a two-storey apartment block, and there were RAF Police guards in white caps guarding all possible approaches. Snipers in the trees for all she knew.

She was still in married personnel quarters—an RAF family

had been pitched out of their home to make a safer place for her. Their personal items were gone, but she could still smell the bacon they'd cooked for breakfast and the scent of aftershave and herbal body wash in the bathroom. She found a note on the breakfast table, in round handwriting with circular dots above the *j*'s and *i*'s.

We hope you enjoy our home.
The hot water takes a little time to come on in the bathroom, and sometimes you need to jiggle the handle on the toilet to stop it running.

Dagmar smiled at the sweet air of hospitality, then went to the kitchen to find her gin. As she passed the toaster, it started talking to her in Greek. She jumped a foot in surprise and banged her hip on the counter.

She stepped closer to the toaster again. The Greek voice resumed. She recognized only the word *tost*.

She examined the toaster but couldn't find a way to turn the voice off. Maybe the British family hadn't managed to turn it off, either. She gave up and put the toaster back on the counter.

The contents of the refrigerator spoke more eloquently than the toaster.

The policewomen hadn't known which items belonged to Judy and which to Dagmar, so they'd brought everything. There was the soy milk that Judy liked and her goat cheese and the Nutella she enjoyed at breakfast.

Sadness fell on Dagmar like cool rain. She closed the refrigerator door, mixed her drink, then left the bottles on the counter rather than open the door to be met again with the ghost of Judy's absence.

Dinner was a frozen meal of pasta primavera heated in the microwave. The creators of the meal apparently hadn't known what *primavera* actually meant: the vegetables were tired and old and tasteless. She had just finished when there was a soft knock on her door.

She had relearned caution in the last twenty-four hours. She took a one-second glance through the front curtains, saw Ismet's silhouette, and opened the door. He kissed her hello, then stepped back to look at her.

"Now I know why Lincoln advised me not to piss you off."

Dagmar felt her cheeks flush.

"I could have handled that better," she said.

"I'd have shot him in the head," Ismet said. She couldn't quite tell whether he was joking or not.

She took his arm, led him toward the couch.

"Please," she said. "Let's not talk about shooting."

"Sorry," he said. "I wasn't thinking."

They sat. Ismet winced, reached behind the cushion, and drew out a leatherette case with a small pair of binoculars.

"Maybe your hosts watch birds," he said. He put the binoculars on the coffee table.

She put a hand on his thigh, rested her head on his shoulder. He put his arm around her. Her head swam, perhaps at his scent, perhaps at her own weariness. Somewhere, just beneath her consciousness, she heard the sound of the sea grating up the shingle at Kouklia. Aphrodite sent a simmering warmth through her groin.

And then she heard Lincoln's voice. *When you turn someone, you get him back to his normal life as soon as possible.* She felt herself stiffen at the memory.

Ismet turned out to be sensitive to her body language.

"What's wrong?" he asked.

"Nothing," she said. "Practically everything. Lots."

"Yes," he agreed. "Lots."

She buried her face in the juncture between his neck and shoulder. He stroked her. She kissed his neck, then licked him there, felt his taste shock her nerves into life.

Ismet brought his lips to hers. They kissed for a long time. Her hands reached for the buttons of his shirt, but then she hesitated.

Damn this, she thought. *Damn this work. It acts against all trust, all humanity.*

He had brought her to his own apartment that night, she remembered. Because his roommate was away and there was more privacy.

But if he'd known that her place was going to be hit and he'd wanted to save her, he would have done exactly that. She'd gone back to her own place only because he'd fallen asleep and she'd wanted a toothbrush.

She wondered how plausible that was. At least that scenario meant Ismet didn't want her killed.

She didn't know what to believe. And of course it had to be admitted that she had a bad history with men.

She leaned on his shoulder again, sighed.

"I'm too tired to do anything else," she said.

"I understand."

"I'd like you to stay tonight, though."

He kissed her cheek.

"Of course."

Tomorrow, she thought, *we'll have the lie detector tests. Then we'll know, maybe.*

He helped her turn the bed to a forty-five-degree angle to the wall. He made no comment as he did so.

The sheets were clean, white with a wide blue stripe and a floral scent—the anonymous British family had made the bed before departing. Dagmar and Ismet slept curled into each other, like a set of quotation marks with no text between them.

In the morning, when she woke, she was astonished that no soldiers had marched through the night, that her mind had not been filled with explosions and blood.

That she could wake on a sunny morning and—for a brief, blessed moment—not feel the feather touch of fear on her nerves.

CHAPTER TEN

Dagmar felt that as the leader, she should take one for the team, and so she took the polygraph test along with the others,. It was only when she was wired into the machine, as the strap went around her rib cage under her breasts, that she realized that she might be asked some questions she didn't want to answer.

The interview took place in a small, warm room in the headquarters building. The operator was a young man with freckles and a truly unattractive set of National Health spectacles. He had a list of questions on an electric display pad and a booklet that turned out to be the operator's manual for the machine. Sometimes, as he wired Dagmar into her chair, he had to flip to one page or another for instructions.

She thought this particular voodoo wasn't very convincing.

The operator had a soft, professional voice, and he kept out of sight, working the machine behind Dagmar's back, so that his words seemed to drift to Dagmar from the sky, as if from an inquisitive angel.

"Are you a citizen of the United States?"

"Yes."

"Are you female?"

"Yes."

Baseline questions designed to establish a kind of psychic background hum against which answers to the more provocative questions could be measured.

"Have you ever stolen money?"

"Yes." After a slight mental stammer.

She'd actually been reclaiming the money that her father had stolen from her, but the protocols here did not involve long explanations.

"Are you working in collaboration with the intelligence service of a country other than the United States?"

"No."

"Do you reside in California?"

"Yes."

The operator alternated provocative questions with innocuous ones, the better to measure the jump in Dagmar's response.

"Do you work in an office?"

"Yes."

"Are you in the pay of a foreign government?"

"No."

"Have you ever cheated on a school exam?"

"No."

If she had, she couldn't remember it.

"Have you ever engaged in a conspiracy to commit murder?"

Well, there it was.

"Yes," she said.

There was a two-second hesitation before the next question, which was, "Do you own an automobile?"

She was nearly as surprised as the operator. She hadn't intended to answer in the affirmative; she'd just fallen into the rhythm of giving truthful answers. She considered what answer she *should* have given — a denial would almost certainly have been detected as a lie. The leap her heart gave at the question would have given her away.

Maybe she just really wanted to talk about it. Confess to somebody.

Still, she wasn't under oath. None of this could be used as evidence. And anyway, it would only confirm what Lincoln already suspected.

Dagmar went on answering questions. She admitted to using marijuana, denied using cocaine.

More questions came along, each layered between trivialities so quotidian that the crucial questions might as well have been shouted aloud.

"Did you kill Judy Strange?"

"No."

"Do you know who killed Judy Strange?"

"No."

"Have you ever killed someone?"

"Yes."

The operator was beyond surprise by now. The next question — about whether or not she liked football — came right on schedule.

"Did you engage in a conspiracy to kill Judy Strange?"

"No."

"Did you tell anyone about the location of the apartment you shared with Judy Strange?"

"No."

The operator gave her a thoughtful look as she rose from the chair at the end of the interview.

She let her police escort take her back to the ops room, where she began her prep for the day's operation. Other members of her crew joined her as their own interviews were completed. Byron arrived last, averting his eyes. As she moved around the room, she could hear him breathing heavily through his nose.

Lincoln returned to the ops room after being briefed by the polygraph operator and called Dagmar into his office. She could see herself reflected in his shades as she took her seat.

"The test suggests you have no complicity in Judy's death," he said.

Dagmar nodded.

"The operator offered an advisory of his own, however."

Dagmar thought about it. "I'd prefer to leave it to my imagination," she said.

He looked at her, folded his hands on the table.

"This is the point at which I'm supposed to say, 'If we don't clear this up, you could be in trouble.'"

"Unless you intend to extradite me to Indonesia," Dagmar said, "there's not a lot of point in digging any further."

Lincoln frowned in surprise.

"Indonesia," he repeated.

"There's a lot of the Indonesian story I haven't told anyone."

Having spent the morning telling the truth, she was now madly sowing lies. Her frantic inventions looped the trail of her life back on itself, obscuring her footprints by running over them with another set of her tracks, all in hopes of concealing her past sins in California.

Lincoln considered this, then held out a hand.

"I said at the beginning," he said, "that I didn't want to know anything."

She nodded.

"I'll stand by that statement," he said.

Dagmar was only too pleased to escape the subject. "How about Ismet?" she asked.

"Also cleared. But we have anomalous readings elsewhere."

"Yes?"

Lincoln opened a manila folder, looked at his own handwritten notes.

"Byron was so angry at being polygraphed that his responses were completely off the scale. The operator was unable to get a baseline to make a judgment concerning what answers were deceptive or not. It's as if Byron answered every single question by screaming and throwing a desk across the room. His blood pressure was so high the operator was afraid he was going to have a stroke."

"Interesting," Dagmar said. She really didn't know what else to say. Angry Man was staying in character.

"On the other end of the scale, Lloyd was uncannily calm throughout his interview. He passed with flying colors, but his lack of normal response indicated that he might have been trained in techniques for beating a polygraph."

Lloyd's father was a retired colonel, Dagmar remembered, perhaps a supporter of the new regime.

"Was he trained to defeat polygraphs by the Company?" she asked.

"I'll ask him. But of course he's been polygraphed before as a matter of course. He might just be able to relax through the whole thing."

"Okay." Not knowing what that meant.

She seemed to specialize in not knowing anything about Lloyd.

Lincoln scrubbed his chin with his hand.

"Polygraphs aren't reliable at the best of times," he said. "Even the most optimistic of the polygraph experts claims only a ninety percent reliability—and that means one in ten black hats walks. And agents would have been trained in beating a lie detector, so the failure rate there is much larger."

"So," Dagmar asked, "why are we bothering with the polygraph at all?"

Lincoln sighed. "Because it's what we've got. I can't afford to ignore any tools at my disposal—and besides, we hit the occasional jackpot." He waved his notes. "Two of the subjects indicated persistent patterns of deception," he said. "Helmuth and Magnus."

Dagmar actually felt her mouth drop open in complete amazement.

"*Helmuth?*" she said.

"Yes."

"*My Eurotrash?*"

Lincoln gave her a cold glance.

"If he doesn't clear this up," he said, "there could be trouble."

"And how is it cleared up, exactly?"

Lincoln spread his hands. "Further interviews."

"Like you're doing now."

"Yes." His shades gazed at Dagmar in their unblinking way. "Do you want to try getting to the bottom of it? Or should I?"

Dagmar considered that her preexisting rapport might do well with Helmuth. Besides, she had enough experience as his boss to maybe know when he was lying.

"I'll take Byron," Lincoln said.

Dagmar called Helmuth into her office. Today he wore soft wool slacks, a polo shirt, and retro Italian shoes with a little gold chain across the instep.

"There's a problem with your polygraph results," she said.

"Really?" he said. His eyebrows lifted in an expression of perfect innocence, an expression that only irritated her.

"You lied like a fucking rug," Dagmar said as viciously as she could. "And I want to know about it."

For perhaps the first time in her experience, Helmuth seemed physically uncomfortable. He shifted in his chair, patted his sleek hair, and pursed his lips.

"It has nothing to do with what we're doing here. Or with Judy being killed."

"Yes?"

He gave her a quick glance.

"There are certain things I'm not prepared to admit to the government," he said. "That's all."

"Such as?"

He gave her a stony look.

"Things that could get my green card revoked," he said. "Which would mean I'd have to lose my lovely job working for you in Los Angeles and return to Germany."

"You may have lost that anyway," Dagmar said.

Again Helmuth shifted in his seat.

"Are you going to tell Lincoln?" he asked.

"Depends."

He looked at the floor for a moment, then looked up.

"I found a hookah bar in Limassol where we could buy hash," Helmuth said. "Magnus and I have been going there every night before we head to the clubs."

Dagmar rolled her eyes. "For Christ's sake!"

Helmuth's eyes flashed "You can't believe the hashish that comes through Cyprus!" he said. "Moroccan, Syrian, Afghan... blond from Lebanon, bhang from Kashmir. It's a connoisseur's paradise!"

"Are you out of your *mind?*" Dagmar demanded. "You didn't remember who you're working for?"

Helmuth gave her a cool look.

"I'm working for you, I believe."

"That," said Dagmar, "is what we're here to decide."

He looked away. A jaw muscle ticked angrily in one cheek.

"Anything else?" Dagmar asked. "Any other little sins I should know about?" He didn't answer, so she named a few: "Women? Cocaine? Meth?"

Helmuth flapped a hand. "Of *course* there were women. I can give you names if you like. But none of them asked me where they could find you or Judy, and I never told them what I was doing here."

"How about Magnus?"

"He's a pro, is Magnus. He was after pussy, okay, but he wouldn't give *information* for it. Not when he had *money*, and he's got plenty of dollars in those little kilt pockets." Helmuth rolled his eyes. "Christ, he's got a house in northern Virginia that looks like Tara."

"Anything else?"

He gave her a resentful look.

"Like what?"

Dagmar waved her hands. "Fuck, Helmuth," she said, "how the hell should *I* know? Black market activities? Artifacts stolen from archaeological sites? Complicated financial instruments designed to destroy Western economies?"

Helmuth dared to offer a sneer.

"Child's play," he said. "I gave all that up years ago."

"Boys being boys, according to our little Pip." Dagmar reporting later, to Lincoln in his office.

"Boys doing what, exactly?" Lincoln asked.

"I believe it all falls into the category of 'victimless crimes.'"

Lincoln gave her a bleak look. "You should have seen Cyprus back in the day. Victimless crimes everywhere you looked. All the victims would just..." He twiddled fingers in the air. "Disappear. Or sometimes simply fly into pieces."

Dagmar dropped into a chair.

"How'd you do with Magnus?"

"Denied everything." He snorted. "Arrogant kilt-wearing shit."

"You might polygraph them again, and avoid those questions about past criminal behavior. Just ask about foreign governments and assassination and Judy."

Lincoln's face wrinkled, as if he'd just bitten into a lemon.

"I'll do that. And—since I don't think this local guy is very experienced—I'm sending for another operator from Langley."

Another voodoo priest, Dagmar thought.

"And how long will that take?"

"They take the murder of U.S. citizens pretty seriously. A few days, I'd guess."

And in the meantime Dagmar would be living under guard, along with the person who had betrayed her.

At least Ismet had done well on the polygraph. That was something, anyway.

"I need the drive with the email addresses," Dagmar said. "Time to send out the two-hour warning."

Lincoln turned to his safe, reached for the number pad.

"Avert your eyes, now."

Have you considered taking advantage of the 105 digital television channels offered by Çankaya Wireless Network? Each is delivered with crystal-clear perfection! We have eight plans, and one of them is certain to be suitable to your budget!

Tuna wore video specs for the demo. Somehow his peculiar shambling gait translated to the subjective image: Dagmar, watching a flatscreen in the ops center, knew she was Tuna's point of view because no one else walked like that. He was marching along Anafartalar, a street named after one of Atatürk's victories over the British.

Dagmar and Lincoln had chosen rush hour for the action again, and the streets were clogged — a good thing, since it would hinder police reaction.

Tuna dodged off the main street and took a secondary street parallel to Anafartalar. There had been a bombing on Anafarta-lar some years earlier, and there were CCTV cameras there now, as well as other cameras atop the Sümer Bank across the street.

While Tuna wasn't under observation he changed his appearance. He paused to reach into his shopping bag for a scarf, which he wrapped around his lower face with a sound that whispered against his microphone, and then a hat that he pulled low over his forehead, cutting off the very top of the video image. Then Tuna hurried on, toward the crowd that could already be seen clustering ahead of him.

The buildings to Tuna's right opened up, and there was Ulus Square, with its equestrian statue of Atatürk on its plinth. Dagmar recognized it perfectly well — she remembered passing by it in August, on her way to Ankara's citadel.

Great Big Idea had returned to the Turkish capital for the first time since Dagmar and the others, glancing nervously over their shoulders, had scuttled away back in August. It was hoped they wouldn't have to run again — if this demo worked, there would be demos every day here, until the generals were driven from the capital or until the resistance was broken.

Anger and outrage was exploding out of the people now. The killings in Izmir had created a fury that might be enough to propel the dissidents into the houses of government.

Video images from the Skunk Works drone overhead showed that Ulus Square was already full, thousands of people standing packed into the small area, with long ropes of people stretched from the square along every major street.

The image on the flatscreen lurched wildly as Tuna vaulted from the road to the elevated square, then looked out over a sea of heads. He was considerably taller than the average Turkish citizen, and he could see clean to the giant bronze statues at the base of Atatürk's plinth.

The place reeked of symbolism. Across the road from Atatürk's statue was the former parliament building, now the Museum of the War of Salvation. Down Atatürk Boulevard was the colorful Victorian-Seljuk pile of the Ankara Palace, the state guesthouse where Atatürk had resided while leading his revolution.

Dagmar could scarcely imagine a better place for a demonstration against the junta, unless it was the Pink House itself.

The image panned down as Tuna reached into his shopping bag for a bullhorn, and then he raised the out-of-focus implement to his lips. Ismet translated Tuna's words as they came from the speakers.

"Take out your greeting cards! Write a message on them, and bring them to the monument!"

Tuna repeated the message several times. Heads bowed as the crowd brought greeting cards out of bundles, bags, and pockets. But though there was a movement toward the plinth, somehow the crowd seemed stalled.

"There's a problem," Lincoln said. He turned to Lloyd. "Can you get us a close-up of what's happening at the statue?"

"Where's Rafet?" Dagmar asked.

"Caught in the crowd across the street," Helmuth said.

Tuna was shouldering his way through the crowd, and then Dagmar's heart lurched as she saw the danger through Tuna's eyes.

The army had put a pair of armed guards on the monument. They were in ceremonial blue tunics, with white belts and white gloves, and clearly intended as a symbolic presence. Their white helmets somewhat resembled those of the Keystone Kops.

But the guards' helmets were not amusing, and their assault rifles were not symbolic. They were real, and they were being brandished at the crowd by the white-gloved hands.

The soldiers had mounted the monument's square foundation, then backed up to the base of the Atatürk plinth and now had nowhere left to go. The crowd formed a half circle around them, silent except for the clicking sound coming from cell phone cameras recording the guards' dilemma. The guards' shoulders were touching—they were giving each other what support they could—and their wide eyes stared wildly at the crowd that had materialized before them.

They probably weren't paying a lot of attention to the hands holding colorful greeting cards. It was the masked, advancing, sinister faces that they would find threatening.

Anything could happen now. If the soldiers panicked they could mow down scores of the close-packed demonstrators before they themselves were either torn to bits or left alone on the scene of their bloody triumph. If the mood of the crowd turned to anger, a mob could attack the guards and bloodied or murdered soldiers seen lying at the feet of Atatürk would be a propaganda triumph for the military government.

Christ, Dagmar thought. *Why does it have to be Tuna?* Tuna was hot tempered and utterly fearless—of all her crew, Tuna would be the one to lose his patience and charge the guards.

Tuna muttered into his microphone.

"You didn't scout the target?" Ismet translated.

"Rafet checked it yesterday," Dagmar said. She didn't bother to transmit the answer—she didn't want to distract Tuna when he was confronted by armed soldiers.

Tuna paused for a moment, and then he stepped onto the monument's meter-high foundation. Dagmar gasped, heart thundering, as both rifles swung toward her—toward *him*—and then he raised his hands, one of them still clutching his bullhorn. He spoke in a soft voice.

"Please, brothers," Ismet translated. "Don't shoot."

The soldiers shuffled a little, but they didn't lower their weapons.

"Brothers," Tuna said, "we just want to write some postcards. We're not here to attack you."

The soldiers looked nervously at each other, and their white-gloved hands loosened their grips on their rifles.

Tuna continued to speak in his soft voice.

"If you wish to leave," he said, "we'll make a way for you." He turned back to the crowd. "Make a path for the brave soldiers!" he called.

In silence, the crowd parted, creating a narrow lane leading across the road toward the old parliament building. Tuna turned back to the soldiers. Their terrified eyes looked like craters in their heads.

"Please, brothers," Tuna said. "Leave in peace."

"Inshallah," Ismet muttered.

The moment that followed seemed to go on forever. The soldiers looked at each other, then at Tuna, then at the lane that had been cleared for them.

And then they raised the barrels of their weapons and walked toward their escape route.

Dagmar, her head swimming, let go the breath she'd been holding since the start of the confrontation.

"Thank you, brothers!" Tuna called. "We know you are not our enemies!" And then, to the crowd, "Give these brave soldiers some presents!"

A woman in the crowd handed one of the soldiers a colorful scarf as he passed, and the soldier, a little embarrassed, took it. There was a cheer and applause and then more scarves. The last the cameras saw of the soldiers, they were walking through the crowd nearly buried beneath great armsful of pashmina blossoms.

Tuna raised his bullhorn.

"Now, let us write on our cards, and make a memorial! And," he added, "be sure not to vandalize the statue!"

No patriotic Turk would want to see demonstrators scrawling over Atatürk's monument.

Cards were laid out in colorful patterns, in messages, stuck in the windowsills of the office buildings that overlooked the square. Cards were stood on end and stacked atop one another in towers.

Scarves were draped over the statues, hung from neighboring buildings, the antennae of the cars trapped in the massive traffic jam caused by the demonstration.

A man in a shabby jacket who earned his living selling pigeon feed off a table made of a cardboard box was so covered in scarves that he looked like the most colorful mummy in the world.

Rafet finally shoved his way through the crowd, jumped up on the monument's foundation, and began to bang his drum. He led the crowd through the usual series of marches and patriotic songs.

"This is the biggest crowd yet!" Lincoln said, and raised a clenched fist into the air.

Only a few days, Dagmar remembered, after the last demo had been shot to bits. The Turks were tough.

The Skunk Works drones showed a few police hanging a respectful distance from the crowd, none of a mind to interfere. The crowd so outnumbered them that they had opted for prudence, even if they were armed and the crowd was not.

Three men in suits and ties jumped up next to Rafet. They pulled scarves off their faces and began to harangue the crowd. Cameras jumped and focused on them.

"Who are these guys?" Dagmar demanded.

Ismet listened for a moment.

"Politicians," he said. "The one in the middle is a guy named Erez—used to be mayor until the generals fired him and banned his party. I didn't catch the other names."

The politicians shouted on, mostly inaudible. The crowd cheered them anyway.

"Someone's trying to hijack our revolution," Helmuth said. He sounded offended.

"That's *supposed* to happen," Lincoln said. "It's not our revolution anyway."

Tuna's video glasses began to pan wildly overhead.

"Police drone," he said in English. "It's up on the north side, moving east."

Lloyd began giving orders to his air force. He was so busy with this that he lost track of the images coming in from the Skunk Works drones, and when he caught up he gave a shout.

"Police convoy coming up from Kizilay!" he said. "Another forming in the Dikmen police complex!"

Dagmar spoke directly to Tuna and Rafet.

"Time to disperse," she said. "Police are coming from the south."

The two acknowledged. Lloyd sent the same message to the camera teams.

Tuna and Rafet raised bullhorns and told everyone to go home. Greeting cards fluttered silver in the air, shimmering like the leaves of olive trees.

For the next few minutes Dagmar was diverted by the entertaining sight of one of the Skunk Works wedges trying to bring down the police drone. The pilot kept missing, and the police drone kept turning its lazy circles undisturbed, like a blind man wandering in a bullring. Finally the wedge managed to clip its target's tail, and presumably the police drone went down—it was impossible to know for certain, because the video feed from the Skunk Works craft went black at the instant of the crash.

Lloyd told the operator to trigger the sequence that would send the drone navigating via GPS to its launch point. They would have to hope for the best.

Dagmar turned back to the screen that was still showing Tuna's point of view. Tuna was looking down at his cell phone and yanking it apart. He pulled out the SIM chip, snapped it in half, and let it fall onto the road. Then he looked up.

He was traveling uphill on a narrow lane between shops and office buildings. Dagmar caught a glimpse of a store called Toys Aras, its façade covered with cavorting Disney characters. How many trademark violations, she wondered, could be packed into a single image?

There were still a large number of the demonstrators walking along with Tuna, but they were rapidly transforming themselves into ordinary, unremarkable people. Hats and scarves were removed. Leftover greeting cards were being stashed atop piles of merchandise or handed to bystanders. Some of the women who, like pious Muslims, had attended the demo with their hair hidden now uncovered to reveal themselves as modern businesswomen in Nikes and designer sunglasses, with BlackBerry earpieces glittering from beneath their hair. Scarves were set decorating the street stalls.

The narrow street came out on a major artery, and Tuna's long legs carried him along, dodging other pedestrians. A minibus with a blue body and tan roof came into sight, and Tuna flagged it down. A door on the right flank opened with a hiss of compressed air, and Tuna stepped aboard.

The minibus was a *dolmuş*, a kind of cross between a bus and taxi. *Dolmuş* was a word that literally meant "stuffed," as in grape leaves, but this minibus was only moderately full, with maybe fifteen people crammed into spaces meant for twelve. Tuna was one of those without a seat.

There was no room for Tuna to approach the front of the bus, so other passengers passed his five-lira note to the driver and then carried his change back. From the little Dagmar could see over the heads of the passengers, it seemed as if the driver was very confident in his ability to drive, smoke, make change, and chat on his phone all at the same time.

The *dolmuş* traveled along at a fine clip until it ran into a jam of vehicles. Horns sounded in vexation. The driver threw up his hands and engaged in what seemed to be a long monologue in which his grievances against the universe were discussed at length.

The creeping pace taxed the patience of a number of the passengers, who left in a clump. Tuna found a seat that had just been vacated. It was upholstered in an unhealthy-seeming aquamarine inflamed by abstract orange-red patterns.

"Well," he ventured to mutter, in English, "it looks like this may take a little while."

Dagmar was surprised that she could still see his video. She would have thought that there would be a hill or something else interfering with the line of sight between Tuna and the receivers that Lincoln had emplaced back in the summer.

The Hot Koans were really doing their job.

"Looks like we've lost the drone," Lloyd said. "If it was coming back, it would have arrived by now."

"Any idea where it went?" Richard asked.

"None. Probably landed on a roof somewhere. We should hope it got completely smashed up."

An instant message appeared on Dagmar's computer; she checked to find that the camera team was now in the safe house. In another minute, she received a text that Rafet was approaching the Haci Bayram Mosque, where he would destroy his cell phone and then attend the next service. Only Tuna was still at large.

She looked up at Tuna's feed and felt her heart sink. Her hands clamped on the arms of her chair.

The minibus had stopped, and a tall paramilitary had just stepped aboard. He carried an Uzi submachine gun around his neck, and his eyes looked at the passengers insolently from beneath the brim of his baseball cap.

Roadblock, Dagmar thought. *Gray Wolves. Oh shit.*

The Wolf was in his late teens, with a mustache and a ring glittering in one ear. He'd stuck a huge saw-toothed knife in his belt, not bothering with a sheath. By his appearance he was young and inexperienced and arrogant and stupid, and Dagmar knew at once that he was going to be trouble.

The Wolf rapped out commands. Dagmar jumped as Ismet's voice came close to her ear.

"He's asking for identification."

The video image panned down to Tuna's big hands, reaching into his jacket for his ID. Then the image panned up again.

The Gray Wolf checked the two passengers at the front of the bus, both elderly men, then moved to a middle-aged woman sitting with a pair of shopping bags on her lap. She reached into her handbag for her identification and knocked one of her shopping bags to the floor. She gave a cry and bent down to retrieve her groceries.

The Wolf yelled at her to get back into her seat and show her ID. He prodded her with the barrel of his gun, and she slid back into her seat with a sob of terror.

Tomatoes rolled on the floor of the bus.

The woman reached for her handbag with shaking hands and knocked it to the floor. She reached for it, then drew her hand back, afraid of the gun, afraid of doing the wrong thing.

Suddenly one of the elderly men was standing and yelling at the Wolf.

"He asks the Wolf to have some respect," Ismet said.

The Gray Wolf was clearly telling the old man to shut up. The old man stepped into the narrow aisle and approached the Wolf.

"He says he's not afraid," Ismet said. "He says he fought for the fatherland."

The Gray Wolf continued to shout back. Ismet didn't bother to translate.

The old man pounded his thin chest with a fist.

"He says he was with the navy in '74," Ismet said. "He says he helped to land the army on Cyprus."

The boy's answer was clearly something along the lines of "Who gives a shit?"

Tuna's point of view kept moving slightly, as if he was quietly shifting his position before going into action. Dagmar watched in horrified fascination, barely breathing. All she could think of was that everyone in the bus was about to die.

The Wolf jabbed the old man with his gun. The old man clearly told him to stop. The Wolf poked him again—and the old man, with admirable timing, slapped the gun away.

The machine pistol went off and put two rounds into the lady with the groceries. Dagmar gave a cry.

Arterial blood spattered from the lady's throat and she began to shriek.

The Gray Wolf stared.

The old man shouted out two angry syllables, threw himself on the Gray Wolf, and tried to wrestle the gun away. The boy shoved the old man back into his seat and then brought his gun around and fired more rounds. Blood flew. The old man collapsed into the lap of the second elderly man, who recoiled. The driver, who seemed to have caught a round himself, was shouting.

The woman with the groceries kept screaming while trying to plug the hole in her neck. Her vegetables rolled around the floor of the bus.

Dagmar watched as the wide eyes of the Gray Wolf surveyed the situation, as his mind tried to grasp the significance of what had happened.

Tuna watched as the boy's mind failed to find anything within itself but the necessity to keep pulling the trigger.

Tuna charged, of course, but by then it was too late.

Tears streamed from Dagmar's eyes as she stared at the blank screen. The video shades continued to record after Tuna had been shot, though the angle showed only boots and the floor. The audio continued to record shots and screams for another fifteen or twenty seconds. Now there were boots marching back and forth, sounds of traffic and distant conversation, the Wolf apparently talking with his teammates.

Ismet was holding her from behind, crouched down behind her with his warm cheek laid against the side of her head. She wiped tears from her face with the back of her hand.

"What's that?" she said. Something was moving in a corner of the frame.

"Jerrican," someone said.

A red plastic container for gasoline. There were flashes of gold, the sound of gurgling.

"No," Ismet said, appalled.

"They're going to torch it," Magnus said.

The flash and explosion ended the transmission. Dagmar hoped the Wolf had been caught in the backblast.

She tried to speak, failed, tried again.

"Copies of this have to go out," she said. "Load it onto every server on the planet."

"No," said Lincoln.

Dagmar was outraged. She broke free of Ismet's arms and swung her chair to him.

"What do you mean, *no*? This is—"

"We wait," Lincoln said. "We wait till the government announces that terrorists have blown up a bus, and then we send out this video to prove what lying bastards they are."

So the Lincoln Brigade did what it normally did with video footage of a demonstration: edited it, sent it to reporters and news agencies, put it on Web pages. They began the lengthy business of assembling the augmented reality version of the demo. Dagmar worked numbly, phantom gunshots rattling in her ears.

At eight P.M. a government minister announced that terrorists, led by Ankara's former mayor, had blown up a bus in the wake of an illegal demonstration. Erez and a number of his associates were being sought by the police.

Tuna's final video was posted on Web sites and sent to news organizations. It went viral very quickly—within hours, Dagmar figured, it would be ubiquitous. A new wanted poster was created for the boy who had shot him.

After ten thirty, most of the Brigade were sent home with their RAF escorts. Lincoln had a conference with Ismet first, then called Dagmar in.

He held out the hard drive with the email addresses on it.

"It's now or never," he said. "You need to tell everyone to head for Ankara. It's time the people took their government back."

He followed as Dagmar took the hard drive to her office and invited everyone on the list to come to Ankara and be slaughtered. She unplugged the drive and gave it back to Lincoln.

"I want a memorial for my friends," she said.

"Of course."

"Tomorrow afternoon, but we'll let everyone know first thing in the morning, so they'll have time to decide what they're going to say."

He bowed his shaggy head gravely.

"Whatever you like," he said.

The RAF Police escort took Dagmar to her apartment. She nodded to the corporal from the RAF Regiment at the bottom of the stair, then walked up the stair to her own floor.

"This is *bullshit*!" Byron's angry voice boiled out of an open window. "We're not *safe* here! Packed in like this, one RPG could kill us all!"

Consistency, she thought, was certainly Byron's strong point.

Ismet opened his door as she passed.

"I got a pizza on my way home," he said. "Shall I come over?"

Ismet, she realized, had lost a roommate as well. Tuna's belongings were still in the apartment, a reminder of the friend who would never return. Like the Nutella that haunted Dagmar's fridge, a visitation from Judy that she would never eat but never remove.

"Give me time to shower," she said.

Under the stream of water she tried to scrub away the sweat and sorrow, the mourning and misery. The result was only an increased consciousness of her own wretched failure. She dried her gray hair, put on a new T-shirt and underwear and a pair of khaki shorts. Trailed by the scent of green tea shampoo, she made herself a gin and tonic and sat by the window and tried to make sense of the thoughts that gyred in her head.

Byron too angry, she thought, *Lloyd too calm. Helmuth and Magnus too stoned.*

This wasn't data; it was just noise. There wasn't a pattern to be found in it.

Tuna and Judy too dead, she thought. There was your pattern.

Ismet knocked and called softly from outside. Dagmar let him in. The cardboard box he carried smelled of garlic and oregano. When the toaster talked to him, he gave a jump, then laughed.

She rattled her glass at him. "Want a drink?"

He raised a can of lager. "I brought my own," he said.

He put the cardboard box on the kitchen table, and Dagmar brought plates from the cupboard. She freshened her drink and brought it to the table.

The pizza had been made with feta and chunks of a local sausage that tasted of fennel and goat. It wasn't entirely awful. Dagmar discovered that she was ravenous and ate her first piece very quickly.

"We'll be doing a memorial for Tuna and Judy tomorrow afternoon," Dagmar said.

"I won't be able to attend," he said. "I'll be on my way to Ankara."

She looked at him in shock, then looked away.

Of course *he'd be going*, she thought. The time for the final confrontation had come, the time when the demonstrators would either take their government back or be crushed in blood, and Ismet was a part of that.

She'd sent out the orders for everyone else less than an hour before. She didn't know why she hadn't realized that Ismet would be included in the next action.

"I won't be going across the Green Line this time," Ismet said in his matter-of-fact way. "They might have my description. So I'll have to fly to Athens, then to Sofia, and take the train to Istanbul and on to Ankara."

"I'll pack you a lunch," she said. It was only a practical thing, but it was all she could manage to say. She couldn't ask the questions that were really in her mind, like *Do you think it's hopeless?* Or *What are your odds of survival?*

She reached for her drink, and it almost slipped through her grease-stained fingers. She wiped her fingers and the glass with a paper napkin.

"Bozbeyli knows about us," she said. "Why hasn't he told everyone?"

Ismet reached for another piece of pizza.

"He must have other plans," he said.

"Can we guess what they are?"

Ismet, mouth full of pizza, gave a jerk of one shoulder, a Turkish way of saying, "I don't care."

She decided that she shouldn't harass him: he'd had a worse day than she had, and his days weren't going to get better anytime soon.

So she asked him if he'd heard from his grandmother and what she'd think of his having an American girlfriend and more about the nomad life on the Anatolian south coast. The change of subject seemed welcome.

They went to bed and his touch set her skin alight. She pressed herself to him, desperate for the reassurance of his body, the solid businesslike whole of him that she could cling to. Ismet was hers, at least for the next few hours.

Even through her pleasure she could hear the whisper in her mind, the voice that suggested that she might already be in mourning for him.

The rioters came in the night, breaking down the wards that Dagmar had so carefully set. Suddenly they were there — bare-chested Indonesian men, rags tied around their heads, hands brandishing machetes or Japanese swords or wavy-edged blades.

She lunged out of bed screaming and fought her way through the intruders into the living room. Ismet called her name over and over and tried to catch her, but she flailed at him and broke free. The coffee table caught the backs of her knees and she tumbled over, still thrashing at the weapons that menaced her... wheezing for breath, she backed into a corner of the room, hitting and kicking at Ismet when he came too close.

There was a pounding on the front door, and shouting. Dagmar shrieked at Ismet not to open the door and let in more of the enemy, but he did anyway, and there was the guard from the RAF Regiment. She screamed at the sight of his assault rifle. His radio crackled loud in the air.

Dagmar shivered and wept and flailed her fists as the Indonesian men circled her. Ismet and the guard had a brief conversation.

"Could you get her a blanket, perhaps?" the corporal said. "I don't like to see her naked like that."

Ismet went to the bedroom and returned with a sheet. He approached Dagmar carefully and offered the sheet. Dagmar snatched it and covered herself. The Indonesian men leered at her.

"I don't know what to do," Ismet said. "I tried holding her, but—"

"Will you stop talking like idiots and *help me!*" Dagmar demanded. Ismet reached for her.

The corporal shook his head. "No," he said. "Don't touch. She'll read it as a threat." He unslung the rifle from around his neck and put it out of sight in the kitchen.

"Let me try something," he said. "One of my mates was in Afghanistan—came back with a similar problem."

He crouched near Dagmar's feet. Dagmar drew her legs up, away from him, and threatened him with her claws.

"Miss," he said. "I'd like you to look at the sheet. Could you do that for me?"

She considered the request and wondered if it was a way to divert her attention so that he could attack. But she decided she could spare the sheet a glimpse and look at it.

The sheet, left behind by the apartment's actual tenants, was fine white cotton with a wide blue Mediterranean stripe. There was the faint aroma of myrrh, Ismet's scent.

"See how stripy it is, miss?" the corporal said. "How smooth?"

"Yes," she said through clenched teeth. Light gleamed wickedly on the Indonesian blades that menaced her.

"Blue and white," the corporal went on, "that's the Greek national colors, miss. It's like their flag."

Dagmar wiped tears from her eyes and considered the sheet and the Greek flag and wondered if she was going to be buried under the Greek flag.

"Maybe you'd like to look at the couch?" the corporal suggested. "It's a different shade of blue, isn't it?"

Slowly the corporal called her attention to the actuality that surrounded her: the couch of robin's egg blue, the lamp with its parchment shade, the ceiling fan with blades that shone with their brass fittings. It was the reality that Dagmar had all along knew was present, lying like an underground river running quietly beneath a surface filled with overwhelming terror and menace. Once her attention was drawn to the quotidian world, the horrors—the Indonesians with their knives and ferocious eyes— began to seem less plausible.

Over time they faded away, though she could still feel their presence, clustered in some other dimension separated from hers only by the thinnest possible membrane.

Dagmar found herself lying naked in the front room, her hand clutching the sheet up to her neck. The soft-voiced corporal squatted at her feet in his camouflage battle dress. Ismet, wearing only his trousers, stood guard by the door, keeping out the others who Dagmar sensed were clustered on the balcony.

The corporal smiled at her. He was dark and square headed, the sleeves of his battle dress peeled back from hairy arms.

"Are you feeling better, miss?" he asked.

Her heart was racing like the engine of a Ferrari.

"I think so," she said. The words felt strange in her mouth, as if she'd never spoken before.

"If you have this problem again, miss," he said, "you just concentrate on your surroundings. The furniture, the ceiling, your clothes—whatever you've got around you, right?"

"All right," she said.

He winked a bright brown eye and grinned at her.

"What's your name?" she asked.

"Poole, miss," he said. "Roger Poole."

"Thank you, Roger Poole," Dagmar said.

"Perhaps you could do with a bit of refreshment," Poole said. "A cup of tea, perhaps?"

"Yes. Why not?" She found herself willing to follow any suggestion at all.

Poole rose carefully to his feet, watching her carefully to make certain she didn't see the movement as a threat. He walked to the kitchen. Ismet approached, watching from a carefully calculated distance.

"I think I'd like to wash my face," she said.

"Of course," he said. Ismet moved toward her to offer a hand, then stepped back. It was the first time Dagmar had ever seen him when he didn't know how to behave. It was almost comical.

Dagmar wrapped the sheet more securely around herself and rose to her feet. A narcotic eddy seemed to swirl into her head, and for a moment she tottered on her feet. She put a hand on the wall to steady herself and then walked to the bathroom.

While she was washing she heard Poole make a report on his radio and Ismet open the door to tell everyone there that whatever happened was over, they could leave. Dagmar ignored this, toweled her face, and looked at herself in the mirror—she saw an older woman there, pale and prematurely aged, hair in disarray, skin sallow in the overhead light. She stared at herself for a moment, stared into her own bleak future, and then picked up her comb. She arranged her hair and then went to the bedroom to put on some clothes.

When she returned, she saw Poole and Ismet both looking at her with cautious anticipation.

"It's over," she said. "I'll be all right."

Till next time, she thought. Which was probably what they were thinking as well.

Poole had the kettle on and had found teas on the kitchen counter. Dagmar picked a Darjeeling over something herbal—she didn't want to be eased back into a sleep where the hallucination could strike again; she much preferred staying awake till dawn.

The three of them sat in the dinette and drank tea and chatted for an hour—chatted about nothing, because Poole proved an expert at harmless blather. He talked about football, pop stars, movies, anything airy and unlikely to send Dagmar back into whatever psychic mine field she'd stumbled into.

After it became obvious that Dagmar was unlikely to relapse into a raving, weeping maniac, Poole washed his cup in the sink, picked up his rifle, said his polite good-byes. He made sure they knew that he'd be on guard till six, then let himself out.

Dagmar looked in wonder at the closed door. "The kindness of strangers..." she murmured.

Ismet placed his cup carefully in his saucer.

"Has this happened before?" he asked.

"It wasn't this bad, usually."

"This bad? Like with police breaking down the door?"

Dagmar shook her head.

"No police," she said.

"How long has it been going on?"

She looked down at her teacup.

"Three years. Since my friends were killed."

He studied her through his spectacles for a long moment.

"Are you... in treatment?" he asked.

She ran her fingers through her gray hair. "I figured it would get better on its own. And it *was*, mostly, until I came here. And now, with people getting killed, it's all coming back."

"Do you think you should see a doctor?"

Dagmar shook her head.

"I have this job. I run a company." She laughed. "I'm running a fucking *revolution*, for Christ's sake! I can't afford any downtime. And I'm often running my company on borrowed money—and there's no way a bank is going to loan money to a crazy person. And—" She shook her head. "We can't afford insurance to cover mental disorders, so I'd basically be on my own."

He considered this, head tilted.

"I think you should see a doctor, anyway."

She waved a hand. "After this is all over."

Apparently Ismet decided not to press the point.

"I'm going to go on the balcony and smoke a cigarette, okay?" he said.

"By all means."

He rose from his chair.

"I only smoke when I'm under stress," he said.

She had already observed this. She offered a faint smile.

"No time like the present," she said.

He collected his shirt and cigarette pack from the bedroom, then stepped out onto the balcony.

Poor man, she thought. He signed up a gaming genius and got a crazy person instead.

Dagmar sighed, rose, washed the tea things. When he returned, she waited on the living room couch. She looked at him, patted the cushion beside her.

He joined her, carrying with him a pleasantly sweet odor of tobacco. She kissed him and rested her head on his shoulder; he put an arm around her.

"It's all right if I touch you now?" he said.

"You can touch me any time I'm not raving."

"Okay." He kissed her forehead. There was bristle on his chin. She nestled against his warmth.

"You don't want to go to bed?" he asked.

"No." The bed had betrayed her to the enemy; she didn't want to lie in it again.

She didn't want to fall asleep, so she talked. She told Ismet about her girlhood in Ohio, her drunken father, her passive but persistent mother. She told him about her time at Caltech, her marriage to an English chemistry professor, her life in England, and her divorce.

"I'm deeply flawed," she said. "You should know that."

Then she reflected that he'd probably worked that out on his own.

She spoke of her return to California to reunite with her friends and start a game company. She told him about being caught in the Indonesian revolt, about Austen's and Charlie's getting killed, about the Maffya hit man she'd tracked through the *Briana Hall* ARG. She stopped short of telling him how she resolved the problem — she wasn't *that* crazy, not yet.

Maybe, toward dawn, she drowsed. She only knew that the daylight caught her by surprise and that she rose from the couch with her mind in a whirl, unclear how she got here, misplaced on Aphrodite's Island, surrounded by the spirits of the dead, lost in the bright Mediterranean air.

CHAPTER ELEVEN

FROM: Rahim

The following proxy sites are still unblocked. Please pass this on to anyone in Turkey.

97.107.137.80:3128

200.65.127.161:3128

202.94.144.73:80

129.82.12.188:3128

212.123.91.165:8080

71.48.222.54:11764

60.6.205.26:808

The following are no longer working:

8.191.16.126:8080

91.103.236.195:8080

193.30.164.3:8080

62.75.219.25:8080

Breakfast was coffee, along with leftover pizza. The latter had not been improved with age. The toaster still talked whenever anyone got near.

The apartment's little shower was too small to hold Ismet and Dagmar both, so they showered separately, then rejoined just in time for Dagmar to kiss Ismet good-bye. His RAF guard checked the Ford to make certain it hadn't been wired with explosives in the night, and then he was gone, off to the war.

Dagmar watched Ismet drive away with a sense of emptiness that she hadn't expected. It was as if all her capacity for emotion had been used up the previous night.

She rather hoped that was the case. At the moment, being an icy logic robot seemed a pretty attractive job.

She took a vacuum flask of coffee and walked down the stairs to encounter a guard from the RAF Regiment. He was a black man with gold-rimmed shades and enormous corded forearms that seemed to burst from the rolled-up sleeves of his battle dress.

"Excuse me," she said.

"Yes, miss?"

"Do you know Corporal Poole?"

The man smiled. "Pooley? Yeah."

"He did me a favor last night, and I'd like to buy him a present. Do you have any idea what he'd like?"

The smile broadened, and the guard took off his shades, revealing a pair of lopsided brown eyes, the right much higher than the left.

"Pooley's a Johnnie Walker man, last I heard."

"Right," Dagmar said. "Thanks."

Anxiety returned as her guard drove her to the ops center. She could picture herself walking in to silence, to the watchful eyes of those who knew she had gone mad the previous night.

But that wasn't what happened. As Dagmar came into the ops center carrying her flask of coffee, she saw activity, people talking and staring at one another's flatscreens.

Something was going on.

But before she could find out what, Lincoln intercepted her in the hall and gestured her into his office. He closed the door behind her and waited to speak until after she'd sat in the visitor's chair. He didn't sit himself; he hovered over her, one hand on the back of her chair.

"Are you going to be all right today?" he asked in a low voice.

She gave a brittle laugh.

"I'll be as all right as I ever am," she said.

"That was a pretty serious report I got."

She looked at him. The blue eyes behind the Elvis glasses were concerned and just a little uneasy.

"It was a serious attack," she said.

"Are you likely to have another?"

Dagmar felt her teeth clack together, some kind of strange nervous reaction. She willed her jaws apart.

"Depends," she said, "on how many more of us get killed."

"I'd like you to see a doctor."

She forced a shrug. "If you think it'll do any good. And so long as no record of the visit will ever exist to fuck up my insurance situation."

"The patient's name will be Briana." Lincoln moved toward his desk. "Shall I make you an appointment with one of the doctors here on the base?"

"Okay." She started to stand, then hesitated.

"One other thing," she said.

"Yes?" His hand on the telephone.

"Make sure I don't have to tell the doc about how I got this way."

She left him to chew on that and headed for the ops room to see what was stirring.

Tuna's killer had been quickly identified by the Group Mind, along with the others in his unit. In response to the killing, the government had announced that the Gray Wolves were being taken off the streets and would no longer be used as a police auxiliary.

Probably that meant that the next time the Wolves conducted a massacre they'd be in civilian dress.

The announcement had heartened the opposition, and now Ankara was a mass of disorder. There appeared to be a number of different demonstrations—or full-fledged riots—and there were videos of demonstrators throwing rocks, of pepper gas being hurled into a chanting crowd, of armored personnel carriers from the army taking up station in front of official-looking buildings, of a police charge on motorcycles. A lot of the action seemed to be taking place on the campuses of Ankara's dozen or more universities. Hundreds of videos and pictures were being uploaded on dozens of Web sites, along with a lot of frantic text in Turkish and broken English.

Dagmar contacted Rafet on satellite phone using encrypted VoIP, but he knew only what he could see from the safe house in Ulus, and that wasn't much. After consultation with Lincoln, it was decided to use some of the Skunk Works drones to cruise over other parts of the city.

Therefore it was pure luck that a drone caught Erez, Ankara's former mayor, marching with a crowd of hundreds into the Ministry of Labor and Social Security—they seized the building, invited the regular workers to leave except for those who wished to join the revolution, hoisted the flag of Erez's banned party beneath the Turkish ensign on the roof, and barricaded the doors against any counterattack. There had been police guards outside the building, but these were severely outnumbered and faded away.

The building was an enormous blocky towerlike structure, glass and cyclopean concrete bulwarks, set in the middle of parks and parking lots and only a short distance from the Atatürk Mausoleum. It would be easy to defend, assuming the mayor's followers were up to defending it.

Soon videos appeared on the Web of the quondam mayor announcing the formation of a provisional government with himself at its head. He invited the people of Ankara to his little fortress to help defend it.

"Is this Yeltsin standing on the tank at the Russian White House?" Dagmar wondered aloud.

"Could be more like Jim Bowie falling down drunk at the Alamo," Lincoln muttered. "But I need to talk to that man."

He went to his office to send off messages. The drama in Ankara continued—and then came the announcement that the mayor of Bodrum, acting in concert with the governor of Muğla Province, had ordered local forces to seal off the Bodrum Peninsula, which he was now prepared to defend against the military government. Bodrum, the fashionable resort town known in ancient times as Halicarnassus, was now in a state of self-imposed siege.

"That's not gonna last," Richard remarked. "The Turks have a freakin' *navy*. They can just sail around that stupid blockade and land however many troops they want."

Hellmuth nodded. "Our allies could benefit from having played more strategy games in their youth, that's for sure."

More news came in, of demonstrations in Manisa, in Denizli, in Edirne, and once again in Trabzon. It was Friday afternoon and a lot of people had started the weekend early, swarming the streets. Hundreds were now waving banners from atop Atatürk Stadium in Beyoğlu, across the Golden Horn from Istanbul. The reaction of the authorities varied: some demonstrations were attacked, others blockaded; others proceeded without opposition. Though Turkish networks didn't mention the demos at all, international news networks were reporting the events live, though their reportage tended to rely heavily on amateur video downloaded from the Web pages created and maintained by the Lincoln Brigade.

Alparslan Topal, the political liaison with the Turkish government-in-exile, appeared in the ops room. Dagmar hadn't seen him in days. He went into conference with Lincoln behind closed doors.

Lola was sent out for sandwiches. Dagmar realized with a guilty start that she had intended a memorial to Tuna and Judy this afternoon and she hadn't even announced it.

At that moment her satellite phone rang.

"Briana," she answered.

"This is Ismet. I'm in hospital."

Driving to the airport in Nikosia he had encountered a police roadblock and upon showing his Turkish passport had been pulled out of the car by Greek Cypriot cops, who had then beaten the shit out of him. If they'd had any reason other than the fact of his Turkish passport, they hadn't mentioned it.

His injuries involved cuts, bruises, sprains, and a possible concussion.

"I'll come get you," Dagmar said.

In a white-hot rage, Dagmar stormed into Lincoln's office to tell him what had happened. He was waiting on the phone — apparently whoever he was talking to had put him on hold.

"You are *not* leaving," he said. "There's too much happening here. I'll send some of our guards to bring him."

"But —"

Lincoln pointed back to the ops room. The sympathy he had demonstrated earlier seemed to have faded.

"*Go do your job,*" he said.

She went, impatient, still furious.

Ismet came in about ninety minutes later. His lips were cut and swollen, one eye was blackened, and there were random cuts and bruises scattered over his face. His glasses were held together with tape. He walked like someone who had been kicked several times in the kidneys.

Dagmar went to him and gently embraced him. He smelled of disinfectant, adhesive, and blood. She kissed an unbruised part of his cheek.

"How are you feeling?" she asked.

He spoke carefully through his cut lips.

"Pain pills help," he said.

Lincoln heard his voice and came out of his office.

"Fuck!" he said. "We can't send you into Turkey like this."

Dagmar turned to him. "No," she said. "You can't."

Lincoln made a disgusted gesture.

"A face that marked up, you'd stand out."

Ismet spoke with careful dignity. "I'll get better," he said.

"Come into my office," Lincoln said.

Dagmar winced at the careful way Ismet lowered himself into a chair. Alparslan Topal was already in the second chair, so Dagmar remained standing. While Topal commisserated with Ismet, Lincoln asked her to close the door, which she did.

"We've both spoken to ex-mayor Erez on the phone," Lincoln said. "I've been able to assure him of support provided that he modifies his original statement proclaiming himself head of the government. Instead he'll say that he's the *provisional* head, until the elected prime minister and president can return to power."

"What support can you give him?" Dagmar said.

"Money," Lincoln said. "Funds to help certain people see the wisdom of democracy. Money to provide a secure retirement for certain officers. And—" He waved a hand in the direction of the ops room. "We have some intelligence that might be useful to him. We've got Rafet on the scene, and the Skunk Works, and our various networks. We have to decide what they're going to do."

"Something a little less hazardous, I hope," Dagmar said, "than forting up in a government ministry and waiting for the government to come and kill them."

Alparslan Topal winced a little at the thought.

"Perhaps Rafet needs to do something more active," Lincoln said. "You need to get into the ops room and work out what's necessary, and how to do it."

Indignation straightened her spine.

"I have damn little information to work with," she said. "We've only got what the demonstrators themselves are putting online, plus some footage from the drones."

"Make your best guess," said Lincoln. "Get Rafet and everyone the network can reach on the streets tomorrow, supporting Erez and the elected government."

Dagmar glanced at Ismet.

"I was hoping to get Is—Estragon comfortably settled in his bed, with his medicines and—"

"We've got guards that can do that," Lincoln said.

"I'd rather stay here," Ismet said. "I won't be any more or less comfortable in the ops room than at home, and I might be useful."

Dagmar saw Ismet settled into his desk chair, then got the disk with the email addresses on it and sent out a preparatory email telling people to be ready before noon the next day. She returned to the ops room and asked for updates. Nothing startlingly new had happened, only more of the same. The Skunk Works drones were having their batteries recharged.

While going about their normal tasks the Lincoln Brigade discussed their options. All agreed that Rafet and the various Brigade-controlled networks should create a major demonstration or marches while the authorities were distracted by demonstrations elsewhere, but it was difficult to tell where some of the actions already were and therefore what locations were safe. And of course it was completely impossible to tell which locations would be safe the next day.

They already had scouting reports on any number of locations, all completed before any actions had even started. Dagmar chose three, then sent orders to the Skunk Works for drones to scout them before nightfall.

It was while Dagmar awaited the news from the drones that she heard a series of exclamations from others in the ops room, all in about a ten-second period.

"Damn!" muttered Richard.

"Fuck!" said Byron.

"Crap!" From Magnus.

Dagmar looked up.

"What's up?"

"*408 Request Timeout*," Richard said. "And I'm looking for a page I just uploaded onto a server I *know* is there."

"Allah kahretsin şu Interneti!" Lloyd snarled at his computer through half-clenched teeth.

"Download's frozen," Magnus said. He reached for his mouse. "I'll cancel and restart."

"And with me it's an *upload*," Byron said. "Motherfucker!"

"*408 Request Timeout*," Magnus said.

"*408*," said Helmuth. He looked up at Dagmar. "What's next? *418 I'm a Teapot?*"

Dagmar thought for a moment, then turned to Richard. "Are we being attacked?"

Richard considered the question, looked at his chronograph, then considered some more.

"Well," he said. "They *do* know we're here. But all the attacks so far have been on Web pages hosted by our proxy sites, and pretty much stopped there." He reached for his phone. "I'll call the base computer centre." He pressed buttons on his phone, then stopped and looked at the display.

"*Out of Area*," he reported in surprise.

"Use the ground line," Dagmar said. She went to her own office, took her own phone from the desk, and tapped the screen to bring it to life.

Out of Area, she read. Plenty of juice in the battery, but no bars.

When she returned to the ops room, she saw everyone sitting very still and watching Richard as he listened on the ground line to someone at RAF Akrotiri's computer centre.

"Right," he said. "Thank you."

Richard turned to Dagmar.

"They're having router trouble," he said. "It's affecting the whole base."

"Any time estimate," Dagmar said, "for when they'll have it up?"

"No."

"Any idea of why cell phones are down?"

"He didn't know they were down until I told him."

The computer centre at Akrotiri was enormous. It shuffled vast quantities of electronic intelligence from the Middle East to GCHQ in Cheltenham, an installation that was sort of the

Barclays Bank of ELINT. Dagmar wondered if she should send Richard down to help the computer centre diagnose its problems, then decided against it—there was no way Richard would have clearance to muck about with their routers. And then she noticed that Byron and Magnus were staring at each other, each with the same expression, stricken and yet glowing with a kind of awe.

"What is it?" she asked.

"Holy fuck," Byron said.

Magnus turned to Dagmar.

"It's the High Zap," he said.

ACT 3

CHAPTER TWELVE

It seemed visibly darker outside, as if a cloud had just smothered the sun. A flight of jets roared overhead, rattling the window in its pane and burying beneath its thunder the sound of ceiling fans and computer cooling systems. Dagmar's heart churned in her chest, as if she were on the edge of panic. Suddenly she was probing the edges of her perceptions, looking for the clues that a burning Ford or a line of police or a horde of knife-wielding Indonesians was about to come storming through the doors of her consciousness.

Not now, she thought. She couldn't have a flashback now.

She and Magnus and Byron stared at each other until the jet blast faded. Dagmar tried to regain control of her heart, her breath.

"High Zap," she said, her mouth dry. "What's that?"

Byron swallowed, suddenly nervous.

"We can't tell you."

Magnus inclined his head toward Lincoln's office. "Ask Chatsworth," he said.

Dagmar looked at Chatsworth's office door, then realized there was something she had to do first.

"In a minute," she said, and looked at the phone in her hand.

Out of Area, it said. She triggered the VoIP function and saw that it was down as well.

Dagmar enabled the sat phone function. Her nerves tautened

as the word *Connecting* swam into sight on the display, repeating over and over again without any actual connection taking place, and then she almost sagged with relief as her handheld indicated that a signal had reached the satellite and been bounced back.

She walked around the room until she found an area with the strongest signal—sat phones didn't work well indoors—and then thumbed in Rafet's number in Ankara. Relief flooded her as the ring tone sang in her ear.

Lincoln had thoughtfully provided the Brigade with sat phones that could connect directly to the satellite, instead of having to go through a ground station at one end or the other.

Rafet answered on the second ring.

"This is Ankara," he said, in English.

"This is Briana," Dagmar said. "We're having some trouble with communications here, and I thought I'd better alert you."

"Here also," Rafet said. "Our cell phones are out, and the government seems to have turned off the Internet."

Dagmar's head swam.

"That's happening here as well," she said.

"So the only way we can communicate is with the satellite phone?"

"Apparently."

Or send a telegram, she thought. *Or a carrier pigeon.*

It was a little late in the game to equip every revolutionary with a satellite phone, and in any case she couldn't afford it. Her plans were in serious trouble.

"Use this phone for primary communication till the Net comes back up," Dagmar said. "Any word from the drones?"

"The drones haven't finished their missions yet. But at least they're still following orders."

"That's good news, at least."

She ended the call and went to Lincoln's office—knocked once and then opened the door. Lincoln sat at his desk and was staring at his phone while annoyance firmed his face.

"My phone's stopped working," he said. "Just as I was about to talk the mayor of Bodrum."

"Cells and the Internet are down," Dagmar said. "Byron and Magnus say it's the High Zap."

Lincoln's mouth opened and the air came out of him in a soft sigh. He seemed to deflate, crumpling into himself like a pumpkin left too long on the shelf.

He was still looking at his phone. He put the phone on the desk and turned to Dagmar. His face was gray.

"Well," he said. "That's one we've lost."

"Lost what?" Dagmar demanded. "Phones? The Internet?"

"The war." Lincoln visibly pulled himself together, his shoulders rising, back growing straight. His hands wandered over his torso as if reassuring himself of his own continued existence. Then he turned to Dagmar, his blue eyes hard.

"Close the door," he said.

Dagmar did so. She sat on one of the brown metal chairs. Lincoln adjusted himself in his Aeron and leaned toward her.

"Are satellite phones working?" he asked.

"Yes."

"In that case I need you to call your company in California — we've got to see how widespread the damage is."

A cold wind blew up Dagmar's spine. This *couldn't* be worldwide, she told herself.

She punched the number on her handheld. In the meantime Lincoln was launching his phone's own satellite function.

In Simi Valley, Helmuth's assistant Marcie answered the phone.

"Hi, Marcie, this is Dagmar. Any problem with the game?"

"Ah —" Marcie seemed surprised. "No, not that I've heard of."

"Could you call up the Handelcorp Web page? Because I'm seeing some strange stuff, here."

She heard fingers tapping a keyboard, followed by the slap of the Enter key.

"Everything looks good here," Marcie said.

"You called it up from the Internet, not our own internal database?"

"Yes."

"Check to see if the links are working."

Marcie reported that everything seemed to be in order.

"No problem with the servers? The routers?"

"No. I'd hear the screaming if there were."

"Right. Thanks. It just must be the local ISP that's buggering up my signal."

She pressed the End key and listened to the last few sentences of Lincoln's conversation with whomever it was he'd called.

"You'll have to do the checking yourself," he said. "I'm not in a position to do anything, here."

Lincoln ended his call and looked at her.

"Everything's fine in Washington except the weather," he said.

"Good," she said.

"I should have realized the problem was local when you told me the satellites were still working."

It can take out communications satellites? she thought.

Lincoln interlaced his fingers, making a single large fist. He placed the doubled fist on the desk before him and leaned toward her.

"The High Zap isn't the real name," he said. "But that's what we'll call it, okay?"

"Call *what?* What are we talking about, Lincoln?"

His lips thinned. His clenched fists thumped once, lightly, on the desk.

"It's hard to know where to begin," he said.

"The beginning usually works," Dagmar said.

"Fine." The fists thumped again on the desk.

"Back in '91," Lincoln said, "a U.S.-led coalition launched Operation Desert Storm to drive the Iraqis out of Kuwait. The allied air forces very quickly achieved superiority in the air and began destroying ground targets virtually at will.

"Throughout the Middle East," he went on, "a rumor spread that the Iraqi air defenses had been knocked out by a computer virus smuggled into an Iraqi defense facility in a printer. The program was supposed to be called 'Devouring Windows.' This rumor persists unto the present day."

Dagmar mentally reviewed the state of cyber arts in 1991, a task made a little uncertain by the fact she'd been a child at the time.

"That couldn't have happened," she said. "Right?"

"No." Lincoln was scornful. "The story originated as an April Fool joke in *InfoWorld* magazine. The reason Iraqi air defense sites went down is that we were burying them in cluster bombs."

"That's what I'd figure," Dagmar said.

"So after the war was over, and the rumor started going around, people in Washington—and I was one of them—began to wonder, *Well, why can't we?* We—the U.S. government, I mean—*created* the Internet; we should have the keys to take it down."

He unclenched his hands and spread them flat on the desk. "It took twenty years and a lot of black ops dollars, but eventually we had the High Zap." He looked around, at the invisible electronic networks that surrounded his cube of an office.

"Now," he said. "We're the High Zap's prisoner."

Dagmar considered this.

"How does it work?" she asked.

One hand twirled in the air, summoning up a memory.

"Remember back in the nineties, when people were talking about the 'Java revolution'?"

"Vaguely."

"Java creates a virtual machine inside the computer that can run programs of its own. The High Zap isn't written in Java, but the program works the same way—it creates a very simple, very clean little engine inside a router, living between layers of the TCP/IP. When it's activated, it refuses any packet that doesn't have the right prefix. Communication is disabled. So communication is completely shut down until a preset time of deactivation has been reached, or until an order arrives that has the correct code prefix ordering it to quit."

"And in the meantime," Dagmar said, "the Internet works perfectly well for anyone with the right codes."

"Correct."

"How does the Zap get into the router?" Dagmar asked.

Lincoln narrowed his eyes. "That was *another* technical problem that took a lot of years to solve. Suffice it to say that it *was* solved, and that it's now in every router made in the last six or seven years."

Does it propagate like a virus? Dagmar wondered. But no—routers were different, had different doors into them, and in any case they were made to route information onward, not keep it in memory... But that meant the Zap had to be *installed* in them, at the factory, and that didn't make sense, either, because routers were made in so many different countries by so many different companies.

"The Zap can be localized, as it seems to be here," Lincoln was saying. "The command can be sent to a particular router, and then forwarded to any other router that responds to a ping in a time of a given fraction of a light-second. Of course, if the area is wide enough, it can go clear up to the Clarke Orbit." He flapped a hand in the general direction of the satellite that had just carried their voices to North America.

"The moon is only—what?" Dagmar tried to remember the figure. "Half a light-second away?"

"Let's just say the Zap has all the reach it needs," Lincoln said.

Dagmar's mind flailed like a drowning man through the sea of fresh information.

"The Zap takes down TCP/IP?" she said.

"Yes."

"But cell phones don't use TCP/IP, and they're down."

"Telephones use PSTN protocol," Lincolon said. "But the *controls for the telephone relays* use TCP/IP—or they do unless they're old-fashioned mechanical relays. So the Zap guarantees a slow degradation of phone service—the phones will be all right until you need to give them an order through TCP/IP, and then they start going mad, and then the network goes into a death spiral and crashes." He gestured to his cell phone. "Apparently the local net ran into a whole complex series of problems and went down fast."

"Jesus," Dagmar muttered. "Is there more bad news?"

"Lots," Lincoln said dryly. "TCP/IP is used by all modern military networks. All modern military satellites. All email. All social media. All local area networks. Voice over Internet. The entirety of the World Wide Web."

An objection occurred to Dagmar.

"But this was designed to bring down military networks, right?" Dagmar said. "Aren't they kept physically apart from other networks? How do you get to them?"

Lincoln raised an eyebrow. "In the event that we can't bring down an enemy by preventing them from ordering online merchandise, sending text messages, and participating in flamewars, we can trash a military net *provided we can gain access.*"

"All it would take," Dagmar said, "is a connection left open at the right moment. But you can't count on that."

"It could be engineered. Or..." He sucked in breath through clenched teeth. "Actually, that's where our problems started. Because it wasn't enough to own the Internet equivalent of an End of Times plague for the Internet, some of our politicians wanted to *actually use it.*"

"So Bozbeyli is just retaliating?" Dagmar asked. "Or—"

"It wasn't used on Bozbeyli," Lincoln said. "Back last spring, the Zap was used on our friends the Syrians—and for good reason, because they were continuing their never-ending quest for weapons of mass destruction. The Israelis wanted to stage an air raid on several sites simultaneously, and they wanted the Syrian air defenses down while they did it."

"So you start with the *rumor* of a secret method for crashing an air defense network," Dagmar said, "and then you end up with an *actual* secret method for crashing an air defense network." She shook her head. "You people are too literal minded."

Lincoln was grim. "I'm a little too close to the action to appreciate any irony, thanks." He leaned back in his Aeron chair. Cold anger haunted his eyes. "I was against the action, quite frankly. I thought the Internet Apocalypse was too big a weapon to use against gnats — I argued that it needed to be held in reserve for a real emergency."

"But you were overruled."

Lincoln shrugged. "I can see their point," he said. "It was in the best possible cause — and I supposed that, if we acted to confirm the 1991 rumor, it would only add to our mystical air of omnipotence."

"But," Dagmar pointed out, "to knock out the Syrian air defense, you still had to get into a military network, not just the Internet."

"You are not cleared for knowing how we could do that," Lincoln said. "But we *could* — provided that we made use of some highly advanced equipment available in a listening station in the mountains of southeastern Turkey — which *itself* exists only because the National Security Agency, which is normally tasked with electronic spying in that area, wouldn't share their raw data with us, only their conclusions." His face assumed the caste of indignation. "When we'd ask how they knew what they claimed to know, they'd just say they couldn't give us that information. It was...vexing. So we got some black ops dollars and built our *own* station, and once we could fact-check them, the NSA grew a lot more tractable. But I digress..."

"Yeah," Dagmar said. "Spare me your D.C. freakin' turf wars."

"Anyway," Lincoln went on, "two technicians with training in the Zap took a copy of the command software to Turkey in a laptop. So that the secret would be safe in the event of the laptop going astray, the software itself was booby-trapped — it required a password within one minute of the laptop's booting, or it would erase itself. The two techs were able to get into the Syrian defense net and bring it down for the one hour and ten minutes necessary to ensure the success of the Israeli strike.

"And then — just hours later — Bozbeyli took over Turkey. We didn't want to send the laptop home through what might be civil disorder, so the laptop stayed on the mountain until Bozbeyli got worried that the listening station might be reporting his *own* phone calls, and sent in the military to shut it down."

He spread his hands in a helpless gesture.

"There was a mix-up. Byron and Magnus got away, but the Turkish military got the laptop with the controls to the High Zap on it. And—as is now apparent—our safeguards failed, and the black hats have now broken into the program and figured out how to use it."

Dagmar was waving her hands, trying frantically to stop the flow of words.

"*Byron and Magnus?*" she said. "Kilt Boy and Angry Man gave the Zap away?"

Lincoln pursed his lips in a gesture of deliberate patience. "Not *gave*," he said.

"And you're still employing them?"

"It wasn't precisely their fault," Lincoln said vaguely. "And they're qualified for what they're doing here. And they have first-hand experience with the Zap; we figured they'd have a better idea than most whether the Zap was being used and where, and what countermeasures might be taken."

Dagmar gazed at Lincoln in weary amazement. She pictured Byron and Magnus high up on the curtain of mountains that rimmed Turkey on the east, bickering and snapping at each other.

At least there were no go-karts to crash up there.

"What did the Turks think of the kilt?" Dagmar asked.

"I'm sure they never saw it." Lincoln flapped a hand. "Magnus would have been instructed to dress inconspicuously."

Dagmar looked at Lincoln. Her fingers tightened on the arms of her chair as anger simmered in her consciousness.

"So," she said, "this whole affair—bringing democracy and a legitimate government back to our allies the Turks—all that is just a way of getting the Zap back?"

Lincoln suddenly looked very tired. He waved a hand.

"Not *just*," he said.

"Uh-huh," Dagmar said.

He turned to her, his face open, his eyes wide.

"You don't have to believe me if you don't want to," he said, "but I *really want this to work*. I like the Turks; I want this region to have a functioning republic; I want the Turks to choose their own leaders. But *my* leaders...they approved this project because the government-in-exile agreed that the Zap would be returned when they came back to power." He turned away, waved a hand again. "Maybe I'm just the perfect idiot for this operation."

Dagmar shook her head. She felt as if her internal buffer had completely filled with unprocessed information and was unable to make headway on any of it.

She threw open her hands.

"What are we supposed to *do* now, Lincoln?" she asked. "I'm completely four-oh-four, here."

Lincoln suddenly seemed very small. His voice seemed to come from far away.

"Defeat the Zap. Somehow."

Suddenly her anger came to the boil. Judy and Tuna and a lot of Turkish citizens had died because Lincoln was hoping to beat the High Zap to the punch, and now he and they had lost...lost the whole war because it turned out the enemy had a trump card to play, the Internet equivalent of a thermonuclear bomb, and had possessed the trump all along, right from the beginning.

In rage Dagmar slapped both hands on Lincoln's desk. The sound made them both jump.

"That's *it*?" she demanded. "That's your whole idea?"

He sat in his chair without moving. She could barely hear him as he spoke.

"It's the only idea we're left with."

Her hand stung.

"Jesus Christ, Lincoln!" she said. "No wonder I'm going crazy!"

He gathered himself again, blue eyes glittering behind smoked lenses.

"I'm sorry about that," he said. "But you can think of yourself as lucky. You can go back to your life when this is over, and create amusements that will thrill your audience of millions. I, on the other hand—" He bent to cough, the sound drawn far from his interior, like the rattle of a dying man. "I have to report to my superiors that every course of action I'd advocated was wrong, that the whole enterprise was a miserable failure and a waste of resources, and that I killed a lot of people for worse than nothing." His voice turned savage. "This is my swan song, you know. My last roundup. I'd hoped to have a little success to console myself with in my wilderness years, but now I'll have nothing to reflect on but the knowledge that I'm a useless failure."

She rose from her chair, far too weary and burdened for sympathy.

"Yeah, you do that," she said. "Meanwhile, I'll try to think of some fucking useful thing to do to fight this plague."

She opened the door, stepped into the ops room, closed the door behind her.

"Update?" she said.

"No change," said Richard. He sat at his desk with a frustrated expression, his fingers tapping the arms of his chair, his Converse sneaks rapping the floor.

Impotence did not suit him.

Dagmar looked over what remained of the Lincoln Brigade, trapped here in this little pocket universe by the suddenly narrowed horizons of their own electronics: Helmuth and Richard, Ismet with his bruised face, Lola, the curly-haired Guardian Sphinx, securing the door, Lloyd on his way from the break room with a cup of coffee in his hand, Byron and Magnus gazing at her with insipid faces.

Those two, she thought, had started the whole project by losing the High Zap in the first place.

She thought of them running down the mountain ahead of Bozbeyli's thugs, juggling the laptop and dropping it or forgetting it in a hotel room, or whatever they were supposed to have done, and then she realized that the more she considered it, the less she believed it.

Dagmar turned, opened the door, and went into Lincoln's office again. He was still in his chair, turned away from her, frowning in silence at the wall.

"Byron and Magnus," she said. "How'd they lose the Zap?"

Lincoln didn't bother turning toward her.

"Like I said. A mix-up. They grabbed the wrong computer and left the laptop at the listening station, where the military found it."

"And then what did they do?"

"They got away. In a car." He looked up at her, puzzlement in his blue eyes.

"Why are you asking?"

"How long were they out of touch?"

"Twenty-four hours or so. They had to be careful. They were in Kurdish country and the military were all over the place." He frowned. "But it doesn't *matter*," he said. "They left the computer *behind*, they didn't lose it on the trip out."

"What I'm trying to tell you," Dagmar said, "is that it was Byron and Magnus who gave us to Bozbeyli. One or both of them, and I'm betting both."

Lincoln's blue eyes opened wide. He swung his chair toward her.

"How do you reckon that?"

"My guess is that when they were on their own, they ran into a roadblock and got arrested. I think they both spilled everything they knew, and that's how the bad guys were able to beat the safeguards on the laptop. I also think they've been in touch with Turkish intelligence since."

Lincoln considered this, scrubbing his hands up and down his cheeks.

"There's not a lot of evidence, there," he said. "And they weren't out of touch for long."

"You said yourself," Dagmar said, "that when you turn someone, you try to get them back to their normal life as soon as possible."

Lincoln nodded, conceding the point. His expression remained unconvinced.

"Lincoln," Dagmar said, "they *hate* each other. They're sharing an apartment, but they never spend time together—Magnus is always off in Limassol with Helmuth, and Byron stays here sending emails to his family. When they do communicate, they argue. Each is always slagging the other behind the other's back. The poison broke out on the go-kart track, remember; they spent the whole time attacking each other. It's as if they're blaming each other for something. Something they can't talk about."

"That doesn't mean..." Lincoln began.

"Byron is scared to death, Lincoln," Dagmar said, then reiterated: "*Scared. To. Death.* Of the Turks, of this whole enterprise. It's one thing for him not to want to go to the Turkish side of the island; it's another to overreact the way he did. I think it's because he knows what it is to be a prisoner, he knows what they can do. If he's still cooperating, it's because he's too afraid not to—they threw such a scare into him, it lasted all the way across the Atlantic. And if Magnus is still a part of it, maybe it's because he's afraid, maybe because he's getting other inducements."

Dagmar leaned forward and leaned her knuckles on Lincoln's desk.

"They fingered Judy and me, Lincoln," she said. "The Turks asked where we were living, and they gave up the information. They both failed their polygraph, remember. It's time to haul them in."

Lincoln reached for the landline, then hesitated with his hand on the telephone.

"I don't know," Dagmar said, "how long I can keep up the pretense of not knowing. So do something fast."

When she left the office he was punching numbers into the phone.

In the ops room she looked around again and saw Web pages flashing on Richard's display, with Helmuth looking over his shoulder. She half-ran to Richard's desk.

"What's happening?" she said, half-running to his place. "Is the Net back up?"

"I'm using a satellite phone as a modem," Richard said.

"Ah. Right."

She should have thought of that herself. It was what she'd done in Indonesia.

Dagmar had her own satellite phone, as did Helmuth and Ismet. She looked at Magnus and Byron—she hoped she wasn't glaring too obviously—and considered asking Lola to requisition a couple more sat phones.

"Ankara's still blacked out," Richard said. "There's no news from there that's less than an hour old." He pointed at a video that had been uploaded via one of their proxy sites. "But there's still action going on in other parts of the country. A demonstration in Antalya, another big one in Konya. It looks like the demo in Istanbul has been suppressed—I saw some pictures earlier of some fighting in that stadium."

Unleashing the Zap on their own capital had given the authorities a huge advantage over their opponents—not only could the opposition no longer easily mobilize their people and get their propaganda before the public, but the police and military had an entire radio net that would be unaffected, and they could muster their own forces and move them without difficulty.

Dagmar didn't hold a lot of hope for Mayor Erez holding out in his stolen ministry building.

She looked up as the door to Lincoln's office opened. But Lincoln didn't come into the ops room; he walked down the hallway to greet Squadron Commander Alvarez as he entered.

Alvarez was followed by a squad of RAF Police, along with

Lieutenant Vaughan. They took Magnus and Byron away. Lincoln followed them out.

The others looked to Dagmar for an answer.

"I think we should assume it's going to be just the few of us for a while," she said.

They looked at her in silence.

"Here's what's happening to our little world," Dagmar said. She gave the others a brief explanation of what the High Zap was and what it did. She left out the history; she left out the part played by Byron and Magnus.

"We need to get the Zap back," she finished.

"I think we just *did*," said Richard. He had listened to Dagmar's lecture with wide eyes, clearly impressed by the ultimate ninja software that had evaded all his firewalls and wrecked his plans, leaving him unable to so much as shift the bits of wreckage around.

Helmuth seemed puzzled.

"We're supposed to beat this thing," he said. "Just the"—he looked over his shoulder at where Lola was guarding the door—"the six of us."

Ismet shifted carefully in his chair. The pain that twitched its way across his face sent a knife through Dagmar's heart.

"Leave me out of it," Ismet said. "I'm not a computer engineer; I'm in advertising."

"We five," Helmuth corrected.

"Yes," Dagmar said. "We five."

Helmuth gave a laugh.

"Well," he said. "At least we have a clear idea of the odds against us."

"We've done the impossible before," Dagmar said. "Remember *Curse of the Golden Nagi?*"

Richard indicated his own modified computer, with its satellite phone cabled in.

"Satellite modems would seem to be the way to go," he said.

280 Walter Jon Williams

"The Zap can take down satellites," Dagmar said. "And if not them, then their ground stations."

"Then telephones," said Lloyd. "Telephony doesn't use TCP/IP. We just need to insulate the switching stations against the Zap."

"How?" Dagmar asked.

He gave the question a moment's thought. "Really old routers?" he offered. "From before they were all infected?"

"Right," Richard said. "We could advertise for them on craigslist."

Dagmar looked at him.

"No mockery, Richard," she said. "All desperate ideas are being considered here."

"Check," said Richard. He gave his glittering Girard Perregaux chronograph a look. It was becoming a nervous tic, Dagmar thought—he didn't have to take his eyes off his flatscreen to know what time it was—but it seemed as if he wanted to reassure himself the item was still on his wrist.

"You know," he said. "Maybe I should call the computer centre and let them know what the problem is. They might be able to get some of their routers offline and restore at least some service."

Dagmar waved a hand. "Carry on."

Richard picked up the handset on his desk, listened for a moment, then returned it.

"No dial tone," he said. He picked up the handset, then joggled the switch on the cradle several times. Eventually Dagmar could faintly hear the distant sound of a dial tone whining from the earpiece of Richard's handset.

"Not all the switches are down," he said, and punched numbers into the handset.

Ismet grasped both arms of his chair, then levered himself to his feet. Dagmar felt a mental shudder as she saw the look of pain on his face.

"Are you all right?" she asked. "Do you need to go lie down?"

"I'll stay here," he said. "I can't help you with your discussion, so I'm just going to go monitor my station."

He walked toward his desk, then paused at the sound of Euro-fighters overhead. He cocked his head and listened.

"I think that's the same flight we've been hearing since the Zap hit," he said. "I think they're circling and waiting for air traffic control to come back online."

"But the traffic control is *radio*," Dagmar said. "The Zap wouldn't take it out."

"But the radars could be controlled through TCP/IP," Richard said. "The controllers might not be able to read their screens right now."

Dagmar paused for a moment of horror at the thought of air-craft wandering lost across the skies.

Ismet walked to his desk and sat. He connected his satellite phone to his computer and tilted the phone antenna toward the windows so that it got better reception. As the discussion developed, Dagmar saw him leaning toward the screen, heard him tapping away on his keyboard

"Look," Helmuth said. "Either we go back to Stone Age fossil-ware or we try to out-evolve the Zap. I say we go forward—there's got to be a way to put a quick and dirty IP together that will keep this thing out."

They discussed this for the next quarter hour and eventually decided that this wasn't their best allocation of resources.

"There must be thousands of people in the Greater D.C. area working on this problem right now," Dagmar said. "They'll do that job much better than we can. We can't save the Internet, not from here. What we need to do is save the revolution."

The faces that turned to her were bleak.

"Look," she said. "If we find a solution, it doesn't need to be pretty. It just needs to work reasonably well most of the time."

Lola rose from her desk and walked to stand in the doorway.

"There was an ARPANET back before there was TCI/IP,"

she said. "It must have used a packet switching system. What was it?"

Dagmar reached for her sat phone, called up its browser, and called up Wikipedia.

"Network Control Program," she said. "NCP. Last used in 1983."

"Over thirty years ago," Helmuth said. "There's no hardware for it now."

Lincoln returned to the ops center at sunset. He walked with a kind of plodding deliberation, as if he were carefully choosing exactly where to place his feet. When he came into the room, he sat on a corner of Byron's desk and looked at the others.

"Byron and Magnus," he said, "have confessed to informing the Turkish government of our projects and our whereabouts. They were responsible for Judy's death."

Helmuth and Richard looked at him in shock. "*Why?*" Richard demanded.

"We're in the process of finding that out. Interrogations are proceeding." He looked down at Dagmar. "Any developments here?"

Dagmar offered him a summary of their discussion.

"Oh lord," he said. "Next you'll be wanting to go back to DOS."

"DOS?" Dagmar asked. "Which DOS?"

"MS-DOS," Lincoln said. "Pre-Windows Microsoft operating system. There's no TCP/IP stack in there anywhere."

Dagmar's first computer had run Windows, and MS-DOS was as foreign to her as, say, Plankalkül.

"So," she said. "Why can't we use it?"

"Because—" A slow light seemed to kindle in Lincoln's eyes. "Because it's awkward and horrible and slow and primitive. Because you'll have to type orders onto a command line instead of just clicking on something. It's not flexible and will only perform limited tasks. And you might end up trying to communicate over a 300bps acoustic coupler, assuming you could steal one from a museum."

"And it bypasses the Zap, right?"

"Yes," Lincoln said. "When you're running DOS, you don't even have an IP address."

"And will it run on our computers?"

"I…" He hesitated. "I don't know why not. You might have to do some special formatting or boot from disks."

"We can create a virtual machine that runs DOS," Richard said. "DOS will see the processor as an—" He looked at Lincoln. "Intel 8086?" he asked. "Eight-oh-eight-eight? Whatever."

Dagmar turned to Helmuth and Richard. "See if you can download a copy over a cell modem. Set it up on a computer and see what we can do."

"Modems are going to be a problem," Lincoln said. "Modem command strings have evolved in the last few decades. I doubt that any of our modems will be able to communicate using DOS."

"We'll find some," Dagmar said. "And when we find them online, there is UPS. There is FedEx. We will prevail."

Richard looked with some amusement at his display.

"Did you know," he said, "that there's a Usenet topic called *alt .comp.DOSRULES*?"

"There's still Usenet?" Lola asked. Lincoln looked at her.

"Sometimes," he said, "people actually go online to *exchange information*, instead of to look stuff up, play games, or to advertise themselves."

Lola took a step back.

"Okay," she said.

"And furthermore," Lincoln insisted, "Usenet isn't a damned dinosaur; it's extremely robust. It's not on a single computer somewhere; it's on millions of computers throughout the world. Just *try* knocking that out."

"Okay!" Lola said, more brightly, and made a patting gesture, as if she were calming an agitated but senile patient.

Dagmar smiled. "Will I find posts from Chatsworth on Usenet?" she asked.

"May not be the same Chatsworth," Lincoln said.

"Do you know what I'm picturing?" Dagmar asked. "I'm picturing old alt-dot-DOS geezer-geeks rocking on their front porches and stamping their canes and talking about the days when bulletin board systems roamed the world."

She heard the room's printer start, and then Ismet rose slowly to his feet and walked to where the printer sat on its table.

"What's happening?" she asked.

"Just taking care of business," he said.

He took some papers out of the printer, then took scissors and carefully trimmed them. He limped to the wall beneath Atatürk's portrait and picked up the hammer and tacks that waited there.

Below Atatürk's blue-eyed glare, below the trophies from earlier demonstrations, Ismet nailed a pashmina scarf, a greeting card, and photographs of Judy and Tuna. Judy's picture had been taken from her own Web site, and Tuna's image had been pulled from one of the team's unedited videos, and it showed him in Istanbul at the first demo, with a shopping bag and a bouquet of brilliant flowers.

Dagmar's heart rose into her throat as she saw Ismet's dogged act of devotion, as she saw the photos of the two lost members of the Lincoln Brigade. She remembered with a stab of guilt that she had planned a memorial for Judy and Tuna for that afternoon, but that the events of the day had been allowed to overtake it.

She rose from her chair.

"We'll get on with our experiments in a minute," she said. "But right now, I think we should take a few minutes to remember our lost friends."

CHAPTER THIRTEEN

Dan the DOS Man says:

The best place to find a dos-compatible modem is in an antique store. Not necessarily a store that sells antiques, though you can find them there, but a genuinely old shop with a modem they've had no reason to change in years. Say the store sends a few credit card checks every day, you don't need an up-to-date modem for that.

You can offer them a free new modem. They may be agreeable to the swap. Of course you can always give them money.

Briana says:

How do I configure a modem for DOS?

Dan the DOS Man says:

What program are you using the modem for in dos? That program should have a setup program for the modem. If it is an internal modem, you may have to go into BIOS and disable the com port that you will be using for the modem.

Dos-capable modems DO NOT USE DRIVERS. If you have a Winmodem you're out of luck. To test: if the modem is on com2, go to dos and type atdt5551212>com2. You might get lucky and hear the modem dial.

Use a hayes compatible modem if you can. Do not use a usb cable as dos doesn't have that many drivers available. Like, none.

Its best to get an external modem. Most internal modems made now are software based and won't work with dos. Many dos programs can't detect com3 and com4.

By the way, be careful if you have a PS2 mouse. An internal hardware modem on com1 or 2 would sometimes conflict with a PS2 mouse. A PS2 mouse is on irq 12, which is okay, but it uses the same serial paths as com1 and com2 to connect to the pci buss. So be wary.

Briana says:

Thnx.

Dan the DOS Man says:

We prefer complete sentences on this bulletin board, Briana. And no slang derived from inferior and incomplete forms of communication such as text messaging.

Briana says:

I totally respect your old-school ethic, boss. Many thanks.

Dagmar contemplated the contents of the bulletin board on her handheld and saved them. She nodded to the RAF guard outside the building—her satellite phone had decided not to work under a roof—and then climbed the stair back to the ops room.

"You know," she said, entering, "DOS is actually kind of cool."

Helmuth glanced up briefly from his workstation.

"We're going to make it cooler," he said.

Helmuth and Richard had gotten their virtual MS-DOS machine working inside Richard's computer the previous evening. But none of the modems in the room were compatible with DOS, so everyone had left the ops room except Lloyd, who was left behind to monitor any new uploads or other developments on the Brigade's various Web pages. He would be relieved about midnight by Lola, who would in turn be relieved by Richard.

Dagmar and their RAF guards had helped Ismet up the stairs to his apartment. His bruises had widened and deepened since the morning, and he looked worse than ever, his face a Rorschach nightmare of purple and yellow and white.

She offered to help Ismet bathe, but he declined. Instead he lay on his sofa, propped up on pillows, while Dagmar sat crosslegged on the floor by his side.

"Can I get you something to eat?" she asked.

"Possibly soup," he said. "I don't have much of an appetite."

"Would you like anything to drink?"

"Tea. Any kind."

She found Turkish tea and a soup can labeled YOĞURT ÇORBASI in the cabinet. Apparently Ismet had brought food supplies across the island from the Turkish side. She poured the soup into a pot and examined it, finding only rice and yogurt and spices— nothing that would be hard for bruised lips and loose teeth to chew—and it smelled faintly appetizing, though with the peculiar heavy aroma common to canned soups.

Ismet came to the dining table to eat. He handled his spoon with care, trying not to splash liquid on the gauze bandages that wrapped two fingers of his right hand.

Watching him was painful. Dagmar wanted to take the spoon herself and feed him, except that she knew he was the kind of man who wouldn't appreciate being spoon-fed. Instead she sat at the kitchen table as a host of anxieties warred in her nerves. She kept a towel in her lap in case he spilled something.

The previous evening she'd had the sense that he would fly today to his death. Instead he'd been saved from that fate by a savage beating, and she felt a strange gratitude to whatever brutal Cypriot cops had rescued Ismet from a deadlier peril. She would have him at least till the bruises faded—and she knew she needed him badly, needed some anchor in this mire of treachery and mendacity, the hopeful, hopeless revolution that had at its heart a misplaced piece of code.

After the meal Ismet took a pain pill with his last swallow of cooling tea. He looked at her.

"I think I will sleep alone tonight," he said. He tried to smile with his cracked, bruised lips. "You might roll over in bed and land on me, and that would hurt."

"I could put a pillow between us."

His look turned somber.

"If you attacked me again," he said, "I could not defend myself."

Shock made her sway in her seat. Tears stung her eyes.

He couldn't trust her not to go mad on him. That was what he was saying.

"You should stay with someone else tonight," Ismet said. "Lola, perhaps."

"I barely know Lola," she said. Her voice broke on the last word.

"Richard and Helmuth, then. Someone you trust."

"I trust *you*." She heard the wail in her voice and told herself to stop, that her emotional need and his physical pain were incompatible right now. The pain could not be suppressed: therefore her need had to be quashed. She would have to take her own solitude upon herself and live in it at least for a while.

Ismet couldn't rescue her every single time. He couldn't save her from the enemies that swam in her own psyche. Those were hers to fight.

"Yes, okay," she said. "I'll crash on Richard's couch."

She washed Ismet's bowl and spoon and saw that he was already half-asleep. She helped him back to the couch, then kissed his cheek, felt the bristles sting her lips. She left his apartment and walked to her own—the promise to stay with Richard and Helmuth was already forgotten—and in the borrowed place, surrounded by others' possessions, she felt the aloneness embrace her.

Without conscious thought Dagmar made tea for herself and put a frozen stuffed pepper in the microwave. She stood for a moment in the kitchen, looking at the furniture and belongings that had been requisitioned for her from another family, and considered the number of betrayals that had brought her to this moment.

Byron and Magnus were vile, but they were at least explicable: whatever reason they had for selling her to Bozbeyli, fear or avarice or opportunism, it was at least an understandable human motivation. They were too transparent to be evil masterminds — they were just very screwed-up human beings, confused, probably deep in denial.

But Lincoln, she thought, was not in denial. He knew what he'd been doing all along. It was Lincoln's lie that had brought her here, selling her the notion that the U.S. government was so devoted to the notion of democracy in Turkey that it would give her the tools to bring it about.

She should, she considered, just pick up her phone and buy a one-way ticket back to Los Angeles. If the government tried to invoke a penalty clause and evade payment, all she had to do was threaten to talk to the press.

It wasn't as if she wasn't an expert at telling convincing stories to strangers. It was only a bonus when the story was true.

Except now, she thought, there were actual revolutionaries in Turkey, whether she had created them or not. And they were fighting the police and the military, staging strikes and demonstrations, occupying a ministry building in Ankara. Living in cages in jails and military bases, screaming under torture, dying, rotting under the ground.

She couldn't fly to her life in California and leave them behind. Not when there was a hope that she could help them succeed.

And besides, she thought, work was the classic cure for depression. Dagmar hooked her laptop to her satellite phone, downloaded a copy of MS-DOS along with a user's manual, and ate her stuffed pepper as she began to acquaint herself with the ancient history of personal computing. She visited the *alt.comp.DOSRULES* forum on Usenet and from this learned of the existence of Dan the DOS Man, along with a number of his colleagues.

Her brain was so charged with her new knowledge and so filled with plans for implementing her ideas that after she fell asleep the nightmares failed to possess her.

In the morning she checked on Ismet and found him in greater pain than he had been the night before. She made him tea, made sure he was comfortable, and then went to the ops center while she conducted her long-distance conversation with Dan.

Soft morning light warmed the ops room, glowed off the ochre yellow walls. The air bore the scent of freshly brewed coffee. The absence of aircraft noise was startling: the planes had all landed, either here or somewhere else, and then not gone up again. The situation was otherwise unchanged: the Zap still possessed Ankara and the southwest corner of Cyprus, including Akrotiri and at least a part of Limassol. Cell phone service and VoIP at Akrotiri were still down, and ground lines were erratic.

Lincoln's door was closed. Dagmar tried to decide what she felt about Lincoln, what she had decided about him. He was either a complete manipulative bastard or as much a fool as she.

Or both, she thought. No reason he couldn't be both.

Dagmar explained her ideas to what was left of her posse, and they began to make plans to travel to Limassol in search of old modems. They would be like the evil sorcerer in *Aladdin*, offering to trade new lamps for old.

Lincoln had come out of his office partway through her exposition. She was too far into her spiel to interrupt herself to decide whether she hated him or not, so she ignored him until he offered a suggestion.

"You might not need to go to Limassol for modems. Akrotiri is huge, and has its own shops and supplies. You might be able to make your deals here."

"Not necessarily," Helmuth said. "Those old modems might be the only cybernetic gear in those shops still working. They might not want to part with them."

"Your guards can't requisition civilian gear," Lincoln said, "and they won't intimidate anyone on purpose, but they're in uniform and carrying guns. They will lend a certain authority to any request you might make."

Dagmar was alarmed by this train of thought. "Be polite," she said.

Richard raised a hand, then spoke.

"We'd have an idea of whether an external modem will work with DOS by looking at the cabling, couldn't we?" he said. "No modem with a USB would function with DOS. Nor would Ethernet, right?"

"You can run an Ethernet IPX network out of DOS," Helmuth said. "I found the instructions online last night while I was researching our brave new operating system."

"And there's no TCP/IP?" Dagmar asked.

"There doesn't have to be. You can set it up either way."

"Terrific," Dagmar said. "We grab those modems, too."

"My point is," Richard said, "that if you find a modem with a twelve-pin cable—or would it be thirty-two?—you make an offer on the spot."

"*We are the junkware,*" Dagmar said. Their new slogan.

"I'll arrange for your escort," Lincoln said. As he walked toward his office, he glanced over his shoulder at Dagmar and gave her a look. She followed.

"I've got transcripts of Magnus's and Byron's confessions," he said, once they were alone. "The Turks caught them at a roadblock outside of Şırnak, practically the minute they came down off the mountains, and the Jandarma so terrified them that they stopped thinking." He shook his head. "They fell for the oldest trick in the world. They were put in separate rooms, and each was told that the other had started talking, and that whoever gave the Jandarma the most information would be treated leniently. They ended up competing to see how fast they could give their secrets away."

"Don't those idiots watch cop shows?" Dagmar said. "They should know better than to tumble for that one."

Lincoln's blue eyes grew serious. "They weren't exactly in a position to demand a lawyer," he said. "And the Jandarma don't bother with explaining Miranda rights."

"That doesn't explain why they sold me and Judy months later," Dagmar said.

"They were being blackmailed," Lincoln said. "The Turks recorded them spilling everything they knew about the Zap, and threatened to release the videos if they didn't, ah, keep in touch. If those videos had been released, they would have lost their security clearances and all their government contracts." He offered a cynical laugh. "They're still blaming each other. They still haven't worked out how they were played."

Dagmar narrowed her eyes.

"And *you* hired these bozos," she said.

Lincoln passed a hand over his forehead.

"It wasn't one of my better decisions," he said. "But at least they're working for us *now*."

"Oh," Dagmar said. "Swell. Just swell."

He offered a grim smile.

"I believe it's been brought home to them that they had confessed not only to espionage on behalf of a foreign power but to being members of a conspiracy to murder an American citizen and were also accessories after the fact. Lieutenant Vaughan and I staged an argument in front of them over whether or not the trial would take place in the UK—I wanted to extradite them to Virginia, which still has the death penalty." He nodded. "So yes—now they're being very cooperative. We can use them to feed false information to their contact in Limassol, if we can figure out what would completely mislead them."

"Have them send their assassins in again," Dagmar said. "That's the only way we'll catch those bastards."

"I doubt they'd send in gunmen again," Lincoln said. "Not with the base on the alert."

Dagmar looked at him sourly.

"I'll try to think of something to tell the Turks that will really fuck them," she said. "But in the meantime I've got to try to work around the technology that those idiots gave to the black hats."

Lincoln nodded.

"You do that," he said.

The modem expeditions went reasonably well. Lola and Lloyd did their best on the Akrotiri aerodrome and scavenged three modems, which they took back to the ops room to see if they'd work with Richard's virtual DOS environment. Helmuth guided Richard and Dagmar through Limassol, first to an electronics store where they bought an armful of the latest internal and external modems, then to the waterfront, where they began moving through a series of small cafés and shops.

"You no want jacket? Nice handbag?"

The merchant at the leather goods store, a portly man with a mustache, was puzzled by Dagmar's line of inquiry.

Dagmar hadn't so much as cast an eye over the store's merchandise before leaning over the counter and noting the dusty modem keeping track of credit card sales. Now she took a look at the coats and jackets hanging on the racks. Some of them seemed quite nice.

"I'll buy a jacket if you'll give me your modem," she said.

This was an offer that was more to the store owner's taste — he understood this kind of bargain better than he could comprehend a strange offer simply to buy his antique modem. The last transaction processed on the modem was a double-breasted belted jacket made of shiny, butter-smooth brown leather, cost €135. It fit Dagmar as if it had been tailored for her. The credit card receipt would be submitted to Lincoln as a business expense. As far as Dagmar was concerned, this was a win-win transaction.

This was Dagmar's only success of the morning, but Helmuth and Richard bagged two modems apiece, and they were in an upbeat mood as they met in a café for a lunch expertly cut from a sizzling cone of pressed beef and lamb by-products. The gyros were as good as any Dagmar had eaten. She received a number of compliments on her jacket.

Their guards, discreetly armed, sat at their own table and ate burgers.

After eating, they ordered Turkish coffee, dark as molasses and nearly as sweet, guaranteed to keep their energy levels high through the afternoon.

Richard showed off his own major purchase—an entire computer, an ancient PC clone in a heavy steel case, which Richard had bought for the sake of its internal modem. The purchase had taken a fair amount of bargaining, with the owner convinced he was somehow being swindled. In the end Richard had simply taken the man to an electronics store and bought him a completely new fully tricked-out office machine, complete with a printer.

"I think I got the better deal," Dagmar said, admiring her jacket.

"Not really," Richard said. "The modem is one thing, but this is another." He pulled the keyboard out of the shopping bag in which he had carried his prize.

"IBM Model M," he said. "Nineteen-eighties technology. The keys use a special patented buckling-spring design. The whole thing is *solid steel*—nothing like the cheap plastic keyboards you see now." He hefted the keyboard, demonstrating how heavy it was. "Built to last for millennia!" he said cheerfully. "In the event of nuclear annihilation, this keyboard will be the only surviving evidence of human achievement."

"That's a Greek keyboard," Dagmar pointed out.

"I'll convert it to English." Richard put the keyboard back in the shopping bag. "Now I've got to find a PS/2 to USB converter; otherwise it's just a nonfunctional antique."

"That keyboard might draw more power than your USB connection gives," Helmuth said.

"I'll work something out." Richard's smile was brilliant.

Dagmar's phone began to sing Thelonious Monk. The display didn't show the number calling her, and she assumed it was the ops center.

"This is Dagmar," she said.

"The Internet is back," Lloyd said.

She straightened in her seat. "We've got Internet!" she said, and saw the others react.

"Has the Internet come back in Ankara as well?" Dagmar asked.

"Yes," Lloyd said. "And we—"

"Is Rafet all right?" Dagmar asked.

"Yes. He's got the drones over Ankara trying to find out what's happening."

Dagmar formed a triumphant fist with her free hand.

"Right, then," she said.

"Dagmar," said Lloyd. "We have the Internet now—but you're in trouble. You need to look at the English online edition of the *Turkish Daily Gazette*."

Alarms began to throb in Dagmar's skull.

"What is this about?" she asked.

Lloyd's voice was crisp and businesslike.

"You've been outed," he said. "Just read the article; then get back here. You and Lincoln need to get together."

ROCK STAR DUPES DEMONSTRATORS

DISSENT ORGANIZED TO PROMOTE POP ALBUM

ISTANBUL, 0621. Sources report to the *Daily Gazette* that recent anti-government demonstrations inside Turkey have been orchestrated by a U.S.-based multimedia firm operating at the behest of English pop star Ian Attila Gordon, whose album *Ararat* has just been released.

Sources say that Gordon, who played James Bond in the recent film *Stunrunner*, filmed in Turkey, engaged Hollywood-based Great Big Idea to promote his album by creating popular enthusiasm in Turkey. Great Big Idea, which normally produces online games, also produced a Turkish-themed game to promote the Bond film.

In Great Big Idea's current promotion, participants are asked to appear in public areas carrying items such as

CDs, scarves, and flowers. The events were presented as gamelike activities, and participants were not told that their involvement would ultimately be used to promote a pop album.

Some of these events have become the focus for antigovernment demonstrations, though it is not known whether Great Big Idea intended this or whether agitators seized the opportunity to use gullible members of the public for their own purposes.

"I'm completely disillusioned," said one participant, a college student giving her name only as "Neriman." "I had been led to believe that the political dimension of these actions was sincere. To find that it was a cynical maneouver intended only to sell pop music is a great disappointment, to say the least."

Great Big Idea has not commented, and in fact their company policy is never to confirm or deny participation in any media event.

The organization is headed by media mogul Dagmar Shaw, described as "a shadowy figure" who was investigated for a series of murders and terror bombings in Los Angeles three years ago.

Ararat is described on its own Web site as "a revolution in music." The album is said to be inspired by Gordon's experience in Turkey filming *Stunrunner* and features Turkish backing musicians.

UPDATE 0945. Mr. Gordon has not offered comment, but a spokesman reached early this morning seemed very surprised and said only, "That's just pure loony tunes, ken?"

"Fuck *me*," Dagmar said, as she followed the link to Gordon's Web site. She had read the story on her handheld as Richard drove the party back to Akrotiri. Their guards followed in a Rover, and behind the guards was a Ford Transit that carried the guards' communications gear, the stuff that actually worked under the influence of the High Zap.

Dagmar was staggered. The article had just enough truth to be believable, just enough power to send the movement she'd created rocking back on its heels.

If Bozbeyli had blamed the CIA for his troubles, it would only have been the sort of thing any dictator was expected to say. Few would have taken the complaints seriously, even if they were shown to be true. But blaming a Scots rock star at least had the advantage of novelty and would guarantee headlines in the tabloid and entertainment press.

If the U.S. government had been blamed, at least the U.S. would have been assumed to have acted for its own rational or political reasons. But bringing Gordon into it tainted the whole enterprise with celebrity and money—no one would want to risk their lives in a political action knowing that the whole point would be to sell records and make someone else famous.

And Dagmar had to admit that the timing was perfect. The story had broken when the Zap had isolated Dagmar in Akrotiri and when her people in California would be asleep. She had been unable to respond to any of the allegations, and any denial would never catch the original story.

The junta had restored the Internet to Ankara because the Zap was costing the local economy far too much money. And they'd restored it to Akrotiri because the damage was already done.

The road curved alongside the sea, a deep brooding azure. Cargo ships swung at anchor waiting for cargo, their waterline high above salt water. Far out to sea, Dagmar could see a patrol boat coasting in British territorial water.

"We're being gamed," she muttered.

"Sorry?" said Richard.

"I said," she repeated, "that we're being gamed."

"Damn right we are!" Helmuth spoke up from the backseat.

Dagmar kept her eyes on the uneasy ocean. Her shock was beginning to fade.

She knew that there was only one thing to do when you were gamed by someone.

Game them back.

Jet noise was back, along with the Internet. The sound of turbo-props thrashing air sounded through Lincoln's office.

"I need to talk to Ian Attila Gordon," Dagmar said.

Lincoln's blue eyes widened in surprise. "You think I've got his number?" he said. "When I was working on *Stunrunner*, it's not like I ever got to talk to the star — I only dealt with PR people."

"Can you call any of them?" Dagmar asked.

"Yeah, sure. But I doubt they've got the star's number, either. If we knew who represented him, we could get him through his management."

Dagmar considered the problem.

"In that case," she said, "I need to talk to Odis Strange."

She had gone into conference in Lincoln's office as soon as she had returned from her errand to Limassol. Richard and Helmuth had carried their spoil into the ops room to begin the business of putting together a DOS network.

Lincoln reached for his handheld.

"I've already had a conversation with Mr. Strange," Lincoln said as he thumbed buttons. "He wants to fly his daughter's body home, but the authorities are flying in a special pathologist from England, and he couldn't come in because of the Zap. I think he's upset — also, I think, high."

"Judy said he was on the wagon," Dagmar said.

"Maybe he was smart enough not to call her when he was out of his mind." Dryly. "By the way, he kept asking awkward questions about what Judy was actually doing out here."

"He'll find that out later today if he tunes in the news," Dagmar said.

"Here's his number," Lincoln said. He held the phone to Dagmar. Dagmar unholstered her own handheld, and Lincoln neatly transferred Odis Strange's number to Dagmar with the press of a virtual button.

Dagmar pressed Send. Lincoln drew his own phone back.

"It's very early in the morning in California," he said.

"I'll have to hope that Odis Strange keeps rock-star hours."

The ring signal repeated five times before Odis Strange answered. During that time Dagmar paced back and forth along the two-yard-long empty strip in front of Lincoln's desk and managed three complete laps.

"Hello." He didn't sound as if Dagmar had dragged him from sleep.

"Mr. Strange," Dagmar said, "my name is Dagmar Shaw. I'm calling from Cyprus. I was Judy's boss."

"I already talked to that guy," Strange said. His tenor voice was crisp, and the words came fast but distinct, *rap-rap-rap*, like the sound from a telegraph key.

"The person you talked to is the man I work for," Dagmar said. "Judy worked directly under me. In fact, we were roommates."

"I'd like to know exactly what Judy was doing out there," Strange said. *Rap-rap-rap.*

"Mr. Strange," Dagmar said. "I'm a game designer. Judy worked for me earlier this year, in the game we ran in Turkey."

"I heard about that," Strange said. "I'd still like to know what the hell was going on."

Dagmar decided to evade that subject.

"The authorities," she said, "tell me they're doing everything they can to locate the men responsible."

"The fucking authorities know more than they're fucking telling." *Rap-rap-rap.* "I should fly out there myself and bring my AR-15 and ask those fuckers some questions. That gun can fire damn near a hundred fifty rounds per minute, and that's on semiautomatic."

"Mr. Strange," Dagmar said, "a situation has come up, and I need your help."

"*Fuck those people up!*" Strange shouted. "*Fuck them up with two-two-three rounds!*"

Dagmar winced and held the phone away from her ear. Lincoln looked at her with saturnine amusement. She turned away from him and stared at the evil eye amulet on his wall.

"Mr. Strange—" she began.

"When can I bring Judy home?" Strange demanded. "Her mother's a damn wreck. The people there are all giving me the runaround."

"I don't know," Dagmar said. "But I promise I'll find out for you."

"I need to go down there and break some heads," Strange said. "Bring a crowbar."

"Mr. Strange," Dagmar said. "I need your help."

The statement seemed to surprise him.

"*My* help?" he said. "What the hell can *I* do?"

"There's a false rumor going around," Dagmar said. "People are saying that I—that Judy and I were hired by Ian Attila Gordon to overthrow the Turkish junta."

"What in God's name—" *Rap-rap-rap* and then a brief pause. "*Attila* was doing this? Attila was trying to overthrow the dictators?"

"Well," Dagmar said, "no, he wasn't."

"It's the CIA that put those guys in power," Strange said. "Those Turkish generals are CIA way back. That's how they got to be Turkish generals in the first place!"

Dagmar tried to stay relentlessly on topic.

"I need to coordinate with Attila," Dagmar said. "I need to talk to him, so we can agree on what to say to the press."

"If you've been fucking with the generals," Strange said, "you're damn right you need to coordinate."

"I didn't say we were doing that." Dagmar couldn't help herself.

"I still can't figure out," Strange said, "how Attila got into this."

"Do you have contact information for him?" Dagmar persisted. "Judy said you knew him." A verbal memory flashed into her mind. "She said you thought he was a tosser."

Strange laughed. "Yeah, he fucking well is," he said. "I've got it on my phone."

"Good, because—" And then the line went dead.

Dagmar looked at her phone in annoyance. Lincoln's window rattled to the sound of Eurofighters crashing the sound barrier somewhere above the Med.

"What happened?" Lincoln asked.

"I think he cut me off accidentally when he was trying to access Attila's number."

Lincoln sighed. "Is he crazy out of his mind?"

Dagmar considered this.

"Who am I to judge?" She shrugged. She hit Redial.

"What the fuck?" She jumped as Strange shouted in her ear before she even heard a ring signal.

"That's what I want to know!" Strange said. "What the fuck? Double-you Tee Eff. Know what I'm saying?"

Persist, she told herself.

"Did you manage to get me Attila's contact information?"

"Yeah. I got it right here."

As he gave the number, she pressed the Write button on her handheld and scribed the number in the air and into her phone's memory.

"Thank you, Mr. Strange," Dagmar said. "I'll get back to you as soon as I can, when I hear anything about Judy."

"Yeah," Strange said. "Thanks."

"I'm very sorry for your loss," Dagmar said. "We all loved Judy here."

She pressed the End button and felt herself sag in relief.

"That seemed to go well," Lincoln said dryly.

"I'm the envy of my friends," Dagmar said as she connected. "Now I have two rock stars on my speed dial."

"Let's hope only one of them is crazy."

The number answered after the first ring.

"Hello?" a Scots voice said. "Who is this? If this is aboot that pish on the telly…"

"Is this Mr. Gordon?" Dagmar asked. She wasn't completely certain: when Ian Attila Gordon sang, it sounded as if he were from Memphis.

"Aye." The voice was cautious.

"Mr. Gordon," Dagmar said, "this is Dagmar Shaw. I'm the person you're supposed to have hired to overthrow General Bozbeyli."

"Thank fuck fir that!" Attila Gordon seemed relieved to have a fellow victim to talk to. "Ah jumped a fuckin mile when Ah heard the phone."

"It's pretty crazy," Dagmar said.

"The arseholes even hacked the Web page! Aw that 'revolution in music' mince wasnae meant tae be there. We couldnae change it back, 'cause thid altered the passwords!"

"They're very good," Dagmar said, "whoever they are."

"Look," Attila said. "The guys are trying tae put thegither a statement denying the story. Maybe we should coordinate—"

"A denial isn't going to work," Dagmar said. "The story's already huge; a denial will never catch up with it."

"What the hell else can we dae!" Attila said. "Mah balls are on the rails here. I mean, I've niver even talked tae yi before, ken? Let alone hired yi—"

"I have an idea," Dagmar said. "It'll get you in front of the story, and it'll put you on the right side of public opinion, but it all depends how much you really want the return of Turkish democracy."

"Cannae hiv they Nazi cunts ruling the roost."

"That's good," Dagmar said, "but when I said *how much*, I actually meant how much in *pounds sterling*."

There was a long silence at the other end. Dagmar held her breath.

She was counting on the idea that rock musicians, when all was said and done, would much rather be God than just be the entertainment.

Please, she thought, *please be a megalomaniac, and not a Scot who's tight with his money.*

"How much?" Attila said.

Dagmar let her breath out in a sigh.

She reckoned she had him.

I am Plot Queen, she thought.

CHAPTER FOURTEEN

There he was on BBC One, Ian Attila Gordon, dressed in blue jeans and a vintage military jacket worn over a white ruffled shirt, with the ruffles dashingly unpinned and hanging over one lapel, a picturesque little piece of asymmetry. He hadn't shaved recently, and heavy whiskers blued his cheeks and chin.

"I wonder who dresses him?" Dagmar said. "That outfit looks good."

"But can he act?" Helmuth said. "The Bond movie sort of left the question open."

"I guess we find out now," Dagmar said.

The Brigade had left the ops room for Lincoln's suite, which had a high-definition television and more comfortable furniture. During the course of the afternoon they'd discovered that four of their scavenged modems would actually function under MS-DOS and they set up their own DOS-based LAN. Instructions had been sent to Rafet and others to put together DOS machines.

But in the meantime, since the Internet was working again, they sent messages to prepare for a demo in Ankara the following day, place and time to be determined later. Rafet and the Skunk Works drones had been sent out to find a suitable place.

Lincoln's rooms, intended for visiting VIPs, resembled those of an upscale hotel, with fabric flowers in vases, gold-and-white-striped wallpaper, and competent but soulless oil paintings on the walls. Lincoln had thrown a packet of Orville Redenbacher in the microwave, and the scent of buttered popcorn floated through the suite. Dagmar sat crosslegged on the floor in front of the television, leaning against the warmth of Ismet's legs. Ismet had joined them in late afternoon, saying that he was bored in his apartment, and now sat on Lincoln's mustard-colored sofa next to Helmuth.

Dagmar ate a handful of popcorn, passed the bowl on to Helmuth, and hoped that Attila would remember his lines.

Attila stepped up to a battery of microphones. He was on the lawn of his East Sussex home, with the last glimmer of the setting sun lighting the ivy-walled house behind him. TV spotlights glowed in his eyes.

Photo flashes lit his cheekbones. He offered a half-shy smile.

I bet he'd look good in a kilt, Dagmar thought.

"I'd like tae address the claims that Ah've somehow masterminded the revolution in Turkey," he said. There was a light in his eye that seemed to suggest he found the notion absurd, that he was just amused by the situation and going through what celebrity and the situation demanded.

"First off," he said, "I'd like tae express mah true love and admiration fae the folk of Turkey. I traveled through the country when Ah filmed *Stunrunner* last year, and I niver failed tae meet with anything but friendship and hospitality. I made some good friends who Ah'd hope tae see again one day."

The amusement went from his eyes.

"I wasnae happy when Ah realized mah new friends would have tae endure a military dictatorship. The coup was an unexpected blow that knocked Turkey's hopes of modernization aw tae hell."

Laughter returned to Attila's eyes. A cocky grin flashed across his face.

"And so Ah decided tae do somethin aboot it, ken? Ah'm here tae tell yis that the claims made this mornin werenae bullshit."

Dagmar clapped in delight as a roar of interest rose from the ranks of the reporters. More flashes lit Attila's face.

"The only bit o story they got wrang was that Ah'm doin all this fae money," he said. "Ah've enough poppy nae tae sell oot mah principles fir a bribe. And tae prove it—" He raised a finger in the air and then brought the finger decisively down on the podium. "Tonight Ahm lettin' yi aw ken that aw mah profits fae the new album *Ararat* will be put into the cause of freedom fae the Turkish people. Ahm committed tae this, and willnae rest until they generals are behind bars."

"*Yes!*" Dagmar pounded fists on the floor, torn between joy and laughter.

Reporters were screeching questions. Attila pretended not to hear, laughed, then cupped a hand behind an ear, the gesture revealing the tattoo on his neck. He answered the question he wanted to.

"What exactly am Ah doin' tae aid the Turks?" he said. He offered an apologetic grin. "Please, Ah cannae exactly go spoutin mah plans over the air, ken? These guys are haudin' enough cairds as it is."

One tenor voice lofted above the others crying questions. It was a nasal, braying cry that carried all the assumed cultural superiority of Thameside, a voice calculated to raise the hackles of anyone born north of the Humber.

In other words, the perfect foil for someone like Attila.

"Are you aware," the voice said, "that it's illegal for a citizen of the United Kingdom to attempt to overthrow a foreign government?"

Attila laughed. "Surely that depends on the government's legitimacy, no?" He shrugged. "Besides, if it aw goes tits up Ah'll only get banged up. Nae great shakes."

Reporters continued to shout questions. Attila affected to be baffled by the volume, then grinned and waved.

"Nae more answers, then," he said, and raised two fingers in a V. "Peace oot," he said.

Brilliant, Dagmar thought.

"What the hell," Helmuth said from the couch, "did that man just say?" English was his second language, and its remote dialects were clearly not his forte.

"He pretty much stuck to the script I wrote for him," Dagmar said. "He just translated it into his own, ah, idiom."

"Does he talk like that all the time?" Richard asked.

Dagmar reviewed their conversations that the afternoon, in which Attila had seemed perfectly competent in Received Standard English, at least when he wasn't upset and in what Dagmar had come to think of as "balls on the rail" mode.

"I think he's exactly as Robbie Burns as he wants to be," she said. "I also think he's underrated as an actor."

Lloyd laughed.

"Imagine some poor bastard trying to translate that into Turkish for Bozbeyli. My god!"

"Are *our* people going to get it, though?" Helmuth said. "I certainly didn't."

Dagmar considered it.

"Attila was doing that deliberately," she said, "and he was winking at the audience the whole time. He's setting up a division between those that get it and those that don't."

"Just as we've been trying to do," Richard said.

"Right," Dagmar said. "You're hip to the Scottish jive or not, just as you're hip to Ozone or not. Our folks will get it, I'm sure."

"Hip," Helmuth said, "isn't going to do much against guns."

"No," Dagmar said. "Events have demonstrated that well enough."

The day's news, generally speaking, hadn't been good. At dawn that morning, under cover of the High Zap, the Turkish military had moved against Ankara's former mayor forted up in the Ministry of Labor. The building had been stormed, apparently with massive loss of life. Now that the Internet had been restored, photos and video was being uploaded by those survivors who had managed to escape. There was little narrative to be discovered in these artifacts, only a lot of confusion, running, screaming, and the sound of automatic weapons fire.

The Turkish media claimed that Mayor Erez had been killed

trying to escape custody, but had not as yet shown pictures of his body. That was promised for later.

If Erez had recorded any last message, any declaration of defiance or principle, it had not yet surfaced. Muzzled by the High Zap, he had died as anonymously and silently as so many of his followers.

Otherwise, as video uploads and Rafet's drones showed, the day in Ankara had been mixed. There hadn't been any big demos, but there had been constant skirmishing between protestors and the security forces. There were videos of a cop being knocked off his motorcycle by a well-thrown brick, an armored car smashing a storefront, ambulances screaming down Atatürk Boulevard, a screaming woman being manhandled into a police car by a party of sweating men in suits and ties. Piles of tires and debris had been set afire to block roads or rally resisters, and the names and addresses of Gray Wolves and police—and their families—had been posted in order to invite popular vengeance.

These scenes were duplicated elsewhere, though with less intensity. There was general unrest in many of the cities, but nothing as well-defined as the demonstrations and occupations of the previous day. It was as if, with the Lincoln Brigade sealed away by the High Zap, the opposition throughout the country was taking a breather and trying to work out a new approach.

The mayor of Bodrum, off in the southeast, still held out on his peninsula. The junta had so far ignored him, perhaps on the theory that his pitiful blockade did more to isolate him than to threaten the generals.

The BBC talking heads were discussing Attila's address. One wondered if Attila weren't taking the role of James Bond far too seriously. Another said that his claims that he was responsible for the disorder in Turkey were absurd.

"It's not Attila Gordon who's making the claim, however," said another. "It's the *official Turkish media* that's claiming he's responsible for the anti-government actions. All Gordon did was confirm their accusations. What are we to make of this extraordinary series of claims?"

Nothing much, as it turned out. They did agree that if any of this was true, Attila Gordon would shortly be in jail.

Dagmar had no worries on that score. The British government knew perfectly well who was stirring up trouble in Turkey and knew it was being done with Whitehall's cooperation, from the Sovereign Base Area of Akrotiri. If they made the ridiculous mistake of arresting Attila, he'd walk.

The talking heads shifted to other news. Lincoln raised the TV remote and turned off the set.

He walked in front of the television and turned to the others.

"Helmuth's right that we're not much good against guns," he said. "But please bear in mind that behind each of those guns is a *person*." He looked at the TV remote in his hand, then placed it on the stand next to the set.

"The average Turkish conscript—in the country he's known affectionately as 'Mehmet'—has more in common with the demonstrators than with the generals," he said. "When Mehmet realizes this and acts on it, the junta is finished. The officer class has a good deal more esprit and ideological solidarity, but they know full well how corrupt their leaders are, and they know how the junta is corrupting the military itself. The best members of the officer class are not natural allies of the generals but obey out of habit, or because they see no other path. When presented with alternatives, they may come over to our side.

"Mehmet is our target," Lincoln said, "but we're not firing bullets. If our people start killing soldiers, they'll close ranks in solidarity. Our strategy has to be to split them, not force them to unite."

"What are the officers going to make of Attila Gordon?" Richard asked.

Lincoln spread his hands. "Lord only knows," he said.

"Well," Helmuth said. "On *that* note . . ." He rose to his feet. "I'll see you all in the morning. Tomorrow's going to be a busy day."

Dagmar rose and helped Ismet escape from the spongy clutches of the mustard-colored sofa. She felt Lincoln's hand on her arm and turned.

"Good save," he said.

"Thanks."

Guards took the Brigade to their quarters. Dagmar paused outside Ismet's door and carefully put her arms around his strained ribs. He carried the scent of soap and antiseptic, as if he carried a part of the hospital around with him.

He kissed her carefully, pressing his bruised lips to hers.

"Were you all right last night?" he asked.

"Slept like a baby," she said.

"Good." His voice took on a precise cast. "You need to see a doctor."

"Lincoln's arranging it."

Resentment crackled in her skull as she realized she didn't want to be the subject of the conversation.

"And you?" she asked. "How are you doing?"

"Still enjoying the pain pills."

She kissed his cheek, the point of his jaw under the ear. Bristles sang against her cheek. He rested his hands lightly on her hips, then kissed her mouth again, a peck that had the air of finality.

"I'm going to bed," he said finally. She dropped her arms and stood back.

"Sleep well," she said.

"You, too."

His door closed behind him, and she heard the lock click. She turned in silence and walked to her own door, feeling all the way the eyes of the RAF Regiment guard posted on the landing. At least it wasn't Corporal Poole who witnessed her rejection.

Serves me right, she thought, *for being crazy.*

It was lucky that she was alone that night, she reflected later, because she had barely gotten into her own room before another flashback struck and suddenly heavily armed intruders were swarming through the door and the windows. They were soldiers, with black scarves wrapped around their faces so only the glittering eyes showed, and they wore the Keystone Kops helmets of the Turkish army. Dagmar lay curled on the couch, whimpering, as they approached.

She felt their hands on her. She felt their hot breath on her neck. Tears shot from her eyes as if under hydraulic pressure.

She remembered how Corporal Poole had returned her to reality two nights before, by calling attention to the ordinary objects around her, and she began to do the same thing, calling to her mind the color and texture of the robin's egg blue couch, the furze of the carpet, the throb of the overhead fan. The soldiers faded.

She sat up, wiped tears from her face, blew her nose. That one hadn't been too bad, she thought: there was no broken furniture, no guards hovering outside her door, no Ismet standing over her, his face alive with shock and embarrassment. She was fine.

Dagmar couldn't face the bedroom. She had slept perfectly well the night before, but now the walls seemed to throb with menace. She couldn't trust the bed that she'd carefully set at an angle—it had betrayed her, and now it looked like nothing but a trap.

She couldn't trust a bedroom ever again. The alternative was simply not to sleep, so she sat up on the couch watching music videos on the telly and laughed when she saw Ian Attila Gordon appear to sing the bombastic theme to *Stunrunner*. They played a lot of Attila that night, seeing as he was in the news, and she heard a fair cross section of his oeuvre.

Harmless, she decided. The music wasn't anything that others hadn't done better.

But he dressed well. And she could imagine him in a kilt. And he kept her entertained long into the night, until exhaustion finally claimed her.

POP STAR ADMITS DECEPTION

Motivations of Anti-Government Movement
Come into Question

Next morning Attila was discussed on all the news programs and one British comic appeared with a subtitled version of Attila's address, in which his Scots was translated variously as "This is really all about me!" and "Can I have my Peace Prize now?"

The body of ex-mayor Erez was shown to selected representatives of the Turkish press.

The Brigade updated the rebel Web pages, editing and uploading the most recent of the videos and photos that had straggled in since the Zap had ended. Also uploaded were pictures of the junta with the label AW TAE HELL. The pictures went viral instantly, appearing on Web sites and blogs, being downloaded and then forwarded to millions who couldn't have pointed to Turkey on a map and who then passed it on to others.

Richard went to work creating a memorial Web page for Erez. Helmuth built a page of worship for Ian Attila Gordon, featuring a video of his interview and a bulletin board for comments. This last was a mistake: it was soon inundated by trolls, ghouls, the insane, Scottish nationalists, Kemalist provocateurs, and dozens of mild Asperger's cases arguing the origin of the phrase "tits up."

That afternoon Rafet successfully led a demonstration of five or six thousand in Kuğulu Park, marching in a chill wind past the lake with its famous Chinese swans. The marchers each carrying a newspaper and a single shoe. Skunk Works drones saw the police response on its way, and the crowd dispersed before the police arrived. A few of the shoes were thrown, a few people arrested off the street, but on the whole it showed that the rebellion still had fight.

The military were not in evidence. According to Lincoln, who had his own sources of information, the Sixty-sixth Motorized Infantry Brigade, part of NATO's Rapid Reaction Corps, had been sent from Istanbul for the express purpose of storming the Ministry of Labor. The brigade had then since been pulled out of the city but was being kept in reserve at a military airfield near the capital.

Ismet watched the developments in Ankara with growing impatience: after Rafet's demo ended he went to Lincoln's office and demanded to be sent to Turkey. Lincoln refused. Anyone in Ismet's condition would be an immediate object of suspicion—Ismet simply looked like someone who had been thrashed recently by police—and Lincoln didn't want Ismet arrested the second he stepped off the train.

When he wasn't arguing with Ismet, Lincoln spent most of the day in his office, sending coded messages to his superiors, receiving intelligence in return, and arguing with the Brits. He emerged in late afternoon to announce that a general strike was going to be called in three days' time. It was time, he thought, to test soft power against the might of the junta.

Dagmar slept alone that night. No ghosts walked.

Monday featured clashes in Kizilay, a rally in Bursa, and small demonstrations elsewhere. Rafet's demonstration in Ulus was called off when police flooded the area before the demonstrators could get there. This meant that the government had gotten inside the Brigade's communications loop—they'd turned someone or gotten hold of a cell phone, or someone had unwittingly recruited an informer. But this had been anticipated and the next day's orders sent people off into a dozen districts, carrying a wide variety of ordinary objects found about the home. Those carrying paperback books, playing cards, pillows, and decks of index cards succeeded in their meet-ups and had successful minidemonstrations that dispersed before the authorities could arrive. But those carrying small jars of condiments were swarmed by police, demonstrating that the condiment carriers' sub-network had been compromised.

That compromised sub-network would be frozen out of future actions, unless of course they were needed to draw police away from something more crucial.

In late afternoon Ismet was checking the video of a demo that had just been uploaded, and he gave a call. Soon the video was being broadcast by the big wall-mounted flatscreen above Helmuth's desk. It showed a file of demonstrators marching past the camera, chanting and waving fists and signs. They carried CDs and towels. There was no audio.

"This demo is supposed to have taken place in Diyarbakır this morning," Ismet said. "The signs are calling for independence for Kurdistan and praising the PPK."

"Crap," Dagmar said. The actions were supposed to be about democracy for Turkey, not self-determination for one of its minorities. Now the authorities could point to the demonstration and say that the movement wasn't really about political freedom but Kurdish separatism.

"This doesn't make sense in a lot of ways," Lloyd said. "Are you sure it's supposed to be Diyarbakır?"

"Yes."

"Diyarbakır is the largest Kurdish city in the country," Lloyd said. "But it's also the largest garrison town. There's the whole Seventh Army Corps in Diyarbakır to make sure demonstrations like this *don't happen*."

Dagmar perched on the edge of Richard's desk and considered the video. "Could the government be gaming us again?" she asked. "Trying to split the movement?"

Lloyd fingered his chin. "I'd say it has to be that way."

"Right," Dagmar said. "Let's watch the video again and look for proof."

On the second viewing, Lloyd jabbed a finger at the screen. "*Stop*," he called. Ismet pressed the Pause button. "Back up." Ismet reversed the video's direction, staying in slow motion. Marchers creeped past, moving backward, swallowing their unheard chanted words.

"There. Stop." The picture froze. Lloyd studied it.

"See the man on the left?" he said. "Red tie? Dark glasses?"

Dagmar located him.

"Yes."

"I think that's Muammar Sengor."

The name meant nothing to Dagmar. Ismet adjusted his spectacles and studied the figure.

"Yes," he said. "That could be him."

"Let's see if Chatsworth recognizes him."

Lincoln was brought from his office to view the video. He shook his head.

"I don't know Sengor. After my time. Sorry."

"I've got his Web page here." Lloyd brought the page up on another screen. It showed a smiling Sengor under a patriotic red banner featuring Turkish stars and crescents. He was a handsome man, in his thirties, with a mustache and a bright white smile.

"It looks like him, all right," Ismet said. "He's even got a red tie in his official photo. Maybe even the same one."

Dagmar cleared her throat. The others turned to her.

"I'm all four-oh-four," she said. "Who is this freakin' Sengor?"

"The unfortunate thing about the Kurds," Lloyd said, "is that they've never been politically united. Some are assimilated into Turkish society—Turkey has had Kurdish generals, Kurdish presidents—and others are tribal and owe allegiance to their sheikhs. The Kurds don't have a common religion—there are Jewish Kurds and Christian Kurds and Yezidis, and even the Muslims are divided between Sunni and Alevi. There are regional dialects of the Kurdish language that make it difficult for Kurds to communicate with each other. And just to complicate things, some Kurds don't even speak Kurdish; they speak Aramaic. When the PKK started calling for an independent Kurdistan, a lot of Kurds probably wouldn't have understood what they were talking about. Ethnic identity has always been a little slippery."

He raised a hand toward Sengor's picture and waved his fingers as if trying to grasp at something elusive.

"Sengor operates in this realm of ambiguity very well. He's an assimilated Kurd who has his own political party based in eastern Turkey. He's supposed to be Alevi, though that's unofficial. He's been a supporter of the military government from the start." His glance shifted to the smiling man on his official Web page. "He's also said to be a gangster. Probably has a piece of the heroin trade, and is supposed to loan gunmen to the government to kill moderate Kurds."

"Right." Dagmar pointed at the frozen picture of the demonstration. "So now we've got him dead to rights, leading a phony demonstration intended to discredit the revolutionary movement. We put out our disclaimer right away."

"That may not be Sengor," Ismet pointed out.

"Doesn't matter," Dagmar said. "The man in the red tie is Sengor from now on."

Ismet and Lloyd went to work on updating the Web pages with the video while simultaneously debunking it in English and in Turkish.

Dagmar followed Lincoln back into his office.

"Do we have to keep calling you 'Chatsworth'?" she asked. "Everyone left in the group knows your real name."

"Squadron Leader Alvarez doesn't know my name," he said. "Neither does Alparslan Topal, or any of the people here at the aerodrome." He took papers off his desk and locked them in his safe. "Now that we're in the habit of maintaining security, let's keep doing it. Just in case."

Dagmar dropped into one of the chrome-and-vinyl seats.

"Someone in the Turkish government is trying to play us," she said. "It's not Bozbeyli or the generals—those were the people who sent gunmen to kill me. This is someone new."

Interest glimmered in Lincoln's blue eyes.

"That's possible," he said.

"You've got access to intelligence reports," Dagmar said. "Do you have any idea who this new person might be?"

Lincoln seemed to give the idea thorough consideration. His eyebrows went up.

"The man who reengineered the High Zap?" he said.

"I wouldn't be surprised," Dagmar said. "Do you have any reports on whatever team deconstructed the Zap?"

Lincoln spread his hands. "I have no information here. I'll make inquiries." He tilted his head. "But this . . . gamester."

"Kronsteen," Dagmar said. "The chess player in *From Russia with Love*."

"Kronsteen," Lincoln echoed. "Do you have any idea what he'll do next?"

"He'll do whatever he can to divide us. He just uploaded a video showing that the rebellion was all about Kurdish independence." Lincoln began to speak, but Dagmar held up a hand. "Don't worry," she said. "I handled it."

He nodded. "I applaud your initiative."

"But what other splits can be engineered in our alliance?"

"Religious Turks versus seculars," Lincoln said immediately. And then, on reflection, "Rich versus poor. City versus rural. Sophisticated, Westernized Istanbul versus the patriotic heartland." He flapped a hand. "Any society has similar fault lines. And any popular movement."

"He'll have a hard time taking this line if he goes too far," Dagmar said. "Within forty-eight hours he's already told us that the rebellion is about both a Scottish rock star and Kurdish separatism."

"Next," said Lincoln, "it'll be a candy mint *and* a breath mint."

"You're dating yourself."

Lincoln sighed. "I roll deep," he said. He looked up.

"By the way," he said, "we may be wearing out our welcome from our friends the Brits. A general officer pointed out to me this morning that we can do our job anywhere—which is true enough—and asked when I thought I'd be finishing up here. I think getting hit with the High Zap has strained their hospitality."

Dagmar considered this. Moving wasn't necessarily a bad idea.

"We need to shift to a place with a lot of bandwidth," she said.

"And we won't have Byron and Magnus to give our location away," Lincoln said.

Dagmar narrowed her eyes.

"Indeed," she said. "How much time do we have?"

"Negotiations are in progress on a number of fronts. Ādaži Military Base has been mentioned—that's in Latvia. So have bases in Germany."

"I don't have the appropriate wardrobe for Latvia," Dagmar said. "I'm used to Southern California, for heaven's sake."

"I believe you can afford a coat on what we're paying you," Lincoln said.

"I can't get another wardrobe out of Uncle Sam?"

"We don't have a regular supplier," Lincoln said, "for T-shirts branded with the logos of failed start-ups."

Dagmar gave a laugh.

"Touché," she said. She thought for a moment.

"We've got Byron and Magnus locked up here, right?" she said. "Why don't we have one of them tell the Turks that we've got evicted and that out little project is canceled?" She thought for a moment. "Byron, for preference. If he defects, he won't see his family again."

Lincoln laughed.

"You're starting to think like me," he said.

"And that," Dagmar said, "is terrifying as hell."

By the next morning Rafet had a backup MS-DOS machine set up inside the safe house, with a modem scavenged from a carpet shop. Instructions for joining the DOS network had gone out to the various heads of the various sub-networks. Richard had put together a bulletin board system within DOS, where instructions to the network could be posted. In the event that the Zap struck Ankara again, Rafet would use a landline to call out of the country, to a number set up in Luxembourg. The Luxembourg number would automatically be forwarded to another number, this one in Milan, and so until it reached the computer humming away in Akrotiri.

If the High Zap lasted long enough, the landlines would go down as well, but Dagmar hoped the Turks wouldn't dare to keep their own cities blacked out for very long. They wouldn't want to crash their own economy, which like the rest of the world was now dependent on the Internet.

Next morning the military staged a formal military parade down Atatürk Boulevard in Ankara, the Sixty-sixth Motorized Infantry

Brigade returning to the scene of their triumph. The junta stood on a reviewing platform in Çankaya and distributed medals. Whose morale the parade was intended to boost was open to question.

What this meant, practically speaking, was that the military and police were busy guarding the parade route, which allowed Rafet to lead a demo near the Cebeci Campus of Ankara University. A swath of old houses had been demolished and not yet replaced, and the demonstrators made a brave sight, waving flags among the ruins and carrying signs in support of the next day's general strike.

The first amateur videos being uploaded, however, seemed to be from some other place altogether. These featured men in shades and galabia and white keffiyehs, who carried flowers and paperback books and waved signs in Arabic. They marched down a wide boulevard past white-walled stucco buildings. Palm trees waved on the horizon.

"What the hell?" Helmuth demanded.

The video was put up on one of the big wall screens. Dagmar studied it.

"No one here reads Arabic, right?"

"A little," said Ismet. "But they're not really showing us the signs; the writing isn't big enough." He squinted at the signs. "It's very idiomatic. I doubt I can make much sense of it."

"The point is," Dagmar said, "this isn't anywhere in Turkey, right? Not even in the far southeast, where there are lots of Arabs?"

Ismet shook his head. "The Gulf States, maybe? Yemen?"

The Arab men reached a park featuring a geodesic-looking jungle gym. Glittering glass buildings shimmered on the horizon. Mercedes and BMWs prowled past the camera. The men began to create designs with their books and flowers.

"Qatar?" Lloyd wondered. "Bahrain?"

"What is going on over there?" Richard wondered aloud.

Helmuth slapped his hand to his forehead. "Fuck," said Helmuth. "It's *revolution creep*." He was utterly disgusted.

Dagmar looked at him, mouth open.

"Revolution creep," she said. "That's it."

The software business had always been prone to what was called scope creep or feature creep, in which shiny, attractive, but poorly conceived new features were added to projects that had already been approved, usually without any changes in budgets or deadlines. The result would be a large, unwieldy, badly functioning piece of bloatware, a prime example being Windows Vista, which jammed together the features of two separate projects, Longhorn and Blackcomb, then jettisoned the original source code to produce a program that glittered with surface appeal but operated with less efficiency than its predecessor. Vista's problems were eventually fixed, but the damage to Microsoft's reputation had been done.

In Dagmar's business, scope creep was a deadly danger. Plots could have so many elements and dimensions that they would run completely out of control. So could the software projects, and the video and audio. Half the anxiety of her job was making sure her projects were streamlined enough to be online by the deadline.

Richard looked at Helmuth.

"They're using our tactics," he said. "But it *doesn't have anything to do with us.*"

"Yes," Dagmar said. "We sent the meme out into the world, and now anyone can use it." And then she studied the men putting down books on the ground, setting them in patterns that might be Arabic writing.

"I wonder if it's Kronsteen," she said.

Ismet looked up at her. Dagmar explained.

"We'll know if it's Kronsteen behind it," Ismet said, "if there are a lot more demos like this in different parts of the world. Because then he'll be trying to trivialize the whole process, show it's just a game that people are playing."

"Yeah," Richard said. "If people are suddenly using these techniques to protest the appointment of a dogcatcher in Aswān, then it's Kronsteen behind it."

Kronsteen's work was revealed later in the day, when Turkish television released an interview with an imam who had allegedly defected from the Tek Organization. He proclaimed that Riza Tek's goal was to restore the caliphate and establish sharia law in Turkey and that Tek's money was behind the rebellion.

"Now we're a Scots rock star, Kurdish rebels, *and* religious zealots," Dagmar said.

"We contain multitudes," Richard said. Dagmar looked at him in surprise. She hadn't reckoned him as the sort of person who would know Whitman.

She turned to Ismet. "Estragon," she said, "can you write an editorial pointing out the insanity of all these competing claims?"

"The nationalists aren't going to see contradictions in this," Lloyd said. "They're going to see *conspiracy*."

"Well," Dagmar said. "Then let's give them one."

They began the editing and uploading of the various videos. Ismet wrote an editorial denouncing the imam and pointed out that his own government said that the rebels were working for a Scotsman.

Lincoln had been away for most of the day. As evening came on, he arrived and called Dagmar into his office. He held out a sheet of paper.

"I've been on the phone with the team in the States working on the High Zap. Turns out they have a clue as to the team—or more likely the individual—who reverse-engineered the High Zap."

"They recognized the way he codes?"

Lincoln looked disgusted. "They haven't managed to decompile the Turkish version yet. Whatever algorithm the guy used was elaborate beyond description." He looked at Dagmar. "He signed it *after* he compiled it—they must have let him compile it himself." He looked skeptical. "Problematic from the security point of view."

"Maybe they were in a hurry."

"Anyway." He opened his briefcase and took out a single sheet of paper. "He signed it with his handle, but we don't know who the handle belongs to. He calls himself 'Slash Berzerker.'"

He put the paper on the table and turned it so that Dagmar could read it.

"Slash Berzerker?" Dagmar said. "What is he, fourteen?" She looked at the paper and checked the spelling. "Fourteen," she said, "and a bad speller?"

Lincoln only shrugged, then retrieved the paper.

"Are you going to burn that?" Dagmar asked.

"If you want me to."

"I've never seen a spy burn an important paper before."

Lincoln shrugged again. "Whatever lifts your luggage."

He crumpled the paper, then looked around the room.

"I don't have an ashtray," he said.

She grinned. "You could swallow it."

Lincoln put the crumped paper on top of his safe, rummaged in his desk for a disposable lighter, and then set fire to the paper. It burned into a gray ash, and the smell of burning began to fill the office. Lincoln batted at the air to disperse the smoke.

"The things I do for people," he muttered. "Are you satisfied now?"

"Yeah." Dagmar rose from her chair. "Because I know exactly how I'm going to find Mr. Berzerker."

CHAPTER FIFTEEN

FROM: Hastur

Mad kung fu proxy for Turkey peoples.

82.215.28.123

Ports 39000–39013

Dagmar sat on her couch, gin and tonic in her hand. Her feet were raised on a pillow, her toes waving at her. She could feel little molecules of alcohol traveling through her body, each going about its happy business of unknitting a ravel'd sleave of care. Or two.

Her phone was pressed to her ear, and California was on the other end of the connection.

"All right," Dagmar said. "You've got Murchison's henchman, right?"

"Yes," Calvin said. "Brickman. He's going to steal Harry's identity and commit enough fraud to get the police after Harry."

"Okay," Dagmar said. "I want you to give Brickman an online handle, okay?"

Calvin was bewildered.

"Why? He doesn't need one."

"Write this down," Dagmar said. "His handle is going to be 'Slash Berzerker.' That's *Berzerker* with a *z*."

"Slash Berzerker?" The words were interrupted by little half breaths as Calvin bent to scrawl the name on a pad.

"You got that? Two words, *Berzerker* with a *z*."

Dagmar heard the tinkling noise of Calvin putting down his pencil.

"Dagmar," he said. "Brickman wouldn't use a handle like Slash Berzerker. He's a total professional; he's been pirating identities for years. He wouldn't use a noob-sounding name like that."

"You can give him some kind of nostalgic reason for using it," Dagmar said, "like maybe it was the handle he used when he was fourteen. But there has to be a reference to Slash Berzerker in Thursday's update." The gin had set her mind spinning; she began to expand on the idea.

"You could use a graphic of a computer login, say," she said. "The username would be Slash Berzerker, but the password wouldn't be visible. It would be hidden somewhere else, and when the players give the password they'll get some new information."

"About Brickman."

"About *anything*. As long as there's a reward for a job well done. Talk to Marcie and see if she can produce something like that on short notice."

"I..." He hesitated. "Can you tell me why I'm doing this, Dagmar?"

"It's a kind of co-production thing," Dagmar said. "With the project I'm working on over here."

"The project that I'm not supposed to know about, but which seems to be the Turkish revolution."

"Yes," Dagmar said. "That one."

"I hope you know what the fuck you're doing, Dagmar," Calvin said.

Dagmar took a sip of her drink. Dioxide bubbles tickled her nose.

"This time," she said, "I think I do."

She had no sooner hit End than " 'Round Midnight" began to play. She thumbed Send.

"Briana," she said.

"Turn on the BBC News right now." Richard's voice. Dagmar lunged for the remote.

"What's happening?" she asked.

"Attila Gordon's on the news again."

She managed to catch the last few seconds of the report. Turned out that Ian Attila Gordon had traveled to Rome for a meeting with the Turkish prime minister and his government-in-exile. There was Attila, leather and blue chin and neck tattoo, smiling and nodding and shaking hands, talking about "coordinating actions," whatever those might be.

"Remember," Attila said to the camera, "the general strike takes place tomorrow. The polis might make yi open your bag, but they cannae make the customer traffic with yi."

"My god," Dagmar said, in something like awe. "My little boy's grown up to be a sociopathic glory-seeking politician."

"Next stop, Downing Street," said Richard.

"Peace oot," Dagmar said, and thumbed End.

She turned off the television, finished her gin and tonic, and lay half-reclined on the sofa as her knotted muscles began to relax. She contemplated making herself another drink and had about decided that was a good idea when there was a knock on her door.

Dagmar flicked aside a corner of the curtain, saw Ismet waiting for her, and felt a flush of pleased surprise.

"Come in," she said as she opened the door. She could smell backyard charcoal grills on the outdoor air.

Ismet stepped inside. He put an arm around her and kissed her cheek. He had shaved, and she could scent more talc than disinfectant on his skin.

"Did you see Attila?" he asked.

"He's making the most of his opportunities," Dagmar said. "I wouldn't be surprised if he visited the Pope tomorrow."

"That's already been announced," Ismet said.

Dagmar laughed. "Would you like a drink?"

Ismet would. She made two drinks, and they carried them to the couch and sat. He put a hand to his ribs as he turned to her, but the pain must have been momentary, since he continued to face her. He raised his glass.

"To Attila."

"To our own little Frankenstein monster."

They touched glasses, drank. He made an interested face.

"In Turkey they make these with lemon, not lime."

"They're good that way, too."

Ismet adjusted himself on the couch, touched his ribs again, then put the hand down.

"I've gone off the narcotics," he said. "Now it's just aspirin for me."

"You must be feeling better."

"I am." He gave her a careful look. "And you? You are all right?"

Dagmar waved a hand. "I have my moments."

He tilted his head. "I am sorry if—if I made any of those moments worse."

She sighed, touched his knee. "You've been hurt," she said. "You've got to look after yourself."

"I did," he said. "I have for a couple days now." He offered a rueful smile. "But now I'm lonely."

She looked up at him, at the purple bruises that discolored his face. "Strange," she said. "So am I."

He leaned toward her—winced, clutched his ribs—leaned closer, then kissed her. His lips were pleasantly moist.

Ismet drew back, hand still on his ribs, and took a few breaths.

"I was going to say," he said, "that I'm no longer afraid that you're going to beat me up."

She nodded. "I'm glad to hear it."

"I was angry when I said that. But I wasn't angry with you."

Dagmar nodded again. She took a sip of her drink, then leaned forward and kissed Ismet again. They kissed a good long while.

When they stopped, Ismet had to take another few quick breaths.

"I forgot to breathe," he said.

"Don't do that."

"You know," he said. "If this is to go any farther, you're going to have to do all the work. I'm not very...flexible."

She laughed. A battered, bruised, half-crippled man and a crazy lady.

"We are the junkware," she said, and kissed him again.

For two days the Lincoln Brigade tried to stay atop the general strike. From the information available, the strike seemed to go well. Amateur videos showed police vandalizing shops that had closed, but even those shops that remained open had few customers. Turkish television showed Ankara streets as jammed with cars as ever, but the images could have been filmed weeks earlier.

At night, everywhere in the country rebels came into the streets and brawled with the police. The Brigade organized a pair of demos. One of them, weaving along Irfan Baştuğ from the Altinpark toward the center of Ankara, was four kilometers long. It was so huge the police didn't dare to try to stop it. The demo eventually dispersed when word came that the Sixty-sixth Motorized Brigade had saddled up and was coming back to town, tanks at the head of the column.

Ian Attila Gordon seemed to be everywhere, on every medium. He had a private audience with the Pope. He appeared on chat shows. His album charted at number eight, with three singles in the top five. A T-shirt with his picture and the label KEN YE REVOLUTION? suddenly appeared at stands and counters throughout the world.

Lincoln said that his colleagues from the American embassies and consulates in Ankara, Istanbul, and Adana were working the phones and visiting generals, trying to get one of the military men to commit to the return of the republic. So far there had been no success.

The Seagram's ARG updated at noon on Friday, Pacific time, which was ten at night in Cyprus. The Lincoln Brigade was still in the ops center, and Dagmar on the phone to Marcie at Great Big Idea, when the new pictures rolled onto the screen.

Now they could only await developments.

Corporal Carrot says:

Googling Slash Berzerker. Nothing here.

Classicist says:

Did you try spelling "Berserker" correctly?

Corporal Carrot says:

Yep. Nada.

Vikram says:

By the way, has anyone noticed that everyone in this game is always drinking whiskey? Which may not be unusual in and of itself, but have you noticed that they ALWAYS DRINK RESPONSIBLY?

Lots of booze, but no alcoholics in this game! Usually these games are full of human wreckage, both addictive and compulsive. THAT'S unusual!

Hippolyte says:

That's an interesting point.

LadyDayFan says:

Harry just found out the police are after him. Do we think he's been committing actual fraud, or do we want to blame Mr. Berzerker for Harry's problems?

Hanseatic says:

This will probably lead nowhere, but I used to play on Blood Harvest with someone who used the Slash Berzerker handle. We must have mowed down tens of thousands of undead between us.

Chatsworth Osborne Jr. says:

Are you still in touch with Slash?

Corporal Carrot says:

Chatty! Haven't seen you here in a long time!

Chatsworth Osborne Jr. says:

I've been overwhelmed by mundane existence in the last few months. But I noticed a new adventure has started, and I'm trying to catch up.

Hanseatic says:

The guy I played online with probably has nothing to do with our current game. He was using that handle at least a couple years before anybody even <u>thought</u> of this game.

Chatsworth Osborne Jr. says:

Still, if it's the only lead we've got . . . Can you message him?

Hanseatic says:

Not until I get home from work and load Blood Harvest. And then I'd have to hope he'll log on.

ReVerb says:

You're playing this ARG at work! That's the spirit!

Chatsworth Osborne Jr. says:

Anyone else out there have an account with Flashpoint Gamez?
You could message him.

Hippolyte says:

My husband has one. But what questions do I ask?

Chatsworth Osborne Jr. says:

Ask him where he is and who he is and what he does for a living.
The answers might be misleading, but even misdirection tells
us something.

Hanseatic says:

I'm in Gdynia, and I played using the mirror site in Bucharest,
so my guess is that Slash was somewhere in Eastern
Europe.

Alaydin says:

Hi everybody, I know that guy. He's not a character in the game;
he's a friend of mine here in Turkey.

Hippolyte says:

I've been worried about the players in Turkey I met during the
Stunrunner game. Are you all right, Alaydin?

Alaydin says:

Well, I'm on strike. My business closed down. There's a lot of
military here in Adana so there's nothing much else that can
be done.

Hippolyte says:

Take care of yourself, Alaydin. Our thoughts and prayers are
with you.

Alaydin says:

Thank you!

Corporal Carrot says:

Your posts are coming through a little funny.

Alaydin says:

Turkısh keyboard.

Corporal Carrot says:

Oh right.

Chatsworth Osborne Jr. says:

Alaydin, I'd like to ask you about your friend Slash. Does he play
ARGs?

Alaydin says:

He played *Stunrunner*, but he wasn't on the bus wıth us. I thınk he
really prefers first-person shooters.

Chatsworth Osborne Jr. says:

If he played *Stunrunner*, then Great Big Idea might have co-opted
him for this game in some way. This might be an attempt to
keep the Turkish audience they captured for *Stunrunner*. Has
Slash ever been an actor or worked in video?

Alaydin says:

He's a computer engineer. He has never been in show business.

Chatsworth Osborne Jr. says:

Can you possibly give us his name? And a way to get ahold of him?

Alaydin says:

I do not want to give away his name without permission.

Chatsworth Osborne Jr. says:

Can you give us email, then?

Alaydin says:

This really is not the same Slash Berzerker. Hes out of the country anyway.

Chatsworth Osborne Jr. says:

Where is he?

Alaydin says:

I think Uzbekistan.

Hanseatic says:

This is beginning to sound suspicious. Maybe he's been sent out of the country for a reason, like to make it hard for us to locate him.

ReVerb says:

He may be hacking Harry's accounts from Uzbekistan.

Alaydin says:

Not same guy!

Chatsworth Osborne Jr. says:

Easiest way to prove that is to contact him. He's the only lead
we've got.

Alaydin says:

I think you're crazy, but ok. N.Üruisamoglu@HasekiNetwork.co.tu.

Chatsworth Osborne Jr. says:

Thanks!

"Nicely done, there, Chatsworth," Dagmar said.

"Sometimes you just have to nag them," Lincoln said, still bent
over his keyboard. The Our Reality Network live feed glimmered
in his Elvis glasses.

"I've got Haseki Network's English-language home page,"
Richard said. "Offices in Turkey, Turkmenistan, Kazakhstan,
Tajikistan, Azerbaijan, and Kyrgyzstan. Mission statement: 'To
provide wireless access where users in the past did not have access
to high speed, high performance, networked communications. To
provide long range point-to-point and point-to-multipoint wireless
connections. To provide a high level of support to our networks
and users.'"

"Slogan," Helmuth said, reading over Richard's shoulder,
"'*Now Your Community is the Whole World.*'"

"When these guys are done," Richard said, "everyone in the
'Stans will be able to receive hot take-out pizza within twenty
minutes."

Helmuth frowned.

"I don't see the connection between Haseki and the High Zap," he said. "These guys are a wireless company, not a bunch of spook hackers."

Lloyd clicked from screen to screen.

"The Turkish pages aren't quite identical to the English pages," he said. "There's a news page in Turkish that mentions that Haseki has completed on schedule a Turkish-inspired, Turkish-engineered secure communications network for the military."

"Bingo," said Richard.

"Still not proven," Helmuth said.

"Slash's name is Nimet Üruisamoglu," Lloyd read from the company Web page. "He's listed as *Vice President, Chief Programmer, Director of Operations (Uzbekistan)*. A recent promotion, apparently."

Helmuth laughed. "He doesn't get credit for being Chief Zombie Killer?"

"His talent for slaughtering the undead," Richard said, "remains unrecognized."

Dagmar, meanwhile, had called up an email program and had typed in Üruisamoglu's email address. She paused as she contemplated the subject line.

"He's about to get hundreds of insane emails from players all over the world," she said. "How can I make sure that mine is the email he's going to open?"

"Offer him money in the subject line," Lincoln suggested. He was still watching the Seagram's mystery unfold on the live feed.

"If I do that," Dagmar said, "he'll think it's spam."

"Tell him you want to hire him for a job," Richard suggested. "Mention Alaydin. Mention stuff from the Haseki Web page."

"Let me write the message in Turkish," Ismet said.

"Oh." Dagmar waved a hand. "Silly of me not to think of that."

They considered the content, then had Ismet draft an email offering a chance for Üruisamoglu to take a well-paid but mysterious contract in Western Europe, and to call Dagmar on her handheld.

"Send several of them," Dagmar said, "with somewhat different content. Just in case he skips over the first few."

"I will," Ismet said. "But let's hope he's not on strike."

Lincoln turned away from the live feed and turned to Dagmar.

"The Group Mind found Slash Berzerker in about twenty minutes," he said. "How long did you expect it would take?"

"A couple hours," Dagmar said. "We got a little bit lucky."

"Even though I'm a part of it," Lincoln said, "I'm always surprised how quickly these missions are completed."

Dagmar smiled. "Things happen fast when you've got tens of thousands of little worker bees to do the job for you."

Lloyd was still looking at his display.

"Üruisamoglu hasn't exactly been hiding his light under a bushel," he said. "He's kind of an IT superstar. I did a search on his name and came up with over a hundred thousand hits." He gestured toward his display. "He's an MIT graduate. He's only twenty-six. He goes to a lot of conventions, gives a lot of speeches. I've got the text for a lot of this stuff here."

"Any of it in English?" Lincoln asked.

"Most of it, in fact."

"Anything political? Anything to indicate whether or not he supports the junta?"

Lloyd shook his head.

"Not so far," he said. "But of course he reverse-engineered the Zap for them."

"It might have been just a job he was paid to do," Lincoln said. "He might just be a mercenary—which is good, from our point of view." He looked up. "Just keep looking," Lincoln said. "We need to know how to approach him."

He turned to Ismet.

"Ideally," he said, "I'd like to get a special ops team to just grab him and drag him to whatever American military bases are still in the 'Stans. But it may take too long to put a snatch team together." He looked at Ismet. "So you'll have to go in and make the approach."

Dagmar's heart gave a lurch.

At least, she thought, Ismet wouldn't be going into the street fighting in Turkey.

"What are we trying to get him to do?" Ismet asked.

"The fact that he signed his work," Lincoln said, "suggests that he compiled it himself, using his own personal compiler and algorithm. And the sort of people who compile programs themselves and then stick their own badge on them are very likely the sort of people who might well leave a back door into the program—they don't code it into a program, because someone might notice; they *add the back door when compiling it.*"

"Ah." Ismet nodded. "So I make contact, I get him to alter the Zap—"

"Putting a gun to his head if necessary," Lincoln said.

Ismet shook his head. "It won't work," he said. "I'll use the gun if I have to, but the fact is that I'm a journalist. He'll know within ten seconds whether I have the knowledge to follow his work— and then he'll make an idiot out of me. How am I going to know if he's doing what I tell him to? Whether I have the gun or not, Slash is the one who will have the advantage."

Lincoln turned somber. He looked over the others, as if numbering them in his head.

"I'll go in," Lloyd said. "I speak Turkish. I've shot a pistol once or twice."

Lincoln looked at him for a moment, then shook his head.

U.S. citizen, Dagmar thought. *Lincoln can't put him in danger. Not without special permission, anyway.*

Lincoln rose. "I'll get busy talking to the good folks in Virginia," he said. "I want the rest of you to prep for your encounter with Slash. He's got a lot of speeches and so forth online—read them; try to figure what it is he wants. Try to work out what we can offer him, or pretend to offer him." He gave the room a lowering look.

"We just may have to *seduce* the bastard," he said. "You figure out what to say, how to say it."

Seduce someone called Slash Berzerker, Dagmar thought. *How hard can* that *be?*

LadyDayFan says:

Assuming that this Üruisamoglu is in fact our Slash Berzerker, and assuming that he answers any of our emails, we should put our heads together and work out what questions we're going to ask him. Should we ask him about Harry right off the bat?

Vikram says:

BTW, have you heard that the Internet is down in New York? I just heard the report here in Bengaluru.

Hippolyte says:

The whole Internet? Doesn't seem very likely.

Corporal Carrot says:

I just checked the news crawl on CNN. They also report that New York is down.

Hippolyte says:

ReVerb is New York based. Are you still here, ReVerb?

Corporal Carrot says:

ReVerb? (ReVerb, reverb, reverb . . .)

Big echo in here.

LadyDayFan says:

Yeah. Big hollow echo.

I think we've lost the Apple.

CHAPTER SIXTEEN

FROM: Rahim

The following proxy sites are still unblocked. Please let any friends in Turkey know this.

86.101.185.112:8080

86.101.185.109:8080

69.92.182.124:2100

128.112.139.28:3124

198.144.36.172:5555

"'Round Midnight" brought Dagmar up from sleep. She flailed awake, arms flying, then knocked her handheld off the bedstand and then had to look under the bed for it.

She located the phone by its glowing screen and grabbed it. She brushed dust from the display, looked blearily at the glowing numbers, and saw Uzbekistan's country code.

Her heart crashed to a sudden surge of adrenaline. She pressed Send.

"This is—" She coughed. "This is Briana."

"Hello." A light, young voice. "You left a message for me to call you. This is Nimet Üruisamoglu."

His voice lilted the unlikely-sounding name, made it almost melodic.

"I'm very pleased to reach you," Dagmar said. She swung her legs out of bed, planted bare feet on the floor. She rose naked and went to the closet for a robe.

"I work for an American IT company," Dagmar said. "We were very impressed by a talk you gave in Germany a couple years ago."

"Which one?" Slash sounded pleased and upbeat.

Dagmar found her robe and got one arm in but couldn't manage the second arm without taking the phone from her ear.

"Ah——" she said, momentarily distracted. "That would be 'Toward the Creation of Neural-Based Communications Systems.'"

Ismet appeared—he'd been in the kitchen brewing coffee—and he used one hand to hold the phone to Dagmar's ear while using the other to guide her arm into the empty sleeve. She shrugged on the robe and gave Ismet a grateful look.

"I'm very pleased that you remember that talk," Slash said.

Dagmar had studied Slash's speeches through online transcripts and chosen the one that seemed the most heartfelt. The speech had been nearly utopian—Slash had envisioned the Internet carrying not simply verbal or written communication, but information about emotional states, transmitted in a kind of holographic form by brain-scanning hardware.

Once people were able to understand one another's true feelings, Slash had suggested, it would lead to greater peace among peoples, possibly the abolition of war itself.

Dagmar, for her own part, had little interest in being able to read the emotions of those she met on the Internet. She knew there were monsters in the human psyche. She had enough creatures lurching about in her own brain, and she preferred to keep them private: she didn't want to broadcast hallucinations of Indonesian rioters or Maffya triggermen to everyone she met, and she very much preferred not to encounter their own needy, ever-hungry Creatures from the Id.

When people found out what others were *really* like, she thought, there would be more wars than peace treaties.

"We found the ideas visionary," Dagmar said. "And I'm pleased to tell you that we may be in a situation to bring your ideas into being."

"But the talk—" Slash stammered a bit. "It was what you call blue-sky. A kind of thought experiment."

"Thanks to our proprietary hardware," Dagmar said, "your vision is a lot closer to reality than you might think."

There was a pause for Slash to digest this.

It was not, she knew, implausible. There were already scanners that could read the areas of the brain that processed speech, so that the scanner would be able to "hear" the words the subject was listening to or be able to print the words the subject was thinking. Processing more complex brain signals such as emotions, she thought, was only a matter of time.

"What company did you say you work for?" he said.

"I can't actually tell you until nondisclosure agreements are in place," Dagmar said. "But the hardware exists, and tests are very promising. Our software at the moment is a kloodge—we could really use a software overhaul—but we also need a vision such as the one you articulated in your German talk."

"I—that's very interesting." He sounded cautiously interested.

Ismet appeared again, bringing a cup of coffee. He pressed it into Dagmar's free hand, and she took a hasty swallow. Coffee scalded its way down her throat.

"I'd very much like to get in the same room with you to discuss this," she said. "Do you think you can fly back to Germany to meet me?"

Germany, where there were plenty of American special ops teams, and military bases where Slash Berzerker could be debriefed.

"I—I'd like to," Slash said. "But unfortunately my next few weeks are committed."

"Oh?" Dagmar tried to sound disappointed. "Where are you?"

"Uzbekistan."

"Really?" Dagmar made an effort to seem genuinely surprised. "Well," she said. "We have people in Europe who might be able to meet with you there. Where in Uzbekistan are you?"

"Unfortunately, I'm in a place that's completely remote. I'm near an oasis called Chechak in the north of the country."

"How do you spell *Chechak*?"

From over the lip of her coffee cup Dagmar gave Ismet a wild grin.

This might just work out.

"Tell me about Uzbekistan," Dagmar said. "The last I heard, they were killing each other."

She and Ismet were in the backseat of the car, being driven to the ops center by their guards. He looked thoughtful.

"Last year they went through another phase of, ah, post-Karimov adjustment. But they're quiet now."

"Who's running the place?"

"A coalition of political parties dividing all the uranium money while it lasts. Or maybe the uranium interests just bought the political parties. I'm sure it's hard to tell."

Dagmar shook her head. "Are they friendly to the U.S.?"

"They're friendly to the American dollar."

Dagmar nodded. "Sounds like people we can work with," she said.

She was nearly skipping in delight when she entered the ops center, but the sight of Lincoln drained the joy from her. He slumped in a chair beneath the picture of Atatürk, a wisp of hair hanging in his face, his face gray and old. A corner of his mouth sagged, as if he'd been hit by a stroke.

Dagmar stopped dead in her tracks and looked at the others. Lloyd and Lola were busy at their desks, expressionless, and the others hadn't arrived yet. Dagmar gathered herself and walked to Lincoln.

"What's wrong?"

"The High Zap hit New York yesterday," Lincoln said. "Just before the stock market closed."

A shock wave rolled through Dagmar till it rebounded off the inside of her skull.

"How long did it last?"

"Only twenty minutes. But that was enough for Bozbeyli to make his point."

Dagmar decided to emphasize the optimistic. "I've talked to Slash Berzerker," Dagmar said. "I knew where he is—alone, apparently, at an oasis called Chechak."

Lincoln slowly shook his head. "Doesn't matter," he said.

"All you have to do is send someone to talk to him," Dagmar said. "Some of those Special Forces guys you were talking about, plus a technician or two smart enough to understand how to rewire the Zap—hell, the techs don't even have to be there in person, just observing in via satellite."

Lincoln waved a hand.

"No," he said. "We can't do any of that. They've canceled our operation."

Dagmar could only stare at him. She heard Ismet walk up behind her, put his arm around her waist.

Lincoln looked up at her.

"From my superiors' point of view," he said, "this op is a complete disaster. We've destabilized an ally, crashed the New York Stock Exchange, lost billions of dollars—"

"The stocks will rebound," Dagmar said.

"I didn't mean the *stocks*." Lincoln's tone was savage. "I meant we lost the *money*. Do you know how much electronic money moves in and out of New York on a given day? How many billions in exchanges were disrupted? Not just the stock market, but the Federal Reserve, the other banks..."

"Oh, come on," Dagmar said. "I could believe those transfers were disrupted, but I can't believe they were *lost*. There's all sorts of error checking—"

"They're checking all those errors now, believe me," Lincoln said. He looked up at Dagmar, his blue eyes wavering behind the tinted lenses.

"When a quake hits Wall Street, it's the foundations of Washington that shake," he said. "Our government is now going to great efforts to convince the Turkish generals that we have their best interests at heart, and that our diplomats and agents will stop trying to subvert the Turkish military. Our op is shut down as of today—we pack up the gear, and head back to the States by the first available transport."

"The first real cyberwar," Dagmar says, "and the U.S. *surrenders?*"

"That's what you do," Lincoln said, "when the apocalypse that the action was trying to prevent *is triggered by the action.*" He shrugged. "They'll probably try for some kind of technological fix—figure out a way to neutralize the Zap, or supplant it with Zap 2.0."

"And Rafet?" Dagmar asked. "The camera crew? What happens to them?"

"They'll be exfiltrated," Lincoln said. "Rafet will go back to his dervish lodge, and the rest—" He shrugged. "Will return to their lives."

"And the revolution?"

Lincoln rose to his feet. Atatürk glowered over his shoulder.

"The Turks are on their own," Lincoln said. He began to walk past Dagmar to his office.

She put out a hand to stop him. When the hand touched his chest, he stopped then looked at her.

"Lincoln," she said, "you can't do this. There has to be an alternative."

His face reddened.

"*I argued with them all night long!*" he said. He sliced the edge of one hand across his jugular. "They cut my fucking throat, okay? We're finished."

He pushed past her and walked toward his office. She turned to Ismet and saw her own stricken look mirrored in his eyes. She drew him to her and pressed her face to his shoulder.

People were dying in Turkey, she thought. *Dying.*

She looked out at the ops room and thought about what they'd done.

They had their MS-DOS network ready to function in case of an attack by the Zap. They had Rafet and his crew in place in the capital. They had dozens of Web pages filled with videos, photos, and propaganda. They had the portable memory with contact information for whole networks of rebels. They had a general strike in progress, one that seemed to be going well.

But the generals had the High Zap, and that trumped everything. They could take down New York, Washington, the country, the world.

Helmuth and Richard walked in together and headed at once for the break room for coffee.

Her posse was down to three, she thought. Richard and Helmuth she paid herself, and she knew that Ismet would soldier on. The three Company employees would have no choice but to return to the States. The Lincoln Brigade didn't even have Lincoln any longer.

She reached for her handheld and looked in the directory for Ian Attila Gordon.

"This is Dagmar Shaw," she said when he answered. "This time I need you to hire me for real."

CHAPTER SEVENTEEN

Duplicity in a Coed Pet-In

It was sabotage, she supposed. Not that she cared, and her guess was that Lincoln didn't, either.

The MS-DOS-capable modems were packed carefully away. Dagmar had to send out one last command, the final message canceling the demonstration that had been previously scheduled for that day…and when she had the portable memory in her hands she copied it to the memory in her personal handheld, the one she'd carried into the ops room that morning, because that was the phone that Slash Berzerker had called and that she could use to call him back.

Dagmar planned to take nothing but the modems and the information. Everything else could be replaced or rebuilt. They all had their own hardware. They were running their bulletin board system on a machine in Luxembourg owned by a colleague of Dan the DOS Man.

We are the junkware, she thought.

Everything else was turned in—the flash drives, the portable disk drives, the phones that hadn't ever been allowed to leave the ops room. Lola checked the bar codes, did the inventory, and didn't seem to notice the personal phone that Dagmar wore in its holster at her waist.

The new modems had never been entered in the inventory, and no one seemed to care that Richard and Helmuth carried them out in a cardboard box.

"Souvenirs," they said.

Helmuth and Richard would be flying to Germany, to bask in luxury at a Sheraton in Frankfurt. In a suite paid for by Attila Gordon, they would try to keep the revolution on its feet.

Ismet and Dagmar had their own destination, in Uzbekistan.

Videos of demonstrations were uploaded from Pakistan, Egypt, and the Philippines. Revolution creep. Kronsteen, Dagmar supposed, trying to devalue the rebellion on his own doorstep.

Late that afternoon Dagmar tracked Lincoln to his office and found him pulling documents from his safe and putting them through a shredder. Something blue glinted amid the strips of paper in the wastebasket. She recognized an evil-eye amulet— flawed, apparently, having failed to keep the mission from catastrophe.

"What happens to Byron and Magnus?" she asked.

"Dennis and Jerry," Lincoln said. "Their real names." He fed another document into the shredder, his eyes not meeting hers. She sensed an evasion.

"What happens to them?" she asked. "Do they get tried here? Back in the States?"

"No trial. Nothing."

She opened her mouth to speak—to *yell*—but he raised his head and lifted a hand.

"This isn't an operation we can ever acknowledge took place," he said. "Putting them on trial would reveal what we tried to accomplish here. So no trial's ever going to happen."

"They're going to *get away with*—"

Lincoln shrugged. Defeat had dug deep trenches in his cheeks, at the corners of his eyes.

"Oh, they'll lose their security clearance. They'll lose their jobs. But they'll be at liberty, and they're talented, so I expect they'll find work somewhere, and never have to see us or each other ever again."

Dagmar clenched her teeth. "Does Byron and Magnus's Turkish control know they've been arrested?"

Lincoln shook his head and dropped another piece of paper in the shredder. "Probably not," he said. "Not unless he has some other source of information beyond those two."

"How did they communicate with him?"

The shredder hummed. "Letter drop via Gmail. The same way you send a message to Rafet."

"Can we send them a message pretending to be Byron and Magnus?"

He frowned, looked up at her.

"To what end?"

"To burn them so the Turks will never trust them again."

Lincoln's blue eyes turned inward. He frowned down at the pages in his hand. "What's your idea?" he asked.

"Send a message to confirm that we're shutting down here and everyone is going home — except for me and Ismet, maybe. We're flying somewhere in Europe to meet an important contact to gain information about the Zap."

Lincoln frowned. "Where?"

"It doesn't matter," Dagmar said. "The point is that when the Turks send a team to observe us or take us out, they get arrested by someone you've warned in advance."

Lincoln reached down and turned off the shredder. He squared his remaining papers and leaned back in his chair.

"Let me think." Frown lines appeared between his eyebrows. "I think I can manage it," he decided. "We'll send them to Berlin and say the meet is in the Hotel Pariser Platz — that's practically next door to the BfV office in Berlin." His eyes sparkled. "And I know just who to call."

Dagmar tried not to show herself as eager as she felt. "So you'll do it?"

"Yes. Why not?" He shrugged. "A last little prank, before we fly off to wretchedness and defeat."

What she hoped was that Bozbeyli's first team—the people he most relied upon to travel to foreign countries and to carry out covert actions—would be busy in Germany, and preferably under arrest, when Dagmar was off in Uzbekistan.

She and Lincoln composed the message, and it was placed in Byron's Gmail account. It placed the meet in the bar of the Pariser Platz at 1700 the next day. Either Byron's control would pick it up or not. Either Bozbeyli's A Team would be diverted to Berlin or not. Either Dagmar would have a little revenge or she wouldn't.

At least she'd have the satisfaction of a little Parthian shot, firing over the rump of her pony as the Lincoln Brigade fled in disorganized retreat.

She stepped out of Lincoln's office and looked over the wreckage of the office. Kemal Atatürk looked back at her with his stern sapphire gaze. Beneath him were the Lincoln Brigade's trophies: the DVD, the wilted flowers, the sad, sagging stuffed bear. The photos of Judy and Tuna, looking out from a world in which they had not been murdered, from a place where they still lived, laughed, and looked forward to the triumphs their lives would bring.

Dagmar took a step toward the wall, to take the memorial down, and then hesitated.

No, she thought. *Let it remain. Let it stay on Cyprus like the ancient memorials of the island, like the stone* wanassa *in its ancient temple, a mystery to those who came after, a phantom touch to their nerves, their hearts. Let it tell them,* she thought, *that something had happened here, something at once sad and profound, something that had started as an insanely fun activity by well-meaning people but had turned into death and betrayal and failure.*

Let it stay, she thought. *Let it remain, a memorial of our own delusion and foundered innocence.*

Disorder in a U.S. Benz Kit

When Lola offered to make travel arrangements, Dagmar said she'd make her own. The next morning, Monday, she hugged Lincoln good-bye at the Nicosia airport. He felt like a sack half-filled with straw. She had told him that she would be flying out later.

She kissed his cheek.

"Stay in touch," she said.

He looked at her, watery blue eyes over the metal rims of his glasses.

"Forgive me?" he asked.

He had lied to her and marched the both of them straight into catastrophe, but he had been as blind and betrayed as she and was now returning home to his own professional purgatory. She couldn't bring herself to hate him.

"Sure," she said. "Why not?"

She watched Lincoln and the others walk through the gate to their waiting aircraft, and then Dagmar turned away and used her phone's satellite function to call Rafet. She explained the situation to him.

"You can wait for Chatsworth's instructions for exfiltration," she said, "or you could carry on, with the understanding that you're working for a purely private concern."

Otherwise known, she thought, *as a demented rock star.*

She told him to consult with the Skunk Works operators and the camera techs, come to a decision concerning what they wanted to do, and then call her back on her private number.

Dagmar's next journey took her to the honey-colored Gulf-stream 550 waiting in the section of the airport reserved for private planes. Stairs were already pushed up to the open door. She climbed the stairs and stepped aboard, and a smiling, shaggy-haired man greeted her.

"Name's Martin," he said, shaking hands. He spoke with a

West Country accent. "Attila would be here himself, but he had a press conference in Glasgow to announce his new justice initiative."

"And what would that be?" Dagmar asked.

"He's setting up a legal fund to aid the defense of those arrested during the demonstrations."

"That's assuming there will actually be trials," Dagmar said.

Martin looked surprised. "Won't there be?" he said.

Dagmar shrugged, then introduced Ismet. Martin showed them to some seats in the rear of the aircraft, for takeoff.

The Gulfstream featured mahogany paneling, gold-plated fixtures, a large oval table of what seemed to be polished black marble, and softly glowing leather couches. Postimpressionist water-colors hung from the bulkheads. Martin showed them to some more conventional seats for takeoff.

"Does Attila actually own this jet?" Dagmar asked.

"No, he rented it from a company in Rome. Can I get you any drinks?"

Ismet asked for orange juice. Dagmar, more interested perhaps in relaxation, ordered a gin and tonic.

One of the two smiling cabin attendants came with their drinks a few minutes later. The attendants were both tall and well-groomed, attractive, and female. They spoke with Italian and French accents, respectively. As there was no eye candy for the heterosexual female, Dagmar gathered that the plane's usual customers were rich men.

The attendants made sure Dagmar and Ismet were strapped in, and the Gulfsteam taxied to the runway, joined the queue behind a Boeing 737, and in its turn launched itself into the air.

The plane refueled in Bucharest, then crossed the Black Sea, the Caucasus, and the Caspian Sea. They kept well clear of Turkish airspace. The cabin attendants served champagne, caviar, blinis, beef stroganoff, and a hearty red burgundy, all appropriate enough for flying over the former Soviet Union. Dessert was bananas caramelized in butter, spices, and brown sugar, then expertly flamed with cognac by the Italian attendant. A movie was offered but declined. The Gulfstream flew over a triangle of Kazakhstan and then entered Uzbek airspace.

"The nearest airport—the nearest we can set this down, I mean—the nearest to your destination is in a town called Zarafshan," Martin said. "We've got a car lined up for you. Attila also explained that you might be wanting these."

He produced a series of cases and produced a pair of Beretta 9mm pistols in holsters and a lightweight semiautomatic shotgun in a nylon scabbard. Dagmar was surprised.

"How did you get these on such short notice?" she asked.

"We were in *Italy*," Martin said. "It's the second-largest arms exporter in the world. They have strict regulations if you live there, but if you're taking the goods out of the country, they practically have a take-away window."

Ismet looked at Dagmar.

"Do you know how to shoot?"

"I've fired pistols," she said. "Not recently, though."

Not, in fact, since she was a teenager and briefly had a boyfriend who was a firearms enthusiast.

"Maybe we'd better give you a refresher."

He very competently field-stripped one of the Berettas, reassembled it, and dry-fired it.

"You've had practice," Dagmar said.

"I was in the army."

"You were?" She was surprised.

"All Turkish men are required to serve. I got to be an officer because I'd been to university, so it wasn't bad."

"What did you do in the army?" Dagmar asked.

"Public relations for the Fifth Corps in Thrace." He smiled. "My service was pretty dull, which was fine with me."

He gave Dagmar a brief course in use of the pistol. She expressed surprise at the pistol's light weight, but Ismet pointed out that adding a magazine stuffed with bullets would increase its mass by a considerable amount.

Dagmar put the pistol down on the marble tabletop. Her hands had a light coating of gun oil, and she reached for a napkin.

"Do you think I might actually need to use this gun?" she said.

"If Slash is not amenable to money," he said. "We've got to make a credible threat."

"You know," she said, "I think we have not worked out all the contingencies of this plan."

"Speaking of money," Martin said. He took another package down from an overhead compartment and opened it in front of them. Packages of Bank of England notes fell out on the table.

"Pounds sterling," he said. "Ten thousand."

Dagmar looked in amazement at Ismet. "We've been working for the U.S. government," he said. "And you know what? They're *pikers*."

One of the cabin attendants appeared. She looked at the guns and money on the table as if they were no more unusual on the plane than copies of *Forbes* and the *Wall Street Journal*, then turned to Dagmar.

"I'm afraid our landing may be delayed," she said. "The pilot is having trouble raising ground control."

A cold warning shimmered up Dagmar's spine.

"I wonder," she said, "how much of the gear on this plane runs on TCP/IP."

"Tell the pilot," Ismet said, "to go ahead and land at Zarafshan whether he can raise them or not."

The attendant looked dubious. "Well," she said, "I—"

"We have to land *somewhere*." Ismet was practical. "It may as well be where we want to go."

Dagmar unholstered her phone and tried to get a cell phone signal.

"Cell networks still okay," she said. "But VoIP is definitely down." She pressed virtual buttons. "I can still get GPS, so the problem is local."

"Local to Zarafshan," Ismet asked, "or to all of Uzbekistan?"

Dagmar didn't have an answer for that. Instead she looked at Martin.

"Attila rented this aircraft, right?" she said. "Did he make any effort to disguise the fact? Working through a shell corporation or anything?"

Bemusement crossed Martin's face.

"He sent me down with his credit card," Martin said. "IAG Productions."

"And I presume the pilot filed a flight plan? Saying he was going to Cyprus, then to Uzbekistan?"

"I imagine so, yeah."

The generals could be expected to keep a watch on the man who had declared himself an enemy of their regime. Attila might as well have drawn a flaming arrow in the sky pointing to their destination.

Dagmar turned to Ismet.

"The plane and the guns and money are nice," she said. "But the advantages of working for a covert branch of the U.S. government are now a lot more apparent."

One of the cabin attendants approached.

"Excuse me, miss, but is that a cell phone you're using?"

"I've got EDET; I can use it on a plane."

"Oh. Very well, then."

Dagmar gave a jump as the phone rang in her hand. She saw it was Helmuth.

"Turkey's down," he said. "The whole country, plus a chunk of Greece and Bulgaria."

"So is Uzbekistan. How's the DOS network doing?"

"Working so far. The landlines are holding up, at least for now."

"What's happening?"

"A bunch of politicans have taken over the old parliament building. The one right near the Atatürk statue in Ulus, where Tuna had his action."

"Don't send Rafet in there. The last time people tried to seize a building, it just made targets out of them."

"I'll tell Rafet."

"Anything else?"

She could almost hear the smile in Helmuth's voice. "The German news is full of it. The cops arrested some terrorists in a Berlin hotel—all heavily armed."

Dagmar gave a triumphant laugh. The first team was out of the picture, and Byron was burned.

Helmuth rang off. The guns were packed away, then stowed in overhead compartments. The money went into pockets and luggage. Dagmar went to look out the window. They were circling a town set in a sandy desert, the Kyzyl Kum, which covered at least half the country. The dunes stood out a brilliant red against deep shadows cast by the westering sun. The town was very, very green—it was amazing in its greenness, especially as contrasted with the brown and rust and alkali that surrounded it. On one side of the town were some kind of mining works, tailing ponds, paved roads. On the other side was the airport, a single strip.

The Gulfstream passed slowly over the airport. Dagmar could see commercial aircraft sitting on concrete aprons near the terminal. There didn't seem to be any planes preparing to take off.

The voice of the pilot—a pleasant Aussie accent—issued from the PA.

"Please prepare for landing."

Ismet and Dagmar shifted to seats with belts. The Gulfstream went into a steep dive, pulled out, touched the end of the runway, bounced, landed again.

Dagmar concluded that the pilot wanted to get out of the way of any other aircraft that might be trying to land, and quickly.

She approved. The faster this was dealt with, the better.

Deranged Scot Sum Amounts to Local Habits

The Gulfstream pulled into an area reserved for foreign aircraft. A polished Honda sedan drew up as the attendants were opening the door, and a man in a uniform got out.

He came aboard the plane and took care of the customs details, stamped Dagmar's and Ismet's passports, and welcomed them to Uzbekistan. Dagmar considered how many long lines she'd stood in at passport control throughout the world, and she turned to Ismet.

"The rich are different from you and me," she said.

"So I understand."

As the customs officer returned to his Honda, a bright yellow vehicle drew up. It resembled a smallish Jeep and was accessorized with running boards, bullbars, and spotlights. A teardrop-shaped luggage compartment was attached to the roof. It looked rather sporty.

"What is that?" Dagmar asked.

"That's a Lada Niva four-wheel drive," Ismet said. "You haven't seen one before?"

"If I have, I probably figured it was a Kawasaki or something."

"I think it's ours."

A man in a suit and tie got out of the Niva. He spoke a sort of English, and he showed Ismet and Dagmar the vehicle. The vehicle seemed rugged enough and ran well for all that the odometer showed 165,000 kilometers. Red plastic jerricans of gasoline had been loaded into the rear compartment for crossing the Kyzyl Kum. Ismet and Dagmar signed papers, and Martin presented a credit card. The gentleman, who had introduced himself as Babür, copied down the number carefully.

"Do you have Internet?" Dagmar asked.

"No," the man said. "No Internet today." He didn't sound as if it was that unusual an occurrence.

Jet noise sounded in the air. Dagmar looked up, held up a hand

against the sun that squatted near the western horizon, and saw a
jet come into view, a smaller craft than the Gulfsteam. It cruised
slowly over the airfield, much as the Gulfstream had done.

Turkish air force markings were clear on the fuselage. Dagmar's heart leaped into her throat.

"Look!" She pointed wildly. Ismet looked up.

"Orospu çocuğu!" he snarled. It must have been impolite,
because Babür looked a little shocked—Uzbek was a Turkic language, and obscenity probably carried across language barriers
easier than anything else.

Dagmar looked across the pavement at the customs officer in
his Honda. He probably knew the other plane was coming, that's
why he was still waiting here.

Dagmar stepped closer to Babür and lightly touched his arm,
then pointed toward the Turkish jet.

"Are you renting them a car?" she said.

"Yes. If you can drive me back to my office, I can bring it."

"I wonder," Dagmar said, "if you can offer me some help?"

Babür smiled pleasantly. "Of course, miss."

"That plane is bringing some people we don't want to meet.
Could you possibly delay bringing their car?"

Babür spread his hands. "Miss, I can't possibly—"

Dagmar reached into her pocket and withdrew a bundle of
English currency. Babür's eyes locked onto the monarch's portrait,
and his words came to a halt.

Dagmar peeled off five hundred-pound notes and handed them
to Babür. He looked both pleased and confused.

"Share this with the people you work with," Dagmar said. "Tell
them to go to dinner. Tell them to have dinner for a *long time*."

The notes vanished into a pocket of Babür's neat suit.

"Yes, miss," he said.

"If they find you and ask why you can't help them, tell them
you can't do anything without the Internet."

Over Babür's shoulder, Dagmar saw a smile flash across Ismet's
face.

"And if their car has a mechanical problem," Dagmar said, "I would also be very grateful." She leaned a little closer and spoke over the sound of the jet. "If this works out to my satisfaction," she said, "I will give you another bonus payment when I return the Niva."

Babür's head bobbed.

"Yes, miss," he said. "Very good."

Baggage was loaded into the Niva. Dagmar was nervous about loading guns into the car right in front of the customs inspector, but he never looked up from whatever document he was reading.

They also took everything from the jet's refrigerator that didn't require cooking: bread, crackers, cans of beluga caviar, cold cuts, hard-boiled eggs, cheese, some beautiful Italian heritage pears, soft drinks, Rock Star, and bottles of water.

They figured they wouldn't have time to stop at a restaurant for a leisurely meal.

The cabin attendants, wearing identical bemused expressions, loaded the spoil into plastic sacks and handed it over. Dagmar said good-bye to Martin on the runway apron.

"You might want to hire a guard on the plane till we leave," she said. She had to shout over the sound of the Turkish jet cruising low over the airfield, one wing tipped down so the crew could view the runways.

"Sorry?" Martin said.

"That plane." She pointed. "They're going to want to kill us. Don't let them sabotage the jet."

Comprehension stitched its way across Martin's features, as if different parts of his face got the message at different times. Dagmar managed to restrain her laughter; then she shook his hand and ran for the Niva.

They drove Babür to his office near the field and left him counting his pound notes.

"You did that very well," Ismet said. "I couldn't have improved on it."

"He's not the first guy I've bribed. You should have seen me handing hundred-dollar bills to New York's finest when we did the *Harry's Crew* live event in Washington Square Park."

"I expect you just gave Babür a month's salary or more."

Dagmar touched the evil eye amulet that dangled from the rearview mirror. "Let's hope that the men in that plane don't have much cash on them."

Zarafshan had an antique feel. The roads weren't in good condition. The town was filled with enormous squat Soviet-era apartment blocs, not all in good repair. They seemed a similar vintage and shared some of the impersonality of the buildings at Akrotiri. One of the buildings seemed to have burned in the country's latest flurry of post-Karimov adjustment.

On the road, a host of vintage Toyotas, Renaults, and Protons testified to a thriving gray market in automobiles. Some of the buildings had metal-and-plastic signs that reminded Dagmar of old Californian road signs from the 1950s, with stylish rockets, satellites, and planets. Decor from the Atomic Café.

"The Zap has bombed this place back to the Space Age," she said.

Ismet smiled. "Good line," he said.

"I stole the sentiment from a Richard Buttner story."

Dagmar craned her head to see if she could find the Turkish airplane. It was on approach to the runway, dropping toward the ground with wheels extended.

She hoped Babür and his fellow employees were having a wonderful time, somewhere else.

Then Zarafshan simply ended, and they were in the Kyzyl Kum, on a two-lane blacktop, old and patched but absolutely arrow straight. Massive, soaring alloy towers carried power lines alongside the road, marching off to the vanishing point on the horizon, the setting sun turning the insulators to red jewels.

On the edge of the desert was a Soviet-era tank, abandoned and with dust drifting over the treads. The huge gun pointed at empty desert. The crew seemed to have just parked it there one day, left, and never returned.

The Niva's engine screamed. The four-by-four rattled, bumped, jounced. The tires thundered on the patched road.

"I don't think I can get above a hundred ten," Ismet said. "The engine isn't big enough, and it's old."

That was something like seventy miles per hour, Dagmar calculated. Not too great.

"Let's hope the...the black hats...don't get a faster car."

She should have ordered a BMW or something, she thought. Attila could afford it.

The desert was reddish sand covered with sparse grass and scrub. Sometimes there were dunes, but mostly it was just flat. Dagmar saw sheep, goats, and occasional camels, their two humps drooping like old, shaggy haystacks.

There were occasional oases, with mud-brick buildings on perfectly straight Soviet-engineered local roads. The fields were very green until the green simply ended, and there the red sands began.

As the sun settled on the horizon the desert took on a brief, roseate beauty, the shadows stark, the sand glowing watermelon red. And then, the sun gone, everything began to fade through gray to black.

Dagmar wondered what the Turks following them were actually after. Would they try to kidnap Slash in order to silence him or simply kill him? Or were they after her and Ismet?

She supposed they'd take whatever they could get. There didn't seem to be a lot of law and order here.

She wondered if the men who had killed Judy were among them. The thought made her turn in her seat, rummage through the bags behind them, and produce a pistol. She fed bullets into a magazine, then slipped the magazine into place with a satisfying click.

They were the second team, she reminded herself. The first team had gotten arrested in Berlin.

The thought didn't make her feel any safer. She loaded a second magazine anyway, then put the pistol and the spare in the holster.

They paused after a couple hours. Full night had descended, with a chill wind that cut through Dagmar's thin leather jacket as she stepped into the desert for a quiet, private pee. When she returned, she found Ismet assembling and loading the shotgun and the other pistol. Then she ate a hard-boiled egg, took a swig of Rock Star, and got behind the wheel.

The Niva would not win prizes for comfort, but it got the job done. The manual shift stuck a bit and the wheel punched her hands every time the vehicle hit a bump, but none of the gauges were in the red and the engine kept turning despite what sounded like its desperate wails for help.

She knew she had to make a left turn here somewhere. She had gotten the latitude and longitude from a Google Earth map and programed these into the GPS on her handheld, but the numbers were, she suspected, fairly approximate. Ismet seemed somehow to have fallen asleep.

There were always tracks leaving the road, most of them probably going to someone's sheep camp. She didn't know which, if any of them, she should take.

If all else failed, the Niva was perfectly capable of driving cross-country.

When the turn finally came she sped right past, then braked and skidded to a stop. Ismet gave a cry and stared wildly in all directions, looking for attackers. It took Dagmar several tries to find reverse with the shift, and then she backed to where a sign pointed to Chechak, giving the name in both the Latin and Cyrillic alphabets.

The turnoff was dirt and broad enough for two trucks to pass abreast, not just a two-rut track like most of the others. The sign was wood and had been jammed in the earth fairly recently, presumably to guide trucks bringing supplies to Slash Berzerker's IT project.

Dagmar put the Niva into four-wheel drive—fortunately she didn't have to get out of the vehicle and mess with locking hubs. Then she jammed her foot down on the accelerator and felt the

Niva lurch forward. She steered into the sign and the bullbars smashed it flat with a satisfying crack of splintered wood. Grinning, she steered onto the turnoff and punched the accelerator again. She looked over her shoulder and could see red sand flying in the tail-lights as the wheels threw up a rooster tail to mark their passage.

The road was mostly sand, but heavy vehicles had compressed it and the four-wheel drive wasn't necessary for traction. She shifted into rear-wheel drive and was soon moving as fast as she dared, about fifty kilometers per hour, dodging potholes and drifts, the back end of the Niva fishtailing through her last-second swerves. The road was for the most part straight, but there were sudden and unanticipated turns or dips or climbs or places where the road had been washed out by a flash flood and she had to shift to four-wheel drive to get through it.

Her GPS showed her that she was getting closer to her destination.

And then the road took a precise right-angle turn to the left, completely unmarked and unexpected, and Dagmar was going too fast to stop or to make the turn. A wall of red sand appeared before them. The Niva struck the sand in an explosion of ruddy dust and suddenly they were airborne. Ismet woke with a yell. Panic flooded Dagmar as she felt weightlessness, and then the vehicle came down with a crash and she was thrown forward against her shoulder belt. Pain flared from forearms braced against the steering wheel. Her foot braced to shove the brake pedal all the way to the floor.

The Niva wasn't moving. Dagmar sat gasping for breath, her heart hammering, a stretch of featureless sand stretching out before the headlamps.

"Are you all right?" Ismet said.

Dagmar blinked. "I think so."

She looked around and saw that the vehicle seemed to be intact. She put the Niva into four-wheel drive, then shifted into reverse. Sand flew from the wheels, but the four-by-four wouldn't move. The Niva wouldn't go forward, either.

"Let me see what's happening." Ismet opened his door and stepped out. A blast of icy wind blew into the vehicle, and Dagmar shivered. Ismet circled the Niva and then came to Dagmar's door. Dagmar rolled down her window, then shivered to another cold gust.

"We're hung up," Ismet said. "We're not going anywhere."

Rage flooded her veins. Dagmar freed herself from her shoulder belt and stepped out onto the Kyzyl Kum.

Sand had been piled just where the road turned, a manmade dune that had since been sculpted into smooth curves by the wind. Either the sand had been scraped from the road and just dumped there or it had been placed there to stop cars that failed to make the turn, a duty that it had performed with faultless efficiency.

The Niva had climbed to the top of the dune, then lost momentum and hung itself on the crest. The sand supported the frame at its midpoint, with the wheels dangling off to either side, unable to gain enough traction to move the vehicle.

"*Shit fuck shit!*" Dagmar restrained herself from kicking the tires.

"We could dig it out," Ismet said. "Do we have a shovel?"

A search revealed that a shovel was not part of the Niva's standard equipment.

"We'll have to use our hands," Dagmar said. She was frozen to the bone and was keeping her teeth from chattering only with effort.

Ismet peered out into the night. He pointed. "I see a light out there," he said. "I can't tell how far it is, not over a flat desert. But they probably have a car or a truck, and we might be able to rent it."

Dagmar narrowed her eyes and peered at the light. It was faint and seemed to glow from somewhere on the edge of the world.

"I'll walk it," Ismet said. He pulled the hood of his windbreaker over his head, then looked back at Dagmar. The headlamps gleamed off his spectacles. He touched her arm.

"Get in the car and stay warm," he said. "I'll be back soon."

Dagmar could only nod in agreement. Ismet equipped himself with a water bottle and some of Dagmar's hundred-pound notes and walked off into the darkness. Dagmar got back in the Niva and cranked up the heater as far as it would go.

As the heater filled the cabin with warmth she began to regret not going off with Ismet. The Turkish gunmen, she thought, could arrive while Ismet was away, and they would see the Niva illuminated in the white splash of its own headlights. If they stopped to investigate, Dagmar would have a hard time explaining that she was just an innocent tourist who took a wrong turn.

She could become less conspicuous by turning off the lights, but then Ismet might not be able to find his way back.

Thoughts of the Turkish assassins sent her digging for her pistol. It had flown forward in the crash and ended up in the footwell. She clipped the holster to her belt. Her search had revealed some of the food they'd plundered from the Gulfstream, and so she made herself some sandwiches with the cheeses and cold cuts and ate them.

She decided that if she saw or heard a car coming, she'd turn off the lights, run into the desert, and hide. If it was Ismet, she'd emerge. If it wasn't, she'd wait for the newcomers to leave.

The cabin was pleasantly warm. She unzipped her leather jacket and reclined the seat. Pain throbbed in her forearms. The desert stretched ahead of her in the headlights, featureless, monotonous. Dagmar closed her eyes.

She must have slept, because she came awake suddenly to the sound of metal on metal. She looked around wildly, clutched at the pistol, and threw the door open. She jumped onto the sand, hand still on the pistol, her head swiveling madly as she tried to make out where the sound was coming from.

"Dagmar, it's me." Ismet's voice.

She sagged with the release of terror. She stepped away from the Niva and saw two large moving shapes looming against the Milky Way. A sound like an enormous belch sounded in the air. In sheer astonishment she beheld a pair of Bactrian camels, their breath steaming in the air.

"This is Ulugbek," Ismet said from atop the camel on the right. "I found him at his sheep camp. His brother is away with the truck, so we rented these instead."

From out of the darkness she saw Ulugbek's smile under a dark mustache. "Assalomu alaykum!" he called.

"Günaydin," she ventured, not knowing if the Turkish greeting would translate or not.

Ulugbek kicked one leg over the front hump of his camel and dropped to the sand. He wore boots and a parka with a MontBell label. He approached Ismet's camel, gave it a series of clucks and commands, and compelled it to kneel. Ismet dismounted awkwardly, staggered on the sand, and recovered.

Ulugbek approached Dagmar and gave her a warm, extended hug. "Hayirli tong!" he said cheerfully. He smelled pleasantly enough of strong tobacco. At a loss for what to do, she patted him on the back.

Ulugbek hugged her twice more, then set to work. The camels were already wearing leather harnesses — that's what Dagmar had heard jingling — and Ulugbek hooked them to nylon towing straps, which he then attached to the Niva's rear bumper. The camels farted and belched. Dagmar and Ismet watched, both shivering in the cold.

"We and the black hats are in a low-speed chase," Dagmar said. "We're moving at camel speed."

"Camels can go pretty fast," Ismet said. "I just found out."

Ulugbek gestured for someone to get into the Niva. Dagmar did so and put the four-by-four into reverse. Ulugbek gave a yell and began hitting the camels with a stick. The animals lurched forward into the harnesses, Dagmar gunned the engine, and the Niva rocked back. Red sand flew from the wheels.

It didn't work; the Niva was still hung on the sand. But Ulugbek had thought ahead and strapped a shovel to his saddle. More sand flew as he dug sand from beneath the Niva, and then the camels were driven forward again.

Still the Niva didn't move. Ulugbek was indomitable: he shifted more sand, then geed up the camels a third time. The Niva lurched backward, then hung. Ulugbek applied himself to the shovel, and more sand flew.

The eastern horizon was turning pale before the Niva finally came free. Ulugbek unhooked the tow straps, then came to Dagmar's door. Dagmar opened the door, and Ulugbek stepped forward and embraced her.

More hugs were in order, apparently. Dagmar submitted with a good grace despite the fact that Ulugbek's efforts at digging had left him covered in sand and sweat. Ismet tipped Ulugbek a can of caviar and then waved farewell as Dagmar gunned the engine and sped in the direction of Chechak.

Ismet sagged in his seat. "My god," he said. "I never want to ride a camel again."

"Was it painful?"

"It was too far above the ground," Ismet said. "I was afraid I'd fall off and break an arm."

When the rising sun at last blazed above the horizon, it showed a dark blotch on the watermelon red sands, a black oasis lying under chalky sandstone mesa. A cluster of receiver dishes and a cell phone tower stood atop the bluff.

"We're there," Dagmar said.

Ismet looked at the new world and yawned.

"Should I open a can of caviar?"

"That might be a little premature. Have a pear."

The oasis grew closer. Houses of mud brick lined roads of sand. There was a general store with gas pumps out front, a coffeehouse, a tiny mosque with a metal dome that looked prefabricated, and several obese dogs lying in the early morning sunshine.

Dagmar slowed as she came into the town. Her GPS said that they had arrived. Wind blew the Niva's rooster tail of dust over the car, and she peered through the ruddy dust. The town's two commercial businesses both seemed closed. No one was yet on the streets.

In the sudden silence, she heard a tinkling waterfall sound. She wondered if it was wind chimes or perhaps a fountain.

She tried to phone Üruisamoglu for directions, but the cell network was down.

"God *damn* it!" she said.

"Go to the mosque," Ismet said.

As she drove to the mosque she discovered the source of the tinkling sound: goats' bells, each tuned to a different note. The herd passed in front of her, urged on by an elderly man in felt boots and an olive green Russian army anorak trimmed with rabbit fur.

More elderly men were found at the mosque, where the dawn service had just ended. They stood in their white skullcaps, carrying their beads and talking with one another. Ismet got out of the Niva, approached, and had a lengthy conversation. He got back in the Niva and gestured toward the bluffs.

"Slash is only in the most obvious place for an IT guy," he said.

Dagmar looked up at the antenna that reared above the town.

"Right," she said, and put the Niva in gear.

"How is your Uzbek, by the way?" she asked.

"Nonexistent," Ismet said. "Uzbek is about as close to modern Turkish as German is to English."

"You managed to talk to them, though. And Ulugbek."

"We found a few words in common."

"Whoah!" They had come to the edge of town, and Dagmar braked at the prow of a strange duck-billed vehicle looming around the corner of a mud wall. The other machine didn't move, and Dagmar realized it was just parked there.

She slowly pulled ahead and saw that she had been startled by a battered old armored vehicle with eight huge tires, its steel flanks studded with little portholes. The original olive drab paint had flaked off it, and it was now spattered with rust, like an old boulder that had been scabbed with fungus.

"Lots of old Soviet military gear lying around the provinces," Ismet said.

"There are license plates on it," she said. "Someone must drive the thing."

The armored vehicle was set up to pull what looked like a long homemade trailer, with a lot of old pipe stacked on it.

"Maybe the owner digs wells," Ismet said.

The Niva descended into a gulch behind the town, then climbed up the other side. Ahead Dagmar saw a two-rut road running past the face of the bluffs, weaving between boulders that had been eroded from above and tumbled down the slope. They came around one craggy rock and saw that a new road had been blazed up the face of the bluffs. She shifted the vehicle into four-wheel drive, cranked the wheel over, and the Niva began to lurch upward.

As they came around a curve they had a view of the oasis and the desert below.

"Look there," Ismet said.

Dagmar braked and saw a red rooster tail crossing the desert, moving fast in their direction.

"That would be our friends from the airport," Ismet said. "I don't think Babür was able to hold them for very long."

"They've got a lot faster car than we do," Dagmar said. She looked at him. "What do we do now? We're stuck on this hill."

"Go up to the top," Ismet said. "We can't turn around here."

The Niva jounced to the top of the road. The tower and the receiver dishes were surrounded by chain link and razor wire. But beyond the tower, to Dagmar's surprise, she saw a yurt, the round felt-walled dwelling that had been a home to the steppe peoples for millennia. Ismet's nomad relatives still lived in similar tents, at least part of the year.

Next to the yurt sat a Volkswagen Rabbit that seemed about the same vintage as the armored vehicle she'd seen in the oasis.

"I'll drive," Ismet said. He jumped out of the passenger door, then paused to look down as the strange car entered the village. "Take your gun."

Heart pounding, Dagmar reached for the gun and its holster and jammed the holster into the back of her jeans.

"What are you doing?"

He turned to look at her. Bruises bled down his face.

"I'm going to lead them off into the desert," he said. "Once we're away, you get Slash into his car"—jerking his head toward the Rabbit—"and then you get him to Zarafshan."

Ismet jumped into the Niva, and there was a shriek of gears as he put it in reverse. As he backed, then turned and began rocking down the bluff, Dagmar was aware that a young man had come out of the yurt and was watching her.

He was small boned and pale skinned, and he huddled in a sheepskin overcoat. He had a unibrow over large brown eyes, and he watched them with a little frown on his face.

She was surprised to see that he was propped up on metal forearm crutches. None of the online material she'd seen about him indicated that he had trouble walking.

Dagmar approached him.

"Hello," she said. "I'm Briana. I talked to you on the phone."

Comprehension dawned on the young man's face, though he still seemed wary.

"I'm Nimet Üruisamoglu," he said.

"Otherwise known as Slash Berzerker."

He flushed slightly. "I started using that name," he said, "when I was fourteen."

Dagmar stepped close.

"You used that name a few months ago," she said. "When you did some work for the Turkish government."

His unibrow darkened, and he looked suspicious.

"What does that matter?" he said.

"Because the government figured out that you put in a back door when you compiled that program and now they've sent people to kill you." She pointed over the edge of the bluff, toward the village.

"They're in Chechak now. As soon as they work out where you are, they're coming up here. Of course maybe they *already* know that you're here."

Slash scowled, deep lines forming in his forehead. The scowl was too old an expression for his young face. His hands clenched on the handgrips of his crutches.

"I don't know what you're talking about," he said.

Dagmar was very aware of the pistol pressing against her spine. She took another step toward Üruisamoglu, hands rubbing her sore forearms.

"They let you compile the program yourself, using your own algorithms. That wasn't a smart thing to do, but then they're not very bright about computers, are they?"

His dark eyes studied her. His upper lip gave a twitch.

"They said it was a weapon," he said. "They said it was something they'd found in a government router, probably planted by a Chinese botnet."

"It *is* a weapon," Briana said. "And the generals are using it now. They shut down New York the other day, and now they've shut down all of Turkey and all of Uzbekistan."

Üruisamoglu's lips parted in surprise.

"That's what's happening *here*?" he said.

"Oh yes."

"I thought our stupid subcontractors in Tashkent had accidentally switched us off. I tried to text them about it, but wireless was down, too."

"They shut down Uzbekistan because they didn't want you to get a warning that you were about to be killed."

His unibrow knit again. "And who are you, exactly?"

"I work for Ian Attila Gordon." She couldn't help but laugh as she said it.

"The rock star?" Üruisamoglu was deeply surprised. "The man who's trying to overthrow the government?"

"The man who's trying to overthrow the government *that's try-ing to kill you.* Yes, that man."

Dagmar could hear the sounds of a car grinding at the base of the bluff. She gave Üruisamoglu a warning look, then crouched down to creep carefully to the edge of the bluff.

A dark sedan was winding along the road. It looked not so much as if it had driven across the desert as physically attacked it: the car was covered in red dust, and there were several fresh dings on the paintwork.

"What—?" Üruisamoglu's voice.

She realized that he had followed her and he was now silhou-etted on the skyline.

"Get down!"

She grabbed his sheepskin coat and pulled him off his crutches. He gave a cry and fell heavily onto the ground. She was afraid he'd cry out and she put a hand over his mouth. His eyes were very large.

The sedan ground on, kicking up alkaline dust. She could see Ismet and the Niva pulled off the road, behind a large block of stone that had at some point in the past tumbled down the bluffs. Ismet was standing by the car, his right arm by his side.

The sedan came closer. Then Ismet stepped out from cover, his right arm pointing at the car.

The sound of rapid fire echoed up the bluffs. The sedan slammed to a halt, then went into reverse. Ismet kept firing. The sedan slewed off the road, and its doors opened. Four men in suits tumbled out of the car and sought cover.

Ismet jumped into the Niva and gunned the vehicle onto the road.

Now it was the others who fired—three of them, Dagmar saw, had pistols. Dagmar felt her nerves leap with every shot. She heard a few bangs as rounds struck the Niva, but the Russian jeep pulled away in a swirl of dust.

The Turkish gunmen ran back to their car. The engine raced. The fourth man—the gunmen had dark suits; he wore something sand colored—was late in getting to the car, and she heard impatient commands. Then doors slammed, and the sedan was racing away.

"Okay," Dagmar said. "Now we get in your car and we run like hell."

Üruisamoglu looked at her.

"We can't," he said. "The car's broken down. They were going to bring me a new one in a day or two."

Dagmar watched the Niva and its pursuer racing away along the bluffs.

"Okay," she said. "We've got to get down to the village and get a ride."

He spread his hands, indicating his crumpled body, the metal crutches.

"How?" he said.

Dagmar was having a hard time believing how quickly it had all gone wrong.

"Let me help you up." She tugged on the sheepskin and helped him rise. He hobbled toward the yurt, and she followed.

She could go down to the village, she thought. Get a car, bring it back up the bluffs. But that would leave Üruisamoglu unguarded. The assassins could return and kill him.

"All right," she said. "You've got a back door into the program. So use it."

Spear Point Flies to Hooters

The yurt was cozy, build on a wooden stage above the ground, with Oriental rugs on the floor and a pellet wood stove. It had a wooden door, a bed on a platform, a large desktop computer, equipment for making tea and warming food. A wood-lattice framework supported the felt walls. There were maps and photos of the Kyzyl Kum, with marks where Üruisamoglu was weaving together his IT infrastructure. He lowered himself carefully onto a large pillow and pulled out his laptop.

"The program will be in your router here," Dagmar said. "You need to configure it so that it will obey you—obey *my*—orders."

"That's going to take a while."

Dagmar was surprised.

"Why?" she said. "All you have to do is use your back door to get into the program, change the government's password to your own—to *my* own—and then tell the program to go dormant again."

Üruisamoglu's unibrow grew darker as he frowned.

"It's not that simple," he said. "The program's...different now."

Dagmar felt a sudden, raging certainty that the kid was lying. She could feel a mad itch where the gun dug into her spine.

"Tell me quick!" she snapped.

The unibrow lifted. He seemed impressed by the force of her anger. Not in a frightened way, exactly, but in a way that absorbed his attention. As if he found strong emotions somehow alien but still the subject of intense interest.

"Okay," he said. "The government was afraid of someone doing...exactly what you want me to do. So when I try to change the program, it queries a central server in Ankara for permission."

Dagmar felt a snarl tug at her lips. She wasn't believing this. "It can contact the central server even when the Net's down?"

"Yes. It will have the correct codes to pass the message through any affected routers." He looked down at his keyboard. "I can get into the central server, I think, because I compiled that program, too, but I'll have to work out how to structure my attack. And I'll have to make certain that Korkut or the other system administrators don't see me working."

"Korkut? Who's Korkut?"

"He's head of computer security for the Intelligence Section. He's smart. I worked for him."

Korkut, she thought. She wondered if he was the man she called Kronsteen, the man who had been behind the attempts to discredit her.

"He was down there," Üruisamoglu said. He gestured toward

where the sedan was roaring off in pursuit. "Korkut was the man in the light-colored suit."

He was the one who wasn't shooting, Dagmar thought. The one the others were yelling at.

Korkut was the geek the assassins had brought along, to make sure Üruisamoglu didn't try to put one over on them.

Dagmar had a lot of questions about Korkut, but she didn't have the time to ask them. Anger jittered in her nerves. But the more she thought about what he'd told her, the more plausible it seemed.

"Better get busy, then," she said.

He didn't answer. Instead he put earbuds into his ears, then began to type. After a few minutes he began to sway back and forth to his music. Dagmar watched him, then ran up to him and pulled one of the buds out of his ears.

"Are you listening to music?" she demanded.

He looked up in surprise. She could hear tinny Europop sounds coming from the bud dangling from her hand.

"What's the problem?" he asked.

"You can't listen to music!" she said. "You'll deplete your battery power!"

"I *always* listen to music when I work."

"Not this time."

She pulled the cord from his laptop and confiscated the earbuds. He looked at her in fury.

"Do you have a miniturbine array for recharging?" she demanded.

Üruisamoglu looked disgusted. "No. I normally have electricity here, but it went out along with everything else."

Dagmar clenched her teeth. She had a recharging unit in her luggage, but her luggage was still in the Niva.

"How much power do you have in your laptop, anyway?"

He waved a finger over the laser sensor to bring up the data, looked up.

"One hour, thirty-nine minutes," he said. "Give or take."

"Can you do the job in that time?"

He shook his head and lifted his shoulders, a Turkish gesture that meant "I don't know."

"Conserve power."

Dagmar went to the door and looked out. Two vehicles were laying dust trails along the road in the distance. She could hear the popping of shots.

She and Ismet should have come up with a better plan, she thought. Though as it happened she couldn't think of one.

Her phone rang, Helmuth calling from Frankfurt.

"Yes?"

"We're getting reports of riots all over Turkey."

Dagmar gave a weary laugh. "Losing the Internet didn't make people stay home; it just pissed them off."

"They were already on strike—maybe they didn't need the Internet so much."

The distant dust trails vanished into the shimmer of the horizon. Dagmar could smell smoke drifting up from the village below.

"What's happening with the old parliament building?" she asked.

"Nothing yet. I'd expect the army to turn up, though." There was a pause. "We also got one report from the east of Turkey, saying the commander of the Second Army has been removed."

"Hm." Dagmar peered at the horizon, saw nothing. "Is that a good thing or a bad thing?"

"I don't know. We need Chatsworth to tell us what it means."

Dagmar considered this and wondered what Lincoln's reaction would be if she told him she was in Uzbekistan.

"You could ask Ismet," Helmuth suggested.

"Last I saw," Dagmar said, "Ismet was driving across the desert being pursued by Turkish gunmen."

There was a long pause.

"Okay," Dagmar said. "Here's what's happening."

She gave a brief outline of the situation. Helmuth muttered something in German under his breath. "So you can't get out?"

"No."

She could hear Helmuth thinking. "I have an idea," he said. "But you're not going to like it."

She cast a glance back into the yurt, at Üruisamoglu sitting motionless at his computer, watching her with his large brown eyes.

"I'm open to suggestions," she said.

"Shoot the kid," Helmuth said. "He works for the damn narco-Nazis anyway, so he's no loss. Take his laptop, grab some supplies, and take off on foot. Hide until the bad guys go away, or until you can reestablish contact with Ismet."

Dagmar felt her mouth go dry.

"That's . . . going to be hard," she said.

"Can you think of a better idea?"

She gave the matter some thought. "I'll have to get back to you," she said. She pressed End and put the phone back in its holster. She looked at Üruisamoglu.

"How are you doing?" she asked.

"It would go faster with music."

She gave him an icy look. "Then *sing*," she said.

She left the yurt and gazed out to the east, where Ismet and his pursuers had disappeared. She saw no dust plumes, heard no vehicle noises or gunshots on the wind.

Dagmar rubbed her sore forearms with her hands. She thought about Ismet dead, Ismet burning in his car, Ismet lying wounded on the sand. Tears stung her eyes.

She had bravely struck off on her own, without any of her support system, and led her lover straight into a fiasco and probably got him killed.

She couldn't save Ismet. She couldn't save Üruisamoglu, and she knew she couldn't kill him. She was useless.

She was Semiramis Orta. She was the spy who failed.

Dagmar clenched her fists, her teeth. Her thin leather jacket didn't seem able to keep out the cold wind at all. She shivered.

God damn *it*, she thought. *Haven't I learned anything?*

Apparently not.

She returned to the yurt and looked over Üruisamoglu's shoulder. He was coding: she recognized structure and syntax but couldn't place the lines in any context. Slash couldn't help clarify; he was off somewhere in his own Deep State—not in the cabal that had taken power in Turkey, but inside the internal realm where art and code and human mind all came together, where mad imagination ran in tandem with the discipline of science, a rigorous internal dreaming that flowed down the arms and through the fingers into the keyboard and then out into the world . . .

Oblivious to her, Üruisamoglu was humming to himself as he worked. Needing the music.

She followed the coding. She did very little coding herself these days, she had Helmuth and others for that, but she still appreciated coding as an art form, and Üruisamoglu was very good. His syntax was clean, he was well organized, and he made few mistakes.

And the original code, the code he was modifying, was astounding. She had never seen anything so clean.

Dagmar looked up as she heard a noise outside the yurt. Sudden terror clutched her. Her heart crashed against her ribs.

Someone was outside.

As quietly as possible, she groped for the pistol at the small of her back. She failed on the first try and on the second managed to ease the Beretta from the holster. She stepped back, looked at the weapon, and remembered how to work it. She took the safety off and pushed the slide back, then let it go. She saw the shiny brass cartridge go into the breech as the slide snapped forward with a clack.

She saw Üruisamoglu jump. He spun around and saw the gun in her hand.

"Ananin ami!" he said. He sounded disgusted.

"I thought I heard something."

"Don't do that!" He was shaking a finger. "Don't do that!"

Dagmar stepped around him, walking toward the door of the

yurt. She wondered how long she had been watching Üruisamo-glu at work, whether she'd become so absorbed in the coding that she hadn't heard someone approach the tent.

Her feet seemed incredibly distant. She could barely feel them touch the carpets. The gun was heavy in her hand and somehow slippery. It wanted to fall out of her grip. She seemed to hear a thin keening on the air, a cry on the very edge of her hearing.

She was absolutely certain that she could hear someone creeping around outside. Someone who was very possibly waiting for her to come out, so that he could shoot her.

She moved closer to the yurt door.

Then Dagmar heard another noise, off to her right somewhere. She gave a cry and snapped the pistol up to aiming level, ready to fire.

She could fire right through the tent walls. But she couldn't see out and didn't trust herself to fire accurately at a sound.

"Did you hear that?" she said. Her voice came out as a husky whisper.

"Hear what?" Üruisamoglu asked.

Dagmar moved closer to the door. If she could fire out, she thought, they could fire in. They could gun her down right where she stood.

She tried to remember all the tactics she had learned playing first-person shooter games. She got down on her knees so as to make a smaller target of herself. She crawled slowly to the door, trying not to make a sound. She knew the enemy were there, waiting.

She thought they were off to the right. She put a hand on the wooden door. Her heart was crashing so loud that she couldn't hear anything else.

Dagmar pushed the door open with her left hand and thrust the pistol out. Her finger was ready on the trigger. She saw only bare ground, with the view of the Kyzyl Kum beyond.

She shoved the door entirely open, swept the pistol around in an arc. Saw no one.

In a sudden murderous frenzy she ran out onto the wooden platform, then dropped from there onto the ground. She peered under the platform, ready to blast away the legs of anyone standing on the other side, but there was no one.

She ran clean around the yurt. No enemy appeared; no gunmen took shots at her. Wind keened through the tower.

Dagmar paused, the gun half-lowered, and listened. She heard nothing but the wind. Then she sagged as she realized what had happened.

She had been hallucinating. If she had actually seen any of the enemy, they would have been Indonesian rioters or maybe Maffya hit men.

She had nearly fired through the yurt wall at something that didn't exist.

Well, she thought, that *would have boosted Slash's confidence.*

Dagmar held out the gun, carefully lowered the trigger to the uncocked position, and slid the safety on. Her hands were trembling so savagely that she had a hard time getting the pistol back in its holster.

She went out onto the edge of the plateau and looked out. No vehicles were in sight. She returned to the yurt and tried to give Üruisamoglu a brave smile.

"Must have been an animal," she said.

"Animal," he repeated, disbelieving. He was still giving her that odd intense look, as if she were some specimen that he was examining under a magnifying glass.

"How's the coding going?" she asked.

He seemed unhappy. "I could use some tea."

There was a hot kettle already on the wood stove, giving off a trickle of steam. Dagmar found a teapot and black tea. A smoky aroma filled the yurt as she made the tea. She gave a cup to Üruisamoglu and took one for herself.

"Thank you," he said.

"You're welcome."

He looked at her. "What are you, a musician like Gordon?"

She managed a smile. "No. I'm a game designer."

He shook his head, skeptical.

"I designed the *Stunrunner* game," she said. "Your friend Alaydin said you played it."

Realization came. He rocked back a little. He pointed a finger at her.

"You're that terrorist woman that Attila Gordon hired. I read about you in the *Gazette.*"

"I'm not a terrorist," Dagmar said.

"My god," he said. "No fucking wonder." He sipped his tea. "This is a real mess."

Dagmar could only agree. She looked down at the forearm crutches lying on the carpet beside him.

"Did you have an accident?" she said.

"A truck hit my car. Six months ago. A friend of mine got killed." He looked up. "That's when the Intelligence Section came to me with the project. I was able to work while I was in recovery." He shook his head. "I should never have come out here."

She looked around the yurt. "Why did you? This is a pretty primitive environment for someone who can't get around very well."

He rubbed the lip of the teacup against his chin. "I wanted to be by myself. I'd been in the hospital; I was in recovery for weeks, doing physical therapy." He looked up at her. "I kept reliving the accident. Every time I saw a truck coming down the road I wanted to run and hide. I kept seeing my friend dead." He looked down at the laptop screen. "I thought if I came up here, I could forget all that."

"It's not so easy," Dagmar said. "I had some friends killed a few years ago and—it's not something one forgets."

Üruisamoglu said nothing, just sipped his tea.

"There are medications that can help," she said. "You could see a doctor."

Üruisamoglu pointed at his head, rotated the finger. "I don't want to lose my edge," he said. He seemed angry.

"There are anti-anxiety drugs and...and others," Dagmar said. She waved a hand vaguely. "They're not supposed to interfere with brain function."

"Anxiety," said Üruisamoglu, "is what keeps me going." His dark eyes flashed beneath the unibrow. "Besides, I don't want anyone thinking I'm crazy."

"It's not crazy; it's supposed to be —"

Üruisamoglu looked up at her savagely. "Do you want me to do the job, or not?"

Dagmar looked at him.

"Do the job," she said.

He put his hands on his keyboard and began to type. Dagmar sipped her own tea—it was deep and smoky, with a tang of the woodlands.

Anxiety is what keeps me going... I don't want anyone thinking I'm crazy. Do you want me to do the job, or not? They were all her own excuses for living with her condition. On Üruisamoglu's lips they sounded pathetic, defensive.

She began to suspect that the excuses didn't sound any better coming from her.

Üruisamoglu began coding steadily. The tea provided a welcome warmth. Dagmar left the yurt again and walked to the edge of the plateau. If she was going to start hallucinating again, she figured it was best she do it out of Üruisamoglu's sight.

Okay, she thought. *I'll see a doc. How much worse can it be?*

The resolution, she thought, lacked a certain force. Possibly because the likely outcome of her current situation was that she would be killed and that she'd never see that doctor.

She huddled into her thin, useless jacket and shivered. Winds had raised a dust devil down in the sands. She watched it for a while, the swirling sand a silvery glitter in the sun, and then saw another trail of dust rising by the bluffs.

Tension sang through her muscles as she realized that the second dust trail was caused by a vehicle moving toward her.

But whose car was it? she wondered. She reached for her

handheld, called up the satellite function, and speed-dialed Ismet.

The ring signal went on for a long time. Dagmar held her breath as the signal went on and on.

Finally she pressed End and returned the phone to its holster. Despair gave a little wail somewhere in her psyche.

She forced herself to remain calm as she walked back to the yurt. She opened the door and went in.

"How long?" she asked.

Üruisamoglu looked briefly up. "Not long," he said.

"We don't have much time."

He circled his hand in that Turkish way that meant he'd heard all this so many times before.

She could carry him out on her back, she thought. But she couldn't see herself clambering along the bluffs that way.

She would just have to buy him time.

Dagmar went out onto the plateau again and tried to work out how the car would come up and where she should hide so that they couldn't see her until the shooting started and where she would stay in cover. She tried several places and checked the field of fire from each. Again she tried to remember what she'd learned in first-person shooter games.

She'd never gotten as good as the best players, the ones who could just run into the middle of a firefight, shoot in all directions while running, killing all the Nazis or the zombies or the Nazi zombies, and never come to harm. Instead she preferred to be a kind of sniper, to settle under cover somewhere and pick the enemy off one by one.

That was the only thing she could do here, fire from ambush. She wasn't a gunfighter, and unlike her character in the video games, she couldn't be sure of hitting anything with a pistol she'd never fired.

The dust plume came closer. Dagmar chose her spot, then jogged back to the yurt. Üruisamoglu was still coding, bent over his work.

"Soon," he said.

"Call me when you're ready."

He waved a hand, telling her to push off. She swallowed her resentment, then returned to her chosen place.

It was another ten minutes before she heard the car laboring up the narrow road. Even though she knew it was coming, she still managed surprise when it finally came into her view.

The car had taken a pounding. The windshield had caved in, leaving only a few silver-glinting remnants around the edges. The body was dinged and covered in dust, one headlight was smashed, and a front fender was flapping loose. The car was a piece of junk now, but that didn't matter. What mattered was that there were still killers in it.

She found it all intensely interesting. Oddly, she wasn't afraid. A short while ago Dagmar had been terrified of hallucinations, but now that the black hats had arrived, the men who could actually kill her, she didn't find them frightening at all.

Dagmar rested her pistol on the rock in front of her and fired. She counted five shots, the pistol kicking against her hand each time, a jolt of pain going up her bruised arm, and she felt a rush of intense pleasure as she saw the sparks thrown up by a bullet as it splashed on the hood.

The driver slammed the brakes, then threw the car into reverse and backed away. A laugh burst past Dagmar's lips as she saw the enemy retreating, and she fired another shot. Someone fired back at her through the windshield — she saw the flash — but the bullet flew away into nothing.

Dagmar thought that she should move now they knew her position, and so she shifted to another of the places she had chosen. She leaned far out from her cover to observe the enemy.

The car backed all the way to the bottom of the bluff, and then the passengers got out. There were still four of them, still in coats and ties, three in dark jackets, one in beige. They consulted with one another briefly, and then the three in dark jackets began to advance up the road. From their posture — crouched down with hands held together in front—it was clear they were holding pistols.

The other one, the one in the light-colored suit, stayed by the car and watched with his arms akimbo. He seemed to be intrigued by what was going on.

The shooters were going to be a lot harder to stop this time. But at least they had only short-range weapons—they'd come prepared to kill a crippled computer scientist in a yurt, not engage in a prolonged firefight.

"Briana! Briana!" Üruisamoglu's voice came from the yurt.

Dagmar hesitated, then broke cover and ran for the yurt. She opened the door.

"What is it?" she asked.

"I've done it. I need you to put in your password."

She ran to him, dropped to her knees, and turned his laptop to her. Passwords swarmed through her mind. It had run blank.

She typed "CONSTANTINOPLE1453," then hit Enter. It was a password that the computers at NSA or other agencies would have no trouble cracking, but she couldn't think of anything else. When she had the opportunity she'd change it.

"Good," Üruisamoglu said. "Now I send it out."

Dagmar jumped to her feet and ran back to her position. The gunmen were a lot closer now. She rested the gun on a rock, aimed, and fired.

The bullet kicked up sand near one of the gunmen's feet, and they all scattered into cover. Return fire began to come up the hill. The bullets sounded like firecrackers going off over Dagmar's head.

There was excitement in being shot at, but the emotion was strangely flattened. This wasn't as involving as a video game. A video game would have better sound effects.

Whenever she saw one of the gunmen she fired, but they were darting from cover to cover and she could never get one in her sights. She emptied her magazine and reached for her second. After that, she realized, she'd be out of bullets.

A bullet whined off the rock close to Dagmar's hand. Her heart leaped. One of the gunman had worked his way onto her flank. She fired wildly at him, jumped to her feet, and ran back to another rock. Bullets snapped through the air near her.

She was breathless. The video game had just gone to another level of intensity. Hordes of zombies would arrive at any second.

Eventually the gunmen drove her all the way back to the yurt. She didn't know how many bullets she had left, but she knew it wasn't many. She dived through the door and dropped prone onto the carpet.

Üruisamoglu, still sitting on his pillow, looked at her.

"What's going on?" he said.

It was the most ridiculous question she'd ever heard. "We're trying to kill each other," she explained, as if to a child. "You'd better get down."

I am about to be killed by three men in ties, she thought.

Someone started firing through the felt walls of the yurt. Üruisamoglu dropped to the floor. His brown eyes were huge.

Voices cried out in Turkish. Üruisamoglu looked at Dagmar.

"They want us to surrender," he said.

"They're here to kill you," Dagmar said. "But you can surrender if you want."

"They have no reason to kill me anymore," Üruisamoglu said. "The Internet's back. It's all out of my hands."

And entirely in mine, Dagmar thought. They'd torture her to get her password.

More bullets began ripping through the felt. One whined off the pellet stove. Üruisamoglu's maps crackled as bullets snapped through them. Dagmar reached for pillows and began to build bulwarks. The gunmen kept shouting.

At least they're not hallucinations, she thought, and almost laughed.

The gunmen called for surrender again. They were probably not looking forward to charging in through the single door.

Dagmar didn't answer. Another pair of shots came in. Maybe, Dagmar thought, they were running low on ammunition as well.

There was a mechanical grinding from outside, the bellowing of engines, the sound of gravel crunching beneath tires. Dagmar wondered if one of the gunmen had gone back for the car.

And then there was more shouting, very desperate sounding, and a lot of shots. A vehicle roared, and Dagmar heard wheels skidding on gravel as it came to a stop right outside the door.

There were huge booms at close range, the sound of a much larger weapon, but no bullets came into the yurt. Then there was a clanking noise, and suddenly Ismet's voice.

"Dagmar! Are you in there? You and Slash come out — fast!"

Dagmar rose to her knees, her head spinning. Üruisamoglu looked at her blankly. She waved at him.

"Come on!" she said.

He crawled across the carpets, dragging his crutches behind him. Dagmar jumped up, ran back to his position, and grabbed his laptop. She ran to the door of the yurt and opened it.

The vehicle outside had eight huge wheels and a duck-billed ramming prow. There were hatches and periscopes and slits for viewing. Hot exhaust smoked from the engines and fouled the air. It was the armored vehicle they'd seen down in the village.

A hatch had opened between the second and the third wheels. Ismet was inside, gesturing.

"Hurry!"

Bullets cracked through the air. Dagmar dived for the hatch, clambered into the interior. It smelled of dust and stale motor oil.

Ismet leaned out, grabbed Üruisamoglu by the shoulders of his sheepskin jacket, and hauled him bodily into the vehicle. The metal crutches clanged on the metal floor. Ismet slammed the hatch shut and yelled something to the driver in the forward compartment. The engine roar increased and the vehicle lurched into reverse.

There were pinging sounds on the metal walls of the vehicle. Dagmar saw little dimples appearing on the inside of the armor. Someone was shooting at them.

Ismet reached for the shotgun on a metal bench seat, thrust it through one of the ports, and fired. The sound in the small metal compartment was enormous.

The big vehicle lurched off. Dagmar and Üruisamoglu clutched at the metal seats in an attempt to stabilize themselves. Dagmar eventually hauled herself into one of the seats, and she looked out through one of the view slits just as one of Ismet's shots caught a gunman in the shoulder, spinning him around.

Then the vehicle dropped nose-first onto the narrow road leading to the Kyzyl Kum, and Ismet lost his footing and crashed to the floor on top of Üruisamoglu.

Ismet scrambled into one of the metal seats and then pulled Üruisamoglu into another. The vehicle swayed and crashed. The engine sound was deafening. The passenger compartment smelled of auto exhaust and cordite.

"This is Shemazar!" Ismet pointed to the driver. "He owns this APC."

Shemazar—a man in late middle age, thin and lined—turned and waved a hand.

"Hi, lady!" he said.

Hi, lady, Dagmar thought. *This guy must have apprenticed as a New York cabbie.*

The APC jounced to the floor of the desert. Ismet shouted instructions. Shemazar waved, shifted into a lower gear, and deliberately drove the APC over the assassins' sedan, leaving it a wreck at the foot of the bluff.

Dagmar looked through one of the slits and saw the man in the light-colored suit. He made no attempt to run away but stood with his hands on his hips, surveying the catastrophe with a disgusted look on his face. Though she doubted he could see her, Dagmar waved at him through the port.

Good-bye, Kronsteen, she thought. *Just think of it as revolution creep.* And then the armored car rolled on.

In a few minutes, they were in the oasis. The Niva waited at Shemazar's house, much the same except for some bullet holes in the hatchback.

"I led them off as far as I could," Ismet said. "Their car was faster, but I had four-wheel drive, so whenever they started to catch me I moved into the open desert, and they couldn't move so fast there. But eventually they realized they weren't going to get me, so they went back to the yurt. I went cross-country to the village, because I thought I might be able to rent this vehicle." He patted the armored side. "We're out another five hundred pounds. Sorry I didn't return your call, but I was in the middle of negotiations."

"You keep saving me," Dagmar said.

He gave her a deadpan look.

"Well," he said, "you keep running into trouble."

In the village they transferred to the Niva. Shemazar cackled and insisted on hugging Dagmar multiple times and kissing her on both cheeks. His lips were excessively moist. Under the circumstances, Dagmar felt, she could scarcely object.

"What about the killers?" Dagmar asked as they pulled away. "What if they catch us again?"

"Not likely," Ismet judged. "We just smashed their car. They're on foot with a wounded man. Nobody in the village is going to give them a car, because the crazy old guy in the armored car isn't going to let them. So I'd say they're walking to Zarafshan."

Unless, Dagmar thought, they could hook up with Ulugbek and his camels.

Lamprey's Appendage Sucks on Ale

Ismet got behind the wheel of the Niva and they left the oasis behind. Dagmar called Helmuth and tried to catch up with events in Turkey.

"Turkey's got Internet again," Helmuth said. "Everything we're hearing says that it's true that the commander of the Second Army got deposed—by his own officers. They've declared for the revolution and they're ready to march on Ankara."

"The Second Army is in the Kurdish provinces," Ismet said. "The general would have been one of Bozbeyli's most loyal subordinates—he was the one who had to keep an eye on the heroin trade. So it's significant that his own people put him under arrest."

As they jounced toward Zarafshan on the highway, as the silver high-tension towers marched past like a long row of saluting soldiers, they heard of the cascade of events that spelled the collapse of Bozbeyli's regime. Other generals—the ones Lincoln had complained were sitting on the fence—began to eye their own subordinates with distrust and to consider that perhaps their choices had been limited to declaring for the rebels or being deposed by their own men.

The First Army commander in Istanbul declared for the rebels, and the Third Army on the Iraq border seemed in chaos, with some units declaring one way and some the other. Only the forces on Cyprus stayed loyal, and they were unable to move to the mainland.

By the time Zarafshan was in sight, it was over. Bozbeyli and the others in his administration had abdicated and flown to Azerbaijan.

"And not only that," Dagmar said. "It turns out I own the Internet. It all belongs to me."

Ismet looked at her. Üruisamoglu pointedly did not.

"It's true," she said. "Though maybe I'll give it back." She cleared her throat. "Maybe. Wouldn't want to leave it in the wrong hands."

She reached for her handheld.

"I'm going to call Attila," she said. "He should know that his triumphant entry into Istanbul is imminent."

"He should be happy about that," Ismet said.

"I don't know. It means he can't hog the headlines any longer."

"Tell him to have the jet ready."

"Yes," Dagmar said. "Only this time, we don't file a flight plan."

Before she could call her phone gave a chirp, and she found that she had a pair of text messages. She called up the first.

Briana love you forever Chatsworth.

A pleasant warmth kindled in the vicinity of her heart. *Manipulative old bastard*, she thought with affection.

"Lv U2," she replied.

Dagmar turned to the second message and saw it was much longer. Richard must have typed it on a keyboard, because it had none of the slang and abbreviations you'd expect in a message thumbed onto a phone pad.

"I have been having problems with my printer," the employee told Dagmar. "Even though the printer was cabled properly to the computer and the driver was installed, and even though the printer responded when it was sent a file, the printer refused to print a document.

"I checked the cable again, and I then uninstalled the printer driver, then reinstalled it. The printer still would not print. Therefore I updated the driver, but the printer still would not function. I swapped out the cables, with no success. I cycled the power on the printer, but still the printer would not print.

"Finally, out of desperation, I uninstalled the operating system, and reinstalled the OS from scratch. And then the printer worked as if nothing had ever been wrong.

"Dagmar, my solution made no sense and was completely inelegant. What am I to understand from this adventure?"

"Persistence," said Dagmar, "also has merit."

She looked at the last line and gave a weary laugh. She read it aloud to Ismet and Üruisamoglu, and they both thought it was funny.

CONSTANTINOPLE1453, she thought. She was going to have to change that, and soon.

She opened a can of beluga, and they ate caviar and hard-boiled eggs all the way to the airport, where the Gulfstream waited, glowing in the sun as if it were made of precious metal, its engines already turning over.

The Niva drew up to the stair that waited in front of the Gulfstream's door. The two cabin attendants were visible at the top of the stairs, waiting with identical white smiles on their faces. The man from customs was in his Honda, and Babür stood waiting for his hundred-pound notes.

Peace oot, Dagmar thought, and reached for her passport.

extras

orbit

meet the author

Walter Jon Williams

WALTER JON WILLIAMS has been nominated repeatedly for every major SF award, including Hugo and Nebula Award nominations for his novel *City on Fire*. His most recent books are *The Sundering, The Praxis, Destiny's Way, The Rift,* and *This Is Not a Game*. He lives near Albuquerque, New Mexico, with his wife. Find out more about the author at www.walterjonwilliams.net.

introducing

**If you enjoyed
DEEP STATE,
look out for**

THE FOURTH WALL

by Walter Jon Williams

I come out of the darkness of the tunnel into the brilliant light and the whole arena erupts with a huge, hollow roaring made by thousands of enthusiastic drunken American males. *Whooooooo.* I'm stunned. I haven't heard anything that enthusiastic in ages. Certainly not for me.

I'm so taken aback that I almost stumble, but my cornerman, Master Pak, keeps me going with steady pressure to my shoulder blades. My eyes are dazzled by camera flashes. People are reaching into the aisles to touch me or to offer high fives. I look to my right and see a whole row of bare-chested guys pumping their fists in the air and barking. They're wearing weird alien bald heads, and their beer bellies are painted baby blue. *Oogh-oogh-oogh-oogh.*

Is that supposed to be my *head?* I think. *These are* my *fans?*

I blink and they're gone, vanished back into the crowd as I advance.

Whoooooo. The sound seems to pick me up and levitate me

toward the sky. My heart pounds. My veins are ablaze with adrenaline.

This is what it's like to be a rock star. This is what it's like to *own* an arena full of people.

Ahead the ring is like a silver crown gleaming in a pillar of light. Outlined in the shining floods, I can see the referee, an enormous 240-pound bodybuilder crammed into a white shirt and bow tie. He wears surgical gloves in the event that I decide to bleed on him. And then an anomaly catches my eye, and I think, *Why is the ref wearing waders?*

When I hop up the stairs to the ring, I find out why.

This is the point where, in my mind's ear, I can hear the television announcer: "This is where the contestant realizes that, without telling him, we've filled the ring with *eight inches of cottage cheese!*"

Oh yeah, I think. *I am so pwned.*

The ring is actually ring shaped, a circle thirty feet across. It's walled off from the rest of the arena by a six-foot curtain of chain link. Overhead, against the rows of floods, I can see automated cameras swooping back and forth on guy wires.

My other corner guy, Ricardo, opens a gate on the chain-link wall, and I step gingerly into the cottage cheese. It's very cold, and it squelches up over my bare feet. I stomp around a bit. The cheese is very slippery. It clings to my feet like buckets of concrete.

Pwned, I think. *Totally pwned.*

The ring announcer, who is wearing a rather smart pair of jackboots with his tux, fills the air with hype as I consider my situation. I have these freakishly long legs and arms, which constitute about my only advantage in a martial arts context. For the last four weeks, Master Pak has been drilling me on stick-and-run maneuvers — when my opponent charges me,

I'm supposed to stop his attack with a stomping kick to the thigh or jab him in the face as I shift left or right.

But I'm hardly going to be able to kick at all, not if I have to scoop my feet out of the muck. Even if I get the kick off, I might slip and fall. And I'm going to have a hard time maneuvering in any case.

I look at Master Pak for help. He's just staring down at the cottage cheese with a stony expression. He has a tae kwon do background, and for him it's all really about the kicking, which is something I suddenly can't do.

I don't know what I can manage in the upcoming fight except stand there and get run down.

Whooooooo. That roaring noise rises again, and I blink off into the darkness and see my opponent and his entourage coming down the aisle from the tunnel.

He's named Jimmy Blogjoy. When he was a kid actor he was Jimmy Morrison, and he starred in a third-rate knockoff of *Family Tree*, but as his career went into decline he renamed himself after his Web log. This happened at roughly the time that everyone on the planet stopped reading blogs. They particularly stopped reading Jimmy's, which gets even fewer hits than mine. You don't want to do the self-revealing thing when all you've got to reveal is the vacuum between your ears.

Jimmy appears in the gate to the ring and looks down at the cottage cheese, which is as much a surprise to him as it was to me. He's redheaded and stocky and short, and there's a mat of rust-colored fur on his chest.

Jimmy looks over at me and snarls. His fists are clenched. He's really angry. Like it's *my* fault he has to step into the cottage cheese.

I snarl back at him. Fucking asshole.

We are in Episode Four of *Celebrity Pitfighter*, a new reality show. The rules for *Celebrity Pitfighter* are that while everyone in the contest has to have been famous at some point in his life, no one can be an actual pitfighter. We are all brand spanking new to the martial arts. Jimmy and I have trained for exactly three weeks. The world is full of drunks lying under bar stools who could take us with one hand behind their backs.

For my three weeks of training I've had cameras following me around at Master Pak's *dojang*, and in addition to the training I've been given little challenges, like learning to toss throwing stars at targets, or being made to hold a padded shield while famously large bruisers tried to kick in my rib cage, or trying to look impressed and competent and grateful when martial arts champions teach me their signature moves.

As with most reality shows, everything was scripted. I'd had to learn lines. The only parts of the show that weren't scripted were the fights—and they were only unscripted *so far as I knew.*

None of my special training will be worth a damn when I'm rolling around in the cottage cheese. Because one of the *other* rules of *Celebrity Pitfighter* is that the contestants have to be given a surprise handicap just before the fight. In past episodes, fighters have had to fight while wearing handcuffs, had fifty-pound weights attached to their right ankles, or the two opponents had their left arms tied together by a six-foot piece of elastic.

Because having a pair of untrained lames pounding each other in the ring *just isn't enough fun.* You just have to have that extra handicap in order to bring the humiliation to its peak. Because humiliation is what reality television is all about—if they can't watch someone utterly destroyed on camera, rejected by his judges and his peers, face not merely lost but annihilated for all time, the audience won't get their sadistic rocks off.

The witless fucks.

The referee calls Jimmy and me together. As he tells us he wants a clean fight Jimmy looks up at me and snarls. He's wearing a green mouthpiece impressed with silver letters that read: *Kill You*. I sneer back.

Bring your worst, you half-assed gump.

We touch gloves and slosh back to our corners. Master Pak touches me and mutters in my ear.

"Look," he says. "You're still bigger than he is. Just beat the shit out of him."

I almost laugh. It's good advice.

I *am* bigger than Jimmy Blogjoy. I'm taller, I have five or six inches of reach on him, and I outweigh him by thirty pounds.

This shouldn't be a fair fight at all. If I knew what I was doing, I'd rip his lungs out.

Master Pak stuffs the mouthpiece in my mouth, leaves the ring, and closes the mesh gate behind him. The audience is baying. It occurs to me that the whole game is set so that Jimmy will win.

"Have Makin train with the TKD guy." I can hear the producer laughing as he says it. "Then put him in goop so he *can't kick*."

I wonder if the production staff has money riding on Jimmy.

The referee looks at me and asks me if I'm ready. I mumble through the mouthpiece that I am. Jimmy is also ready. The ref punches the air in front of him.

"*Let's rock the world!*" he says.

Whooooo. My heart is crashing in my chest. I can't see anything outside the ring. Master Pak is shouting at me, but I can't hear what he's saying.

The audience noise reaches a crescendo as I slosh forward a

couple of steps, then pause to await developments. Jimmy is coming straight on, balled fists on guard, his eyes fixed on my face. I raise my guard. He keeps on. He gets in range and I jab him in the face.

Nothing happens. Jimmy keeps coming. I jab again and he throws a pair of wild punches that miss. I jab and try to maneuver.

The jabs aren't working, even though I can feel them connect and feel the shock all the way to my shoulder. They're supposed to stop Jimmy or rock him back on his heels, but he just absorbs the punch and keeps coming. So I kick Jimmy somewhere in his midsection.

This works, because Jimmy goes down. Except that I go down, too, because my support leg slips in the cottage cheese.

In wild panic I flounder to my feet, cold cheese chilling my torso. Jimmy's already up, charging me, swinging wildly again. He's actually *growling*. I jab, but there's cottage cheese on my glove and the punch slips off him. He wraps his arm around me and smashes up under my chin with the top of his head. I see stars and the next thing I know I'm back in the cottage cheese with Jimmy on top of me.

He's sitting on my chest raining punches down. I cover my face and try some of the techniques that Master Pak taught me to reverse someone on top of me, but the cheese is everywhere and we keep slipping. At least he isn't hurting me much.

I wriggle and thrash and manage to slide a leg free from beneath his weight. I put my foot against his chest and push and he slides off me.

As I thrash to my feet blackness is swimming before my eyes. The fight's just a few seconds long and already I've run out of steam.

Before I can quite come on guard Jimmy socks me on the

side of the head. I see stars. I back up, trying to put distance between us, and come up against the chain-link wall. Jimmy clamps onto me again and tries to wrestle me into the cheese. It's like fighting a rabid badger. My chest is heaving with the effort of staying on my feet.

In a rage I pound Jimmy uselessly in the body and the back of the head and try to break free, but the punches are too short to be effective, or I'm too out of breath—and then our legs get tangled and I fall into the goop again, twisting away from Jimmy, facedown. A tidal wave of cottage cheese surges across the ring. Suddenly Jimmy's on my back. He snakes a forearm around my throat, but I grab his hand and manage to pull it away and save my windpipe. His feet—his "hooks" as they are called in Mixed Martial Arts—wrap around me and pull my thighs apart. I sprawl face-first into the cottage cheese, and Jimmy begins a flurry of angry punches to the back of my head. None of them are particularly damaging, but there are a lot of them.

I can't see. I can't breathe. Cottage cheese fills my mouth, my nostrils, my ears. Jimmy's punches rock my world every half second. I try to push myself up from the floor of the ring, but I'm pushing up Jimmy's weight as well as my own, and my hands keep slipping out from under me. My lungs are about to explode.

I'm drowning. The thought sends me into a spasm of activity. I wriggle, I slither, I manage to get out from under Jimmy long enough to catch a breath, but he grabs my head and shoves me under again. The bland, salty taste of cottage cheese fills my throat.

Surrender! I've got to surrender! I'm supposed to tap the mat as a signal that I give up, but the floor is covered by cottage cheese and no one can see the gesture when I try it. I begin to flail, clawing at the cottage cheese. My head is full of whirling stars. Pain erupts in my chest, as if my aorta has just exploded.

In the moment before I die, I think of the next day's headline.

Has-been Drowns While Trying to Resurrect His Career. That's what they'll carve on my tombstone.

Then the bodybuilder referee pulls Jimmy off me, reaches his gloved hands under my armpits, and peels me out of the cottage cheese as if I were made of soggy cardboard.